# THE BOOK OF
# SONGS

# THE BOOK OF
# SONGS

✦

*Translated by Arthur Waley*

*Edited with Additional Translations
by Joseph R. Allen*

*Foreword by Stephen Owen*

*Postface by Joseph R. Allen*

GROVE PRESS
*New York*

*Published simultaneously in Canada*
*Printed in the United States of America*

Library of Congress Cataloging-in-Publication Data
Shih ching. English
    The book of songs / translated by Arthur Waley; edited with
additional translations by Joseph R. Allen; foreword by Stephen Owen;
postface by Joseph R. Allen.
        p.      cm.
    Includes bibliographical references.
    ISBN 0-8021-3477-7
    I. Waley, Arthur.   II. Allen. Joseph Roe.   III. Title.
    PL2478.F813        1996
895.1'1108—dc20                    96-23037

Design by Laura Hammond Hough

Grove Press
841 Broadway
New York, NY 10003

00 01 02 03  10 9 8 7 6 5 4 3 2

# Contents

✦

# *Preface*

✦

This edition of *The Book of Songs* offers Arthur Waley's translations of the Chinese classic in a new format, supplemented by additional translations, accompanied by new interpretative materials, and updated in several ways. I hope these changes allow readers to appreciate *The Book of Songs* in a new, revitalized light; toward that goal I have done the following:

For the first time these translations are presented in the "Mao" format and order that they have known in the Chinese original for over two millennia; the nature and history of that format are discussed in the Postface at the end of the volume. This order replaces the seventeen topical categories that Waley devised when he originally published his translations in 1937 (see the Appendix for those categories and order). Now readers can enjoy Waley's excellent translations in the poems' original contextual frame, a frame that has its own elegant structure and offers a view into the principles of organization and canonization of early Chinese literature.

I have also included translations of the fifteen poems that Waley omitted from his edition (poems number 191–99, 253–54, 257–58, and 264–65), thus yielding a translation of the entire Chinese corpus of 305 poems. Waley claimed that these fifteen poems were uninteresting and textually corrupt; they are indeed very difficult poems, but they have been integral to the classic since its inception, and it behooves us to include them here. Although I have freely consulted other translations and commentaries,[1] I have sought to model my translations on those by Waley, both in specific vocabulary and phrasing as well as in tone and style. Needless to say, trying to write in another's voice when that voice is as strong as Waley's has been both exciting and daunting.

1. Principally, Bernhard Karlgren's *Glosses on the Book of Odes* (1942–46), Qu Wan-li's *Shi jing shi yi* (1958), and Cheng Jun-ying and Jiang Jian-yuan's *Shi jing zhu xi* (1991).

For each of the translations I have added a title that is derived from the one by which the poem is commonly known in Chinese. The Chinese titles are generally taken from the opening lines of the poems, and thus I have drawn on Waley's translations (with a few exceptions) in producing these English titles.

The reader will find several types of material designed to articulate and explain the new format: a map of the Zhou feudal kingdom, a table of important legendary and historical figures that appear in the text, brief introductions to the sections and subsections of the collection, a Postface dealing with the literary history of the Chinese text, and a Selected Bibliography.

Finally, all Chinese names and terms have been cast into the pinyin romanization system that is now the international standard. In an effort to aid readers unfamiliar with Chinese, I have, however, used hyphens between syllables, except in common place-names.

In reordering Waley's translations I have retained as many of his notes and explanations as possible, recasting them to fit the new format when necessary. Occasionally I have deleted notes no longer applicable and supplemented others with additions of my own (so marked). With one exception, which I am certain is a printing error, I have retained Waley's stanza breaks. I have only on rare occasions altered his translations.

Arthur Waley's *The Book of Songs* remains a masterpiece of translation, appreciated by general readers, students of Chinese literature, and Sinologists. Like no other scholar or translator, Waley has negotiated the demands of both Sinological accuracy and the beauty of language. Stephen Owen's Foreword offers an equally eloquent appreciation of this collection. I hope this new format and additional materials will help the reader know better the power and beauty of this classic text in its original design.

JOSEPH R. ALLEN
*University of Minnesota, Twin Cities*

## Important Sites Mentioned in *The Book of Songs*

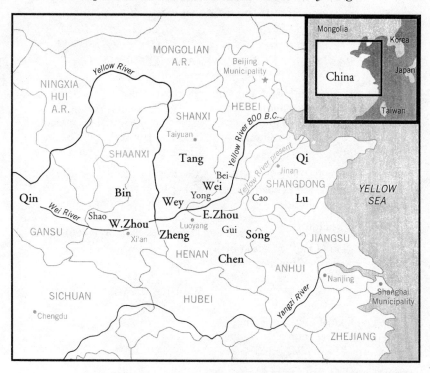

This map shows the approximate locations of royal and feudal states mentioned in *The Book of Songs*. The names of relatively minor and short-lived principalities are set in a smaller font. The location of the Western Zhou and Eastern Zhou are both depicted, although they existed only prior to and after 771 B.C., respectively. Current political borders and important cities are indicated in gray, along with the present course of the lower Yellow River.

(Based on maps in *Zhongguo lishi dituji,* Vol. 1 [Shanghai: Ditu chubanshe, 1982].)
© Joseph R. Allen and Kevin Tseng

# Important Legendary and Historical Figures

These are the most important figures mentioned in the *Songs*, along with their traditional dates (all B.C.).

## PERIOD OF MYTH AND LEGEND

Yu (Great Yu), controller of the flood

**Pre-dynastic Zhou**

**Shang-Yin**

Jiang Yuan, mother of Hou Ji, impregnated when she trod on god's footprint

Jian Di, impregnated by an egg from the dark bird, gives birth to Xie, ancestor of the Shang people

Hou Ji (Lord Millet), mythical male ancestor of the Zhou people, inventor of agriculture

Xie, the Dark King, has grandson Xiang-tu

Bu-ku, son of Hou Ji

. . .

Duke Liu (Liu Gong), grandson of Bu-ku, brought the Zhou people to the land of Bin

Tang the Victorious (1766), founder of the Shang kingdom

. . .

. . .

Wu Ding, 23rd Shang king (of 31), c. 1300

Dan-fu (Duke of Old, Great King), moved the Zhou people to Mount Qi, married Lady Jiang, sired sons:

. . .

Tai-bo, fled south to yield the throne to younger brother, Wang Ji

Wang Ji, married Lady Ren (Tai-ren), sired Chang, who became King Wen

# ZHOU ROYAL PERIOD

Wen Wang (King Wen, the Civil), originally Earl of West (Xi bo) under the Shang, married Tai-si, Lady Xin, designated first king of Zhou (1134)

Wu Wang (King Wu, the Martial), (r. 1122–16) son of King Wen, defeated the Shang, established the Zhou dynasty in his father's name, capital at Hao

  Duke of Zhou, younger brother of King Wu, regent for young King Cheng

  Duke of Shao, half brother of King Wu

King Cheng (r. 1115–1079)

King Kang (r. 1078–53)

. . .

King Li (r. 841–28)

King Xuan (r. 827–782), had adviser Zhong Shan Fu

King You (r. 781–71), took consort Bao Si, lost western capital

King Ping (r. 770–20)

**Feudal States**

  In order of the Airs of the States

Bei
Yong
Wei
Zheng
Qi
Wey
Tang
Qin
Chen
Gui
Cao
Bin

In the Hymns

Lu

Song (under Shang designation)

# *Foreword*

✦

Our age is one of complexities, in which the causes of events and their meanings are never entirely clear. Perhaps for this reason, in the poetry of our age we respect an answering complexity, which interprets the world and offers no clear answers. Difficulty is our common measure of depth. However, as we read more poetry, particularly early poetry, we often make a surprising discovery: that there is in some poetry a magic of simplicity, which can be even more forceful and alluring than modern complexity. We find it, for example, in some of the medieval English lyrics:

> Ich am of Irlaunde,
> And of the holy londe
> Of Irlaunde.
>
> Good sire, pray ich thee,
> For of sainte charite,
> Come and daunce with me
> In Irlaunde.

At least on one level we still feel we are included by such poems, included in the archaic invitation to go off with the singer and dance with her in that mysterious land, Irlaunde. The poem can still address us; however, we also recognize we can no longer accept such an invitation with simple delight, nor could we ourselves be able to offer such an unself-conscious invitation. A poetry as simple and open as this is somehow beyond our capacities. And at the moment we recognize this, we may have an intuition that the complexity and "depth" of our own modern poetry is not entirely a progress, but also a falling away and loss. In reading a poem like "Ich am of Irlaunde," we

may have a moment of something like shame, recognizing a basic
humanity that can address us, even though we no longer speak back
to it. If we are given such a moment of revelation, we can grasp
something of the role of *The Book of Songs* in Chinese civilization.

There are many poems in *The Book of Songs* which are, like "Ich
am of Irlaunde," invitations. They can speak desire without the wink
of embarrassment or the self-conscious crudeness that reacts against
embarrassment—the qualities that touch almost all statements of desire
in modern popular songs.

> That the mere glimpse of a plain coat
> Could stab my heart with grief!
> Enough! Take me with you to your home. (147)

> A very handsome gentleman
> Waited for me in the lane;
> I am sorry I did not go with him. (88)

> Cold blows the northern wind,
> Thick falls the snow.
> Be kind to me, love me,
> Take my hand and go with me. (41)

Even more wondrous, it is a world in which people can speak not
only desire but also the contentment of desire, a happy life between
man and woman. The husband can want to sleep just a little longer,
and the wife can sing him out of bed with a vision of shared joys:

> The lady says: "The cock has crowed";
> The knight says: "Day has not dawned."
> "Rise, then, and look at the night;
> The morning star is shining.
> You must be out and abroad,
> Must shoot the wild-duck and wild-geese.

> When you have shot them, you must bring them home
> And I will dress them for you,
> And when I have dressed them we will drink wine
> And I will be yours till we are old." (82)

As joy can be spoken, pain can be spoken as well and with an equal honesty. A woman, driven to a marriage she doesn't want, can respond with a voice that has no gender, that speaks simply as a human being:

> My heart is not a mirror,
> To reflect what others will. (26)

And as she continues her complaint, she finds her metaphors not in a literary tradition, but in the griminess of everyday life:

> O sun, ah, moon,
> Why are you changed and dim?
> Sorrow clings to me
> Like an unwashed dress. (26)

Such a direct and honest world could probably never have existed in a real human society, but somehow it did exist in poetry.

The Book of Songs is both poetry and scripture, a work of literature and one of the Confucian classics. Over the past two and a half millennia, The Book of Songs has been interpreted and understood in very different ways; but while the significance of the Songs changed from age to age and from reader to reader, the texts always retained their allure, promising access to something basic in the human spirit.

For the tradition of Chinese poetry The Book of Songs was a beginning that was never forgotten; echoes of the Songs appear throughout classical Chinese poetry, even in this century. For many the Songs represented the ideal for all poetry, with an archaic honesty and simplicity that seemed forever just out of reach to more sophisticated and self-conscious ages. In addition, the songs seemed to their readers to be a permanent embodiment of the inner lives of people in the remote past: in the Songs one could discover "what it was like then" more perfectly than in any history. Finally, for the Confucian thinker the Songs played a central role in the great Confucian project of educating the human heart back to its natural goodness; it was assumed that if a person heard the songs performed, especially as they had once been performed with their lost ancient music, the emotions of the listener would be shaped to decent, balanced, and, at the same time, natural responses to the events of life.

Behind all these different approaches to the Songs was a simple definition of what a poem was (the term "song," shi, in the title The

*Book of Songs* being the same generic word used later for all classical poetry). This definition first appeared in another of the Confucian classics, *The Book of Documents,* and its authority was immense (as if God had decided to offer a brief pronouncement on the nature of poetry in Genesis). The definition is: "Poetry gives words to what the mind is intent upon." This seemingly innocuous statement had immense consequences: readers found in the *Songs* not an "art" of words, produced by a special class of human beings called "poets," but rather a window into another person's heart, a person like themselves. Behind every song one might find some powerful concern— desire, anger, reverence, pain—set in its living context. Other Confucian classics treated outward things: deeds, moral precepts, the way the world worked. But *The Book of Songs* was the classic of the human heart and the human mind.

Each reader of *The Book of Songs* has sought to understand the poems as they "originally" were, and each reader has found in them his or her own vision of the remote past, a vision of basic humanity. Confucian scholars discovered their own idea of a genuinely moral society; Arthur Waley, a twentieth-century Western reader, discovered a folk poetry that confirmed modern Western notions of archaic society; contemporary Chinese Marxist interpreters find their own version of social history. However, in one sense each different interpretation of the *Songs* has discovered the same thing: that original core of humanity that we all still have within us.

*The Book of Songs* is an anthology of 305 poems of varying length, drawn from various levels of Zhou society. It contains folk songs, songs of the nobility, ritual hymns, and ballads on significant events in the history of the Zhou people. The oldest poems, the temple hymns of the royal house of Zhou, may date as early as 1000 B.C.; but most of the songs seem to have reached their present versions shortly before the anthology was put together, probably around 600 B.C. Although it is likely that versions of many of the individual poems continued to be sung in peasant society, the anthology itself clearly belonged to the Zhou court and the courts of the feudal states into which the Zhou kingdom had disintegrated.

Western and modern Chinese scholars have often expressed puzzlement that early China, unlike so many other cultures, has no epic, in which some central myth of the people is shaped into a narrative whole. In Chinese literature *The Book of Songs* occupies the place where Western notions of literary history assume an epic ought to be. However, when we reflect on the nature of *The Book of Songs,* we find in it a different vision of wholeness, and one perhaps more persuasive than the narrative unity of an epic. *The Book of Songs* is a work that attempts to embrace every aspect of its world: the dead ancestors and the living, past history and present, men and women, the ruling house and the common people. And between each of these divisions in their world, the songs create relations that bind them together: the living do homage to the ancestors and the ancestors watch over the living; the present acts with past examples in mind; men and women speak to one another in love or anger; the common people praise or blame their rulers, and the best rulers act in the interest of the common people. The anthology constitutes a whole without possessing any simple unity. Moreover, its wholeness has an ideological basis which would preclude the possibility of epic. Epic unity demands a focus that speaks for one group and excludes other voices: the voices of the common people, the voices of women, voices from all aspects of life outside the heroic ethos. When Andromache begs Hektor not to go out to fight in the *Iliad,* her voice is only a foil against which Hektor can declare his fatal commitment to heroic values. Odysseus' commoners exist poetically only to serve the hero in his hour of need. But the legacy of Zhou culture prohibited deafness to those other voices: it was essential that they have their say, that attention be paid to them.

One of the most remarkable tenets of the Zhou monarchy was the notion of "Heaven's charge," that the right to rule was given to the house of Zhou by Heaven only so long as the Zhou watched over the interests of the people it ruled. The real Mycenaean warrior who fought below the walls of Troy might well have worried about the peasants at home, who were tilling the fields and keeping the sheep; but to the literary warrior in Homer these are invisible or allowed to appear to aid the hero's progress: each warrior seeks his own private glory. The rulers of Zhou were less confident: archaic Chinese writings, including many of the songs, are filled with notes of anxiety lest the ruler stray and Heaven, in its wrath, withdraw its charge from Zhou:

> Mighty is God on high,
> Ruler of His people below;
> Swift and terrible is God on high,
> His charge has many statutes.

> Heaven gives birth to the multitudes of the people,
> But its charge cannot be counted upon.
> To begin well is common;
> To end well is rare indeed. (255)

This anxiety is reminiscent of the caution that the house of Israel needed to show, always under the watchful eye of God; but the situation of the Zhou was even more precarious: they were not, like the people of Israel, chosen forever, but merely given an office which they could keep only so long as they carried out its duties and remained successful. And the clearest evidence of Heaven's support was to be found in the voices of the common people. The Zhou were constantly reminded of the fate of the dynasty they had conquered, the Yin or Shang dynasty, which had in its day enjoyed Heaven's favor and then lost it:

> Bright they shone on earth below,
> Majestic they blaze on high.
> Heaven cannot be trusted;
> Kingship is easily lost.
> Heaven set up a foe to match the Yin;
> Did not let them keep their frontier lands. (236)

That "foe" was the Zhou itself. Kingship is indeed easily lost. Although the power of the Zhou monarchy had disintegrated and largely passed to the Zhou's feudal lords by the time *The Book of Songs* was compiled, a concern for the attitude of the common people remained part of the Zhou legacy. The warrior class of early Greece and the later citizens of the city states, who looked back fondly on that warrior past, were content to listen to the deeds of heroes alone. And, with very few exceptions, the folk poetry of Greece is lost to us. The same is true of archaic India. But over half of *The Book of Songs* is either folk poetry, modified folk poetry, or inspired by folk poetry.

There is a noticeable lack of violence in *The Book of Songs*.[1] There is some glorification of Zhou military power—fast chariots,

---

1. For a longer discussion of this question and the avoidance of violence, the reader might consult C. H. Wang, "Toward Defining a Chinese Heroism," *Journal of the American Oriental Society* (95), January–March 1975, pp. 25–35.

blazing valor, rank upon rank of warriors—but blood is hardly ever shed. Among the songs of the dynasty are those that bear the memories of the great folk migrations that brought the Zhou people into the Chinese heartland. Here we might expect the stuff of epic, monumental struggles in which the Zhou people show their power and fitness to rule. But this is how "stalwart Duke Liu" begins the migration into the land of Bin:

> He stacked, he stored,
> He tied up dried meat and grain
> In knapsacks, in bags;
> Far and wide he gathered his stores.
> The bows and arrows he tested,
> Shield and dagger, halberd and battle-axe;
> And then began his march. (250)

The value of wholeness, which governs the compilation of the anthology, can also be seen in these individual poems: the ordinary work of provisioning the people must be celebrated along with the conquest, for in this activity Duke Liu also shows his fitness to rule. Indeed, the only point where the principle of wholeness is violated is in the presentation of violence. Having made ready "Shield and dagger, halberd and battle-axe," Duke Liu must anticipate some resistance from the people into whose lands he is leading the migration, but:

> He made his royal progress, proclaimed his rule;
> There were no complaints, no murmurings
> Either high up in the hills
> Or down in the plains. (250)

Duke Liu's fitness to rule is demonstrated by the willing acceptance of his overlordship on the part of the people whose land he has invaded. It is as sure a mark of Heaven's favor as David's strong sling-arm or Diomedes' prowess.

There is military heroism in *The Book of Songs*, but it is directed more often to public rather than private glory. The Zhou's heroes are praised for their valor, but also for their sagacious execution of state policy. The army is essentially a collective force, "the king's claws and fangs" (185):

The king's hosts swept along
As though flying, as though winged,
Like the river, like the Han,
Steady as a mountain,
Flowing onward like a stream,
Rank on rank, in serried order,
Immeasurable, unassailable;
Mightily they marched through the land of Xu. (263)

However, such exultation in Zhou military might represents a threat of violence, which must be balanced by some statement justifying the use of force, as in the stanza that immediately follows the one above:

The king's plans have been faithfully effected,
All the regions of Xu have submitted,
All the regions of Xu are at one;
It was the Son of Heaven's deed.
In the four quarters all is peace;
The peoples of Xu come in homage.
The regions of Xu no longer disobey;
The king goes back to his home. (263)

Moral power and peace here are a transparent disguise for the brute conquest of Xu. The peoples of Xu had probably thought of themselves as independent rather than "disobedient." We must never forget that here we are reading the values of Zhou rather than social fact. We must not suppose that Zhou was any less bloody than any other branch of the human family. But they felt uneasy enough about their acts of violence to try to conceal them in royal propaganda.

The principle of wholeness in the anthology does not allow such praises of Zhou military might to go unquestioned. Poems by soldiers complaining of military service are even more numerous than ballads glorifying Zhou campaigns:

Minister of War,
Truly you are not wise.
Why should you roll us from misery to misery?
We have mothers who lack food. (185)

> What plant is not faded?
> What day do we not march?
> What man is not taken
> To defend the four bounds?
>
> What plant is not wilting?
> What man is not taken from his wife?
> Alas for us soldiers,
> Treated as though we were not fellow-men! (234)

What Homeric warrior would have declared that he was prevented from desertion only by fear of punishment?

> Oh, bright Heaven high above,
> Shining down upon the earth below,
> Our march to the west
> Has led us to the desert wilds!
> . . . . . . . . . . . . . . . . . . . .
> Of course I long to come home,
> But I fear the meshes of crime. (207)

The "meshes of crime" are what we would call "the arm of the law," which will catch him if he deserts the campaign.

The songs of courtship and marriage are generally the least marked by cultural differences and perhaps the easiest of the songs for a modern Western reader to appreciate immediately. Many of these poems might have come from any tradition of folk lyric in the world. There is an *alba,* or dawn song (96), in which the anxious girl urges her unwilling lover to get away before he is discovered, that might just as easily be a translation from the Provençal or Old French or medieval German. There is a voice for each step in the delicate dance of courtship: invitation; celebration of the dashing good looks or beauty of the beloved; exchanges of love-gifts and love-words; love-tests; the laments of women seduced and abandoned; and the man who waits for the girl who never comes.

> By the willows of the Eastern Gate,
> Whose leaves are so thick,
> At dusk we were to meet;
> And now the morning star is bright. (140)

The native speaker of English has difficulty avoiding reading the second line "Whose leaves *they* are so thick," thus assimilating the stanza entirely to our own folk lyric. And here, as so often, what at first seems only incidental finally proves essential to the scene: the willows are not simply the place chosen for meeting: their thick leaves, now observed wistfully, would have served to hide the lovers.

The Zhou was an agrarian dynasty, and their sense of beauty and order is closely related to the cycles and abundance of the agricultural year. In a society of warriors life is directed to a single intense and uncertain moment of decision, crisis; this plays a powerful role in understanding the structure of time and events, hence of narrative. Agrarian time is cyclical, a complete and repeating series of acts and events, all of which are equally necessary and all of which contribute to the whole. In *The Book of Songs* we often sense a sheer delight in naming all the parts of things: all the different kinds of millet, every activity to be performed in its season. Poems of *The Book of Songs* never begin "in the middle of the matter," *in medias res,* as Horace advised the writer of the epic; the songs begin at the beginning and follow through to the end. The need for wholeness in this poetry of the Zhou goes far deeper than the dynasty's need for assurance of universal support: it embodies a larger sense of how the world and events in it are structured. Each actor and act must be placed on the stage. The farming hymns are filled with that pleasure in abundance and order in the following celebration of the planting:

> They clear away the grass, the trees;
> Their ploughs open up the ground.
> In a thousand pairs they tug at weeds and roots,
> Along the low grounds, along the ridges.
> There is the master and his eldest son,
> There the headman and the overseer.
> They mark out, they plough.
> Deep the food-baskets that are brought;
> Dainty are the wives,
> The men press close to them.
> And now with shares so sharp
> They set to work upon the southern acre.
> They sow the many sorts of grain,
> The seeds that hold moist life. (290)

It is not enough to say that the lowlands were weeded; we must remember the ridges too. The absence of suspense, the delight in things in their expected order, is one of the most difficult qualities for the Western reader to appreciate in these earliest poems of *The Book of Songs*. It is a world with anxiety but without terror: there is no incomprehensible divinity, god the hunter, who tracks men down, good men like Job and men who follow the proper customs like Pentheos, whom Dionysos destroyed. There are, however, a few poems that recall a darker and even more archaic past, times when retainers were killed and buried with their lords, to keep them company in the afterlife. One of the few datable poems in *The Book of Songs* comes from 621 B.C., the date of the death of Duke Mu of the state of Qin, a border duchy where the old customs still survived:

> "Kio" sings the oriole
> As it lights on the thorn-bush.
> Who went with Duke Mu to the grave?
> Yan-xi of the clan Zi-ju.
> Now this Yan-xi
> Was the pick of all our men;
> But as he drew near the tomb-hole
> His limbs shook with dread.
> That blue one, Heaven,
> Takes all our good men.
> Could we but ransom him
> There are a hundred would give their lives. (131)

The stanzas of the song continue with the oriole alighting on a series of different plants; and each time it alights, a new member of the Zi-ju clan is sent to join Duke Mu in the grave. Many of the songs begin with some natural image whose relation to the topic of the song is oblique (as the English "Green grow the rushes, o"), but in this case there seems to be some magic correspondence between the plant on which the bird stops and the man named in the following lines, as if an augur were present who could read Heaven's choice of victim in the movements of the bird.

The sense of arbitrary and inescapable doom in the poem above stands out from all other poems in *The Book of Songs*. The anthology presents the full human share of unhappiness and pain, but usually the reasons behind suffering are quite clear: desertion by a lover, misgovernment, the hardships of forced military service. In the increasingly turbulent and violent centuries that followed the seventh century B.C., much in *The Book of Songs* seemed indeed to come from a lost era in which the world was comprehensible; and the anthology contributed much to the Chinese myth of the Zhou as the ideal polity.

Out of this diverse body of hymns, ballads, and folk songs current in the seventh century *The Book of Songs* took shape. We know that the songs were performed in the feudal courts of the period, and that they became an authoritative body of texts with which everyone in the courts was familiar. They served as one of the few unifying cultural legacies of the Zhou in an age of political fragmentation and interstate warfare. Like the Homeric epics in Greece, an aura gathered around the songs, and, known to all, they were frequently quoted in court discussions to lend force to arguments. This practice of quotation would usually involve taking lines or stanzas out of context and applying them, with varying degrees of appropriateness, to contemporary situations. From this custom (and from the reaction against its egregious abuses) individual songs gradually acquired general interpretations.

Confucius (551–479 B.C.) placed great emphasis on the study of *The Book of Songs,* both as an essential part of a moral education and as training for political life in the courts. In his *Analects,* we can see the *Songs* well on its way to becoming a classic; the poems are recommended as paradigms of the moral heart: "There are three hundred Songs and one phrase covers them all: 'No straying from the path'" (*Analects* 2.2). However, since many of the songs, as honest as they may seem to our eyes, did not conform to certain aspects of Confucian morality, they were reinterpreted to make them accord with their presumed moral perfection. The Traditionalists, whom we now call "Confucians," made *The Book of Songs* a central text in their schools; they based ethical discourses on them and, as earlier in the courts, cited the *Songs* to prove their points. This practice is amusingly illustrated in a cruel parody by the greatest foe of the Traditionalists, the Daoist Zhuang-zi (c. 369–286 B.C.). Note that the verse quoted isn't really from the *Songs,* but does sound like one:

> Some Confucians were robbing graves according to *The Book of Songs* and Rites. The senior Confucian gave a dictum to his subordinates, "Sun riseth in the east; how goeth the matter at hand?" A junior Confucian answered,

"We haven't stripped off his robes yet, but there's a pearl
in his mouth."

The senior Confucian: "Ah, indeed it is as the *The
Book of Songs* says:

> 'The millet is green, so green,
> It groweth on the slopes.
> If ungenerous in life,
> What good a pearl in the lips when dead?'

"I'll grab his whiskers in one hand and yank down on his
beard with the other. You prop his jaws open with a metal
spike, then gently, gently spread his cheeks so as not to
damage the pearl in his mouth."

If the Traditionalists believed that the *Songs* could make a person good,
Zhuang-zi saw them as a potential disguise of evil. There is a vener-
able Daoist principle in this: when interpretation and practical ap-
plication appear, possibilities of misinterpretation and misapplication
appear with them.

When Confucianism finally was fully institutionalized in the
Han dynasty, *The Book of Songs* became a standard part of the scho-
lastic curriculum, each poem carrying with it an orthodox interpre-
tation, which explained how that poem responded to the moral and
social conditions of the age in which it was produced. By this point
the anthology had come to lead the double life mentioned earlier,
both as literature and as a Confucian classic. There was always some
tension between the clear and natural surface of the text and the
weight of moral interpretation attached to it. Perhaps the best anal-
ogy in the Western tradition would be the Song of Solomon in the
Bible, where a surface of erotic love poetry played counterpoint to
orthodox interpretation as the soul's love for God (or Christ's love
for the Church). And as with the Song of Solomon, that tension in
*The Book of Songs* worked both ways, lending the natural responses
of the *Songs* a quality of moral value, and casting on moral positions
given in the exegeses the glow of natural response.

The interpretation of *The Book of Songs* is filled with difficul-
ties, for the philological interpretation both of individual words and
lines and of whole poems. Arthur Waley was a scholar in his own
right, as well as being a remarkably gifted translator; and he has done

his best in these translations (which are at the same time interpreta-
tions) to restore to the *Songs* some of the freshness of its Zhou ori-
gins. Many aspects of these poems will always seem strange to us:
unfamiliar place names and vanished folkways. Very few readers in-
deed have ever ridden in a chariot, nor do we wear belts with carved
stones dangling from them (Waley's "girdles"). But in many of the
songs something basic is still transmitted, even across the barriers of
translation, a different culture, and over two and a half millennia of
history. And when we catch that basic human note, we may recog-
nize that it is we who have become strange and alien, not the songs.
We find in them words we can feel but no longer say, such as the
following words of a woman to a lover who has abandoned her:

> If along the highroad
> I caught hold of your sleeve,
> Do not hate me;
> Old ways take time to overcome. (81)

—STEPHEN OWEN
*Harvard University*
1987

# THE AIRS OF THE STATES,
## POEMS 1–160

◆

*The Book of Songs* opens with the youngest and most celebrated part of the collection: "The Airs of the States" (*Guo feng*). The origins of these 160 poems are clearly in popular songs; they are strongly stanzaic in structure, simple in language, and direct in emotion. If we imagine these poems being sung a cappella or to the simple accompaniment of a zither (instead of being paralyzed on the printed page) we can easily hear their lyric appeal. Ranging from the complaints of weary troopers to the teasing of risqué women, the poems in the Airs celebrate village festivals, the agricultural calendar, and daily life of the town. While poems of courtship are found throughout much of the *Songs* and there is a variety of other topics in the Airs, still the girl-meets-boy songs are the ones that draw our attention in this part of the collection. Moreover, those poems sent later Confucian scholars scurrying to construct their most speculative didactic interpretations, in which desirous lovers are transformed into distant lords and royal consorts.

The "Airs of the States" are grouped in fifteen sections by geographic area. The first two are specially named "southern" (*nan*) groups associated with important ducal states of the Zhou royal house. Although the *nan* do not differ substantially from the other airs, they do hold a special place in the literature: the opening poem, "The Ospreys Cry," is one of the most discussed poems in the Chinese critical tradition. The other thirteen sections are identified with various feudal states and areas of the Zhou feudal kingdom.

There is an obvious editorial hand at work here. Most of these sets come in "decades" of poems and often have elements that link them loosely together. Of these sets perhaps the most famous (or infamous) is the "Airs of Zheng," which has carried the stigma of licentiousness since the pronouncement by Confucius that, "The Airs of Zheng are licentious . . . I detest them for disrupting the orthodox music" (*Analects* 17.18). Clearly, in the beginning what was most disturbing about the Zheng poems was their music, but the lyrics of many are also suggestive. Poem no. 95, "The Zhen and Wei," has been perhaps the most scandalous with its clear statement of female desire.

# South of Zhou, 1–11
✦

This set is one of the four airs associated with the Zhou royal house. The poems in this group are said to come from the Zhou ancestral settlement near Mount Qi, which was said to be under the control of the Duke of Zhou. The set is integral to the long exegetical traditional of the *Songs*; this is especially so for poem no. 1, which has been traditionally linked to the royal consort of King Wen. The commentaries attribute this set (as well as the next) with the civilizing influence by the Zhou on their neighbors, presumably to the south.

## 1 ✦ *The Ospreys Cry*

"Fair, fair," cry the ospreys
On the island in the river.
Lovely is this noble lady,
Fit bride for our lord.

In patches grows the water mallow;
To left and right one must seek it.
Shy was this noble lady;
Day and night he sought her.

Sought her and could not get her;
Day and night he grieved.
Long thoughts, oh, long unhappy thoughts,
Now on his back, now tossing on to his side.

In patches grows the water mallow;
To left and right one must gather it.
Shy is this noble lady;
With great zither and little we hearten her.

In patches grows the water mallow;
To left and right one must choose it.
Shy is this noble lady;
With bells and drums we will gladden her.

## 2 ✦ *The Cloth-Plant Spreads*

How the cloth-plant[1] spreads
Across the midst of the valley!
Thick grows its leaves.
The oriole in its flight
Perches on that copse,
Its song is full of longing.

How the cloth-plant spreads
Across the middle of the valley!
Close grow its leaves,
I cut them and steam them,
Make cloth fine and coarse,
For clothes that will not irk me.

I will go to my nurse,
I will tell her I am going home.
Here I sud my shift,
Here I wash my dress.
Which things are clean and which not?
I am going to comfort my parents.

---

1. *Ge* is the name applied to various sorts of creeper from the fibers of which cloth was made—and species of *Pachyrhizus,* including the yam bean. (Waley translates the term as both cloth-plant and cloth-creeper. *Ed.*)

## 3 ✦ *Cocklebur*

Thick grows the cocklebur;
But even a shallow basket I did not fill.
Sighing for the man I love
I laid it there on the road.

"I am climbing that rocky hill,
My horses stagger,
And I stop for a little to drink from that bronze ewer
To still my heart's yearning.

I am climbing that high ridge,
My horses are sick and spent,
And I stop for a little while to drink from that horn cup
To still my heart's pain.

I am climbing that shale;
My horses founder,
My groom is stricken,
Oh, woe, oh, misery!"

In the first verse it is the lady left at home who speaks; in the remaining
verses it is the man away on a perilous journey.

## 4 ✦ *Drooping Boughs*

In the south is a tree with drooping boughs;
The cloth-creeper binds it.
Oh, happy is our lord;
Blessings and boons secure him!

In the south is a tree with drooping boughs;
The cloth-creeper covers it.
Oh, happy is our lord;
Blessings and boons protect him!

In the south is a tree with drooping boughs;
The cloth-creeper encircles it.
Oh, happy is our lord;
Blessings and boons surround him!

## 5 ✦ *Locusts*

The locusts' wings say "throng, throng";
Well may your sons and grandsons
Be a host innumerable.

The locusts' wings say "bind, bind";
Well may your sons and grandsons
Continue in an endless line.

The locusts' wings say "join, join";[1]
Well may your sons and grandsons
Be forever at one.

## 6 ✦ *Peach-Tree*

Buxom is the peach-tree;
How its flowers blaze!
Our lady going home
Brings good to family and house.

Buxom is the peach-tree;
How its fruit swells!
Our lady going home
Brings good to family and house.

Buxom is the peach-tree;
How thick its leaves!
Our lady going home
Brings good to the people of her house.

---

1. The three noises that the locusts' wings make are punned upon and interpreted
as omens.

## 7 ✦ *Rabbit Nets*

Firmly set are the rabbit nets,
Hammered with a *ding, ding*.
Stout-hearted are the warriors,
Shield and rampart of our elder and lord.

Firmly set are the rabbit nets,
Spread where the paths meet.
Stout-hearted are the warriors,
Good comrades for our elder and lord.

Firmly set are the rabbit nets,
Spread deep in the woods.
Stout-hearted are the warriors,
Belly and heart of our elder and lord.

When women were going to have babies they ate plantain in order
to secure easy delivery. This plant has always had a high reputation
as a drug in the West as well as in the East. In the Highlands it was
called the Plant of Healing. It was one of the nine sacred herbs of the
Saxons, and Pliny held that it was a cure for hydrophobia. Its use in
childbirth is, so far as I know, peculiar to China.

## 8 ✦ *Plantain*

Thick grows the plantain;
Here we go plucking it.
Thick grows the plantain;
Here we go gathering it.

Thick grows the plantain;
Here we hold it between the fingers.
Thick grows the plantain;
Here we are with handfuls of it.

Thick grows the plantain;
Here we have our aprons full of it.
Thick grows the plantain;
Now apronfuls are tucked in at our belts.


9 ✦ *The Han Is Broad*

In the south is an upturning tree;
One cannot shelter under it.
Beyond the Han a lady walks;
One cannot seek her.
Oh, the Han it is so broad,
One cannot swim it,
And the Jiang, it is so rough
One cannot boat it!

Tall grows that tangle of brushwood;
Let us lop the wild-thorn.
Here comes a girl to be married;
Let us feed her horses.
Oh, the Han it is so broad,
One cannot swim it,
And the Jiang, it is so rough
One cannot boat it!

Tall grows that tangle of brushwood;
Let us lop the mugwort.
Here comes a girl to be married;
Let us feed her ponies.
Oh, the Han it is so broad,
One cannot swim it,
And the Jiang, it is so rough
One cannot boat it.

I call the Yangtze the Jiang, to distinguish it from the Yellow River,
which I call simply "the River." The mention of the Han River and

the Yangtze together fixes the scene of this song somewhere near modern Hankou, in east-central Hubei.

## 10 ✦ *Banks of the Ru*

I go along the high banks of the Ru[1]
Cutting faggots from the bough.
I have not yet seen my lord;
I feel a pang as of morning hunger.

I go along the high banks of the Ru
Cutting boughs that have been lopped and grown again.
At last I have seen my lord;
He has not left me for ever.

"The bream has a red tail;
The royal house is ablaze.
But though it is ablaze,
My father and mother are very dear."

## 11 ✦ *Unicorn's Hoofs*

The unicorn's hoofs!
The duke's sons throng.
Alas for the unicorn!

The unicorn's brow!
The duke's kinsmen throng.
Alas for the unicorn!

1. A tributary of the Huai, in southeastern Henan. In the last verse the returning husband speaks. A fish with a bleeding tail, floating helplessly downstream, is the symbol of a ruined kingdom, as we may see from a passage in the *Zuo zhuan* chronicle (Duke Ai, 17th year).

> The unicorn's horn!
> The duke's clansmen throng.
> Alas for the unicorn!

That this was a dance song is shown by its extreme likeness to no. 25, which we know to have been a dance song. There is a "unicorn-dance" in Annam. It takes place at the full moon of the eight month.[1] Masked dances sometimes end by the chief mask being set up and shot at.[2] That, I think, is what is happening here. The archers shoot away first its hoofs, then its brow, then its horn.

---

1. Van Huyen, *Les Chants Alternés . . . en Annam,* p. 18. "*L'homme qui sait bien danser avec une tête de licorne. . . .*"

2. F. E. Williams, "Mask Ceremonies on the Papuan Gulf," Congrès International des Sciences Anthropologiques, *Compte Rendu* (1934), p. 274.

# South of Shao, 12–25

✦

The second of the two "southern" sets, this one is associated with the Duke of Shao, half brother to King Wu. He was given the more western part of the older Zhou lands, with the capital at Shao, where these poems are said to have been collected. "In the Wilds Is a Dead Doe" (23) has stirred much discussion throughout the ages and is certainly memorable in its imagery and poignancy.

### 12 ✦ Magpie's Nest

Now the magpie had a nest,
But the cuckoo lived in it.
Here comes a girl to be married;
With a hundred coaches we'll meet her.

Now the magpie had a nest,
But the cuckoo made a home in it.
Here comes a girl to be married;
With a hundred coaches we'll escort her.

Now the magpie had a nest,
But the cuckoo filled it.
Here comes a girl to be married;
With a hundred coaches we'll gird her.

The Chinese believed it was an honor for other birds to rear the cuckoo's young, as we may see by this poem of Du Fu (eighth century A.D.) on the small cuckoo:

It gets its young reared in many birds' nests,
And the many birds do not dare complain,
But continue to care for the feeding of its young
With mien as reverent as one who serves a god.

Here the bride coming as an honored stranger into the family is compared to the young cuckoo.

Some time after marriage the wife was solemnly presented to her husband's ancestors. It is this rite, and not the arrival of the bride from her father's house, which from the religious point of view really constitutes the wedding. It is thus the counterpart to what takes place in church in Western marriage ritual. It will be noticed that the bride wears a wig or head-covering of false hair. This was only worn while serving the ancestors. Modern Hasidic Jewish brides go further, shaving their heads and wearing a wig during the whole of their married life.

## 13 ✦ *Gathering White Aster*

See, she gathers white aster
By the pools, on the little islands.
See, she uses it
At the rituals of her prince and lord.

See, she gathers white aster
Down in the ravine.
See, she uses it
In the ancestral hall of prince and lord.

Her tall wig nods
At dawn of night, while she plies her task.
With tall wig gently swaying
Here she comes back to her room.

## 14 ✦ *The Cicada*

Anxiously chirps the cicada,
Restlessly skips the grasshopper.
Before I saw my lord
My heart was ill at ease.
But now that I have seen him,
Now that I have met him,
My heart is at rest.

I climbed that southern hill
To pluck the fern-shoots.
Before I saw my lord
My heart was sad.
But now that I have seen him,
Now that I have met him,
My heart is still.

I climbed that southern hill
To pluck the bracken-shoots.
Before I saw my lord
My heart was sore distressed.
But now that I have seen him,
Now that I have met him,
My heart is at peace.

## 15 ✦ *Gathering Duckweed*

Here we are gathering duckweed
By the banks of the southern dale.
Here we are gathering water-grass
In those channeled pools.

Here we are packing them
Into round basket, into square.
Here we are boiling them
In kettles and pans.

Here we lay them beneath the window
Of the ancestral hall.
Who is the mistress of them?[1]
A young girl purified.


### 16 ✦ Sweet Pear-Tree

Young and tender is this sweet pear-tree;
Do not lop it or knock it,
For the Lord of Shao took shelter under it.

Young and tender is this sweet pear-tree;
Do not lop or harm it,
For the Lord of Shao rested under it.

Young and tender is this sweet pear-tree;
Do not lop it or uproot it,
For the Lord of Shao reposed beneath it.

This song is supposed to have been made by the people of the south,
in grateful memory of the Lord of Shao's services to their country.


### 17 ✦ Paths with Dew

The paths are drenched with dew.
True, I said "Early in the night";
But I fear to walk in so much dew.
Who can say that the sparrow has no beak?
How else could it have pierced my roof?
Who can say that you have no family?
How else could you bring this suit?
But though you bring a suit,
Not all your friends and family will suffice.

1. I.e., for whose benefit is the ceremony performed?

Who can say that the rat has no teeth?
How else could it have pierced my wall?
Who can say that you have no family?
How else could you bring this plaint?
But though you bring this plaint,
All the same I will not marry you.[1]

## 18 ✦ *Young Lamb*

In skins of the young lamb
Sewn with white silk of five and twenty strands,
Going home to supper from the palace
With step grave and slow!

In hides of the young lamb
Sewn with white silk of a hundred strands,
With step grave and slow
From the palace going to his supper!

In skins of the young lamb sewn
With white silk of four hundred strands,
With step grave and slow
Going home to supper from the palace!

The more numerous the strands the more potent the personal magic
(*de*) of the wearer. Thread of a fixed number of strands is often used
in attaching amulets, charms, and the like.

1. Literally, "I will not follow up" the love-meeting. Compare poem no. 151,
verse 3.

### 19 ✦ *Deep Rolls the Thunder*

Deep rolls the thunder
On the sun-side of the southern hills.
Why is it, why must you always be away,
Never managing to get leave?
O my true lord,
Come back to me, come back.

Deep rolls the thunder
On the side of the southern hills.
Why is it, why must you always be away,
Never managing to take rest?
O my true lord,
Comc back to me, come back.

Deep rolls the thunder
Beneath the southern hills.
Why is it, why must you be always away,
Never managing to be at home and rest.
O my true lord,
Come back to me, come back.

### 20 ✦ *Plop Fall the Plums*

Plop fall the plums; but there are still seven.[1]
Let those gentlemen that would court me
Come while it is lucky!

Plop fall the plums; there are still three.
Let any gentleman that would court me
Come before it is too late!

Plop fall the plums, in shallow baskets we lay them
Any gentleman who would court me
Had better speak while there is time.

---

1. This poem is akin to love-divinations of the type "Loves me, loves me not" and "This year, next year, sometime, never." Seven, as with us, is a lucky number.

The following is the song of the handmaids in some princely household. They had to leave their master's side before daybreak, to "fade out" before dawn, and therefore compare themselves to stars; whereas the wife could remain with her lord all night.

## 21 ✦ Small Stars

Twinkle those small stars,
Three or five in the east.
Shrinking, through the dark we walk
While it is still night in the palace.
Truly, fates are not equal.

Twinkle those small stars,
In Orion, in the Pleiades.
Shrinking, through the dark we walk
Burdened with coverlet and sheet.
Truly, fates are not alike.[1]

## 22 ✦ The Jiang Parts and Joins

The Jiang[2] parts and joins.
Our lady went to be married
And did not take us.
She did not take us,
But afterward she was sorry.

The Jiang has its islands.
Our lady went to be married
And did not bring us.
She did not bring us,
But afterward she found room for us.

1. For a comparatively modern parallel, see J. K. Shryock, "Ch'ên Ting's Account of the Marriage Customs of the Chiefs of Yünnan," *American Anthropologist,* vol. 36, no. 4, 1934.

2. The Jiang is the Yangtze River. *Ed.*

The Jiang divides and joins.
Our lady that went to be married
Did not move us with her.
She did not move us with her,
But in the end she has let us come.

This is a song of bridesmaids who suffered the indignity of being left behind when the bride removed to her husband's house. The image of a river dividing and joining again, as a symbol of temporary parting, occurs in early Japanese poetry: "Like the torrent whose course is barred by a great rock, though now we are parted, in the end I know that we shall meet," *Warete mo suye ni awamu to zo omou.*[1] The last line, "But in the end she has let us come," is corrupt, and the sense can only be guessed at.

If people find a dead deer in the woods, they cover it piously with rushes. But there are men who "kill" a girl, in the sense that they seduce her and then fail to "cover up" the damage by marrying her. Such is the burden of the next poem, its last three lines calling up elliptically the scene of the seduction.

### 23 ✦ *In the Wilds Is a Dead Doe*

In the wilds there is a dead doe;
With white rushes we cover her.
There was a lady longing for the spring;
A fair knight seduced her.

In the wood there is a clump of oaks,
And in the wilds a dead deer
With white rushes well bound;
There was a lady fair as jade.

"Heigh, not so hasty, not so rough;
Heigh, do not touch my handkerchief.[2]
Take care, or the dog will bark."

1. *Shìkwa Wakashū,* book 7 no. 228.

2. Which was worn at the belt.

## 24 ✦ *Gorgeous in Their Beauty*

Gorgeous in their beauty
Are the flowers of the cherry.
Are they not magnificent in their dignity,
The carriages of the royal bride?

Gorgeous in her beauty
As flower of peach or plum,
Granddaughter of King Ping,
Child of the Lord of Qi.

Wherewith does she angle?
Of silk is her fishing-line,
This child of the Lord of Qi,
Granddaughter of King Ping.

We know nothing further about this royal marriage, but it must have taken place about the middle of the eighth century. Fish, in the *Songs*, are symbols of fertility. In no. 190 a dream of fishes is interpreted as a promise of good harvests. In general, the fish that get caught in one's nets and traps are indications of other blessings that Heaven will send. Fish (and fishing, as in the present song) figure in several of the marriage songs. In India, fishing was part of the marriage ceremony, and the fertility and prosperity of the marriage was augured from the catch. Thus, according to the *Grhyasu-tra*,[1] the bridal pair go into the water up to their knees and catch fish in a new garment. They ask a Brahmin who accompanies them what he sees, and he replies, "Children and cattle." Similar customs still survive in modern India.[2] A rite of this kind probably once existed in ancient China; but all memory of it was forgotten by the time the commentators set to work upon the *Book of Songs*.

1. See R. Pischel, *Sitzungsberichte der Akademie der Wissenschaften*, Berlin, 1905, p. 529.

2. See W. Crooke, *Religion and Folklore of Northern India*, p. 244 and p. 478. Also Westermarck, *History of Human Marriage*, vol. 2, p. 484, and W. Logan, *Malabar*: "Bride and bridegroom stand beside a tub of water in which several small live fish are placed and by means of a cloth capture these fish" (vol. 1, p. 128).

### 25 ✦ *The Zou-yu*

Strong grow the reeds;
At one shot I kill five swine.
Alas for the Zou-yu!

Strong grows the wormwood;
At one shot I kill five hogs.
Alas for the Zou-yu!

In the section on music in the *Book of Rites* it is said that in the pantomime which represented the victory of King Wu of Zhou over Shang, at the end of the dance, "to the left they shoot the Wild Cat's Head and to the right the Zou-yu," which was a mythological animal, parallel to the unicorn. Here we have the song that the archers, boasting of their prowess, sing while they "shoot the Zou-yu." Heroes in Russian epics shoot through thirty trees, so that we need not be surprised to find these bowmen claiming incredible feats.

The Confucians were in the habit of concocting a sort of pseudohistory by investing mythological figures, both animal and human, with bureaucratic functions. Thus in the first book[1] of the *Shu jing,* various monsters such as the dragon are enrolled into the civil service. The same thing happened to the Zou-yu, who already in the *Book of the Lord Shang* (third century B.C.) appears as Keeper of the King's Paddocks. Some commentators have taken the name Zou-yu in this song as the name of an official!

---

1. Or the second, according to the current arrangement.

# Airs of Bei, 26–44

✦

Bei was a small principality that, along with Yong, is generally considered to have been subordinate to the larger state of Wei, which absorbed both at a later date. Bei was located in the north-central region of the Chinese plain, occupying part of the territory of the former Shang domain, on the border of present-day Hebei and Henan. This large set, twice the size of most other sets, begins with the first of two "Cypress Boat" poems and includes numerous famous love poems, such as "Of Fair Girls" (42).

This is the song of a lady whose friends tried to marry her against her inclinations:

### 26 ✦ *Cypress Boat*

Tossed is that cypress boat,
Wave-tossed it floats.
My heart is in turmoil, I cannot sleep.
But secret is my grief.
Wine I have, all things needful
For play, for sport.

My heart is not a mirror,
To reflect what others will.
Brothers too I have;
I cannot be snatched away.
But lo, when I told them of my plight
I found that they were angry with me.

My heart is not a stone;
It cannot be rolled.
My heart is not a mat;
It cannot be folded away.
I have borne myself correctly
In rites more than can be numbered.

My sad heart is consumed, I am harassed
By a host of small men.
I have borne vexations very many,
Received insults not few.
In the still of night I brood upon it;
In the waking hours I rend my breast.

O sun, ah, moon,
Why are you changed and dim?
Sorrow clings to me
Like an unwashed dress.
In the still of night I brood upon it,
Long to take wing and fly away.


## 27 ✦ *The Green Coat*

THE LADY:   Heigh, the green coat,
           The green coat, yellow lined!
           The sorrow of my heart,
           Will it ever cease?

           Heigh, the green coat,
           Green coat and yellow skirt!
           The sorrow of my heart,
           Will it ever end?

THE MAN:   Heigh, the green threads!
           It was you who sewed them.
           I'll be true to my old love,
           If only she'll forgive me.

Broad-stitch and openwork[1]
Are cold when the wind comes.
I'll be true to my old love
Who truly holds my heart.

The specific designation of speakers here and in later poems does not
appear in the original; Waley is extrapolating from the apparent dia-
logue; see his note to no. 100. *Ed.*

### 28 ✦ *Swallow, Swallow*

Swallow, swallow on your flight,
Wing high, wing low.
Our lady that goes home,
Far we escort beyond the fields.
Gaze after her, cannot see her,
And our tears flow like rain.

Swallow, swallow on your flight,
Now up, now down.
Our lady that goes home,
Far we go with her.
Gaze after her, cannot see her,
And stand here weeping.

Swallow, swallow on your flight,
Call high, call low.
Our lady that goes home,
Far we lead toward the south.
Gaze after her, cannot see her,
Sad are our hearts indeed!

1. Symbol of the new mistress.

A lady Tai-ren is she,
Her heart so faithful and true!
So gentle, so docile,
Clean and careful of her person,
Mindful of her late lord,
Making provision for his helpless ones.

This, as has always been recognized, is a song about a lady who, after the death of her husband, returns to her father's house. In the last verse she is compared to Tai-ren, the mother of King Wen,[1] a model of womanly virtues.

### 29 ✦ *Sun and Moon*

O sun, ah, moon
That shine upon the earth below,
A man like this
Will not stand firm to the end.
How can such a one be true?
Better if he had never noticed me.

O sun, ah, moon
That cover the earth below,
A man like this
Will not deal kindly to the end.
How can such a one be true?
Better if he had not requited me.

O sun, ah, moon
That rise out of the east,
A man like this,
Of whom no good word is said,
How can he be true?
I wish I could forget him.

---

1. The founder of the Zhou dynasty, traditionally supposed to have died in 1122 B.C.

O sun, ah, moon
That from the east do rise,
Heigh, father! Ho, mother,
You have nurtured me to no good end.
How should he be true?
He requited me, but did not follow up.[1]


## 30 ✦ Wild and Windy

Wild and windy was the day;
You looked at me and laughed,
But the jest was cruel, and the laughter mocking.
My heart within is sore.

There was a great sandstorm that day;
Kindly you made as though to come,
Yet neither came nor went away.
Long, long my thoughts.

A great wind and darkness;
Day after day it is dark.
I lie awake, cannot sleep,
And gasp with longing.

Dreary, dreary the gloom;
The thunder growls.
I lie awake, cannot sleep,
And am destroyed with longing.


## 31 ✦ They Beat Their Drums

They beat their drums with a loud noise,
Leaping and prancing weapon in hand,
Building earth-works at the capital or fortifying Cao.
We[2] alone march to the south.

1. Our love-meeting.

2. The people of Wei, whose capital at the probable date of this poem was north
of the Yellow River; Chen and Song lay to the south of the river.

We were led by Sun Zi-zhong
To subdue Chen and Song.
He does not bring us home;
My heart is sad within.

Here we stop, here we stay,
Here we lose horses
And here find them again
Down among the woods.

"For good or ill, in death as in life;
This is the oath I swear with you.
I take your hand
As token that I will grow old along with you."

Alas for our bond!
It has not lasted even for our lifetime.
Alas for our troth!
You did not trust me.

The last verse but one is the wife's marriage-vow. This song, like
no. 156, is about a soldier who comes home only to find that his
wife has given him up for dead and married again.

## 32 ✦ A Gentle Wind

When a gentle wind from the south
Blows to the heart of those thorn-bushes
The heart of the thorn-bushes is freshened;
But our mother had only grief and care.

A gentle wind from the south
Blows on that brushwood of the thorn-tree.
Our mother was wise and kind;
But among us is no good man.

Yonder is a cold spring
Under the burgh of Xun.
There were sons, seven men;
Yet their mother had only grief and care.

Pretty is that yellow oriole
And pleasant its tune.
There were sons, seven men,
Yet none could soothe his mother's heart.

Xun was a place in Northern Henan. This poem reads to me like a song taken from or connected with a folk-story. The commentators explain it as "a eulogy on filial sons," an interpretation which they can only justify by very tortuous means. The bad sons are contrasted with the pretty and innocent bird.

### 33 ✦ Cock-Pheasant

SHE: That cock-pheasant in its flight
    Flaps feebly with its wings;
    By this passion of mine
    What have I brought myself but misery?
    That cock-pheasant in its flight
    Cries low, cries high;
    Ah, my lord, truly
    You have broken my heart.

HE: Look up at the sun, the moon.
    Not less enduring is my love.
    But the way is long;
    How could I possibly come?

    Oh, all you gentlemen,[1]
    You give me no credit for my good deeds.
    I harmed none, was foe to none,
    I did nothing that was not right.

1. Who are judging this case.

### 34 ✦ *The Gourd Has Bitter Leaves*

HE:   The gourd has bitter leaves;
       The ford is deep to wade.
SHE:  If a ford is deep, there are stepping-stones;
       If it is shallow, you can tuck up your skirts.

HE:   The ford is in full flood,
       And baleful is the pheasant's cry.
SHE:  The ford is not deep enough to wet your axles;
       The pheasant cried to find her mate.

On one note the wild-geese cry,
A cloudless dawn begins to break.
A knight that brings home his bride
Must do so before the ice melts.

The boatman beckons and beckons.
Others cross, not I;
Others cross, not I.
"I am waiting for my friend."[1]

### 35 ✦ *Valley Wind*

Zip, zip the valley wind,
Bringing darkness, bringing rain.
"Strive to be of one mind;
Let there be no anger between you."
He who plucks greens, plucks cabbage
Does not judge by the lower parts.
In my reputation there is no flaw,
I am yours till death.

---

1. She says this to the boatman.

Slowly I take the road,
Reluctant at heart.
Not far, no, near;
See, you escort me only to the gateway.[1]
Who says that sow-thistle is bitter?
It is sweeter than shepherd's-purse.
You feast your new marriage-kin,
As though they were older brothers, were younger brothers.

"It is the Wei that makes the Jing look dirty;
Very clear are its shoals."[2]
You feast your new relations,
And think me no fit company.
"Do not break my dam,
Do not open my fish-traps.
Though for my person you have no regard,
At least pity my brood."[3]

Where the water was deep
I rafted it, boated it;
Where the water was shallow
I swam it, floated it.
Whether a thing was to be had or no
I strove always to find it.
When any of your people were in trouble
I went on my knees to help them.

Why do you not cherish me,
But rather treat me as an enemy?
You have spoilt my value;
What is used, no merchant will buy.
Once in times of peril, of extremity
With you I shared all troubles.
But now that you are well-nurtured, well-fed,
You treat me as though I were a poison.

---

1. He hustles her off the premises without courtesy.

2. It is only in comparison with the new wife that I seem shabby. These lines are no doubt a proverb; the poem comes from Henan and not from Shaanxi. The Jing flows into the Wei to the east of the old Zhou capital in Shaanxi.

3. These lines, several times repeated in the *Songs,* must be a quotation.

I had laid by a good store,
Enough to provide against the winter;
You feast your new kin,
And that provision is eaten up.
Then you were violent, were enraged,
And it gave me great pain.
You do not think of the past;
It is only anger that is left.


## 36 ✦ *How Few*

How few of us are left, how few!
Why do we not go back?
Were it not for our prince and his concerns,
What should we be doing here in the dew?

How few of us are left, how few!
Why do we not go back?
Were it not for our prince's own concerns,
What should we be doing here in the mud?


## 37 ✦ *High Mound*

The cloth-plant on that high mound,
How its joints stretch on and on!
O my uncles, O my elders,
Why so many days?

Why are you tarrying?
There must be a reason.
Why does it take so long?
There must be a cause.

Our fox-furs are messed and worn;
There is not a wagon that we have not brought to the east.
O uncles, O elders,
You do not share our toils with us.

Pretty little creatures
Were the children of the owl;[1]
O uncles and elders
With your ear-plugs[2] so grand!


### 38 ✦ *So Grand*

So grand, so tall
He is just going to do the Wan dance;[3]
Yes, just at noon of day,
In front of the palace, on a high place,
A big man, so warlike,
In the duke's yard he dances it.

He is strong as a tiger,
He holds chariot reins as though they were ribbons.
Now in his left hand he holds the flute,
In his right, the pheasant-plumes;
Red is he, as though smeared with ochre.
The duke hands him a goblet.

"On the hills grows a hazel-tree;
On the low ground the licorice.
Of whom do I think?
Of a fair lady from the West.
That fair lady
Is a lady from the West."[4]

1. But grow up baleful and hideous; so, too, the uncles and elders fail to come up to expectation.

2. For ear-plugs, see no. 98. There is the suggestion that they stop up their ears and do not listen to our appeal. (Waley's original cross-reference was to the wrong poem. *Ed.*)

3. Despite all that commentators have written on the subject, I do not think that we really know what "Wan" means. (In his editions, Waley includes an essay on the Wan dance in the Appendix. *Ed.*)

4. This is the song that accompanies the dance.

### 39 ✦ *Fountain Waters*

High spurt the waters of that fountain,
Yet it flows back into the Qi.
My love is in Wei,
No day but I think of him.
Dear are my many cousins;[1]
It would be well to take counsel with them:

"On the journey you will lodge at Ji,[2]
You will drink the cup of parting at Ni,
A girl that goes to be married,
Leaving parents, leaving brothers."
I will ask all my aunts
And next, my elder sister:

"On the journey you will lodge at Gan;
You will drink the cup of parting at Yan,
Grease wheels, look to axle-caps,
And the returning carriages will go their way:
A quick journey to the Court of Wei,
And may you get there safe and sound."

I think of the Forked Fountain,
Long now I sigh for it.
I think of Mei and Cao,
And how my heart yearns!
Come, yoke the horses, let us drive away,
That I may be rid at last of my pain.

1. Literally, "the various female members of the Ji clan," the speaker's clan. The scene of the poem is northern Henan.

2. This is their answer; so, too, in verse 3.

## 40 ✦ *Northern Gate*

I go out at the Northern Gate;
Deep is my grief.
I am utterly poverty-stricken and destitute;
Yet no one heeds my misfortunes.
Well, all is over now.
No doubt it was Heaven's doing,
So what's the good of talking about it?

The king's business came my way;
Government business of every sort was put upon me.
When I came in from outside
The people of the house all turned on me and scolded me.
Well, it's over now.
No doubt it was Heaven's doing,
So what's the good of talking about it?

The king's business was all piled upon me;
Government business of every sort was laid upon me.
When I came in from outside
The people of the house all turned upon me and abused me.
Well, it's over now.
No doubt it was Heaven's doing,
So what's the good of talking about it?

## 41 ✦ *Northern Wind*

Cold blows the northern wind,
Thick falls the snow.
Be kind to me, love me,
Take my hand and go with me.
Yet she lingers, yet she havers!
There is no time to lose.

The north wind whistles,
Whirls the falling snow.
Be kind to me, love me,
Take my hand and go home with me.
Yet she lingers, yet she havers!
There is no time to lose.

Nothing is redder than the fox,
Nothing blacker than the crow.[1]
Be kind to me, love me,
Take my hand and ride with me.
Yet she lingers, yet she havers!
There is no time to lose.

## 42 ✦ *Of Fair Girls*

Of fair girls the loveliest
Was to meet me at the corner of the Wall.
But she hides and will not show herself;
I scratch my head, pace up and down.

Of fair girls the prettiest
Gave me a red flute.
The flush of that red flute
Is pleasure at the girl's beauty.

She has been in the pastures and brought for me rush-wool,
Very beautiful and rare.
It is not you that are beautiful;
But you were given by a lovely girl.

1. And no one truer than I.

## 43 ✦ The New Terrace

Bright shines the new terrace;
But the waters of the river are miry.
A lovely mate she sought;
Clasped in her hand a toad most vile.

Clean glitters the new terrace;
But the waters of the river are muddy.
A lovely mate she sought;
Clasped in her hand a toad most foul.

Fish nets we spread;
A wild goose got tangled in them.
A lovely mate she sought;
But got this paddock.

This song may refer to a story about a bridegroom who was changed into a toad, which is, of course, a very widely spread type of folk-story, common in Asia as well as in Europe. The scene of the song is Northern Henan. "River" does not necessarily mean the Yellow River.

## 44 ✦ Off in a Boat

The two of you[1] went off in a boat,
Floating, floating far away.
Longingly I think of you;
My heart within is sore.

The two of you went off in a boat,
Floating, floating you sped away.
Longingly I think of you.
Oh may you come to no harm!

---

1. We can only construe *er zi* as "two sirs"; but I suspect that it is a corruption of a single name.

# Airs of Yong, 45–54

✦

Yong (present-day northern Henan) was the second of two small principalities later absorbed into the large state of Wei, which appears next in the collection. This set can be seen as a companion set to the "Airs of Bei," with a parallel opening poem, the second "Cypress Boat" of the collection.

## 45 ✦ Cypress Boat

Unsteady is that cypress boat[1]
In the middle of the river.
His two locks looped over his brow[2]
He swore that truly he was my comrade,
And till death would love no other.
Oh, mother, ah, Heaven,
That a man could be so false!

Unsteady is that boat of cypress-wood
By that river's side.
His two locks looped over his brow
He swore that truly he was my mate,
And till death would not fail me.
Oh, mother, ah, Heaven,
That a man could be so false!

1. Symbol of fluctuating intention.

2. Before his coming of age. Compare no. 102.

## 46 ✦ *On the Wall There Is Star-Thistle*

On the wall there is star-thistle;
It must not be swept away.[1]
What is said within the fence[2]
May not be disclosed.
But what could be disclosed[3]
Was filthy as tale can be.

On the wall there is star-thistle;
It must not be cleared away.
What is said within the fence
May not be reported in full.
But what could be reported in full
Was lewd as tale can be.

On the wall there is star-thistle;
It must not be bundled for firewood.
What is said within the fence
May not be openly recited.
But what could be recited
Was shameful as tale can be.


## 47 ✦ *Companion of Her Lord till Death*

Companion of her lord till death,
The pins of her wig[4] with their six gems,
Easy and stately,
Like a mountain, a river
Worthy of her blazoned gown.
That our lady is not a fine lady
How can any man say?


1. Because its prickles keep out intruders.

2. I.e., at the secret hearing of love-disputes.

3. The matrimonial dispute here referred to is traditionally supposed to have taken place in Wei, about 699 B.C. See Additional Notes.

4. Compare no. 13.

Gorgeous in its beauty
Is her pheasant-wing robe,
Her thick hair billows like clouds,
No false side-lock does she need.
Ear-plugs of jade,
Girdle pendants of ivory,
Brow so white.
How comes it that she is like a heavenly one,
How comes it that she is like a god?

Oh, splendid
In her ritual gown!
Rich the crepes and embroideries
That she trails and sweeps.
Clear is our lady's brow,
That brow well-rounded.
Truly such a lady
Is a beauty matchless in the land.

## 48 ✦ *She Was to Wait*

I am going to gather the dodder
In the village of Mei.[1]
Of whom do I think?
Of lovely Meng Jiang.
She was to wait for me at Sang-zhong,
But she went all the way to Shang-gong
And came with me to the banks of the Qi.

I am going to gather goosefoot
To the north of Mei.
Of whom do I think?
Of lovely Meng Yi.
She was to wait for me at Sang-zhong,
But she went all the way to Shang-gong
And came with me to the banks of the Qi.

1. The places mentioned in the song were all in northern Henan.

I am going to gather charlock
To the east of Mei.
Of whom do I think?
Of lovely Meng Yong.
She was to wait for me at Sang-zhong,
But she went all the way to Shang-gong,
And came with me to the banks of the Qi.

## 49 ✦ *How the Quails Bicker*

How the quails bicker,
How the magpies snatch!
Evil are the men
Whom I must call "brother."

How the magpies snatch,
How the quails bicker!
Evil are the men
Whom I must call "lord."

In 658 B.C. the people of Wei, continually harassed by the Di tribes, were forced to abandon their capital north of the Yellow River, in northern Henan, and transfer it to the southern enclave of Hebei that runs in a narrow strip between Shandong and Henan. In their move they were assisted and protected by Duke Huan of Qi, who sent a gift of three hundred horses,[1] presumably because most of the Wei people's horses had been captured by the Di. The following song describes the building of the new capital. We do not know its exact site, nor what is meant by "Tang" and the "Jing hills."

1. *Guo yu* (Qi yu). Multiplied in this song to three thousand.

## 50 ✦ *The Ding Star in the Middle of the Sky*

The Ding-star[1] is in the middle of the sky;
We begin to build the palace at Chu.
Orientating them by the rays of the sun
We set to work on the houses at Chu,
By the side of them planting hazels and chestnut-trees,
Catalpas, Paulownias, lacquer-trees
That we may make the zithers great and small.

We climb to that wilderness
To look down at Chu,
To look upon Chu and Tang,
Upon the Jing hills and the citadel.
We go down and inspect the mulberry orchards,
We take the omens and they are lucky,
All of them truly good.

A magical rain is falling.
We order our grooms
By starlight, early, to yoke our steeds;
We drive to the mulberry-fields and there we rest.
Those are men indeed!
They hold hearts that are staunch and true.
They have given us mares three thousand.

## 51 ✦ *A Girdle*

There is a girdle in the east;
No one dares point at it.
A girl has run away,
Far from father and mother, far from brothers young and old.

There is dawnlight mounting in the west;
The rain will last till noon.
A girl has run away,
Far from brothers young and old, far from mother and from
father.

1. Part of Pegasus; also called the Building Star.

Such a one as he
Is bent on high connections;
Never will he do what he has promised,
Never will he accept his lot.

The girdle is the rainbow. Its appearance announces that someone
who ought not to is about to have a baby; for the arc of the rainbow
typifies the swelling girdle of a pregnant woman. No one dares point
at it, because pointing is disrespectful, and one must respect a warn-
ing sent by Heaven. The second verse opens with a weather prov-
erb. The "mounting" here typifies the swelling girdle; the rain means,
I think, the tears she will shed when she finds that she has been
deceived. For the lover is bent on forming powerful marriage con-
nections that will improve his lot in life, and whatever promises he
may make now, he will certainly not fulfill them.

### 52 ✦ *Look at the Rat*

Look at the rat; he has a skin.
A man without dignity,
A man without dignity,
What is he doing, that he does not die?

Look at the rat; he has teeth.
A man without poise,
A man without poise,
What is he waiting for, that he does not die?

Look at the rat; he has limbs.
A man without manners,
A man without manners[1]
Had best quickly die.

1. But *li* includes a great deal that we should call religion; for example, sacrificing
at the right time.

## 53 ✦ *Pole-Banners*

High rise the pole-banners
In the outskirts of Jun,[1]
With white bands braided.
Oh, fine horses, four abreast!
Such great gentlemen,
What can we offer them?

High rise the pole-banners
By the gate-house of Jun,
With white bands bound.
Oh, fine horses, five abreast!
Such great gentlemen,
What can we give them?

High rise the pole-banners
By the walls of Jun,
With white bands plaited.
Oh, fine horses, six abreast![2]
Such great gentlemen,
How can we feed them?

## 54 ✦ *Gallop*

I ride home, I gallop
To lay my plaint before the lord of Wei,
I gallop my horses on and on
Till I come to Cao.
A great Minister, post-haste![3]
How sad my heart.

1. Near the capital of the Wei state, in northern Henan.

2. Evidence of six horses having drawn one chariot has been found in excavations of Zhou tombs.

3. Sent to bring her back.

He[1] no longer delights in me;
I cannot go back.
And now, seeing how ill you use me,
Surely my plan is not far-fetched!

He no longer delights in me;
I cannot go back across the river.
And now, seeing how ill you use me,
Surely my plan is not rash!

I climb that sloping mound,
I pick the toad-lilies.
A woman of good intent
Has always the right to go.
That the people of Xu should prevent it
Is childish, nay, mad.

I walk in the wilderness;
Thick grows the caltrop.
Empty-handed in a great land,
To whom could I go, on whom rely?
Oh, you great officers and gentlemen,
It is not I who am at fault;
All your many plans
Are not equal to what I propose.

The general situation in this poem is quite clear. The speaker is a
lady of Wei, unhappily married in Xu, a small state to the southeast
of Wei. She attempts to go back to her own people and home, but
is detained by the men of Xu. She speaks of Xu as a "great land" out
of conventional courtesy. Tradition says that she was Mu Fu-ren, a
Wei princess married to the Lord of Xu about 671 B.C.

1. Her husband in Xu.

# Airs of Wei, 55–64

✦

Wei was closely associated with the Zhou royal house (first enfeoffed to a brother of King Wu) and was one of the most powerful and longest-lived feudal states throughout the Zhou and Warring States periods. The River Qi, which appears throughout the set, is a principal tributary of the Yellow River, crossing the Wei territory west to east. This set, which can be grouped with the two preceding sets,[1] contains a number of outstanding poems, especially the early narrative of "A Simple Peasant" (58) and the naive lyric "A Quince" (64). The set later became linked with the licentious "Airs of Zheng."

### 55 ✦ Little Bay of the Qi

Look at that little bay of the Qi,
Its kitesfoot[2] so delicately waving.
Delicately fashioned is my lord,
As thing cut, as thing filed,
As thing chiseled, as thing polished.
Oh, the grace, the elegance!
Oh, the luster, oh, the light!
Delicately fashioned is my lord;
Never for a moment can I forget him.

1. This is seen, for example, in the description of a performance of the *Songs* in 543 B.C., which is discussed in the Postface.

2. A kind of reed-like grass.

Look at that little bay of the Qi,
Its kitesfoot so fresh.
Delicately fashioned is my lord,
His ear-plugs are of precious stones,
His cap-gems stand out like stars.
Oh, the grace, the elegance!
Oh, the luster, the light!
Delicately fashioned is my lord;
Never for a moment can I forget him.

Look at that little bay of the Qi,
Its kitesfoot in their crowds.
Delicately fashioned is my lord,
As a thing of bronze, a thing of white metal,
As a scepter of jade, a disc of jade.
How free, how easy
He leant over his chariot-rail!
How cleverly he chaffed and joked,
And yet was never rude!

## 56 ✦ *Drumming and Dancing*

Drumming and dancing[1] in the gully
How light-hearted was that tall man!
Subtler than any of them at capping stories.
And he swore he would never forget me.

Drumming and dancing along the bank,
How high-spirited was that tall man!
Subtler than any at capping songs.
And he swore he would never fail me.

1. Literally "bending the legs." That particular kind of dancing (with bent knee), so common in the Far East, must be meant.

Dancing and drumming on the high ground,
How gay was that tall man!
Subtler than any at capping whistled tunes.
And he swore his love would never end.

I think that too many of the songs have been explained by M. Granet
as being connected with a festival of courtship in which the girls and
boys lined up on opposite sides of a stream—a type of festival well
known in Indochina. This song, however, is clearly connected with
such a meeting. An interesting book on courtship by exchange of
songs has been published by N. van Huyen (*Chants Alternés des Garçons
et des Filles en Annam,* 1934).

## 57 ✦ *A Splendid Woman*

A splendid woman and upstanding;
Brocade she wore, over an unlined coat,
Daughter of the Lord of Qi,
Wife of the Lord of Wei,
Sister of the Crown Prince of Qi,
Called sister-in-law by the Lord of Xing,
Calling the Lord of Tan her brother-in-law.

Hands white as rush-down,
Skin like lard,
Neck long and white as the tree-grub,
Teeth like melon seeds,
Lovely head, beautiful brows.
Oh, the sweet smile dimpling,
The lovely eyes so black and white.

This splendid lady takes her ease;
She rests where the fields begin.
Her four steeds prance,
The red trappings flutter.
Screened by fans of pheasant-feather she is led to Court.
Oh, you Great Officers, retire early,
Do not fatigue our lord.

Where the water of the river, deep and wide,
Flows northward in strong course,
In the fish-net's swish and swirl
Sturgeon, snout-fish leap and lash.
Reeds and sedges tower high.
All her ladies are tall-coiffed;
All her knights, doughty men.

This poem celebrates the most famous wedding of Chinese antiquity, that of Zhuang Jiang, daughter of the Lord of Qi (northern Shandong), who married the Lord of Wei in 757 B.C. Wei centered around the modern Wei-hui in northern Henan. Xing was farther north, on the borders of Henan and southern Hebei. Tan was the modern Cheng-zi-ai, near Long-shan, in central Shandong. It has become famous because of the excavations carried out there in recent years.[1] One has to bear in mind that the bridegroom and bride are in other parts of the world often treated as though they were a king and queen. It is not impossible that such a song as this, though royal in origin, was afterward sung at ordinary people's weddings.

### 58 ✦ *A Simple Peasant*

We thought you were a simple peasant
Bringing cloth to exchange for thread.
But you had not come to buy thread;
You had come to arrange about me.
You were escorted across the Qi
As far as Beacon Hill.
"It is not I who want to put it off;
But you have no proper match-maker.
Please do not be angry;
Let us fix on autumn as the time."

1. See, for example, *Academia Sinica*, 4.2 (1933).

I climbed that high wall
To catch a glimpse of Fu-guan,[1]
And when I could not see Fu-guan
My tears fell flood on flood.
At last I caught sight of Fu-guan,
And how gaily I laughed and talked!
You consulted your yarrow-stalks[2]
And their patterns showed nothing unlucky.
You came with your cart
And moved me and my dowry.

Before the mulberry-tree sheds its leaves,
How soft and glossy they are!
O dove, turtle-dove,
Do not eat the mulberries![3]
O ladies, ladies,
Do not take your pleasure with men.
For a man to take his pleasure
Is a thing that may be condoned.
That a girl should take her pleasure
Cannot be condoned.

The mulberry-leaves have fallen
All yellow and seared.
Since I came to you,
Three years I have eaten poverty.
The waters of the Qi were in flood;
They wetted the curtains of the carriage.[4]
It was not I who was at fault;
It is you who have altered your ways,
It is you who are unfaithful,
Whose favors are cast this way and that.

1. Where her lover was. The scene is northern Henan.

2. Used in divination. See no. 169, verse 4.

3. Which are supposed to make doves drunk.

4. Which was a good omen.

Three years I was your wife.
I never neglected my work.
I rose early and went to bed late;
Never did I idle.
First you took to finding fault with me,
Then you became rough with me.
My brothers disowned me;
"Ho, ho," they laughed.
And when I think calmly over it,
I see that it was I who brought all this upon myself.

I swore to grow old along with you;
I am old, and have got nothing from you but trouble.
The Qi has its banks,
The swamp has its sides;
With hair looped and ribboned[1]
How gaily you talked and laughed,
And how solemnly you swore to be true,
So that I never thought there could be a change.
No, of a change I never thought;
And that *this* should be the end!

## 59 ✦ *Bamboo Rod*

How it tapered, the bamboo rod
With which you fished in the Qi!
It is not that I do not love you,
But it is so far that I cannot come.

The Well Spring is on the left;
The Qi River on the right.
When a girl is married
She is far from brothers, from father and mother.

1. While still an uncapped youth.

The Qi River is on the right,
The Well Spring is on the left;
But, oh, the grace of his loving smile!
Oh, the quiver of his girdle stones!

The Qi spreads its waves;
Oars of juniper, boat of pine-wood.
Come, yoke the horses, let us drive away,
That I may be rid at last of my pain.

## 60 ✦ *Vine-Bean*

The branches of the vine-bean;[1]
A boy with knot-horn at his belt!
Even though he carries knot-horn[2] at his belt,
Why should he not recognize me?
Oh, so free and easy
He dangles the gems at his waist!

The branches of the vine-bean;
A boy with archer's thimble at his belt!
Even though he has thimble at belt,
Why should he not be friends with me?
Oh, so free and easy
He dangles the gems at his waist!

---

1. Generally identified as *Metaplexis stauntoni*, which would fit quite well.

2. The knot-horn, a pointed instrument for undoing knots, was worn by adult men, presumably symbolizing their right to undo the knot of a bride's girdle; while the wearing of the bowman's thimble signified that a man was of age to go to war.

## 61 ✦ *The River Is Broad*

Who says that the River is broad?
On a single reed you could cross it.
Who says that Song[1] is far away?
By standing on tip-toe I can see it.

Who says that the River is broad?
There is not room in it even for a skiff.
Who says that Song is far away?
It could not take you so much as a morning.

## 62 ✦ *Bo Is Brave*

Heigh, Bo is brave;
Greatest hero in the land!
Bo, grasping his lance,
Is outrider of the king.

Since Bo went to the east
My head has been tousled as the tumbleweed.
It is not that I lack grease to dress it with;
But for whom should I want to look nice?

Oh, for rain, oh, for rain!
And instead the sun shines dazzling.
All this longing for Bo
Brings weariness to the heart, aching to the head.

Where can I get a day-lily[2]
To plant behind the house?
All this longing for Bo
Can but bring me heart's pain.

1. Song lay to the south of the Yellow River, Wei to the north.

2. An herb of forgetfulness; the *wasuregusa* of Japanese love poetry which was worn at the belt.

## 63 ✦ *There Is a Fox*

There is a fox dragging along
By that dam on the Qi.
Oh, my heart is sad;
That man of mine has no robe.

There is a fox dragging along
By that ford on the Qi.
Oh, my heart is sad;
That man of mine has no belt.

There is a fox dragging along
By that side of the Qi.
Oh, my heart is sad;
That man of mine has no coat.

## 64 ✦ *A Quince*

She threw a quince to me;
In requital I gave a bright girdle-gem.
No, not just as requital;
But meaning I would love her for ever.

She threw a tree-peach to me;
As requital I gave her a bright greenstone.
No, not just as requital;
But meaning I would love her for ever.

She threw a tree-plum to me;
In requital I gave her a bright jet-stone.
No, not just as requital,
But meaning I would love her for ever.

I have here used the term "requital" because it is technical in our
own pastoral poetry. For example, in Michael Drayton's *Pastorals*:

His lass him lavender hath sent
Showing her love, and doth requital crave;
Him rosemary his sweetheart . . . [etc.]

Modern botanists identify the fruit of verse 1 as *Cydonia sinensis* (Chinese quince), that of verse 2 as *Cyndonia japonica,* and that of verse 3 as the common quince. The names of the stones very likely indicate their shape and their position in the girdle-pendant rather than their quality.

# Airs of the Royal Domain, 65–74

✦

This set of poems is associated with the royal domain of King Ping (770–20 B.C.) of the Eastern Zhou period, which located its capital near present-day Luoyang. As such, the poems were read as emblematic of the decline of Zhou power. The two "cloth-plant" poems (nos. 71 and 72) are part of a large group of poems throughout the Airs that utilize similar imagery and themes.

### 65 ✦ The Wine-Millet Bends

That wine-millet bends under its weight,
That cooking-millet is in sprout.
I go on my way, bowed down
By the cares that shake my heart.
Those who know me
Say, "It is because his heart is so sad."
Those who do not know me
Say, "What is he looking for?"[1]
Oh, azure Heaven far away,
What sort of men can they be?

---

1. Seeing his bowed head, they think he is looking on the ground for something he has dropped.

That wine-millet bends under its weight,
That cooking-millet is in spike.
I go on my way bowed down
By the cares that poison my heart within.
Those who know me
Say, "It is because his heart is so sad."
Those who do not know me
Say, "What is he looking for?"
Oh, azure Heaven far away,
What sort of men can they be?

That wine-millet bends under its weight,
That cooking-millet is in grain.
I go on my way bowed down
By the cares that choke my heart within.
Those who know me
Say, "It is because his heart is so sad."
Those who do not know me
Say, "What is he looking for?"
Oh, azure Heaven far away,
What sort of men can they be?


66 ✦ *My Lord Is on Service*

My lord is on service;
He did not know for how long.
Oh, when will he come?
The fowls are roosting in their holes,
Another day is ending,
The sheep and cows are coming down.
My lord is on service;
How can I not be sad?

My lord is on service;
Not a matter of days, nor months.
Oh, when will he be here again?
The fowls are roosting on their perches,
Another day is ending,
The sheep and cows have all come down.
My lord is on service;
Were I but sure that he gets drink and food!

## 67 ✦ *My Lord Is All Aglow*

My lord is all aglow.
In his left hand he holds the reed-organ,
With his right he summons me to make free with him.
Oh, the joy!

My lord is care-free.
In his left hand he holds the dancing plumes,
With his right he summons me to sport with him.
Oh, the joy!

In 771 B.C. the Zhou capital was sacked by barbarian tribes, and the Western Zhou dynasty came to an end. A new capital was set up near Luoyang in Henan, but henceforward the Zhou (now known as Eastern Zhou) ceased to have any real political power, the Zhou king becoming merely the religious head of the affiliated states. The strong states of Qin and Jin kept the barbarians in check to the north and west. The real danger to the diminished Zhou kingdom came from the rising power of the Chu people in the south. In nos. 68 and 259 we find the king's soldiers defending Shen, Fu, and Xu in southern Henan. In no. 153 we find the people of Cao in south-western Shandong lamenting the decline of Zhou and ready to march to its assistance.

## 68 ✦ *The Spraying of the Waters*[1]

The spraying of the waters
Cannot float away firewood that is bundled.[2]
Yet those fine gentlemen
Are not here with us defending Shen.
Oh, the longing, the longing!
In what month shall we get home?

The spraying of the waters
Cannot float away thornwood that is bundled.
Yet those fine gentlemen
Are not here with us defending Fu.
Oh, the longing, the longing!
In what month shall we get home?

The spraying of the waters
Cannot float away osiers that are bundled.
Yet those fine gentlemen
Are not here with us defending Xu.
Oh, the longing, the longing!
In what month shall we get home?

## 69 ✦ *In the Midst of the Valley Is Motherwort*

In the midst of the valley is motherwort
All withered and dry.
A girl on her own,
Bitterly she sobs,
Bitterly she sobs,
Faced with man's unkindness.

---

1. This title appears three times in the collection (cf. nos. 92 and 116), although
Waley translates it slightly differently each time. *Ed.*

2. An image of cohesion.

In the midst of the valley is motherwort
All withered and seared.
A girl on her own,
Long she sighs,
Long she sighs,
Faced with man's wickedness.

In the midst of the valley is motherwort
All withered and parched.
A girl on her own,
In anguish she weeps,
In anguish she weeps;
But what does grief avail?

*Tui*, Siberian motherwort, is also called "The herb good for mothers."

## 70 ✦ *The Gingerly Hare*

Gingerly walked the hare,
But the pheasant was caught in the snare.
At the beginning of my life
All was still quiet;
In my latter days
I have met these hundred woes.[1]
Would that I might sleep and never stir!

Gingerly walked the hare;
But the pheasant got caught in the trap.
At the beginning of my life
The times were not yet troublous.
In my latter days
I have met these hundred griefs.
Would that I might sleep and wake no more!

1. The fall of the Western Zhou dynasty?

Gingerly walked the hare;
But the pheasant got caught in the net.
At the beginning of my life
The times were still good.
In my latter days
I have met these hundred calamities.
Would that I might sleep and hear no more!

## 71 ✦ *Close the Cloth-Plant Spreads*

Close the cloth-plant spreads its fibers
Along the banks of the river.
Far from big brothers, from little brothers
I must call a stranger "Father,"
Must call a stranger "Father";
But he does not heed me.

Close the cloth-plant spreads its fibers
Along the margin of the river.
Far from big brothers, from little brothers
I must call a stranger "Mother,"
Must call a stranger "Mother";
But she does not own me.

Close the cloth-plant spreads its fibers
Along the lips of the river.
Far from big brothers, from little brothers
I must call strangers kinsmen,
Must call strangers kinsmen;
But they do not listen to me.

## 72 ✦ *Plucking Cloth-Creeper*

Oh, he is plucking cloth-creeper,
For a single day I have not seen him;
It seems like three months!

Oh, he is plucking southernwood,
For a single day I have not seen him;
It seems like three autumns!

Oh, he is plucking mugwort,
For a single day I have not seen him;
It seems like three years!

## 73 ✦ *My Great Carriage*

"I brought my great carriage that thunders
And a coat downy as rush-wool.
It was not that I did not love you,
But I feared that you had lost heart.

I brought my great carriage that rumbles
And a coat downy as the pink sprouts.[1]
It was not that I did not love you,
But I feared that you would not elope."

Alive, they never shared a house,
But in death they had the same grave.
"You thought I had broken faith;
I was true as the bright sun above."

## 74 ✦ *Among the Hillocks Grows the Hemp*

Among the hillocks grows the hemp;
There works Zi-jue of Liu
There works Zi-jue of Liu.
If only he would come in and rest!

1. Of red millet.

Among the hillocks grows the wheat;
There works Zi-guo of Liu,
There works Zi-guo of Liu.
If only he would come in to supper!

Among the hillocks grow the plum-trees;
There work those good men of Liu,
There work those good men of Liu
That gave me jet-stones for my girdle.

# Airs of Zheng, 75–95

✦

Beginning with Confucius, commentators have long disparaged this large set of poems for its "licentiousness" (first for its music and then for its lyrics). That official displeasure might be seen as directly proportional to the power of the poetry, especially in the strong voice it gives to female desire, found in a number of poems and culminating in the last two, "Out in the Bushlands a Creeper Grows" and "The Zhen and Wei" (94, 95). Zheng was a powerful state located south of the Yellow River in present-day western Henan and was an important ally of the Eastern Zhou court.

## 75 ✦ *Your Black Coat*

How well your black coat fits!
Where it is torn I will turn it for you.
Let us go to where you lodge,
And there I will hand your food to you.

How nice your black coat looks!
Where it is worn I will mend it for you.
Let us go to where you lodge,
And there I will hand your food to you.

How broad your black coat is!
Where it is worn I will alter it for you.
Let us go to where you lodge,
And there I will hand your food to you.

## 76 ✦ I Beg You, Zhong Zi

I beg of you, Zhong Zi,
Do not climb into our homestead,
Do not break the willows we have planted.
Not that I mind about the willows,
But I am afraid of my father and mother.
Zhong Zi I dearly love;
But of what my father and mother say
Indeed I am afraid.

I beg of you, Zhong Zi,
Do not climb over our wall,
Do not break the mulberry-trees we have planted.
Not that I mind about the mulberry-trees,
But I am afraid of my brothers.
Zhong Zi I dearly love;
But of what my brothers say
Indeed I am afraid.

I beg of you, Zhong Zi,
Do not climb into our garden,
Do not break the hard-wood we have planted.
Not that I mind about the hard-wood,
But I am afraid of what people will say.
Zhong Zi I dearly love;
But of all that people will say
Indeed I am afraid.

## 77 ✦ Shu Is Away in the Hunting-Fields

Shu is away in the hunting-fields,
There is no one living in our lane.
Of course there *are* people living in our lane;
But they are not like Shu,
So beautiful, so good.

Shu has gone after game.
No one drinks wine in our lane.
Of course people *do* drink wine in our lane
But they are not like Shu,
So beautiful, so loved.

Shu has gone to the wilds,
No one drives horses in our lane.
Of course people *do* drive horses in our lane.
But they are not like Shu,
So beautiful, so brave.

## 78 ✦ *Shu in the Hunting-Fields*

Shu in the hunting-fields
Driving his team of four,
The reins like ribbons in his hand,
His helpers[1] leaping as in the dance!
Shu in the prairie.[2]
The flames rise crackling on every side;
Bare-armed he braves a tiger
To lay at the Duke's feet.
Please, Shu, no rashness!
Take care, or it will hurt you.

Shu in the hunting-fields
Driving his team of bays.
The yoke-horses, how high they prance!
Yet the helpers keep line
Like wild-geese winging in the sky.
Shu in the prairie.
Flames leap crackling on every side.
How well he shoots, how cleverly he drives!
Now giving rein, now pulling to a halt
Now letting fly,
Now following up his prey.

1. The two outside horses.

2. That has been fired to drive the game into the open.

Shu in the hunting-fields,
Driving a team of grays.
The two yoke-horses with heads in line,
The two helpers obedient to his hand.
Shu in the prairie,
Huge fires crackling on every side.
His horses slow down,
Shu shoots less often.
Now he lays aside his quiver,
Now he puts his bow in its case.

## 79 ✦ Men of Qing

The men of Qing are in Peng,
Their armored teams very strong.
Two spears, pennon out-topping pennon
Above the river[1] they move at ease.

The men of Qing are in Xiao,
Their armored teams very swift.
Two spears, hook topping hook;
Above the river they course at will.

The men of Qing are in Zhou,
Their armored teams move free.
The Left circles its banners, the Right raises them,
While the Center shouts "Well done!"

---

1. The scene of the song is near Kaifeng in Henan, apparently on both banks of
the Yellow River. I do not think it is possible to connect it with any definite his-
torical incident, but the traditional date (c. 660 B.C.) is quite a likely period. There
was probably more point in it than meets the eye. As it stands, the song is singu-
larly flat and uninteresting.

## 80 ✦ *Furs of Lamb's Wool*

His furs of lamb's wool so glossy!
Truly he is steadfast and tough.
That great gentleman
Would give his life rather than fail his lord.

His furs of lamb's wool, facings of leopard's fur!
He is very martial and strong.
That great gentleman
Is the upholder of right in this land.

His furs of lamb's wool so splendid,
His three festoons so gay!
That great gentleman
Is the first in all our land.

## 81 ✦ *Along the Highroad*[1]

If along the highroad
I caught hold of your sleeve,
Do not hate me;
Old ways take time to overcome.

If along the highroad
I caught hold of your hand,
Do not be angry with me;
Friendship takes time to overcome.

1. This poem is discussed at length in the Postface. *Ed.*

## 82 ✦ *The Lady Says*

The lady says: "The cock has crowed";
The knight says: "Day has not dawned."
"Rise, then, and look at the night;
The morning star is shining.
You must be out and abroad,
Must shoot the wild-duck and wild-geese.

When you have shot them, you must bring them home
And I will dress them for you,
And when I have dressed them we will drink wine
And I will be yours till we are old.
I will set your zithers before you;
All shall be peaceful and good.

Did I but know those who come to you,
I have girdle-stones of many sorts to give them;
Did I but know those that have followed you,
I have girdle-stones of many sorts as presents for them.
Did I know those that love you,
I have girdle-stones of many sorts to requite them."

This song and no. 96 could be paralleled by many "albas," dawn-songs, in European traditional poetry. The word used for "shoot" does not mean shooting with an ordinary bow and arrow but fowling with a short dart attached to a string. Xu Zhong-shu has written an interesting article on the subject.[1]

## 83 ✦ *There Was a Girl with Us in Our Carriage*

There was a girl with us in our carriage
Whose face was like the mallow-flower.
As we swept along,
Oh, at her belt the bright girdle-gems!
That fair eldest Jiang
Was fair and fine indeed.

1. See *Academia Sinica*, vol. 4, no. 4.

There was a girl with us in the same carriage-line
Whose face was like the mallow blossom.
As we swept along,
How those girdle-stones jingled!
That lovely eldest Jiang,
All that was told of her is true.


### 84 ✦ The Nutgrass Still Grows on the Hill

The nutgrass still grows on the hill;
On the low ground the lotus flower.
But I do not see Zi-tu;
I only see this madman.

On its hill the tall pine stands;
On the low ground the prince's-feather.
But I do not see Zi-chong;
I see only a mad boy.

The "madmen" were young men dressed up in black jackets and red
skirts who "searched in the houses and drove out pestilences."[1] In
order to do this they must have been armed, for disease-demons are
attacked with weapons, just like any other enemy. It is therefore not
surprising that the *Zhou li*[2] lists them among various categories of
armed men. Their nearest European equivalents are the Căluşari danc-
ers of Romania, who created such a stir in London when they at-
tended the International Folk Dance Festival in 1935. Professor Vuia
describes[3] the dance of the Căluşari as having originally been "a dance
with arms, intended to drive away demons of ill-health." Closely
analogous were the famous "Flower Boys" of Korea, who reached
their zenith in the sixth century A.D.

1. Commentary on *Zuo zhuan* chronicle; Duke Min, second year. For the medley
garb of these "wild men," see *Guo-yu*, the story of Prince Shen-sheng of Jin.

2. Chapter 54.

3. *Journal of the English Folk Dance and Song Society*, 1935, p. 107, where a note by
me on the Korean parallel is also printed.

The *you-long* of verse 2 has been identified as *Polygonum orientale* ("prince's-feather").

This is presumably the song with which the people of the house greeted the exorcists.

## 85 ✦ *Fallen Leaves*

Fallen leaves, fallen leaves,
The wind, he blows you.
O uncles, O elders,
Set the tune and I will sing with you.

Fallen leaves, fallen leaves,
The wind, he buffets you.
O uncles, O elders,
Set the tune and I will follow you.

## 86 ✦ *Mad Boy*

That mad boy[1]
Will not speak with me.
Yes, all because of you
I leave my rice untouched.

That mad boy
Will not eat with me.
Yes, it is all because of you
That I cannot take my rest.

1. For "mad boys," see no. 84.

## 87 ✦ *Gird Your Loins*

If you tenderly love me,
Gird your loins and wade across the Zhen;
But if you do not love me—
There are plenty of other men,
Of madcaps maddest, oh!

If you tenderly love me,
Gird your loins and wade across the Wei;
But if you do not love me—
There are plenty of other knights,
Of madcaps maddest, oh!

## 88 ✦ *Handsome*

A very handsome gentleman
Waited for me in the lane;
I am sorry I did not go with him.

A very splendid gentleman
Waited for me in the hall;
I am sorry I did not keep company with him.

I am wearing my unlined coat, my coat all of brocade.[1]
I am wearing my unlined skirt, my skirt all of brocade!
Oh uncles, young and old,
Let me go with him to his home!

I am wearing my unlined skirt, my skirt all of brocade.
And my unlined coat, my coat all of brocade.
Oh uncles, young and old,
Let me go with him to his home!

---

1. I do not here or elsewhere use these textile terms in a technical sense. Words for needlework and weaving are hopelessly confused in ancient Chinese; as they were also in medieval English.

THE AIRS OF THE STATES, POEMS 1–160

## 89 ✦ *By the Clearing at the Eastern Gate*

HE:    By the clearing at the Eastern Gate
        Where madder grows on the bank—
        Strange that the house should be so near
        Yet the person distant indeed!

SHE:   By the chestnut-trees at the Eastern Gate
        Where there is a row of houses.
        It is not that I do not love you,
        But that you are slow to court me.

## 90 ✦ *Wind and Rain*

Wind and rain, chill, chill!
But the cock crowed kikeriki.
Now that I have seen my lord,
How can I fail to be at peace?

Wind and rain, oh, the storm!
But the cock crowed kukeriku.
Now that I have seen my lord,
How can I fail to rejoice?

Wind and rain, dark as night,
The cock crowed and would not stop.
Now that I have seen my lord,
How can I any more be sad?

The weather, just how the cock crows, markings on the horses of
the bridegroom's carriage (no. 126)—everything that happens or is
seen on a wedding-day is ominous. The notes I ascribe to the cock
are not exact transcriptions but merely convenient equivalents.

### 91 ✦ *You with the Collar*

Oh, you with the blue collar,
On and on I think of you.
Even though I do not go to you,
You might surely send me news?

Oh, you with the blue collar,
Always and ever I long for you.
Even though I do not go to you,
You might surely sometimes come?

Here by the wall-gate
I pace to and fro.
One day when I do not see you
Is like three months.

### 92 ✦ *Even the Rising Waters*

Even the rising waters
Will not carry off thorn-faggots that are well bound.
Brothers while life lasts
Are you and I.
Do not believe what people say;
People are certainly deceiving you.

Even the rising waters
Will not carry off firewood that is well tied.
Brothers while life lasts
Are we two men.
Do not believe what people say;
People are certainly not to be believed.

## 93 ✦ *Outside the Eastern Gate*

Outside the Eastern Gate
Are girls many as the clouds;
But though they are many as clouds
There is none on whom my heart dwells.
White jacket and gray scarf[1]
Alone could cure my woe.

Beyond the Gate Tower
Are girls lovely as rush-wool;
But though they are lovely as rush-wool
There is none with whom my heart bides.
White jacket and madder skirt
Alone could bring me joy.

## 94 ✦ *Out in the Bushlands a Creeper Grows*

Out in the bushlands a creeper grows,
The falling dew lies thick upon it.
There was a man so lovely,
Clear brow well rounded.
By chance I came across him,
And he let me have my will.

Out in the bushlands a creeper grows,
The falling dew lies heavy on it.
There was a man so lovely,
Well rounded his clear brow.
By chance I came upon him:
"Oh, Sir, to be with you is good."

1. Denoting a humble lover.

## 95 ✦ *The Zhen and Wei*

When the Zhen and Wei
Are running in full flood
Is the time for knights and ladies
To fill their arms with scented herbs.
The lady says, "Have you looked?"
The knight says,"Yes, I have finished looking;
Shall we go and look a little more?
Beyond the Wei
It is very open and pleasant."
That knight and lady,
Merrily they sport.
Then she gives him a peony.

The Zhen and Wei
Run deep and clear;
That knight and lady,
Their flower-basket is full.
The lady says, "Have you looked?"
The knight says, "Yes, I have finished looking;
Shall we go and look a little more?
Beyond the Wei
It is very open and pleasant."
That knight and lady,
Merrily they sport.
Then she gives him a peony.

The commentators, no doubt rightly, connect this poem with a spring festival at which there was a custom of general courtship and mating. So we must take our knight and lady not as an individual romance, but as typical of the general courtship that went on in the land of Zheng in the third month. The peony has, of course, a great reputation for medicinal and magical powers, both in the West and in China. It shares some of the mythology of the mandrake. It was probably the root rather than the flower that first interested the Chinese; for the second element in the name (*Shao-yao*) means "medicinal herb," and it is the root of the peony that has always been used in medicine. It probably figured in courtship first as a love-philter, and later (as in this poem) merely as a symbol of lasting affection, like our rosemary. A popular etymology makes it mean the "binding herb."

# Airs of Qi, 96–106

✦

The state of Qi was one of the oldest and largest in the Zhou feudal domain, located in the northern part of present-day Shandong; it was a companion state to Lu to the south, which instead of "airs" has a section of "hymns" (nos. 297–300). Several of the poems in this set are specifically about weddings, in which the most important event is the transportation of the bride to her husband's home, as seen in "Southern Hill" (101) and "Here They Gallop" (105).

## 96 ✦ *The Cock Has Crowed*

THE LADY:    The cock has crowed;
It is full daylight.

THE LOVER:    It was not the cock that crowed,
It was the buzzing of those green flies.

THE LADY:    The eastern sky glows;
It is broad daylight.

THE LOVER:    That is not the glow of dawn,
But the rising moon's light.
The gnats fly drowsily;
It would be sweet to share a dream with you.

THE LADY:    Quick! Go home!
Lest I have cause to hate you!

## 97 ✦ *Splendid*

How splendid he was!
Yes, he met me between the hills of Nao.[1]
Our chariots side by side we chased two boars.
He bowed to me and said I was very nimble.

How strong he was!
Yes, he met me on the road at Nao.
Side by side we chased two stags.
He bowed to me and said "well done."

How magnificent he was!
Yes, he met me on the south slopes of Nao.
Side by side we chased two wolves.
He bowed to me and said "that was good."

## 98 ✦ *The Gate-Screen*

He waited for me at the gate-screen, heigh-ho!
His ear-plugs[2] were white, heigh-ho!
And over them, a bright flower, heigh-ho!

He waited for me in the courtyard, heigh-ho!
His ear-plugs were green, heigh-ho!
And over them, a bright blossom, heigh-ho!

He waited for me in the hall, heigh-ho!
His ear-plugs were yellow, heigh-ho!
And over them, a blossom bright, heigh-ho!

1. In northern Shandong.

2. I take it that ear-rings were only worn on state occasions and that the "plugs" took their place at other times.

## 99 ✦ *Sun in the East*

Sun in the east!
This lovely man
Is in my house,
Is in my home,
His foot is upon my doorstep.

Moon in the east!
This lovely man
Is in my bower,[1]
Is in my bower,
His foot is upon my threshold.

## 100 ✦ *Toward the East It Is Still Dark*

Toward the east it is still dark,
But he bustles into jacket and skirt.
He bustles into them and hustles into them;
From the palace they have sent for him.

The dew of night is not yet dry,[2]
But he bustles into skirt and coat,
Hustles into them and bustles into them;
To the palace they have summoned him.

1. The word that I have translated "bower" means the back part of the house, where the women lived. The sun and moon are symbols of his beauty, and do not mark (as one might at first sight suppose) the time of his visit. Compare no. 143.

2. The original says, "Toward the east it is not yet dry." The first two characters have been erroneously repeated from verse 1.
   For a different rendering of this song, see *Chinese Poems* (1946), p. 21. I am still not sure which is right. Here, and elsewhere in this book, the allocation of lines to different speakers is my own, and is not indicated in the original (except in no. 82. *Ed.*)

"He is breaking the willows of the fenced garden,
The mad fellow in his flurry—
Never can he judge the time of night;
If he's not too late, then he's too early."


## 101 ✦ Southern Hill

Over the southern hill so deep
The male fox drags along,
But the way to Lu is easy and broad
For this Qi lady on her wedding-way.
Yet once she has made the journey,
Never again must her fancy roam.

Fiber shoes, five pairs;
Cap ribbons, a couple.[1]
The way to Lu is easy and broad
For this lady of Qi to use.
But once she has used it,
No way else must she ever go.

When we plant hemp, how do we do it?
Across and along we put the rows.
When one takes a wife, how is it done?
The man must talk with her father and mother.
And once he has talked with them,
No one else must he court.

When we cut firewood, how do we do it?
Without an axe it would not be possible.
When one takes a wife, how is it done?
Without a match-maker he cannot get her.
But once he has got her,
No one else must he ever approach.[2]

---

1. Marriage gifts.

2. With a view to marriage. It does not, of course, mean that he may not have concubines.

## 102 ✦ *Too Big a Field*

Do not till too big a field,
Or weeds will ramp it.
Do not love a distant man,
Or heart's pain will chafe you.

Do not till too big a field,
Or weeds will top it.
Do not love a distant man,
Or heart's pain will fret you.

So pretty, so lovable,
With his side-locks looped!
A little while, and I saw him
In the tall cap of a man.

## 103 ✦ *Here Come the Hounds*

Here come the hounds, ting-a-ling,
And their master so handsome and good:
The hounds, with double ring,
Their master so handsome and brave.
The hounds, with double hoop;
Their master so handsome and strong.

## 104 ✦ *Wicker Fish-Trap*

In the wicker fish-trap by the bridge
Are fish, both bream and roach.
A lady of Qi goes to be married;
Her escort is like a trail of clouds.

In the wicker fish-trap by the bridge
Are fish, both bream and tench.
A lady of Qi goes to be married;
Her escort is thick as rain.

In the wicker fish-trap by the bridge
The fish glide free.
A lady of Qi goes to be married;
Her escort is like a river.


## 105 ✦ *Here They Gallop*

Here they gallop, pak, pak,
Bamboo awning, red leatherwork.
The Lu road is easy and wide;
A lady of Qi sets out at dusk.

Four black horses well-groomed,
Dangling reins all glossy.
The Lu road is easy and wide;
All happiness to this lady of Qi!

The waters of the Wen stretch broad;
The escort has splendid steeds.
The Lu road is easy and wide;
A pleasant journey to the lady of Qi!

The waters of the Wen rush headlong;
The escort has swift steeds.
The Lu road is easy and wide;
Good love-sport to the lady of Qi!

The River Wen runs east to west through the middle of central
Shandong and divides the states of Qi and Lu.


## 106 ✦ *Hey-ho*

Hey-ho, he is splendid!
Magnificent in stature,
Noble his brow,
His lovely eyes so bright,
Nimble in running,
A bowman unsurpassed.

Hey-ho, he is glorious!
Lovely eyes so clear,
Perfect in courtesy,
Can shoot all day at a target
And never miss the mark.
Truly a man of my clan.

Hey-ho, he is lovely!
His clear brow well-rounded,
When he dances, never losing his place,
When he shoots, always piercing.
Swift his arrows fly
To quell mischief on every side.

# Airs of Wey,[1] 107–13

✦

Wey was a small state in the eastern part of present-day Shanxi, which was absorbed into the large state of Jin to the east in the seventh century B.C. The last poem of this relatively small set, "Big Rat" (113), is by far the most noteworthy. It foreshadows the political laments that are so common in the "Minor Odes" but uses figurative language that is unusual for the *Songs*, both in the direct metaphor of calling the rapacious government a rat and in the invocation of the mysterious "happy land."

### 107 ✦ *Fiber Shoes*

Fiber shoes tightly woven
Are good for walking upon the dew.
A girl's fingers, long and slender,
Are good for sewing clothes.
Hem them, seam them;
The loved one shall wear them.

The loved one is very dutiful;
Humbly she steps aside.
Jade plugs at her ears,[2]
Ivory pendant at her belt.
Only—she is mean,
That is why I make this stab.

1. Here and elsewhere I alter the spelling of this name (usually "Wei") to distinguish it from the other state of Wei of present-day Henan (cf. nos. 55–64). *Ed.*

2. The meter shows that a line is missing. I supply one on the analogy of other poems.

I take this to be the "stab," the wounding, spiteful song of a girl who considered she had not been properly rewarded for her toil in making the bride's trousseau.


### 108 ✦ *Oozy Ground by the Fen*

There in the oozy ground by the Fen[1]
I was plucking the sorrel;
There came a gentleman
Lovely beyond compare,
Lovely beyond compare,
More beautiful than any that ride
With the duke in his coach.

There on a stretch by the Fen
I was plucking mulberry-leaves;
There came a gentleman
Lovely as the glint of jade,
Lovely as the glint of jade,
More splendid than any that attend
The duke in his coach.

There in the bend of the Fen
I was plucking water-plantain;
There came a gentleman
Lovely as jade,
Lovely as jade,
More splendid than any that escort
The duke in his coach.

1. A tributary of the Yellow River in the southwestern corner of Shanxi.

### 109 ✦ *In the Garden Is a Peach-Tree*

In the garden is a peach-tree;[1]
But its fruits are food.
It is my heart's sadness
That makes me chant and sing.
Those who do not know me
Say, "My good sir, you are impudent.
That man is perfectly right.
What is this that you are saying about him?"
My heart's sorrow,
Which of them knows it?
Which of them knows it?
The truth is, they do not care.

In the garden is a prickly jujube;
But its fruits are good to eat.
It is my heart's sadness
That makes me travel from land to land.
Those who do not know me
Say, "My good sir, you are a scamp.
That man is perfectly right.
What is this that you are saying about him?"
My heart's sorrow,
Which of them knows it?
Which of them knows it?
The truth is, they do not care.

### 110 ✦ *Climb the Wooded Hill*

I climb that wooded hill
And look toward where my father is.
My father is saying, "Alas, my son is on service;
Day and night he knows no rest.
Grant that he is being careful of himself,
So that he may come back and not be left behind!"

---

1. As it balances the prickly jujube, it cannot be the ordinary peach that is meant, but the *yang-tao*, "sheep's peach," which was thorny. See no. 148.

I climb that bare hill
And look toward where my mother is.
My mother is saying, "Alas, my young one is on service;
Day and night he gets no sleep.
Grant that he is being careful of himself,
So that he may come back, and not be cast away."

I climb that ridge
And look toward where my elder brother is.
My brother is saying, "Alas, my young brother is on service;
Day and night he toils.
Grant that he is being careful of himself,
So that he may come back and not die."

## 111 ✦ *In the Ten-Acre Field*

In the ten-acre field
A mulberry-picker stands idle,
Says: "If you're going, I will come back with you."

Beyond the ten-acre field
A mulberry-picker has strayed,
Says: "If you're going, I will stroll with you."

## 112 ✦ *Cutting Hardwood*

Chop, chop they cut the hardwood
And lay it on the river bank
By the waters so clear and rippling.
If we did not sow, if we did not reap,
How should we get corn, three hundred stack-yards?
If you did not hunt, if you did not chase,
One would not see all those badgers hanging in your courtyard.
No, indeed, that lord
Does not feed on the bread of idleness.

Chop, chop they cut cart-spokes
And lay them beside the river,
By the waters so clear and calm.
If we did not sow, if we did not reap,
How should we get corn, three hundred barns?
If you did not hunt, if you did not chase,
One would not see the king-deer hanging in your courtyard.
No, indeed, that lord
Does not eat the bread of idleness.

Chop, chop they cut wheels
And lay them on the lips of the river,
By the waters so clear and wimpling.
If we did not sow, if we did not reap,
How should we get corn, three hundred bins?
If you did not hunt, if you did not chase,
One would not see all those quails hanging in your courtyard.
No, indeed, that lord
Does not sup the sup of idleness.


## 113 ✦ *Big Rat*

Big rat, big rat,
Do not gobble our millet!
Three years we have slaved for you,
Yet you take no notice of us.
At last we are going to leave you
And go to that happy land;
Happy land, happy land,
Where we shall have our place.

Big rat, big rat,
Do not gobble our corn!
Three years we have slaved for you,
Yet you give us no credit.
At last we are going to leave you
And go to that happy kingdom;
Happy kingdom, happy kingdom,
Where we shall get our due.

Big rat, big rat,
Do not eat our rice-shoots!
Three years we have slaved for you.
Yet you did nothing to reward us.
At last we are going to leave you
And go to those happy borders;
Happy borders, happy borders
Where no sad songs are sung.

# Airs of Tang, 114–25

✦

"Tang" is an old designation for what would become the very powerful state of Jin in the north-central part of the Zhou feudal area; the "Airs of Tang," along with the preceding set, are thus associated with Jin. Here and in many other poems in the collection, beauty (often of a loved one) is depicted with sartorial images rather than with direct reference to the body—see, for example, "Your Lamb's Wool" (no. 120).

## 114 ✦ *Cricket*

THE FEASTERS:    The cricket is in the hall,
                   The year is drawing to a close.
                   If we do not enjoy ourselves now,
                   The days and months will have slipped by.

THE MONITOR:    Do not be so riotous
                   As to forget your homes.
                   Amuse yourselves, but no wildness!
                   Good men are always on their guard.

THE FEASTERS:    The cricket is in the hall,
                   The year draws to its end.
                   If we do not enjoy ourselves now,
                   The days and months will have gone their way.

THE MONITOR:    Do not be so riotous
                   As to forget the world beyond.
                   Amuse yourselves, but no wildness!
                   Good men are always on the watch.

| THE FEASTERS: | The cricket is in the hall, |
|---|---|
| | Our field-wagons are at rest. |
| | If we do not enjoy ourselves now, |
| | The days and months will have fled away. |
| THE MONITOR: | Do not be so riotous |
| | As to forget all cares. |
| | Amuse yourselves, but no wildness! |
| | Good men are always demure. |

## 115 ✦ *On the Mountain Is the Thorn-Elm*

On the mountain is the thorn-elm;
On the low ground the white elm-tree.
You have long robes,
But do not sweep or trail them.
You have carriages and horses,
But do not gallop or race them.
When you are dead
Someone else will enjoy them.

On the mountain is the cedrela;
On the low ground the privet.
You have courtyard and house,
But you do not sprinkle or sweep them.
You have bells and drums,
But you do not play on them, beat them.
When you are dead
Someone else will treasure them.

On the mountain is the varnish-tree;
On the low ground the chestnut.
You have wine and meat;
Why do you not daily play your zither,
And perhaps once in a way be merry,
Once in a way sit up late?
When you are dead
Someone else will enter into your house.

## 116 ✦ *Spray Rises from Those Waters*

SHE: Spray rises from those waters;
The white rocks are rinsed.
White coat with red lappet,
I followed you to Wo;
And now that I have seen my lord,
Happy am I indeed.

Spray rises from those waters;
The white rocks are washed clean.
White coat with red stitching,
I followed you to Hu;
And now that I have seen my lord,
How can I be sad?

HE: Spray rises from those waters;
The white rocks are dabbled.
I hear that you are pledged;
I dare not talk to your people.

The places mentioned are all in south-central Shanxi. In the first two verses the white rocks are symbols of the man's fresh, clean (*sauber,* as the Germans say) appearance. In the third verse they symbolize his tears shed because he knows that the lady has been *ming,* bidden by her parents to marry someone else, and that it is hopeless for him to *gao,* talk to her parents, ask for her hand.

## 117 ✦ *Pepper-Plant*

The seeds of the pepper-plant[1]
Overflowed my pint-measure.
That man of mine,
None so broad and tall!
Oh, the pepper-plant,
How wide its branches spread!

The seeds of the pepper-plant
Overflowed my hands as well.
That man of mine
Big, tall, and strong!
Oh, the pepper-plant,
How wide its branches spread!

## 118 ✦ *Fast Bundled*

Fast bundled is the firewood;
The Three Stars[2] have risen.
Is it to-night or which night
That I see my Good Man?
Oh, masters, my masters,[3]
What will this Good Man be like?

Fast bundled is the hay;
The Three Stars are at the corner.[4]
Is it to-night or which night
That shall see this meeting?
Oh, masters, my masters,
What will that meeting be like?

1.  The fine stature of the lover is compared to the luxuriance of the pepper-plant, which at the same time symbolizes the heat of his passion.

2.  The belt of Orion.

3.  May merely be a meaningless exclamation.

4.  Of the house, as seen from inside.

Fast bundled is the wild-thorn;
The Three Stars are at the door.
Is it to-night or which night
That I see that lovely one?
Oh, masters, my masters,
What will that lovely one be like?


## 119 ✦ *Tall Pear-Tree*

Tall stands that pear-tree;[1]
Its leaves are fresh and fair.
But alone I walk, in utter solitude.
True indeed, there are other men;
But they are not like children of one's own father.
Heigh, you that walk upon the road,
Why do you not join me?
A man that has no brothers,
Why do you not help him?

Tall stands that pear-tree;
Its leaves grow very thick.
Alone I walk and unbefriended.
True indeed, there are other men;
But they are not like people of one's own clan.
Heigh, you that walk upon the road,
Why do you not join me?
A man that has no brothers,
Why do you not help him?


## 120 ✦ *Your Lamb's Wool*

In your lamb's wool and cuffs of leopard's fur
From people like me you hold aloof.
Of course, I have other men;
But only you belong to old days.

---

1. The image of the pear-tree works by contrast, exactly as in no. 169.

In your lamb's wool and sleeves of leopard's fur
To people like me you are unfriendly.
Of course, I have other men;
But it is only you that I love.


121 ✦ *The Bustard's Plumes*

*Suk, suk* go the bustard's plumes;
It has settled on the oak clump.
But the king's business never ends;
I cannot plant my cooking-millet and wine-millet.
Where can my father and mother look to for support?
O blue Heaven so far away,
When will this all be settled?

*Suk, suk* go the bustard's wings;
It has settled on the thorn-bushes.
But the king's business never ends;
I cannot plant my wine-millet and cooking-millet.
What, then, are my father and mother to eat?
O blue Heaven so far away,
When will it all end?

*Suk, suk* goes that row of bustards;
They have settled on the mulberry clump.
But the king's business never ends;
I cannot plant my rice and spiked millet.
Then how shall my father and mother be fed?
O blue Heaven so far off,
When will things go back to their wonted ways?

## 122 ✦ *No Bedclothes?*

"How can you say you have no bedclothes?
                Why, you have seven!"
"But not like your bedclothes, so comfortable and fine."
"How can you say you have no bedclothes?
                Why, you have six!"
"Yes, but not like your bedclothes, so comfortable and warm."

## 123 ✦ *Tall Is the Pear-Tree*

Tall is the pear-tree
That is on the left side of the road.
Ah, that good lord
At last[1] has deigned to visit me.
To the depths of my heart I love him.
Had I but drink and food for him!

Tall is the pear-tree
That is at the turn of the road.
Ah, that good lord
At last is willing to come and play with me.
To the depths of my heart I love him.
Had I but drink and food for him!

## 124 ✦ *The Cloth-Plant Grew*

The cloth-plant grew till it covered the thorn-bush;
The bindweed spread over the wilds.
My lovely one is here no more.
With whom? No, I sit alone.

---

1.  Play of words on "tall" and "at last"? Both approximately *died* in Archaic Chinese.

The cloth-plant grew till it covered the brambles;
The bindweed spread across the borders of the field.
My lovely one is here no more.
With whom? No, I lie down alone.

The horn[1] pillow so beautiful,
The worked coverlet so bright!
My lovely one is here no more.
With whom? No, alone I watch till dawn.

Summer days, winter nights—
Year after year of them must pass
Till I go to him where he dwells.
Winter nights, summer days—
Year after year of them must pass
Till I go to his home.


## 125 ✦ *Plucking Licorice*

I was plucking licorice, licorice,
On the top of Shou-yang.[2]
The stories that people tell—
Do not believe them at all.
Let be, let be!
It is not so at all.
The stories that people tell—
What is to be got from them?

1. A pillow of wood inlaid with horn.

2. Near Ping-yang, in south-central Shanxi. The first two lines in each verse may
be comparisons; but I think they imply an alibi.

I was plucking sow-thistle, sow-thistle
At the bottom of Shou-yang.
The stories that people tell—
Do not heed them at all.
Let be, let be!
It is not so at all.
The stories that people tell—
What is to be got from them?

I was plucking cabbage, wild cabbage
To the east of Shou-yang.
The stories that people tell—
Do not be led by them at all.
Let be, let be!
It is not so at all.
The stories that people tell—
What is to be got from them?

# Airs of Qin, 126–35

✦

The state of Qin rose in the far west to challenge and finally defeat all other feudal states, in the end replacing the Zhou royal house with China's first imperial dynasty (221–06 B.C.), ruled by the infamous Qin Shi-huang (First Emperor of the Qin). Yet these poems come from a time when Qin was a relatively minor player in feudal politics. In legend and official history the people of Qin are described as descendants of the "barbarian" tribes of the west, which is said to account for their martial prowess and able horsemanship. Whether by cultural legacy or editorial hindsight, many of the poems in the set do refer to that association. The famous poem "The Oriole" (131) depicts a people fierce even in death.

### 126 ✦ *Coach-Wheels Crunch*

The coach-wheels crunch;
There is one horse with a white forehead.
I have not yet seen my lord;
I am waiting till they send for me.

On the hillside grows the lacquer-tree,
On the lowlands the chestnut-tree.
Now I have seen my lord;
He sits opposite me, playing his zither:
"If today we are not merry,
In time to come we shall be too old."

On the hillside grows the mulberry-tree,
On the lowlands the willow.
Now I have seen my lord;
He sits opposite me, playing his reed-organ:
"If today we are not merry,
In time to come we shall be gone."


## 127 ✦ *Team of Grays*

His team of grays pull well;
The six reins in his hand
The duke's well-loved son
Follows his father to the hunt.

Lusty that old stag,
That stag so tall.
The duke says: "On your left!"
He lets fly, and makes his hit.

They hold procession through the northern park,
Those teams so well trained,
The light carts, bells at bridle;
Greyhound, bloodhound inside.


## 128 ✦ *Small War-Chariot*

The small war-chariot with its shallow body,
The upturned chariot-pole, with its five bands,
The slip rings, the flank-checks,
The traces stowed away in their silvered case.
The patterned mat, the long naves,
Drawn by our piebalds, our whitefoots.
To think of my lord,
Gracious as jade,
In his plank hut
Brings turmoil to every corner of my heart.

His four steeds so strong,
The six reins in his hand;
The piebald and the bay with black mane are inside,
The black-mouthed brown and the deep-black horse are outside.
The dragon shields are held touching,
Silvered too the buckle straps.[1]

My thoughts are of my lord
So gracious at home in the town.
When can I expect him?
How can I endure thus to think of him?

The team lightly caparisoned, perfectly trained,
The trident spear with silvered butt,
The shield many-colored with its coating of feathers,
The tiger-skin quiver with its chiseled collar,
The two bows stretched one against the other
To the bamboo-frame lashed with rattan.
My thoughts are of my lord
Whether I sleep or wake.
Gentle is my good man,
Flawless is his fair name.


## 129 ✦ Rush Leaves

Thick grow the rush leaves;
Their white dew turns to frost.
He whom I love
Must be somewhere along this stream.
I went up the river to look for him,
But the way was difficult and long.
I went down the stream to look for him,
And there in mid-water
Sure enough, it's he!

1. Actually, the strap buckles were silvered. The inversion is for the sake of rhyme.

Close grow the rush leaves,
Their white dew not yet dry.
He whom I love
Is at the water's side.
Upstream I sought him;
But the way was difficult and steep.
Downstream I sought him,
And away in mid-water
There on a ledge, that's he!

Very fresh are the rush leaves;
The white dew still falls.
He whom I love
Is at the water's edge.
Upstream I followed him;
But the way was hard and long.
Downstream I followed him,
And away in mid-water
There on the shoals is he!

## 130 ✦ *Mount Zhong-nan*

On Mount Zhong-nan[1] what is there?
There are peach-trees, plum-trees.
My lord has come
In damask coat, in fox furs,
His face rosy as though rouged with cinnabar.
There is a lord for you indeed!

On Mount Zhong-nan what is there?
The boxthorn, the wild plum-tree.
My lord has come
In brocaded coat, embroidered skirt,
The jades at his girdle tinkling.
Long may he live, long be remembered!

1. South of Xi'an, Shaanxi.

## 131 ✦ *The Oriole*

"Kio" sings the oriole
As it lights on the thorn-bush.
Who went with Duke Mu to the grave?
Yan-xi of the clan Zi-ju.
Now this Yan-xi
Was the pick of all our men;
But as he drew near the tomb-hole
His limbs shook with dread.
That blue one, Heaven,
Takes all our good men.
Could we but ransom him
There are a hundred would give their lives.

"Kio" sings the oriole
As it lights on the mulberry-tree.
Who went with Duke Mu to the grave?
Zhong-hang of the clan Zi-ju.
Now this Zhong-hang
Was the sturdiest of all our men;
But as he drew near the tomb-hole
His limbs shook with dread.
That blue one, Heaven,
Takes all our good men.
Could we but ransom him
There are a hundred would give their lives.

"Kio" sings the oriole
As it lights on the brambles.
Who went with Duke Mu to the grave?
Qian-hu of the clan Zi-ju.
Now this Qian-hu
Was the strongest of all our men.
But as he drew near the tomb-hole
His limbs shook with dread.
That blue one, Heaven,
Takes all our good men.
Could we but ransom him
There are a hundred would give their lives.

Duke Mu of Qin died in 621 B.C., so that the exact date of No. 131 is known. (Of course, the composition of the poem could have occurred later. *Ed*.) The extent to which kings were followed into the grave by their servitors differed very much at various times and in various localities. The practice existed on a grand scale during the dynasty which preceded Zhou. It was disapproved of by the Confucians, but revived by the Qin when they conquered all China (middle of the third century B.C.). So far as I know it was never revived after the rise of the Han in 206 B.C.

## 132 ✦ *Falcon*

Swoop flies that falcon;
Dense that northern wood.
Not yet have I seen my lord;
Sore grieves my heart.
What will it be like, what like?
I am sure many will forget me.

On the hill is a clump of oaks
And in the lowlands, the piebald-tree.
Not yet have I seen my lord;
My grief I cannot cure.
What will it be like, what like?
I am sure many will forget me.

On the hill is a clump of plum-trees;
And on the lowlands, planted pear-trees.
Not yet have I seen my lord;
With grief I am dazed.
What will it be like, what like?
I am sure many will forget me.

The theme of the comparisons is that everything in nature goes its wonted way and is in its proper place; but I am embarking on a new, unimaginable existence.

## 133 ✦ *No Wraps?*

How can you plead that you have no wraps?
I will share my rug with you.
The king is raising an army;
I have made ready both spear and axe;
You shall share them with me as my comrade.

How can you plead that you have no wraps?
I will share my under-robe with you.
The king is raising an army,
I have made ready both spear and halberd;
You shall share them with me when we start.

How can you plead that you have no wraps?
I will share my skirt[1] with you.
The king is raising an army,
I have made ready both armor and arms;
You shall share them with me on the march.

## 134 ✦ *North of the Wei*

I escorted my mother's brother
As far as the north of the Wei.
What present did I give him?
A big chariot and a team of bays.

I escorted my mother's brother;
Far my thoughts followed him.
What present did I give him?
A lovely ghost-stone,[2] a girdle-pendant of jade.

1. As a rug at night.
2. So the word is written; but the "ghost" element may merely be phonetic.

### 135 ✦ *As We Sprouted*

Oh, what has become of us?
Those big dish-stands that towered so high!
To-day, even when we get food, there is none to spare.
Alas and alack!
We have not grown as we sprouted.

Oh, what has become of us?
Four dishes at every meal!
To-day, even when we get food, there is never enough.
Alas and alack!
We have not grown as we sprouted.

# Airs of Chen, 136–45

✦

From the selection here, one would assume that city gates, which are featured in half of these poems, are somehow especially significant to the singers of Chen. In fact, the city wall and its gate are important throughout Zhou civilization, and in that liminal space things often happened and stories began. Chen, itself, was at the southern edge of the Zhou domain and would in the end be absorbed into the southern state of Chu, noted for its unique cultural makeup, especially its practice of shamanism. This culture was sometimes also associated with Chen, but there certainly is no sign of that here; these are simple, engaging love songs, which are the main fare of "The Airs of the States."

### 136 ✦ Hollow Mound

How you make free,
There on top of the Hollow Mound!
Truly, a man of feeling,
But very careless of repute.

Bang, he beats his drum
Under the Hollow Mound.
Be it winter, be it summer,
Always with the egret feathers in his hand.

Bang, he beats his earthen gong
Along the path to the Hollow Mound.
Be it winter, be it summer,
Always with the egret plumes in his hand.

## 137 ✦ *Elms of the Eastern Gate*

Elms of the Eastern Gate,
Oaks of the Hollow Mound—
The sons of the Zi-zhong
Trip and sway beneath them.

It is a lucky morning, hurrah!
The Yuan girls from the southern side
Instead of twisting their hemp
In the market trip and sway.

It is a fine morning at last!
"Let us go off to join the throng."
"You are lovely as the mallow."
"Then give me a handful of pepper-seed!"


## 138 ✦ *The Town-Gate*

Down below the town-gate
It is easy to idle time away.
Where the spring flows by
It is easy to satisfy one's desires.[1]

Must the fish one sups off
Needs be bream from the river?
Must the girl one weds
Needs be a Jiang[2] from Qi?

Must the fish one sups on
Needs be carp from the river?
Must the girl one weds,
Needs be a Zi from Song?[3]

---

1. Not by drinking the water, as has usually been supposed, but by picking up one of the girls who haunted the fringes of the town.

2. Name of the clan to which the rulers of Qi belonged.

3. Clan name of the rulers of Song. *Ed.*

### 139 ✦ *The Pond by the Eastern Gate*

The pond by the Eastern Gate
Is good for steeping hemp.
That beautiful Shu Ji[1]
Is good at capping songs.

The pond by the Eastern Gate
Is good for steeping cloth-grass.
That beautiful Shu Ji
Is good at capping proverbs.

The pond by the Eastern Gate
Is good for steeping rushes.
That beautiful Shu Ji
Is good at capping stories.

### 140 ✦ *By the Willows of the Eastern Gate*

By the willows of the Eastern Gate,
Whose leaves are so thick,
At dusk we were to meet;
And now the morning star is bright.

By the willows of the Eastern Gate,
Whose leaves are so close,
At dusk we were to meet;
And now the morning star is pale.

1. Literally, "third daughter of the clan Ji."

### 141 ✦ *Tomb Gate*

By the Tomb Gate are thorn-trees;
With an axe they are felled.
Man, you are not good,
And the people of this country know it,
Know it, but do nothing to check you;
For very long it has been so.

By the Tomb Gate are plum-trees;
Owls roost upon them.
Man, you are not good;
I make this song to accuse you.
Accused you do not heed me;
After your fall[1] you will think of me.

The magpie's nest, so cleverly contrived, and the other many-colored things in the following poem, are symbols of specious invention.

### 142 ✦ *On the Dike There Is a Magpie's Nest*

On the dike there is a magpie's nest,
On the bank grows the sweet vetch.
Who has lied to my lovely one,
And made my heart so sore?

The middle-path has patterned tiles,
On the bank grows the rainbow plant.
Who has lied to my lovely one,
And made my heart so sad?

1. When punished by "all the gentlemen." The metaphor is perhaps one of wrestling. (Waley's original note uses an incorrect cross-reference; but, as David Schaberg has suggested, it should be no. 35, stanza 5. *Ed.*) The owl is an evil bird. Owls roosting means evil deeds being "brought home" to the doer.

## 143 ✦ *Moon Rising*

A moon rising white
Is the beauty of my lovely one.
Ah, the tenderness, the grace!
Heart's pain consumes me.

A moon rising bright
Is the fairness of my lovely one.
Ah, the gentle softness!
Heart's pain wounds me.

A moon rising in splendor
Is the beauty of my lovely one.
Ah, the delicate yielding!
Heart's pain torments me.

## 144 ✦ *In Zhu-lin*

"How do you manage to be in Zhu-lin?"
"We are the escort of Xia Nan.
He has come to Zhu-lin;
We are the escort of Xia Nan.

We drove our four horses;
We did not pause till the outskirts of Zhu.
We drove our four colts,
And were in time for breakfast at Zhu."

Xia Nan was a grandee of the Chen state, in east-central Henan; his castle was at Zhu-lin, not far from the Chen capital. The satirical intention which the commentators attribute to the song does not fit in with its wording. In any case the date is about 600 B.C., or somewhat earlier.

### 145 ✦ *Swamp's Shore*

By that swamp's shore
Grow reeds and lotus.
There is a man so fair—
Oh, how can I cure my wound?
Day and night I can do nothing;
As a flood my tears flow.

By that swamp's shore
Grow reeds and scented herbs.
There is a man so fair—
Well-made, big, and strong.
Day and night I can do nothing;
For my heart is full of woe.

By that swamp's shore
Grow reeds and lotus-flowers.
There is a man so fair—
Well-made, big, and stern.
Day and night I can do nothing;
Face on pillow I toss and turn.

# Airs of Gui, 146–49

✦

Gui (also read *Kuai*) was a small state absorbed into Zheng in the eighth century B.C. Because of that, some argue that these four poems belong to the "Airs of Zheng"; others point out that these poems originate from a time when Gui was still sovereign and thus have their own designation. The small size of the set does suggest that the poems should be seen as remnants of something larger, and similarities with the following set suggest parallel provenances.

## 146 ✦ *Your Lamb's Wool*

In your lamb's wool sauntering,
In your fox-fur at Court—
Oh, how can I help thinking of you?
My heart throbs with pain.

In your lamb's wool roaming,
In your fox-fur there in the Hall—
Oh, how can I but think of you?
My heart is sad and sore.

In your lamb's wool glossy
As the first rays of dawn—
How can I help thinking of you?
My heart is sick within.

### 147 ✦ *Plain Cap*

That the mere glimpse of a plain cap
Could harry me with such longing,
Cause pain so dire!

That the mere glimpse of a plain coat
Could stab my heart with grief!
Enough! Take me with you to your home.

That a mere glimpse of plain leggings
Could tie my heart in tangles!
Enough! Let us two be one.

### 148 ✦ *In the Lowlands Is the Goat's-Peach*

In the lowlands is the goat's-peach;[1]
Very delicate are its boughs.
Oh, soft and tender,
Glad I am that you have no friend.

In the lowlands is the goat's-peach;
Very delicate are its flowers.
Oh, soft and tender,
Glad I am that you have no home.

In the lowlands is the goat's-peach;
Very delicate is its fruit.
Oh, soft and tender,
Glad I am that you have no house.

---

1. The goat's-peach was later identified with the Chinese gooseberry, which now
only grows a long way south of the Yangtze. The same names were applied to the
*Actinidia chinensis*, which grows in the north and is probably what is meant here.

### 149 ✦ *No Breeze*

No breeze stirs,
No cartwheel grates.
I gaze down the highway
And my heart is sad within.

No breeze blows,
No cartwheel whirrs.
I gaze down the highway
And my heart within is sore.

If there is anyone who offers to cook the fish
One is glad to wash the cauldrons for him.
If anyone will make cause with the west,[1]
That's a tune I'll gladly join in!

---

1. Gui lay immediately to the east of the new Zhou capital. The singer, I think,
wanted to make cause with Zhou instead of with Qi.

# Airs of Cao, 150–53

♦

Again we have a very small set of poems from a minor feudal kingdom. Cao, located in southwestern Shandong, was absorbed by a larger state to the south, Song, in the seventh century B.C. (cf. nos. 301–05).

### 150 ♦ *Mayfly*

Wings of the mayfly—
Dress so bright and new.
My heart is grieving;
Come back to me and stay.

Wing-sheaths of the mayfly—
Clothes so bright and gay.
My heart is grieving;
Come back to me and bide.

A mayfly that breaks out from its hole—
Hemp clothes, spotless as snow.
My heart is grieving;
Come back to me and rest.

### 151 ♦ *Man at Arms*

That man at arms
Bears halberd and spear;
That fine gentleman,
Ribboned head cloth and red greaves.[1]

1. More accurately, demijambes.

The pelican stays on the bridge;
It has not wetted its wings.
That fine gentleman
Has no right to his dress.

The pelican stays on the bridge;
It has not wetted its beak.
That fine gentleman
Has not followed up his love-meeting.

Oh, pent, oh, packed as they mount,
Those dawn-mists on the southern hill!
Oh, gentle, oh, fair,
Those young girls[1] left to pine.

## 152 ✦ *The Cuckoo*

The cuckoo is on the mulberry-tree;
Her young go astray;
But good people, gentle folk—
Their ways are righteous.
Their ways are righteous,
Their thoughts constrained.

The cuckoo is on the mulberry-tree;
Her young on the plum-tree.
Good people, gentle folk—
Their girdles are of silk.
Their girdles are of silk,
Their caps of mottled fawn.

The cuckoo is on the mulberry-tree;
Her young amid the thorns.
Good people, gentle folk—
Their ways are faultless.
Their ways are faultless,
They shape our land from end to end.

1. Whom he has seduced; or we may take it in the singular.

The cuckoo is on the mulberry-tree,
Her young on the hazel.
Good people, gentle folk—
Shape the people of this land.
Shape the people of this land,
And may they do so for ten thousand years!


## 153 ✦ *The Falling Spring*

Splash, that falling spring
Soaks that clustering henbane.
With a groan I start from my sleep
When I think of the city of Zhou.

Splash, that falling spring
Soaks that clustering southernwood.
With a groan I start from my sleep
When I think of Zhou and its city.

Splash, that falling spring
Soaks that clustering yarrow.
With a groan I start from my sleep
When I think of the city camp.

Strong grow the millet shoots;
Heavy rains have fattened them.
All the lands must march;
The Lord of Xun[1] will reward them.

1. Duke Wen, of Jin, who was acclaimed as duke by the troops at Xun, in south-
ern Shanxi, after his return from exile in 636. In 632 he organized a federation of
states pledged to support the king of Zhou. The people of Cao belonged to the
confederacy.

# *Airs of Bin, 154–60*

✦

Bin was the ancestral land of the Zhou royal house in present-day central Shaanxi and was associated with the Zhou legendary ancestor Lord Millet (cf. no. 245). These poems are some of the most important in the collection, with numerous references to the "eastern campaign" of the Duke of Zhou, presumably because he drew his troops from this stronghold of Zhou power when he went east to subdue a rebellion of Shang loyalists. The first poem in the set, "The Seventh Month," is an important rhapsody on the activities of the agricultural year.

The piece which follows is not a calendar but a song made out of sayings about "works and days," about the occupations belonging to different seasons of the year. There is no attempt to go through these in their actual sequence. "Seventh month," "ninth month," and so forth, means the seventh and ninth months of the traditional, popular calendar, which began its year in the spring; whereas "days of the First," "days of the Second" means, according to the traditional explanation, the days of the first and second months in the Zhou calendar, which began its year round about Christmas, that is to say, at the time of the winter solstice. "The Fire ebbs" is explained as meaning "Scorpio is sinking below the horizon at the moment of its first visibility at dusk." Did this happen in northern China round about September during the eighth and seventh centuries B.C., the probable period of this song? That is a question which I must leave to astronomers.

### 154 ✦ *The Seventh Month*

In the seventh month the Fire ebbs;
In the ninth month I hand out the coats.
In the days of the First, sharp frosts;
In the days of the Second, keen winds.
Without coats, without serge,
How should they finish the year?
In the days of the Third they plough;
In the days of the Fourth out I step
With my wife and children,
Bringing hampers to the southern acre
Where the field-hands come to take good cheer.

In the seventh month the Fire ebbs;
In the ninth month I hand out the coats.
But when the spring days grow warm
And the oriole sings
The girls take their deep baskets
And follow the path under the wall
To gather the soft mulberry-leaves:
"The spring days are drawing out;
They gather the white aster in crowds.
A girl's heart is sick and sad
Till with her lord she can go home."

In the seventh month the Fire ebbs;
In the eighth month they pluck the rushes,
In the silk-worm month they gather the mulberry-leaves,
Take that chopper and bill
To lop the far boughs and high,
Pull toward them the tender leaves.
In the seventh month the shrike cries;
In the eighth month they twist thread,
The black thread and the yellow:
"With my red dye so bright
I make a robe for my lord."

In the fourth month the milkwort is in spike,
In the fifth month the cicada cries.
In the eighth month the harvest is gathered,
In the tenth month the boughs fall.
In the days of the First we hunt the raccoon,
And take those foxes and wild-cats
To make furs for our Lord.
In the days of the Second is the great Meet;
Practice for deeds of war.
The boar one year old we keep;
The three-year-old we offer to our lord.

In the fifth month the locust moves its leg,
In the sixth month the grasshopper shakes its wing,
In the seventh month, out in the wilds;
In the eighth month, in the farm,
In the ninth month, at the door.
In the tenth month the cricket goes under my bed.
I stop up every hole to smoke out the rats,
Plugging the windows, burying the doors:
"Come, wife and children,
The change of the year is at hand.
Come and live in this house."

In the sixth month we eat wild plums and cherries,
In the seventh month we boil mallows and beans.
In the eighth month we dry the dates,
In the tenth month we take the rice
To make with it the spring wine,
So that we may be granted long life.[1]
In the seventh month we eat melons,
In the eighth month we cut the gourds,
In the ninth month we take the seeding hemp,
We gather bitter herbs, we cut the ailanthus for firewood,
That our husbandmen may eat.

---

1. Wine increases one's *de* (inner power) and consequently increases the probability of one's prayers being answered. That is why we drink when we wish people good luck.

In the ninth month we make ready the stack-yards,
In the tenth month we bring in the harvest,
Millet for wine, millet for cooking, the early and the late,
Paddy and hemp, beans and wheat.
Come, my husbandmen,
My harvesting is over,
Go up and begin your work in the house,
In the morning gather thatch-reeds,
In the evening twist rope;
Go quickly on to the roofs.
Soon you will be beginning to sow your many grains.

In the days of the Second they cut the ice with tingling blows;
In the days of the Third they bring it into the cold shed.
In the days of the Fourth very early
They offer lambs and garlic.
In the ninth month are shrewd frosts;
In the tenth month they clear the stack-grounds.
With twin pitchers they hold the village feast,
Killing for it a young lamb.
Up they go into their lord's hall,
Raise the drinking-cup of buffalo-horn:
"Hurray for our lord; may he live for ever and ever!"


## 155 ✦ Kite-Owl

Oh, kite-owl, kite-owl,
You have taken my young.
Do not destroy my house.
With such love, such toil
To rear those young ones I strove!

Before the weather grew damp with rain
I scratched away the bark of that mulberry-tree
And twined it into window and door.
"Now, you people down below,
If any of you dare affront me. . . ."

My hands are all chafed
With plucking so much rush flower;
With gathering so much bast
My mouth is all sore.
And still I have not house or home!

My wings have lost their gloss,
My tail is all bedraggled.
My house is all to pieces,
Tossed and battered by wind and rain.
My only song, a cry of woe!

This poem is traditionally associated with the legend of King Cheng and his protector, the Duke of Zhou. It figures in the *Metal-Clasped Box*,[1] a fairly late work which, however, incorporates a good deal of early legend. The song is said to have been given to King Cheng by his good uncle. Naturally the kite-owl, always classed as a "wicked bird" by the Chinese, symbolizes the wicked, rebellious uncles. The persecuted bird, who is the speaker in the poem, would seem most naturally to be the Duke of Zhou, and the young whom the bird had reared with such love and care would then be the boy king. But the allegory does not work out very closely, and it is possible that the song had a quite different origin, and was only later utilized as an ornament to the legend of King Cheng.

1. One of the books of the *Shu jing*.

## 156 ✦ *Eastern Hills*

I went to the eastern hills;
Long was it till I came back.
Now I am home from the east;
How the drizzling rain pours!
I am back from the east,
But my heart is very sad.
You made for me that coat and gown
"Lest my soldier should go secret ways."[1]
Restless the silkworm that writhes
When one puts it on the mulberry-bush;
Staunch I bore the lonely nights,
On the ground, under my cart.

I went to the eastern hills;
Long, long was it till I came back.
Now I am home from the east;
How the drizzling rain pours!
The fruit of the bryony
Has spread over the eaves of my house.
There are sowbugs in this room;
There were spiders' webs on the door.
In the paddock were the marks of wild deer,
The light of the watchman[2] glimmers.
These are not things to be feared,
But rather to rejoice in.[3]

1. Be untrue.

2. The "night-goer," i.e., the glow-worm.

3. All these things can be interpreted as good omens. For example, *lu,* "deer,"
suggests *lu,* "luck." The spider is called "happy son" and other such names.

I went to the eastern hills;
Long, long was it till I came back.
When I came from the east,
How the drizzling rain did pour!
A stork was crying on the ant-hill;
That means a wife sighing in her chamber.
"Sprinkle and sweep the house,
We are back from our campaign."
There are the gourds piled up,
So many, on the firewood cut from the chestnut-tree.
Since I last saw them
Till now, it is three years!

I went to the eastern hills;
Long, long was it till I came back.
When I came from the east,
How the drizzling rain did pour!
"The oriole is in flight,
Oh, the glint of its wings!
A girl is going to be married.
Bay and white, sorrel and white are her steeds.
Her mother has tied the strings of her girdle;
All things proper have been done for her."
This new marriage is very festive;
But the old marriage, what of that?

This song is a typical "elliptical ballad," in which themes are juxta-
posed without explanation. Thus "the oriole . . ." down to "All things
proper have been done for her," is a marriage-song theme, which
lets us know that during the soldier's absence his wife has assumed
his death and married again.

### 157 ✦ *Broken Axes*

Broken were our axes
And chipped our hatchets.[1]
But since the Duke of Zhou came to the east
Throughout the kingdoms all is well.
He has shown compassion to us people,
He has greatly helped us.

Broken were our axes
And chipped our hoes.
But since the Duke of Zhou came to the east
The whole land has been changed.
He has shown compassion to us people,
He has greatly blessed us.

Broken were our axes
And chipped our chisels.
But since the Duke of Zhou came to the east
All the kingdoms are knit together.
He has shown compassion to us people,
He has been a great boon to us.

### 158 ✦ *Axe-Handle*

How does one cut an axe-handle?
Without an axe it is impossible.[2]
How does one take a wife?
Without a matchmaker she cannot be got.

Cut an axe-handle? Cut an axe-handle?
The pattern is not far to seek.
Here is a lady with whom I have had a love-meeting;
Here are my dishes[3] all in a row.

---

1. I.e., the whole state was in a bad way. The Duke of Zhou was sent to rule in Lu, the southern part of Shandong.

2. I.e., someone who has already been married himself.

3. Of ritual offerings.

This song represents, I think, the popular view that marriage was a very simple matter, and a matchmaker by no means necessary.

159 ✦ *Minnow-Net*

"The fish in the minnow-net
Were rudd and bream.
The lover I am with
Has blazoned coat and broidered robe."

"The wild-geese take wing; they make for the island.
The prince has gone off and we cannot find him.
He must be staying with you.

The wild-geese take wing; they make for the land.
The prince went off and does not come back.
He must be spending the night with you."

"All because he has a broidered robe
Don't take my prince away from me,
Don't make my heart sad."

160 ✦ *The Wolf*

The wolf may catch in its own dewlap
Or trip up upon its tail.
But this nobleman, so tall and handsome,
In his red shoes stands sure.

The wolf may trip upon its tail
Or be caught in its dewlap.
But this nobleman, so tall and handsome—
In his fair fame is no flaw.

# THE MINOR ODES,
## POEMS 161–234

✦

"The Minor Odes" (*Xiao ya*) marks a transition away from the quotidian concerns of the Zhou feudal countryside, so prominent in "The Airs of the States," toward a more aristocratic and courtly level of that society. To be sure, there is still a good measure of romantic desire and everyday distress in this section of seventy-four poems—witness the lover's complaint of being treated like slop-water in "Valley Wind" (201) or the soldiers' lament against war in "Tall Pear-Tree" (169). Yet there is a difference. Throughout "The Minor Odes" we find frequent mentions of the palace chamber, the feasting table, and the general's chariot. Moreover, these poems often specify historical terms: naming the Xian-yun enemy of the north and the Chinese general Nan-zhong who opposed them, dating poems with astronomical and calendrical precision, and lamenting the ill-advised actions of King You and his consort. These events are apparently unfolding at the same time and in coordination with the comings and goings described in "The Airs of the States," yet they often seem to be two steps removed from each other: as "The Greater East" (203) says, "Ways that are for gentleman to walk / And for commoners to behold."

Most important, "The Minor Odes" is pervaded by clan allegiances and other mechanisms for the maintenance of political and social power. Men (and it is almost exclusively men) come and go, are welcomed and sent off, plot wars together, and (perhaps most noticeably) eat and drink at clan gatherings. Wine flows through these poems, lubricating their negotiations of power—wine is mentioned four times more often in "The Minor Odes" than in the rest of the collection. And rather than the somber libations of the ancestral rituals that we see in the last part of the collection, it is boisterous drinking that celebrates the here and now: "Set out your dishes and meat-stands, / Drink wine to your fill; / All you brothers are here together, / Peaceful, happy, and mild." (164) Perhaps not coincidentally, "The Minor Odes" also has the most references to the "king's business," which was inevitably war. That feudal obligation to the royal house engendered some of the most powerful political laments in the collection, such as in "Bringing Out the Carts" (168) and "Diminutive" (196).

Traditionally, "The Minor Odes" and "The Major Odes" have been divided into decades (*shi*), which I have marked with section breaks.

## 161 ✦ *The Deer Cry*

*You, you,* cry the deer
Nibbling the black southernwood in the fields.
I have a lucky guest.
Let me play my zither, blow my reed-organ,
Blow my reed-organ, trill their tongues,
Take up the baskets of offerings.
Here is a man that loves me
And will teach me the ways of Zhou.

*You, you,* cry the deer
Nibbling the white southernwood of the fields.
I have a lucky guest,
Whose fair fame is very bright.
He sees to it that the common people do not waver,
Of all gentlemen he is the pattern and example.
I have good wine;
Let my lucky guest now feast and play.

*You, you,* cry the deer
Nibbling the wild garlic of the fields.
I have a lucky guest.
I play my zithers, small and big,
Play my zithers, small and big.
Let us make music together, let us be merry,
For I have good wine
To comfort and delight the heart of a lucky guest.

For the "luckiness" of guests, compare the *Odyssey,* book 6, line 207,
"All guests and beggars are envoys of Zeus."

## 162 ✦ *Four Steeds*

My four steeds are weary,
The high road is very far.
Indeed, I long to come home;
But the king's business never ends.
My heart is sick and sad.

My four steeds are weary,
They pant, those white steeds with black manes.
Indeed, I long to come home,
But the king's business never ends;
I have no time to tarry or stay.

See how they fluttered, those doves,[1]
Now rising, now dropping;
Yet they settled on the bushy oaks.
But the king's business never ends;
I have no time to feed my father.

See how they fluttered, those doves,
Now rising, now hovering.
Yet they settled on the bushy boxthorn.
But the king's business never ends;
I have no time to feed my mother.

I must yoke my white horses with black manes,
I must gallop at top speed.
Indeed, I long to come home.
That is why I made this song,
To tell how I long to feed my mother.

---

1. The ancient Chinese believed the turtle dove was very assiduous in feeding its parents. But I think the meaning here is simply that the dove rests at last; whereas the soldier gets no rest.

### 163 ✦ *Bright Are the Flowers*

Bright are the flowers
On those plains and lowlands.
In a great host go the travelers,
Each bent on keeping his place.

"My horses are colts,
My six reins are glossy;
I will speed, I will gallop,
Everywhere asking for counsel."

"My horses are dappled,
My six reins are like the threads of a loom.
I will speed, I will gallop,
Everywhere asking for instructions."

"My horses are white with black manes,
My six reins are all greased.
I will speed, I will gallop,
Everywhere asking for good plans."

"My horses are brindled,
The six reins very level.
I will speed, I will gallop,
Everywhere asking for advice."

This song is nominally a song of envoys, about to embark on a dip-
lomatic mission. I have a feeling, however, that the words may be
those of the "visiting" movement in a dance or dance-game.

### 164 ✦ *Cherry-Tree*

The flowers of the cherry-tree,
Are they not truly splendid?
Of men that now are,
None equals a brother.

When death and mourning affright us
Brothers are very dear;
As "upland" and "lowland" form a pair,
So "elder brother" and "younger brother" go together.

There are wagtails[1] on the plain;
When brothers are hard pressed
Even good friends
At the most do but heave a sigh.

Brothers may quarrel within the walls,
But outside they defend one another from insult;
Whereas even good friends
Pay but short heed.

But when the times of mourning or violence are over,
When all is calm and still,
Even brothers
Are not the equal of friends.

Set out your dishes and meat-stands,
Drink wine to your fill;
All you brothers are here together,
Peaceful, happy, and mild.

Your wives and children chime as well
As little zither with big zither.
You brothers are in concord,
Peaceful, merry, in great glee.

Thus you bring good to house and home,
Joy to wife and child.
I have deeply studied, I have pondered,
And truly it is so.

1. Symbols of agitation.

## 165 ✦ *The Woodman's Axe*

*Ding, ding* goes the woodman's axe;
*Ying, ying* cry the birds,
Leave the dark valley,
Mount to the high tree.
"Ying" they cry,
Each searching its mate's voice.

Seeing then that even a bird
Searches for its mate's voice,
How much the more must man
Needs search out friends and kin.
For the spirits are listening
Whether we are all friendly and at peace.

"Heave ho," cry the woodcutters.
I have strained my wine so clear,
I have got a fatted lamb
To which I invite all my fathers.[1]
Even if they choose not to come
They cannot say I have neglected them.

Spick and span I have sprinkled and swept,
I have set out the meats, the eight dishes of grain.
I have got a fatted ox,
To which I invite all my uncles,
And even if they choose not to come
They cannot hold me to blame.

They are cutting wood on the bank.
Of strained wine I have good store;
The dishes and trays are all in rows.
Elder brothers and younger brothers, do not stay afar!
If people lose the virtue that is in them,
It is a dry throat that has led them astray.

1. Paternal uncles.

When we have got wine we strain it, we!
When we have none, we buy it, we!
Bang, bang we drum, do we!
Nimbly step the dance, do we!
And take this opportunity
Of drinking clear wine.

## 166 ✦ *May Heaven Guard*

May Heaven guard and keep you
In great security,
Make you staunch and hale;
What blessing not vouchsafed?
Give you much increase,
Send nothing but abundance.

May Heaven guard and keep you,
Cause your grain to prosper,
Send you nothing that is not good.
May you receive from Heaven a hundred boons,
May Heaven send down to you blessings so many
That the day is not long enough for them all.

May Heaven guard and keep you,
Cause there to be nothing in which you do not rise higher,
Like the mountains, like the uplands,
Like the ridges, the great ranges,
Like a stream coming down in flood;
In nothing not increased.

Lucky and pure are your viands of sacrifice
That you use in filial offering,
Offerings of invocation, gift-offerings, offering in dishes and
        offering of first-fruits
To dukes and former kings.
Those sovereigns say: "We give you
Myriad years of life, days unending."

The Spirits are good,
They will give you many blessings.
The common people are contented,
For daily they have their drink and food.
The thronging herd, the many clans[1]
All side with you in deeds of power.

To be like the moon advancing to its full,
Like the sun climbing the sky,
Like the everlastingness of the southern hills,
Without failing or falling,
Like the pine-tree, the cypress in their verdure—
All these blessings may you receive!

The next two poems (along with no. 177 and no. 178) deal with or mention the campaigns of the Zhou people against the fierce Xian-yun tribes. The two Chinese generals, Nan-zhong, in no. 168, and Ji-fu, in no. 177, are both traditionally placed in King Xuan's reign (827–782 B.C.). Of the Xian-yun we know very little. All that we can be certain of is that they were a dreaded foe who invaded Shaanxi, the home-country of the Zhou, and were driven back in a series of campaigns, some of which took place round about 800 B.C.

### 167 ✦ *Plucking Bracken*

We plucked the bracken, plucked the bracken
While the young shoots were springing up.
Oh, to go back, go back!
The year is ending.
We have no house, no home
Because of the Xian-yun.
We cannot rest or bide
Because of the Xian-yun.

---

1. Into which the Zhou overlords were divided.

We plucked the bracken, plucked the bracken
While the shoots were soft.
Oh, to go back, go back!
Our hearts are sad,
Our sad hearts burn,
We are hungry and thirsty,
But our campaign is not over,
Nor is any of us sent home with news.

We plucked the bracken, plucked the bracken;
But the shoots were hard.
Oh, to go back, go back!
The year is running out.
But the king's business never ends;
We cannot rest or bide.
Our sad hearts are very bitter;
We went, but do not come.

What splendid thing is that?
It is the flower of the cherry-tree.
What great carriage is that?
It is our lord's chariot,
His war-chariot ready yoked,
With its four steeds so eager.
How should we dare stop or tarry?
In one month we have had three alarms.

We yoke the teams of four,
Those steeds so strong,
That our lord rides behind,
That lesser men protect.
The four steeds so grand,
The ivory bow-ends, the fish-skin quiver.
Yes, we must be always on our guard;
The Xian-yun are very swift.

Long ago, when we started,
The willows spread their shade.
Now that we turn back
The snowflakes fly.
The march before us is long,
We are thirsty and hungry,
Our hearts are stricken with sorrow,
But no one listens to our plaint.


## 168 ✦ *Bringing Out the Carts*

We bring out our carts
On to those pasture-grounds.
From where the Son of Heaven is
Orders have come that we are to be here.
The grooms are told
To get the carts loaded up.
The king's service brings many hardships;
It makes swift calls upon us.

We bring out our carts
On to those outskirts.
Here we set up the standards,
There we raise the ox-tail banners,
The falcon-banner, and the standards
That flutter, flutter.
Our sad hearts are very anxious;
The grooms are worn out.

The king has ordered Nan-zhong
To go and build a fort on the frontier.
To bring out the great concourse of chariots,
With dragon banners and standards so bright.
The Son of Heaven has ordered us
To build a fort on that frontier.
Terrible is Nan-zhong;
The Xian-yun are undone.

Long ago, when we started,
The wine-millet and cooking-millet were in flower.
Now that we are on the march again
Snow falls upon the mire.
The king's service brings many hardships.
We have no time to rest or bide.
We do indeed long to return;
But we fear the writing on the tablets.[1]

"Dolefully cry the cicadas,
Hop and skip go the grasshoppers.
Before I saw my lord
My heart was full of grief.
But now that I have seen my lord
My heart is still."[2]
Terrible is Nan-zhong;
Lo, he has stricken the warriors of the West!

The spring days are drawn out;
All plants and trees are in leaf.
Tuneful is the oriole's song.
The women gather aster[3] in crowds.
We have bound the culprits;[4] we have captured the chieftains,
And here we are home again!
Terrible is Nan-zhong;
The Xian-yun are leveled low.

1. The king's command.

2. Bridal-hymn formula, spoken by the wives.

3. For use in the ancestral temple.

4. For trial. Enemies are criminals and their instigators must be tried at law, like criminals. See Additional Notes.

## 169 ✦ *Tall Pear-Tree*

WIFE:    Tall grows that pear-tree,
              Its fruit so fair to see.[1]
              The king's business never ends;
              Day in, day out it claims us.

CHORUS:    In spring-time, on a day so sunny—
              Yet your heart full of grief?
              The soldiers have leave!

WIFE:    Tall grows that pear-tree,
              Its leaves so thick.
              The king's business never ends;
              My heart is sick and sad.

CHORUS:    Every plant and tree so leafy,
              Yet your heart sad?
              The soldiers are coming home!

SOLDIER:    I climb that northern hill
              To pluck the boxthorn.
              The king's business never ends;
              What will become of my father, of my mother?

CHORUS:    Their wickered chariots drag painfully along,
              Their horses are tired out.
              But the soldiers have not far to go.

WIFE:    If he were not expected and did not come
              My heart would still be sad.
              But he named a day, and that day is passed,
              So that my torment is great indeed.

CHORUS:    The tortoise and the yarrow-stalks agree;
              Both tell glad news.
              Your soldier is close at hand.

The tortoise and the yarrow-stalks represent two methods of divination. The first consisted of heating the carapace of a tortoise and

---

1. "The tree flowers in its season; but the soldiers cannot lead a natural existence" (earliest commentator). This use of contrast was completely misunderstood by later interpreters.

"reading" the cracks that appeared; the second, of shuffling stalks of the Siberian milfoil. (For a reference on tortoise-shell oracles see my note 5 to poem no. 237. *Ed.*)

### 170 ✦ *Fish in the Trap*

The fish caught in the trap
Were yellow-jaws and sand-eels.
Our lords have wine
Good and plentiful.

The fish caught in the trap
Were bream and tench.
Our lords have wine
Plentiful and good.

The fish caught in the trap
Were mud-fish and carp.
Our lords have wine
Good and to spare.

Things they have in plenty,
Only because their ways are blessed.
Things they have that are good,
Only because they are at peace with one another.
Things they have enough and to spare,
Only because their ways are lovely.

### 171 ✦ *In the South There Are Lucky Fish*

In the south there are lucky fish,
In their multitudes they leap.
Our lord has wine;
His lucky guests shall feast and rejoice.

In the south there are lucky fish,
In their multitudes they glide.
Our lord has wine;
His lucky guests shall feast and be merry.

In the south there is a tree with drooping boughs;
The sweet gourds cling to it.
Our lord has wine;
His lucky guests shall be feasted and comforted.

Winging, winging, the doves
In their flocks they come.[1]
Our lord has wine;
His lucky guests shall be feasted, shall be surfeited.

### 172 ✦ *Nutgrass Grows on the Southern Hills*

On the southern hills grows the nutgrass;
On the northern hills the goosefoot.
Happiness to our lord
That is the groundwork of land and home!
Happiness to our lord!
May he live for evermore.

---

1. Birds are the messengers of Heaven; when they come in flocks, it means that Heaven will send many blessings.

On the southern hills the mulberry;
On the northern hills the willow.
Happiness to our lord,
That is the light of land and home.
Happiness to our lord!
May he live for ever and ever.

On the southern hills the aspen;
On the northern hills the plum-tree.
Happiness to our lord
That is the father and mother of his people.
Happiness to our lord!
May his fair fame be for ever.

On the southern hills the cedrela;
On the northern hills the privet.
Happiness to our lord,
Yes, and life long-lasting!
Happiness to our lord!
May his fair fame never droop.

On the southern hills the boxthorn;
On the northern hills the catalpa.
Happiness to our lord,
Yes, till locks are seer and face is gray!
Happiness to you, our lord!
To your descendants, safety and peace!


173 ✦ *Thick Southernwood*

Thick grows that southernwood;
The falling dew drenches it.[1]
Now that I have seen my lord
My heart is eased.
So peaceably he laughs and talks
That I am happy and at rest.

1. A symbol of the bride's tears.

Thick grows that southernwood;
The falling dew lies heavy upon it.
Now I have seen my lord,
He has become my protector, my light.[1]
May his power[2] have no flaw,
May he live for evermore!

Thick grows that southernwood;
The falling dew dabbles it.
Now that I have seen my lord
I am happy and at peace.
May he bring good to his elder brothers, his younger brothers,
May he have magic power and great longevity!

Thick grows that southernwood;
The falling dew soaks it.
Now I have seen my lord,
His rein-ends jingling,
His chariot-bells and bridle-bells chiming,
In whom all blessings meet.


174 ✦ *Sopping Dew*

Sopping lies the dew;
Not till the sun comes will it dry.
Deep we quaff at our night-drinking;
Not till we are drunk shall we go home.

Sopping lies the dew
On that thick grass.
Deep we quaff at our night-drinking,
Here at the clan-gathering we will carry it through.[3]

1. Reading very doubtful.

2. Wherever the word "power" occurs in the translations it represents the Chinese word *de*. (But *de* does not always translate as "power." *Ed.*)

3. Meaning doubtful.

Sopping lies the dew
On those boxthorns and brambles.
Renowned are you, our guests,
None of you failing in noble power.

Those oil-trees, those paulownias,
Their fruits hang thick.
Blessed and happy are you, my lords,
None failing in noble ways.

## 175 ✦ *The Red Bow*

The red bow is unstrung,
When one is given it, one puts it away.
I have a lucky guest;
To the depths of my heart I honor him.
The bells and drums are all set;
The whole morning I feast him.

The red bow is unstrung,
When one is given it, one stores it.
I have a lucky guest;
To the depths of my heart I delight in him.
The bells and drums are all set;
The whole morning I ply him.

The red bow is unstrung,
When one is given it, one puts it in its press.
I have a lucky guest;
To the depths of my heart I love him.
The bells and drums are all set;
The whole morning I drink pledges with him.

The next piece is a marriage song adapted to celebrate not the meeting between bride and bridegroom but an audience given by a feudal superior to his vassal. No doubt most of the other marriage songs in this book were often used in the same way; but this is the only one in which the wording has manifestly been altered to fit the new purpose. The line which has been changed is the last in verse 3: "He gave me a hundred strings of cowries." Vast numbers of inscriptions record the giving of cowries by feudal lords to their vassals, as a reward for faithful services. There is not the slightest reason to suppose that a bridegroom ever gave his bride a gift of cowry shells. "A hundred" probably only means "a great many." A good account of the use of cowries as currency in ancient China is given by H. G. Creel in *The Birth of China*, p. 92. Judging by the analogy of numerous similar songs, the line must originally have run, "My spirits rise" (*wo xin ze xing*), or something to that effect.

## 176 ✦ *Thick Grows the Tarragon*

Thick grows the tarragon
In the center of that slope.
I have seen my lord;
He was pleased and courteous to boot.

Thick grows the tarragon
In the middle of that island.
I have seen my lord,
And my heart is glad.

Thick grows the tarragon
In the center of that mound.
I have seen my lord;
He gave me a hundred strings of cowries.

Unsteady is that osier boat;
It plunges, it bobs.[1]
But now that I have seen my lord
My heart is at rest.

---

1. I was uneasy about what sort of reception I should get.

## 177 ✦ *The Sixth Month*

In the sixth month all is bustle,
We put our war-chariots in order,
Our four steeds are in good fettle,
We load our bow-cases and quivers.
The Xian-yun are ablaze,
We have no time to lose.
We are going out to battle,
To set aright the king's lands.

Our team of blacks is well-matched,
A pattern of perfect training.
It is the sixth month;
We have finished all our field-work,
We have finished all our field-work
Throughout the thirty leagues.[1]
We are going out to battle
To help the Son of Heaven.

Our four steeds are tall and broad,
Hugely high they stand.
We fall upon the Xian-yun,
We do great deeds,
So stern, so grim
We fulfill the tasks of war,
Fulfill the tasks of war
That the king's lands may be at rest.

1. Compare no. 277. A league (*li*) was three hundred paces.

The Xian-yun were scornful of us,
They encamped at Jiao-huo.[1]
They invaded Hao and Fang.
As far as the north banks of the Jing.
With woven pattern of bird blazonry
Our silken banners brightly shone.
Big chariots, ten of them,
Went first, to open up a path.

Those war-chariots were well balanced
As though held from below, hung from above.
Our four steeds were unswerving,
Unswerving and obedient.
We smote the Xian-yun
As far as the great plain.[2]
Mighty warrior[3] is Ji-fu,
A pattern to all the peoples.

Ji-fu feasts and is happy;
He has received many blessings from Heaven:
"Here I am, back from Hao;
I have been away a long time
And must give a drinking-party to my friends,
With roast turtle and minced carp."
And who was with him?
Zhang Zhong, pious[4] and friendly.

1. Generally supposed to have been near modern Fu-feng, west of the Zhou capital. The meaning of Hao and Fang is very uncertain. It would be rash to build geographical theories on the order in which the places are mentioned, for this may be dictated by the necessities of rhyme.

2. Probably not the modern Tai-yuan in Shanxi.

3. Or "mighty in peace and war."

4. To his ancestors. But the "pious and friendly" may easily be a corruption of another personal name.

## 178 ✦ *Plucking White Millet*

Lo, we were plucking the white millet
In that new field,
In this fresh-cleared acre,
When Fang-shu arrived
With three thousand chariots
And a host of guards well-trained.
Yes, Fang-shu came
Driving his four dappled grays,
Those dappled grays so obedient,
In his big chariot painted red,
With his awning of lacquered bamboo and his fish-skin quiver,
His breast-buffers[1] and metal-headed reins.

Lo, we were plucking the white millet
In that new field,
In this middle patch,
When Fang-shu arrived
With three thousand chariots,
With banners shining bright.
Yes, Fang-shu came
With leather-bound nave and metal-studded yoke,
His eight bells jingling,
Wearing his insignia—
The red greaves so splendid,
The tinkling onion-stones at his belt.

1. Pear-shaped buffers which hung from the horse's shoulder-girth.

Swoop flew that hawk
Straight up into the sky,
Yet it came here to roost.
Fang-shu has come
With three thousand chariots
And a host of guards well-trained.
Yes, Fang-shu has come
With his bandsmen beating the drums,
Marshaling his armies, haranguing his hosts.
Illustrious truly is Fang-shu,
Deep is the roll of the drums,
Shaking the hosts with its din.

Foolish were you, tribes of Jing,[1]
Who made a great nation into your foe.
Fang-shu is old in years,
But in strategy he is at his prime.
Fang-shu has come,
He has bound culprits, captured chieftains.
His war-chariots rumble,
They rumble and crash
Like the clap of thunder, like the roll of thunder.
Illustrious truly is Fang-shu,
It was he who smote the Xian-yun,
Who made the tribes of Jing afraid.

## 179 ✦ Chariots Are Strong

Our chariots are strong,
Our horses well matched.
Team of stallions lusty
We yoke and go to the east.

Our hunting chariots are splendid,
Our teams very sturdy.
In the east are wide grasslands;
We yoke, and a-hunting we go.

---

1. The people later called Chu. At this period they were between the Han River and the Yangtze, in northern Hubei.

My lord follows the chase
With picked footmen so noisy,
Sets up his banners, his standards,
Far afield he hunts in Ao.

We yoke those four steeds,
The four steeds so big.
Red greaves, gilded slippers—
The meet has great glamour.

Thimbles and armlets are fitted,
Bows and arrows all adjusted,
The bowmen assembled
Help us to lift the game.

A team of bays we drive;
The two helpers do not get crossways,
Faultlessly are they driven,
While our arrows shower like chaff.

Subdued, the horses whinny;
Gently the banners wave.
"If footmen and riders are not orderly
The great kitchen will not be filled."

My lord on his journeys
Without clamor wins fame.
Truly, a gentleman he;
In very truth, a great achievement.

## 180 ✦ Lucky Day

A lucky day, fifth of the week,[1]
We have made the sacrifice of propitiation,[2] we have prayed.
Our hunting chariots so lovely,
Our four steeds so strong,
We climb that high hill
Chasing the herds of game.

1. The ten-day week.

2. Compare no. 241, verse 8.

A lucky day, seventh of the cycle;[1]
We have picked our steeds.
Here the beasts congregate,
Doe and stag abound,
Along the Qi and Ju,[2]
The Son of Heaven's domain.

Look there, in the midst of the plain,
Those big ones, very many!
Scampering, sheltering,
Some in herds, some two by two.
We lead hither all our followers,
Anxious to please the Son of Heaven.

We have drawn our bows;
Our arrows are on the bowstring.
We shoot that little boar,
We fell that great wild ox.
So that we have something to offer, for guest, for stranger,
To go with the heavy wine.

✦ ✦ ✦

1. Sixty-day cycle.
2. Northeast of the Zhou capital.

## 181 ✦ *Wild-Geese*

The wild-geese are flying;
*Suk, suk* go their wings.
The soldiers are on the march;
Painfully they struggle through the wilds.
In dire extremity are the strong men;
Sad are their wives, left all alone.

The wild-geese are flying;
They have lighted in the middle of the marsh.
The soldiers are walling a fort;
The hundred cubits[1] have all risen.
Though they struggle so painfully,
At last they are safely housed.

The wild-geese are flying;
Dolefully they cry their discontent.
But these were wise men
Who urged us in our toil,
And those were foolish men
Who urged us to make mischief and rebel.

## 182 ✦ *What of the Night?*

What of the night?
The night is not yet spent.
The torches in the courtyard are alight.
But my lord has come;
Tinkle, tinkle go his harness-bells.

What of the night?
The night is not yet old.
The torches in the courtyard are bright.
But my lord has come;
Twit, twit go the bells.

---

1.  Cubit-square frames held the earth in position when the walls were being built.

What of the night?
The night nears dawn.
The torches in the courtyard gleam.
My lord has come;
I can see his banners.


## 183 ✦ *In Flood*

In flood those running waters
Carry their tides to join the sea.
Swift that flying kite
Now flies, now lights.
Alas that of my brothers,
My countrymen and all my friends,
Though each has father, has mother,
None heeds the disorders of this land!

In flood those running waters
Spread out so wide, so wide.
Swift that flying kite;
Now flying, now soaring.
Thinking of those rebellious ones
I arise, I go.
The sorrows of my heart
I cannot banish or forget.

Swift that flying kite
Makes for that middle mound.
The false words of the people,
Why does no one stop them?
My friends, be on your guard;
Slanderous words are on the rise.

The meaning is: we are heading for rebellion swift as a kite or as a
stream in flood.

## 184 ✦ *A Crane Cries*

When a crane cries at the Nine Swamps
Its voice is heard in the wild.
A fish can plunge deep into the pool
Or rest upon the shoals.
Pleasant is that man's garden
Where the hardwood trees are planted;
But beneath[1] them, only litter.
*There are other hills whose stones*
*Are good for grinding tools.*

When a crane cries at the Nine Swamps
Its voice is heard in Heaven.
A fish can rest upon the shoal
Or plunge deep into the pool.
Pleasant is that man's garden
Where the hardwood trees are planted.
But beneath them are only husks.
*There are other hills whose stones*
*Are good for working jade.*

## 185 ✦ *Minister of War*

Minister of War,
We are the king's claws and fangs.
Why should you roll us on from misery to misery,
Giving us no place to stop in or take rest?

Minister of War,
We are the king's claws and teeth.
Why should you roll us from misery to misery,
Giving us no place to come to and stay?

---

1. The "beneath" certainly has a double sense and hints that the lower classes are treated as of no account. The refrain is a cryptic threat to emigrate. Compare no. 113.

Minister of War,
Truly you are not wise.
Why should you roll us from misery to misery?
We have mothers who lack food.

186 ✦ *The White Colt*

Unsullied the white colt
Eating the young shoots of my stack-yard.[1]
Keep it tethered, keep it tied
All day long.
The man whom I love
Here makes holiday.

Unsullied the white colt
Eating the bean leaves of my stack-yard.
Keep it tethered, keep it tied
All night long.
The man whom I love
Is here, a lucky guest.

Unsullied the white colt
That came so swiftly.
Like a duke, like a lord
Let your revels have no end.
Prolong your idle play,
Protract your leisure.

Unsullied the white colt
In that deserted valley,
With a bundle of fresh fodder.
"Though you, its master, are fair as jade
Do not let the news of you be rare as gold or jade,
Keeping your thoughts far away."

---

1. Used as a vegetable garden when not required for stacking crops.

## 187 ✦ *The Oriole*

O oriole, yellow bird,
Do not settle on the corn,
Do not peck at my millet.
The people of this land
Are not minded to nurture me.
I must go back, go home
To my own land and kin.

O oriole, yellow bird,
Do not settle on the mulberries,
Do not peck my sorghum.
With the people of this land
One can make no covenant.
I must go back, go home
To where my brothers are.

O oriole, yellow bird
Do not settle on the oaks,
Do not peck my wine-millet.
With the people of this land
One can come to no understanding.
I must go back, go home
To where my own men[1] are.

## 188 ✦ *I Went into the Country*

I went into the country;
Deep the shade of the ailanthus.
It was as bride and wife
That I came to your house.
But you did not provide for me—
Sent me back to land and home.

---

1. Literally "fathers," i.e., her adult kinsmen, whether father or father's brothers.

I went into the country;
I plucked the dockleaf.
It was as bride and wife
That I came to live with you.
But you did not provide for me—
Back to my home you sent me.

I went into the country;
I plucked the pokeweed.
You thought nothing of the old marriage—
Found for yourself a new mate.
Not for her wealth, oh no!
But merely for a change.

189 ✦ *The Beck*

Ceaseless flows that beck,
Far stretch the southern hills.
May you be sturdy as the bamboo,
May you flourish like the pine,
May elder brother and younger brother
Always love one another,
Never do evil to one another.

To give continuance to foremothers and forefathers
We build a house, many hundred cubits of wall;
To south and west its doors.
Here shall we live, here rest,
Here laugh, here talk.

We bind the frames, creak, creak;
We hammer the mud, tap, tap,
That it may be a place where wind and rain cannot enter,
Nor birds and rats get in,
But where our lord may dwell.

As a halberd, even so plumed,
As an arrow, even so sharp,
As a bird, even so soaring,
As wings, even so flying
Are the halls to which our lord ascends.[1]

Well leveled is the courtyard,
Firm are the pillars,
Cheerful are the rooms by day,
Softly gloaming by night,
A place where our lord can be at peace.

Below, the rush-mats; over them the bamboo-mats.
Comfortably he sleeps,
He sleeps and wakes
And interprets his dreams.
"Your lucky dreams, what were they?"
"They were of black bears and brown,
Of serpents and snakes."

The diviner thus interprets it:
"Black bears and brown
Mean men-children.
Snakes and serpents
Mean girl-children."

So he bears a son,
And puts him to sleep upon a bed,
Clothes him in robes,
Gives him a jade scepter to play with.
The child's howling is very lusty;[2]
In red greaves shall he flare,
Be lord and king of house and home.
Then he bears a daughter,

1. This verse is corrupt and not intelligible with any certainty.

2. *Huang*, "lusty," suggests the *huang*, "flare," of the red greaves. These could only be worn by the king's command and constituted a decoration similar to the British Garter. Women (see the next verse) received no such marks of distinction.

And puts her upon the ground,
Clothes her in swaddling-clothes,
Gives her a loom-whorl to play with.
For her no decorations, no emblems;
Her only care, the wine and food,
And how to give no trouble to father and mother.


190 ✦ *No Sheep?*

Who says you have no sheep?
Three hundred is the flock.
Who says you have no cattle?
Ninety are the black-lips.
Here your rams come,
Their horns thronging;
Here your cattle come,
Their ears flapping.

Some go down the slope,
Some are drinking in the pool,
Some are sleeping, some waking.
Here your herdsmen come
In rush-cloak and bamboo-hat,
Some shouldering their dinners.
Only thirty brindled[1] beasts!
Your sacrifices will not go short.

Your herdsman comes,
Bringing faggots, bringing brushwood,
With the cock-game, with hen-game.
Your rams come,
Sturdy and sound;
None that limps, none that ails.
He beckons to them with raised arm;
All go up into the stall.

---

1. I.e., the rest are whole-colored and therefore suitable for sacrifice.

Your herdsman dreams,
Dreams of locusts and fish,
Of banners and flags.
A wise man explains the dreams:
"Locusts and fishes
Mean fat years.
Flags and banners
Mean a teeming house and home."[1]

---

1. This helps to explain why flag-waving plays such a prominent part in the
fertility-rites of peasant Europe.

The following nine poems are translated by Joseph R. Allen.

### 191 ✦ *High-Crested Southern Hills*

High-crested are those southern hills,
With rocks piled high and towering.
Majestic are you, Master Yin,[1]
To whom all the people look.
Grief is burning in their hearts.
But they dare not even speak in jest.
The state lies in ruins,
Why do you not see to this?

High-crested are those southern hills,
Filled with tortuous terrain.
Majestic are you, Master Yin,
But now so unfair we know not what to say.
Heaven has sent a plague down upon us,
Death and destruction are everywhere.
The people's words are full of spite,
Why does no one stop this sadness?

Mr. Yin, Grand Master,
Be the bedrock of Zhou,
Hold the state's even balance,
Control all these lands,
Aid the Son of Heaven himself;
Thereby the people will not go astray.
Mighty Heaven, now unkind,
Do not oppress our people so.

---

1. Qu Wan-li, following Chen Huan, understands *shi yin* (here Master Yin) as a truncation of *tai-shi yin-shi* of stanza 3, which he reads as two separate terms, as found in no. 263. There Waley translates the terms as "Grand Leader" and "officer." All other commentators, including Karlgren, follow this traditional reading.

You have not attended to this yourself,
Thus the common folk have no trust.
If you do not investigate, do not serve,
Then at least do not neglect the noble ones.
Be impartial, be resolute,
Then there will be no danger from petty men,
And trivial relatives and sycophants
Will not hold high office again.

Mighty Heaven now inconstant,
Brings down on us this hardship;
Mighty Heaven now uncaring,
Brings down on us this great pain.
If you, sir, were strict in rule,
The peoples' hearts would be relieved.
If you, sir, brought peace to reign,
Evil and anger would be sent away.

Now inconstant is mighty Heaven,
Disorder is forever on the land,
Month upon month it arises,
And people live unsettled lives.
Grief fills their hearts like bad wine,
Who will control state's good order?
If one does not himself take over,
Our families will long toil and suffer.

Driving forth those four steeds,
Four steeds with thick necks stretched.
I look out over the four quarters,
Increasingly troubled, I have no place to ride.

When your cruelty is in full form,
We will indeed meet your spears;
But if you are constant and kind to us,
Then we shall pledge ourselves to you.

Mighty Heaven is now unfair,
Our king is not at peace,
He does not take heed his own heart,
And turns on those who complain.

Jia-fu made this ballad[1]
To delve the King's disorder.
If you would change your heart,
The myriad states would be well-nourished.


## 192 ✦ *The First Month*

Heavy frost in the first month of summer
Fills my heart with grief and pain,
And the lies and rumors of others
Make it hurt so much the more.
To think of me all alone,
My grieved heart is overwhelmed;
Take pity on my timid worries,
I am sick with loneliness and grief.

When my parents gave birth to me,
What brought on this affliction?
Why not before my coming?
Why not after?
First they shower me with sweet words,
Then their words are vile.
More and more I have a grieved heart,
And for this I am abused.

My grieved heart is helpless,
To think of me without sustenance.
And people quite innocent
Are sentenced to be slaves and servants.
Oh, take pity on us people,
Where will sustenance be secured?
Look, the ominous raven swoops,
On whose house will he alight?

1. Commentators all understand Jia-fu as a person's name (with some variant readings), and Zhu Xi notes there is an officer of the Zhou by that name mentioned in the *Spring and Autumn Annals* (years 703, 696 B.C.); this would place the poem about eighty years after its traditional dating. I follow Waley in translating *song* (to chant, recite) as "ballad"—cf. no. 260, "Ji-fu made this ballad."

Look in the middle of those woods
There is only firewood and brush.
The people are now in great danger,
See how Heaven is all beclouded.
It could surely stand firm,
Then there would be none it could not overcome.
Oh, august God on High,
Is there any whom you despise?

Yes, you say the mountains are low,
But they have hills and have ridges.
The lies and rumors of others,
Why does no one stop them?
We call in the elders for counsel,
Ask them to divine our dreams;
They all say "we are sagely,"
But who can tell the cock-raven from the hen?

Yes, you say that Heaven is high,
Yet we dare not but stoop under it.
Yes, you say the earth is solid,
But we dare not but tip-toe on it.
Those who cry out these words
Have their good sense and reason.
Take pity on people now;
Why be such snakes and serpents?[1]

See how on that barren, hilly field
The rich grain rises above all others.
Heaven beat me down,
But it could not overcome me.
First they took me as model,
But they could not reach that high;
Then they treated me as enemy,
But they too could not overpower me.

---

1. I understand the "serpents" to refer to evil officials or the like; and we should pity the people (*ren*) who suffer under them. This follows glosses by Zheng Xuan and Zhu Xi.

Alas, the grief in my heart
Feels like it is tied in knots.
How can these rulers now
Be so very vicious?
When the flames are first rising high,
How can they be extinguished?
Majestic was the capital of Zhou,
But Lady Bao Si destroyed it.[1]

Till the end is this ever-lasting worry,
And we are beleaguered by a driving rain.
After the carriage is already loaded,
You then toss the side-boards away,
Whereupon your load tumbles over;
I ask you, sir, to help us here.[2]

Do not toss your side-boards away,
Or all will fall into your spokes.
If you take heed of your driver,
Your load will not tumble over.
And you will pass by dangerous places.
Have you not given thought to this?

The fishes are in the pond,
But still they cannot be happy,
For the deeper they dive,
The clearer they shine.
My grieved heart is deeply saddened
Thinking about the state's vicious ways.

1. Bao Si was the femme fatale blamed for causing the fall of the Western Zhou in 771 B.C. According to the account in the *Shi ji,* King You became thoroughly infatuated with her, thereby alienating his feudal lords, whereupon the capital of Hao, referred to here as "noble Zhou," fell to barbarian forces.

2. Commentators often read this as a statement by the carriage owner addressed to his superiors; it seems more logical that it is the voice of subordinates to the owner saying, essentially, "give us a break."

There are those with tasty wine,
And they also have fine dishes.
They gather together with their neighbors,
Their relatives are very numerous.
To think of me all alone,
My grieved heart is deeply pained.

Petty men have their fine houses,
The base their hefty emoluments;
But the people are now without sustenance,
For Heaven's calamities have struck them down.
The rich are doing well indeed;
Take pity on the lonely and helpless.

## 193 ✦ *Alignment in the Tenth Month*

With the alignment in the tenth month,
On the first day, *xin-mao* of the cycle,[1]
The sun was eclipsed,
And it was so very frightening.
First the moon grew dim,
Then the sun grew dim too.
All of the folk here below
Were in great lament.

The sun and moon foretell disaster
When they do not follow their normal path.
No state in the realm is well-governed
When it fails to use its good men.
The eclipse of the moon,
Is something often seen.
But this eclipse of the sun!
Where have we gone astray?

1. *Xin-mao* is the designation for the twenty-eighth day of the sixty-day cycle, which revolved independent of the monthly calendar. This date is identified by Legge with an eclipse on August 29, 775 B.C.—see Legge, *The Chinese Classics*, vol. 6, p. 321. Qu Wan-li and Cheng and Liang place the date in 776. In his *T'ien Hsia* essay Waley argues for a dating of 735.

Slashing was the lightning with its thunder
Nothing was settled, nothing well run,
All the streams boiled and overflowed,
Mountaintops crashed and tumbled down.
High ledges became deep valleys,
And valleys rose up into ridges.[1]
Take pity on people now;
Why does no one stop this?

Huang-fu was Prime Minister,
Fan was Master of Lands,
Jia-bo was Chief of Officials
Zhong-yun, Steward of the Table,
And Zou-zi, Royal Scribe,
Jue was Master of the Stables,
Ju was Captain of the Guard;
The lovely consort, so resplendent, had just taken her position.[2]

Come now, Huang-fu,
How can things be so untimely?
Why do you send us off to labor
Without considering our pressing needs?
Fallen down are our walls and houses,
The fields unkept and overgrown,
And you say, "I am not mistreating you,
These are just the rules."

Huang-fu, you are so very wise;
Choosing Xiang as your new city site,[3]
You select three ministers to serve,
Truly many are stores and treasures.
You were unwilling to leave even one old guard behind
Whereby to protect our king.
You selected those with carriages and horses
To resettle them off in Xiang.

1. These lines are said to describe the earthquake and attending disaster in the second year of King You's reign (780 B.C.), as recorded in the *Guo-yu*—see Qu Wan-li, p. 156.

2. The traditional commentaries identify this royal consort as Bao Si (see no. 192, verse 8).

3. This apparently refers to the choice of a capital-city site after the fall of Hao in 771 B.C.; the Xiang referred to here presumably was in present-day Henan.

Hard we have worked in your service,
Daring not complain about the toil.
Without offense, I am quite innocent,
But slanderous mouths clamor on.
The hardships of the folk here below
Are not brought on by Heaven;
No, nice to meet, then a stab in the back,
Violence comes from the acts of men.

Unending is my malady,
Making me so very pained.
Abundance fills every land,
I alone am lost in grief.
The people all are slipping away,
I alone do not dare take rest.
The decrees of Heaven are unfathomable;
Yet I dare not imitate my colleagues and slip away myself.


194 ✦ *Rain Without Limit*[1]

Broad and vast is mighty Heaven,
Yet it keeps its grace from us,
But rather brings death and famine,
War and destruction to all the states.
Foreboding Heaven is a cruel affliction,
It does not ponder, does not plan.
It pays no attention to the guilty,
Who have admitted their crimes.
But the ones who are innocent,
These, without exception, suffer.

---

1. This title does not seem to follow from the poem, and there is some evidence of textual corruption and missing verses.

The house of Zhou was destroyed,[1]
There was no place to rest or reside.
The great officials scattered across the land,
No one knew how we toiled.
The three high ministers
All refuse to serve at dawn or at dusk.
Princes and feudal lords
All refuse to meet in the morning or at night.
One wished they could be good,
But no, they continue their wayward ways.

How can it be, mighty Heaven,
That the word of rule is untrue?
Like those who walk along,
With no place in the end to go.
You, our many lords,
Take special care of yourselves.
How could you not fear the others,
Or hold no fear of Heaven?

There is war, but we do not withdraw;
There is famine, but we do not progress.
I am but a common attendant
Deeply saddened, exhausted every day.
You, our many lords,
All refuse to take counsel.
When words are well-considered, you should respond;
When words are slanderous, then withdraw.

How pitiful I am, unable to speak.
Not that my tongue has problems,
But rather I am exhausted.
To be able to speak would be good indeed;
Then the clever words would flow
And I would finally find some rest.

---

1. Again referring to the fall of the western capital in 771 B.C. *Zhou zong* may be
an inversion of the term for capital, as above, or a generic reference to the Zhou
royal clan; see no. 193, verse 6.

"Go serve in office," is what they say;
But it is so difficult, so full of danger.
Some orders cannot be carried out,
And thus you incur the Son of Heaven's blame.
Other orders can be carried out,
But rancor can reach even to your friends.

They say you should return to the royal city,
But you say, "There I have no house or home."
So lonely I weep till my eyes bleed;
Of these words not one does not pain.
In the past when you moved away,
Who was there to build a house for you?


## 195 ✦ *Foreboding*

Foreboding Heaven is a cruel affliction,
Spreading out over the lands below.
Plans and counsels are twisted and vile;
When will we ever see their end?
Plans of benefit are not followed,
But yet, those with none are put to use.
Considering their plans and counsels
I am filled with much agony.

Gathering in groups, they spread their gossip;
So very pitiful it is to me.
When plans made are beneficial,
Then they all are turned aside.
But when the plans are harmful
These are taken as their guide.
Considering their plans and counsels,
I wonder where are we bound?

Our tortoise shells are exhausted,
They do not offer good counsel.[1]
Master planners we have so very many,
Yet with them nothing is achieved.
Debates fill the court with words,
But with failure who dares takes the blame.
We are like wayfarers asking for directions,
On we go, never finding our proper way.

How pitiful are the plans they make;
They do not follow the patterns of former times,
They do not take great counsel as their standard.
Shallow words are what they heed,
And shallow words make their debate.
Like architects consulting others along the road,
With them one will not have quick success.

Although the state is not large,
There are sages and those who are not.
Although the people are few,
Some are thinkers, some are planners,
Some respectful, others disciplined.[2]
Do not allow them, like the gushing spring,
To plunge down together in defeat.

No one dares fight a tiger bare-handed,
No one dares cross the River without a boat;
Yet people know only about one thing,
And nothing about all the others.
Be careful, be cautious,
As if you were approaching an abyss,
As if you were treading on thin ice.

1. Tortoise shells were used in traditional divination practices, especially those of the Shang royal house (see no. 237, footnote 5).

2. Something seems to be wrong with the parallel phrasing here, especially in conjunction with the closing couplet. Both Zheng Xuan and Karlgren offer interesting solutions, but I have translated the text as it seems to appear.

## 196 ✦ *Diminutive*

Diminutive is the calling dove,
Who soars to the Heavens above;
My heart is filled with grief and pain,
Thinking of men of former times.
I lie awake till the dawn does break,
Missing the two people of my life.[1]

People enlightened and wise,
Drink wine but remain mild and restrained.
Those who are benighted and dumb,
Get drunk and are ever more extravagant.
Each of you, take heed of your demeanor,
Heaven's charge is never to be repeated.

The large beans grow in the plain,
The common folk go to pluck them.
The eggs laid by the mulberry bug
Are nourished by the mother wasp.[2]
Teach your children well,
Then fortune like this will be theirs.

See that wagtail bird,
How it flies, how it calls.
Each day there I go forth,
Every month, I journey off.
Up early in the morn, to bed late at night;
Be sure not to bring shame to those who bore you.

Flitting about is the mourning dove
Across the threshing yard eating the grain.
Take pity on us forever alone—
Off to prison, off to jail,
Grasping straws for divination,
Whence will fortune ever come?

1. I.e., one's parents, according to commentaries.

2. According to folklore the eggs (or young) of the mulberry bug are carried on
the back of a certain bee who nourishes them.

Be mild and modest with others,
As if you were alighting in a high tree.
Be fearful, be timid,
As if you were approaching a ravine.
Be careful, be cautious,
As if you were treading on thin ice.


## 197 ✦ Wings Flapping

Wings flapping, those small crows
Return to roost, flock on flock.
Good fortune comes to all;
I alone am in distress.
Why this curse from Heaven?
What is my offense?
Indeed my heart is grieved,
What can I do or say?

Level and easy was the way of Zhou,
But now it is over-grown with weeds.
My heart is filled with grief and pain,
My ponderings make me sick of heart.
With deep sighs, I need to sleep;
It's not just grief, but also age.
Indeed my heart is grieved;
My head pounds, fevers rage.

Certainly the mulberry and catalpa of home
Are to be remembered and adored.
Whom do we revere if not our fathers?
Whom do we need if not our mothers?
But I do not know outer garments
Or even inner linings.[1]
Heaven bore and nourished me,
How was I born under such a star?

1. These lines are much in dispute. Traditional commentaries have construed them to refer to the speaker's attachment to his parents, but that does not fit the following lines. I have translated them rather close to the original, accepting Karlgren's sartorial (rather than somatic) reading of the terms.

In the heavy hanging willows
Cicadas buzz their raspy buzz.
Deep is that dark ravine,
Reeds and rushes are full and thick.
As a boat in the current floats,
We know not where we go.
Indeed my heart is grieved;
Yet there's no time to get the sleep I need.

There the deer run along
On nimble and easy legs;
The pheasants coo in the morning light,
Calling to their mates.
Yet like that decaying tree,
Diseased and without limbs,
My heart is grieved indeed;
For no one understands me.

Look there, a trapped hare,
Perhaps someone will save it.
Along the path, a dead man lies,
Perhaps someone will bury him.
My lord has a heart
Cruel and callous to our lot.
Indeed my heart is grieved;
My tears fall because of it.

My lord follows slanderers,
As if responding to their toasts.
My lord treats me unkindly
Taking no care to ponder.
Falling a tree, first you lean it;
Splitting wood, always with the grain.
You release those with offenses
And pile them high upon me.

Nothing is high if not a hill;
Nothing is deep if not a spring.
My lord should go easy with those words,
Ears are listening through the walls.
Do not break my dam,
Do not open my fish-traps.
Though for my person you have no regard,
At least pity my brood.[1]


## 198 ✦ Clever Words

Mighty Heaven, vast and wide,
Whom we call father and mother,
Without blame, without offense,
Yet such disorder is upon us.
Mighty Heaven's terror is immense,
But I am truly without blame.
Mighty Heaven's power is great,
But I am truly without offense.

When disorder first came,
Calumny did soon reign.
Now that disorder has come again,
My lord follows those slanderers.
But if my lord were angry with them,
Disorder would quickly end.
If my lord were pleased with others,
Disorder would quickly cease.

My lord had many covenants made,
And for that the disorder deepened.
My lord has followed slanderous thieves,
And with that the disorder turned mean.
The words of those thieves are sweet,
And with them the disorder is fed.
They are not doing their duty,
But instead are the king's affliction.

---

1. The last four lines also occur at the end of stanza 3 of no. 35.

Grandly made is the temple complex;
My lord had it so built.
Well-ordered is the great plan;
The sagely ones decided it.
Others have their secrets,
But I can see through them.
Dashing about is the crafty rabbit,
But even a dumb dog can catch it.

Supple are those softwoods
That my lord had planted there.
The talk of those who come and go
Can be figured in your heart;
Thin and shallow are their inflated words,
Out from their mouths they spew,
Clever words like a tooted reed;
How thick-skinned they are indeed.

Whoever are those people
Living along the river's edge?
Without strength, without courage,
They promote the instruments of disorder.
Trivial and yet swollen too,
Where is this courage of yours?
The plans you make may be many,
But just how many are there of you?

## 199 ✦ *What Sort of Person*

Just what sort of person is this,
His heart full of vengeful spite?
Why does he pass by our bridge,
But does not deign to enter my door?
And who does he follow in this?
It must be the one from Bao.

Those two come along together,
But which one makes this trouble?
Why does he pass by our bridge,
And does not come in to comfort me?
In the beginning he was not like this,
Saying he now cannot stand me.

Just what sort of person is this?
Why does he come along our pathway?
I can hear his voice over there,
But I do not see him.
With others he has no regrets;
Of Heaven he has no fear.

Just what sort of person is this?
He moves like a whirlwind;
Why not off to the north?
Why not off to the south?
Why does he pass by our bridge
Only to upset my thoughts?

Slowly you drive along,
And have no time to rest;
Then quickly you go,
With time to grease your wheels.
When you first came to me,
Oh, how I was in anguish.

Then you returned and came in,
And my heart was at ease.
You returned again and did not,
Why is it so difficult to know?
The first time you came
Caused me such pain.

Elder brother plays the clay whistle,
Younger brother the bamboo flute.
Like cash on a string we two are tied together
But you truly do not know me.
I offer these three animals
In sacrifice and in pledge.

If you were ghost or gremlin,
Then of course I could not have you.
But I see in your expression
Someone who knows no limits.
Thus I have made this good song
To express my restless heart.


## 200 ✦ *The Chief of Attendants*

An ornament here, a decoration there
Make up this shell-embroidery.
Those slanderers of men
Indeed have gone too far!

A spread here, a gape there
Make up the Southern Fan.[1]
Such slanderers of man,
Who would consent to join their counsels?

Jibber-jabber, blither-blather!
Their idea of "counsel" is to slander men.
And if you speak with any caution
They say that you are not loyal.

Gabble-gabble, tittle-tattle!
Their idea of "counsel" is to slander men.
You think they won't get *you*?
Already they are moving your way.

The proud man enjoys himself,
The toiler lives in woe.
Oh, Heaven, azure Heaven,
Take note of that proud man,
Take pity upon that toiler!

---

1. The constellation of the Winnowing Fan; part of Sagittarius.

Those slanderers of men,
Who would consent to join their counsels?
I take those slanderers of men
And throw them as an offering to the jackals and tigers.

If jackals and tigers will not eat them
I throw them as an offering to Him of the North.[1]
If He of the North will not accept them
I throw them as an offering to Him on high.

The way through the willow garden
Leads to the acred hill.
The palace-attendant[2] Meng Zi
Made up the words of this song.
May all gentlemen, whosoever they be
Listen to it with attention!

✦ ✦ ✦

1. The Spirit of the Pole-star?

2. The word came to mean "eunuch"; but we do not know at what date eunuchs
were first used in Chinese palaces.

## 201 ✦ *Valley Wind*

Zip, zip the valley wind!
Nothing but wind and rain.
In days of peril, in days of dread
It was always "you and I."
Now in time of peace, of happiness,
You have cast me aside.

Zip, zip the valley wind!
Nothing but wind and duststorms.
In days of peril, in days of dread
You put me in your bosom.
Now in time of peace, of happiness,
You throw me away like slop-water.

Zip, zip the valley wind
Across the rocky hills.
No grass but is dying,
No tree but is wilting.
You forget my great merits,
Remember only my small faults.

## 202 ✦ *Thick Tarragon*

Thick grows that tarragon.
It is not tarragon; it is only wormwood.
Alas for my father and mother,
Alas for all their trouble in bringing me up!

Thick grows that tarragon.
It is not tarragon; it is mugwort.
Alas for my father and mother,
Alas for all their toil in bringing me up!
"That the cup should be empty
Is a humiliation to the jar."[1]
Than to live the life of the common people
Better to have died long ago!

1. Proverb?

Without a father, on whom can we rely?
Without a mother, whom can we trust?
At every turn we should encounter trouble,
At every turn meet failure.

My father begot me,
My mother fed me,
Led me, bred me,
Brought me up, reared me,
Kept her eye on me, tended me,
At every turn aided me.
Their good deeds I would requite.
It is Heaven, not I, that is bad.

The southern hills, they rise so sharp,
The storm-wind blows so wild.
Other people all prosper;
Why am I alone destroyed?

The southern hills, they rise so jagged,
The storm-wind blows so fierce.
Other people all prosper;
I alone can find no rest.

The situation in the next song is very clear. A man of the east (Shandong) complains that all the best jobs go to the men of the west, to the people from the Zhou capital, while all the real work is done by local people. Members of the Zhou aristocracy who are supposed to administer the country, are given positions with high-sounding titles, but do none of the work that these titles imply. Hence they are compared to the stars, which bear the names of all sorts of useful things but perform no useful function: "In the south there is a Winnowing Fan; but it cannot sift, or raise the chaff," and so on. Tradition says that the song was made by a minister of the Lord of Tan, a small state that was thirty miles east of the modern port Jinan. The date of the song has generally been supposed to be the reign of King You of Zhou (781–771 B.C.). It is certainly more likely that it dates from western Zhou times, when the dynasty was still powerful, than after its virtual eclipse in 771. But the ascription to King You's time is no doubt merely due to the fact that he ranks in history as a "bad king." It may in point of fact just as well belong to the reign of one of the "good kings." In order not to disfigure the page with too great a mass of footnotes, I will explain the star-names here. The Han River in Heaven is the Milky Way. The Weaving Lady and the Draught Ox are constellations on opposite sides of the Milky Way. Later legend turned the Ox into a Herdboy and made him the lover of the Weaving Lady. The Opener of Brightness is the Morning Star; the Long Path, the Evening Star. The Net is the Hyades; the Winnowing Fan, part of Sagittarius.

### 203 ✦ The Greater East

Messy is the stew in the pot;
Bent is the thornwood spoon.
But the ways of Zhou are smooth as a grindstone,
Their straightness is like an arrow;
Ways that are for gentlemen to walk
And for commoners to behold.
Full of longing I look for them;
In a flood my tears flow.

In the Lesser East and the Greater East[1]
Shuttle and spool are idle.
"Fiber-shoes tightly woven
Are good for walking upon the dew."[2]
Foppishly mincing the young lords
Walk there upon the road.
They go away, they come back again;
It makes me ill to look at them!

1. Fu Si-nian discusses the meaning of these terms in *Academia Sinica,* vol. 2, pt. 1. Roughly speaking, the Lesser East means the extreme west of Shandong; the Greater East means central Shandong, between Jinan and Dai'an. Cf. no. 300, verse 5.

2. An allusion to no. 107, or at any rate a utilization of the same theme.

That spraying fountain so cold
Does not soak firewood that is gathered and bundled.
Heigh-ho! I lie awake and sigh.
Woe is me that am all alone!
Firewood that is gathered firewood
May still be put away.
Woe is me that am all alone!
I too could do with rest.

The men of the East, their sons
Get all the work and none of the pay.
The men of the West, their sons,
Oh, so smart are their clothes!
The men of Zhou, their sons
Wear furs of bearskin, black and brown.
The sons of their vassals
For every appointment are chosen.

Fancy taking the wine
And leaving the sauce,
Having a belt-pendant so fine
And not using its full length!

In Heaven there is a River Han
Looking down upon us so bright.
By it sits the Weaving Lady astride her stool,
Seven times a day she rolls up her sleeves.
But though seven times she rolls her sleeves
She never makes wrap or skirt.
Bright shines that Draught Ox,
But can't be used for yoking to a cart.
In the east is the Opener of Brightness,
In the west, the Long Path.
All-curving are the Nets of Heaven,
Spread there in a row.

In the south there is a Winnowing Fan;
But it cannot sift, or raise the chaff.
In the north there is a Ladle,
But it cannot scoop wine or sauce.
Yes, in the south is a Winnowing Fan;
There it sucks its tongue.
In the north there is a Ladle,
Sticking out its handle toward the west.


## 204 ✦ *The Fourth Month*

The fourth month was summer weather;
The sixth month, blistering heat.
Have our ancestors no compassion
That they can bear to see us suffer?

The autumn days were bitterly cold;
All plants and grasses withered.
I am sick of turmoils and troubles;
When shall we go home?

The winter days were stormy and wild;
The whirlwinds, blast on blast!
Other people are all in comfort;
Why should we alone be harmed?

On the hill were lovely trees,
Both chestnut-trees and plum-trees.
Cruel brigands tore them up;
But no one knew of their crime.

Look at that spring water;
Sometimes clear, sometimes foul.
But we every day meet fresh disaster.
How can we be expected to feed?[1]

---

1. Our parents.

On flow the Jiang and the Han,
Main-threads of this southern land.
We are worn out with service;
Why does no one heed us?

Would that I were an eagle or a falcon
That I might soar to Heaven.
Would I were a sturgeon or snout-fish
That I might plunge into the deep.

On the hill grows the bracken,
In the lowlands, the red-thorn.
A gentleman made this song
That his sorrows might be known.


205 ✦ *Northern Hills*

I climb those northern hills
And pluck the boxthorn.
Very strenuous are the knights,
Early and late upon their tasks;
The king's business never ends.
But for my father and mother I grieve.

"Everywhere under Heaven
Is no land that is not the king's.
To the borders of all those lands
None but is the king's slave."[1]
But the ministers are not just;
Whatever is done, I bear the brunt alone.

[Like] a team of steeds so strong
The king's business bears down upon me.
Everyone congratulates me on my youthfulness,
Is surprised I am still so strong,
That with muscles still so tough
I build the frontiers on every hand.

1. A proverbial saying?

Some people sit quietly at home;
Others wear themselves out in serving their country.
Some lie peacefully in bed;
Others are always on the move.

Some senselessly yell and bawl;
Others fret and toil.
Some loll about at their ease;
Others in the king's business are engrossed.

Some sunk in pleasure swill their wine;
Others are tortured by the fear of blame.
Some do nothing but scold or advise;
Others in every trouble must act.


## 206 ✦ Don't Escort the Big Chariot

Don't escort the big chariot;
You will only make yourself dusty.
Don't think about the sorrows of the world;
You will only make yourself wretched.[1]

Don't escort the big chariot;
You won't be able to see for dust.
Don't think about the sorrows of the world;
Or you will never escape from your despair.

Don't escort the big chariot;
You'll be stifled with dust.
Don't think about the sorrows of the world;
You will only load yourself with care.


1. This song uses the same formula as no. 102.

### 207 ✦ *Minor Bright*[1]

Oh, bright Heaven high above,
Shining down upon the earth below,
Our march to the west
Has led us to the desert wilds!
It was in the early days of the second month;[2]
We have suffered cold and heat.
Oh, the sadness of my heart,
Its poison is very bitter.
Thinking of those who nurtured me
My tears fall like rain.
Of course I long to come home,
But I fear the meshes of crime.

Long ago when we set out
The days and months[3] were just becoming mild.
When shall I get back?
The year is drawing to its close.
When I think I am single-handed
And my affairs very many,
Oh, the sadness of my heart!
Truly, I cannot get leave.
Thinking of those that nurtured me,
Full of longing I turn and gaze.
Indeed, I long to come home,
But I am afraid of the wrath that would ensue.

1. "Minor" in this title is assumed to be derived from the section name ("The Minor Odes"), as opposed to "Major Bright" (236) in the next section ("The Major Odes"). *Ed.*

2. That we got here.

3. I.e., the weather.

Long ago when we set out
The days and months were just becoming warm.
When shall I get back?
The affairs of the campaign press upon me more and more.
The year is drawing to its close;
They are plucking southernwood, cutting the beans.
Oh, the sadness of my heart!
I only make myself miserable by thinking.
When I remember those who nurtured me
I rise and leave the place where I lie.
Indeed, I am longing to go home;
But I dread the commotion that would follow.

*Listen to that, you gentlemen,*
*And do not forever take your ease.*
*Fulfill the duties of your station;*
*God sides with the upright and straight.*
*The spirits, they are listening*
*And will give good to you.*
*Listen to that, you gentlemen,*
*And do not forever take your rest.*
*Fulfill the duties of your station.*
*God loves the upright and straight.*
*The spirits, they are listening*
*And will give you blessings for evermore.*[1]


## 208 ✦ *Drums and Bells*

Drums and bells jingle
Where the Huai flows broad.
Sad is my heart and sore;
That good man, my lord—
I long for him and cannot forget.

---

1. The word "God" in this verse is not expressed, but it or "Heaven" must be understood as the subject of the sentence. In the last verse the minstrel addresses his audience.

The drums and bells blend their sound;
The waters of the Huai sweep on.
Sad is my heart and wretched.
That good man, my lord—
In his power no flaw.

Bells play, the great drum is beaten;
The Huai has three islands.
Sad is my heart and shaken.
That good man, my lord—
In his power no fault.

Din of drums and bells,
Sound of the small zither, the great.
Reed-organ and stone chimes make music together.
There are songs of the capital, songs of the south,
And flute unfaltering.

It is possible that this song is a lament for someone who lost his life during the southern campaigns of the late western Zhou. But this is very uncertain.

The only unfamiliar conception in the sacrificial songs is the "Dead One." The word (*shi*) literally means to "lay out" and consequently can be applied to "laying" meals (as in no. 185, last line) or to the "laying out" of the dead. It is thus a euphemism, a softened word, less direct than our word "corpse." At Chinese sacrifices a young man, usually the grandson of the sacrificer, impersonated the ancestor to whom the sacrifice was being made. For the time being the spirit of the ancestor entered into him. It was, however, no frenzied "possession," like that of the Siberian shaman; on the contrary, the demeanor of the Dead One was extremely quiet and restrained.

## 209 ✦ *Thick Star-Thistle*

Thick grows the star-thistle;
We must clear away its prickly clumps.
From of old, what have we been doing?
We grow wine-millet and cooking-millet,
Our wine-millet, a heavy crop;
Our cooking-millet doing well.
Our granaries are all full,
For our stacks were in their millions,
To make wine and food,
To make offering, to make prayer-offering,
That we may have peace, that we may have ease,
That every blessing may be vouchsafed.

In due order, treading cautiously,
We purify your oxen and sheep.
We carry out the rice-offering, the harvest offering,
Now baking, now boiling,
Now setting out and arranging,
Praying and sacrificing at the gate.
Very hallowed was this service of offering;
Very mighty the forefathers.
The Spirits and Protectors[1] have accepted;
The pious descendant shall have happiness,
They will reward him with great blessings,
With span of years unending.

1. Generally understood by modern scholars as being a title of the Dead One. I think it means the Ancestors; but there is not much difference; for the time being the Impersonator *is* an Ancestor.

We mind the furnaces, treading softly;
Attend to the food-stands so tall,
For roast meat, for broiled meat.
Our lord's lady hard at work
Sees to the dishes, so many,
Needed for guests, for strangers.
Healths and pledges go the round,
Every custom and rite is observed,
Every smile, every word is in place.
The Spirits and Protectors will surely come
And requite us with great blessings,
Countless years of life as our reward.

Very hard have we striven
That the rites might be without mistake.
The skillful recitant conveys the message,
Goes and gives it to the pious son:
"Fragrant were your pious offerings,
The Spirits enjoyed their drink and food.
They assign to you a hundred blessings.
According to their hopes, to their rules,
All was orderly and swift,
All was straight and sure.
For ever they will bestow upon you good store;
Myriads and tens of myriads."

The rites have all been accomplished,
The bells and drums are ready.
The pious son goes to his seat
And the skillful recitant conveys the message:
"The Spirits are all drunk."
The august Dead One then rises
And is seen off with drums and bells;
The Spirits and Protectors have gone home.
Then the stewards and our lord's lady
Clear away the dishes with all speed,
While the uncles and brothers
All go off to the lay feast.

The musicians go in and play,
That after-blessings may be secured.
Your viands are passed round;
No one is discontented, all are happy;
They are drunk, they are sated.
Small and great all bow their heads:
"The Spirits," they say, "enjoyed their drink and food
And will give our lord a long life.
He will be very favored and blessed,
And because nothing was left undone,
By son's sons and grandson's grandsons
Shall his line for ever be continued."

## 210 ✦ *Truly, Southern Hills*

Truly, those southern hills—
It was Yu[1] who fashioned them;
Those level spaces, upland and lowland—
The descendant tills them
We draw the boundaries, we divide the plots,
On southern slopes and eastern we set out acres.

A great cloud covers the heavens above,
Sends down snows thick-falling.
To them are added the fine rains of spring.
All is swampy and drenched,
All is moistened and soft,
Ready to grow the many grains.

The boundaries and balks are strictly drawn;
The wine-millet and cooking-millet give good yield,
To be harvested by the descendant;
That he may have wine and food
To supply the Dead One and the guests,
And so get life long-lasting.

1. This is the mythological Great Yu, the controller of floods and the architect of the mountains and rivers of China. *Ed.*

In the midst of the field are the huts;
Along the boundaries and balks are gourds.
He dries them, pickles them,
And offers them to his great forefathers.
So shall the descendant live long,
Receiving Heaven's favor.

He makes libation with clear wine,
Then follows with the Ruddy Male,[1]
Offering it to the forefathers, to the ancients.
He holds the bell-knife
To lay open the hair;
He takes the blood and fat.

So he offers the fruits, offers the flesh
So strong-smelling, so fragrant.
Very hallowed was this service of offering,
Very mighty his forefathers.
They will reward him with great blessings,
With span of years unending.

✦ ✦ ✦

1. Kenning for the bull.

People performing a ritual, such as that of offering of sacrifice, often call the things connected with the ritual by "kennings," substitute names of an allusive kind. Thus, according to the Book of Rites (*Li ji*), in the ancestral temple the bull is called First Great Warrior; the pig, Fatty; the hare, Bright Look. Other words are "semi-tabooed" by having a fixed epithet. Thus jade is called "blessed jade." Compare our "semi-taboo" when we feel the necessity of putting the epithet "poor" in front of the name of dead people whom we mention. In no. 211 "the Thing Purified" is probably the bowl, and "the Thing Bright" ("bright" being the stock epithet of things connected with the spirits) is the grain brought in the bowl. The sacrificer himself has a kenning. He is called "the Descendant" (it is only later that the word means specifically "great-grandson") in his relationship to offerings in general and to the offerings of harvest ritual in particular. The Field Grandad is defined as meaning "the previous harvest."[1] Agriculturalists in many parts of the world believe that the virtue of the crop is concentrated in the last sheaf to be cut. This sheaf, known in England as "The Old 'Un" and in Germany as "Der alte Mann," is kept till the next year (it is often nailed to a cowshed) and imparts its virtue to the fresh crop.

In Morocco young locusts, not yet able to fly, are dealt with by putting straw in their path and setting fire to it. Perhaps the last sheaf was used in China in the same way (no. 212, verse 2).

---

1. In later times the meaning of this phrase was no longer understood. The "Field Grandfather" was identified with the culture hero Shen Neng, who belongs to a very different circle of ideas. Compare *Zhou li,* chapter 46, folio 51.

## 211 ✦ *The Large Field*

"Far it stretches, that large field;
Every year we take ten thousand.
I take last year's crop
And feed my laborers.
For a long time we have had good harvests,
And now they are off to the southern acres,
Some weeding, some banking.
The wine-millet and cooking-millet are as lusty
As we prayed for, as we willed.
Fine, my chosen men!"

"With the Thing Purified, the Thing Bright,
With our bullocks for sacrifice, and our sheep
We come to honor the Earth Spirit, to honor the quarters.
For our fields have all done well,
The laborers have had luck.
We twang zithers, beat drums
To serve Field Grandad,
To beg for sweet rain,
So that our millet may be blessed,
Our men and women well fed."

Here comes the Descendant,
With his wife and children,
Bringing dinner to the southern acres.
The laborers come to take good cheer,
Break off a morsel here, a morsel there,
To see what tastes good:
"On the crop-balks and the long acre
All is fine and plentiful.
I don't think the Descendant will find fault;
The laborers have worked hard."

The Descendant's crops
Are thick as thatch, tall as a shaft;
The Descendant's stacks
Are high as cliffs, high as hills.
We shall need thousands of carts,
Shall need thousands of barns,
For millet, rice, and spiked millet;
The laborers are in luck.
"Heaven reward you with mighty blessings!
Long life to you, age unending!"

## 212 ✦ *The Big Field*

The big field brings a heavy crop.
We have chosen the seed, have seen to our tools;
We have got everything ready for you.[1]
With our sharp ploughs
Let us begin on the southern acre.
Now we sow our many crops;
They grow straight and tall;
The Descendant is well pleased.

There are no bare patches, everywhere our crops sprout,
They are firm, they are good,
There is no foxtail, no weeds.
Avaunt, all earwigs and pests,
Do not harm our young crops.
The Field Grandad has holy power,
He can take you and offer you to the flaming fire.

1. The bailiff.

A damp air comes chill,
Brings clouds that gather,
Raining on our lord's fields
And then on our private plots.
There stand some backward blades that were not reaped,
Here some corn that was not garnered,
There an unremembered sheaf,
Here some littered grain—
Gleanings for the widowed wife.

Here is the Descendant
With his wife and children
Bringing dinner to the southern acres.
The laborers come to take good cheer.
Then he makes offering to the quarters,
Smoke-offering and sacrifice,
With his red bull and his black,
With his wine-millet and cooking-millet,
Makes offering and sacrifice,
That blessings may be ours for evermore.

## 213 ✦ *Look There at the Luo River*

Look there at the Luo[1] River,
Its waters so deep and wide.
Our lord has come,
Blessings heaped upon him thick as thatch;
In his madder knee-caps so red
He is raising the king's six hosts.

Look there at the Luo River,
Its waters so deep and wide.
Our lord has come,
With his scabbard-gems that blaze.
May our lord for ten thousand years
Keep safe his house and home.

1. We cannot tell whether the Luo in Shaanxi or the Luo in Henan is meant.

Look there at the Luo River,
Its waters so deep and wide.
Our lord has come,
In whom all blessings join.
May our lord for ten thousand years
Keep safe his home and land.


214 ✦ *Gay the Flower*

Gay the flower,
Lush its leaves.
I have seen my lord,
And my heart is at rest,
My heart is at rest.
Small wonder that he is praised!

Gay the flower,
Gorgeous its yellow.
I have seen my lord,
And magnificent he is,
Magnificent he is.
Small wonder that he is blessed!

Gay the flower,
With its yellow and white.
I have seen my lord
Driving white horses with black manes,
Four white horses with black manes,
And six reins all glossy.

Put them to the left, to the left,
And gentlemen do what is best.
Put them to the right, to the right;
Gentlemen know what to do.
And knowing so well what to do,
Small wonder that they continue!

## 215 ✦ *Mulberry-Finch*

How it chirrups, the mulberry-finch!
Beautifully mottled its wing.
Our lord is happy and at ease;
He has received the blessings of Heaven.

How it chirrups, the mulberry-finch!
Beautifully mottled its throat.
Our lord is happy and at ease,
He, the shelterer of all the lands.

The shelter, the prop,
A pattern to the many chieftains;
Peaceable and mild,
Receiver of blessings innumerable.

His drinking horn high-curving,
His good wine so soft;
No self-glory, no pride,[1]
So that all blessings he wins.

## 216 ✦ *Mandarin Ducks*

Mandarin ducks were in flight;
We netted them, snared them.
Long life to our lord,
Well may blessings and rewards be his!

There are mandarin ducks on the dam,
Folding their left wings.[2]
Long life to our lord,
Well may blessings forever be his!

1. There are many variants.
2. Wing folded on wing portends blessing heaped upon blessing.

When there is a team of horses in the stable
We give it fodder, give it grass.
Long life to our lord,
May all blessings nurture him!

When there is a team of horses in the stable
We give it grass, give it fodder.
Long life to our lord,
May all blessings safely bind him!

## 217 ✦ *The Cap Is Tall*

A cap so tall,
What is it for?
Your wine is good,
Your viands, blessed.
Why give them to other men?
Let it be to brothers and no one else.
Do not the mistletoe and the dodder
Twine themselves on cypress and pine?
Before I saw my lord[1]
My sad heart had no rest;
But now that I have seen my lord,
What happiness is mine!

A cap so tall,
What is it for?
Your wine is good,
Your viands, blessed.
Why give them to other men?
Your brothers must all come.
Do not mistletoe and dodder
Twine about the top of the pine?
Before I saw my lord
My sad heart knew no peace;
But now I have seen my lord,
What good times are at hand!

1. Bridal-song formula.

A cap so tall
Is for putting on the head.
Your wine is good,
Your viands high heaped.
Why give them to other men?
Send for brothers, nephews, uncles.
When a snowstorm is coming
Sleet falls in its van.
But death and loss may come any day;
Not for long are we together.
Enjoy wine to-night;
Our lord holds feast!


## 218 ✦ *Axle-Pin of a Coach*

GUESTS: Slim and fine is the axle-pin of a coach,
And lovely the young girl that has come.
Of hunger we made light, of thirst;
For her fair fame had reached us.

HOST: Though I have no fine friends to meet you,
Pray feast and rejoice.

GUESTS: Such shelter gives that wood on the plains
That the pheasants all roost there.
Truly of this great lady
The magic Powers are strong.[1]

HOST: Pray feast and be at ease,
Good friends, of whom I cannot weary.

Although this wine is not good,
Try to drink just a little.
Although these meats are not fine,
Try to eat just a little.
Although I have no Power that I can impart to you,
Pray sing and dance.

---

1. Her *de* has drawn us to this place.

GUESTS:     We climbed that high ridge
            To cut firewood from the oak-tree,
            To cut firewood from the oak-tree.
            And ah, its leaves so wet!
            But now that in the end we have seen you
            All our sorrows are at rest.

            High hills we breasted,
            Long ways we went,
            Our four steeds prancing,
            Six reins like zither strings.
            But the sight of your new bride
            Brings good comfort to our hearts.

## 219 ✦ *The Bluebottles*

Buzz, buzz the bluebottles
That have settled on the hedge.
Oh, my blessed lord,
Do not believe the slanders that are said.

Buzz, buzz the bluebottles
That have settled on the thorns.
Slanderers are very wicked;
They disturb the whole land.

Buzz, buzz the bluebottles
That have settled on the hazel-bush.
Slanderers are very wicked;
They have joined[1] the two of us.

---

1. Joined our names in scandal? This may, of course, be a love poem; the meaning
of the last line is uncertain.

220 ✦ *The Guests Are Taking Their Seats*

The guests are taking their seats,[1]
To left, to right they range themselves.
The food-baskets and dishes are in their rows,
With dainties and kernels displayed.
The wine is soft and good,
It is drunk very peaceably.
The bells and drums are set,
The brimming pledge-cup is raised.
The great target is put up,
The bows and arrows are tested,
The bowmen are matched.
"Present your deeds of archery,
Shoot at that mark
That you may be rewarded with the cup."

Fluting they dance to reed-organ and drum.
All the instruments perform in concert
As an offering to please the glorious ancestors,
That the rites may be complete.
For when all the rites are perfect,
Grandly, royally done,
The ancestors bestow great blessings;
Sons and grandsons may rejoice,
May rejoice and make music:
"Let each of you display his art."
The guests then receive the pledge-cup,
The house-men enter anew
And fill that empty cup,
That you may perform your songs.

1. Literally, their mats.

When the guests first take their seats,
How decorous they are, how reverent!
While they are still sober
Their manner is dignified and correct;
But when they are drunk
Their manner is utterly changed.
They leave their seats and roam,
Cut capers, throw themselves about.
While they are still sober
Their manner is dignified and grave;
But when they are drunk
It becomes unseemly and rude;
For when people are drunk
They do not know what misdemeanors they commit.

When guests are drunk
They howl and bawl,
Upset my baskets and dishes,
Cut capers, lilt, and lurch.
For when people are drunk
They do not know what blunders they commit.
Cap on one side, very insecure,
They cut capers lascivious.
If when they got drunk they went out,
They would receive their blessing like the rest.
But if they get drunk and stay,
The power of the feast is spoilt.
Drinking wine is very lucky,
Provided it is done with decency.

It is always the same when wine is drunk;
Some are tipsy, some are not.
So we appoint a master of ceremonies,
Or choose someone as recorder.
"That drunk man is not behaving nicely;
He is making the sober feel uncomfortable.
Pray do not mention at random
Things that do not belong together, that are quite silly.
What are not real words, do not say;
What leads nowhere, do not speak of,
Led on by drunkenness in your talk,
Bringing out 'rams' and 'hornless' side by side.
After the three cups[1] you don't know what you are saying;
What will become of you if you insist on taking more?"

❖ ❖ ❖

1.  The three ritual cups. To talk of a hornless ram is like talking of a Manx cat's tail.

## 221 ✦ *Fish and Water-Plants*

The fish are at home, at home among their water-plants,
Beautifully streaked are their heads.
The king is at home, at home in Hao,[1]
Content and happy he drinks his wine.

The fish are at home, at home among their water-plants,
Very pliant are their tails.
The king is at home, at home in Hao,
Drinking his wine, happy and content.

The fish are at home, at home among their water-plants,
Snuggling close to their reeds.
The king is at home, at home in Hao,
Very soft he lies.

## 222 ✦ *Gathering Beans*

When one gathers beans, gathers beans,
One puts them in baskets square or round.
The princes have come to Court;
With what gift can I present them?
Although this is nothing to give them,
It shall be a great coach and four.
What besides this shall I give them?
Black robe and broidered skirt.

---

1. Said to have been the capital of Zhou in the early days of the dynasty. When this poem was written, Hao had probably become a pleasure-palace, a sort of Versailles. We do not know at what date the later conception of a "capital" began. When we discuss where the earliest kings had their "capital," we are perhaps committing an anachronism. Possibly in early times the center of government was where the king was at the moment.

High spurts that fountain;
Come, pluck the cress that grows by it.
The princes have come to Court;
Let us look at their banners.
Their banners flutter, flutter,
Their harness bells ring.
Driving teams of three, teams of four,
The princes arrive.

Red greaves on their legs,
Cross-laced below.
Not that they are wanton or loose;
These are what the Son of Heaven gave.
Oh, happy princes,
To whom the Son of Heaven gave his charge!
Oh, happy princes,
Before whom all blessings were spread!

The branches of the oak,
Their leaves cluster close.
Oh, happy princes
That guard the Son of Heaven's land!
Oh, happy princes,
In whom all blessings unite!
On this side and that, to left and right,
We join in your procession.

It was adrift, that willow boat;
Now to our tow-line we have tied it.
Oh, happy princes,
Whom the Son of Heaven measures.[1]
Oh, happy princes,
May all blessings shelter them!
Let us play, let us sport;
For the princes have come.

1. Probably corrupt. We need a meaning parallel to "tied."

### 223 ✦ *Horn Bow*

Pliant the horn bow;
Swiftly its ends fly back.
But brothers and kinsmen by marriage
Ought not to keep their distance.

If you are distant
The common people will be so too;
But if you set a good example
The common people will follow it.

These good brothers
Are generous and forgiving;
But bad brothers
Do each other all the harm they can.

Common people are not good;
They turn their backs on one another, each his own way.
He who has got the cup won't pass it on,
Until there is already nothing left in it.

Like[1] the old horse that was changed into a colt,
They don't look behind them.[2]
When they eat, it must be till they are gorged,
When they pour out drink, they take huge quantities.

1. "Like" is not expressed in the original.

2. I.e., don't consider those who come "after them," who have not yet been served. The old horse, delighted by its own capers, did not notice that the village boys were laughing at it "behind its back."

Don't teach monkeys to climb trees,
Or put wet plaster on wet plaster.[1]
If gentlemen set good rules
The lesser folk will fall in with them.

Thick though the snow may have fallen,
When sunshine warms it, it melts.
But none of you offers to step down or retire;
You remain proudly on high.

Fast though the snow may have fallen,
When sunshine warms it, it flows away.
That you should be so unseeing, so purblind—
That is what makes me sad.

## 224 ✦ *Leafy Willow-Tree*

Very leafy is that willow-tree,
But I would not care to rest under it.[2]
God[3] on high is very bright;
Don't go too close to him!
Were I to reprove him,
Afterward I should be slaughtered by him.

Very leafy is that willow-tree,
But I would not care to repose under it.
God on high is very bright;
Don't hurt yourself on him!
Were I to reprove him,
Afterward I should be torn to pieces by him.

1. The common people are bad enough already. Do not by your bad example add fresh wickedness to their wickedness.

2. Because *liu* (willow) also means "slaughter."

3. I.e., the ruler.

There is a bird, flies high,
Yes, soars to Heaven.
But that man's heart
Never could it reach.
Why should I rebuke him,
Only to be cruelly slain?


## 225 ✦ *Knight of the City*

That knight of the city,
His fox-furs so brown,
His pose unchanging,
His speech well-cadenced.
He was coming back to Zhou,
And all the people stood gazing.

That knight of the city
In traveling hat and black headcloth;
That lady his daughter,
Thick and lovely her hair![1]
Me, alas, she did not see!
Sad is my heart within.

That knight of the city
With his ear-stops of precious stone;
That lady his daughter
They called her Yin Ji.
Me, alas, she did not see!
Sorrow is pent up within.

That knight of the city
Dangled a sash cut so as to hang.
That lady his daughter
Curled her hair like a scorpion
Me, alas, she did not see!
Where can I go to seek her out?

1. This line is corrupt in the original and the sense can only be guessed at.

No, it was not made to dangle;
The sash had length to spare.
No, it was not that she made it curl;
Her hair curled of itself.
Me, alas, she did not see!
But what use to pine and sigh?


### 226 ✦ *Gathering Green*

The whole morning I gathered green;
And in the end had not a handful.
My hair is all wispy;
I must go home and wash it.

All the morning I gathered blue;
But did not get a skirtful.
On the fifth day he was to come;
It is the sixth; and he is not here.

When he went hunting
I put his bow in its case;
When he went fishing
I reeled his line.

And what did he catch?
Bream and tench,
Aye, bream and tench;
On a line I strung them.

In the above song a girl, about to be married, goes to gather plants
with which to make green and blue dyes for her trousseau-dresses.
She fails to fill her basket, which is a bad omen. Sure enough, the
man does not turn up on the wedding-day. She recalls the happy
days of their courtship and the time when the omens were still good.
When he was fishing he caught a great haul of bream and tench, which
meant that they would be married and have many children.

We have seen from poem no. 178 that simultaneously with the attacks of the Xian-yun, the Zhou had trouble on their southern frontier. As an ally against their southern enemies they made friends with the chieftain of Shen,[1] and King Xuan's successor, the last king of western Zhou,[2] married a Shen princess. The Lord of Shao, a fief near the Zhou capital, was sent with an army to the south, to fortify Xie, a stronghold of the Shen people. During the same period great campaigns, of which we hear much in the bronze inscriptions, were carried on against the tribes of the Huai Valley.

### 227 ✦ *Young Millet*

Lusty is the young millet;
Copious rains have fattened it.
Long, long was our march to the south;
But the Lord of Shao has rewarded it.

Oh, our loads, our barrows,
Our wagons, our oxen!
But now the marching is over
And at last we are going home.

Oh, our footmen, our chariot-drivers,
Our armies, our hosts!
But now our marching is over
And at last we are going back.

Noble is the palace at Xie;
The Lord of Shao planned it.
Glorious was the army on its march;
The Lord of Shao gave it victory.

The highlands and the lowlands were made safe;
The springs and streams cleared.
The Lord of Shao has vanquished,
And the king's heart is at rest.

1. In southern Henan.
2. King You, 781–72 B.C.

### 228 ✦ *Mulberry on the Lowland*

The mulberry on the lowland, how graceful!
Its leaves, how tender!
Now that I have seen my lord,
Ah, what delight!

The mulberry on the lowland, how graceful!
Its leaves, how glossy!
Now that I have seen my lord,
What joy indeed!

The mulberry on the lowland, how graceful,
Its leaves, how fresh!
Now I have seen my lord,
His high fame holds fast.

Love that is felt in the heart,
Why should it not be told in words?
To the core of my heart I treasure him,
Could not ever cease to love him.

### 229 ✦ *The White-Flower*

The white-flower is twisted into bast,
The white reeds are bound in bundles.
But my lord is estranged from me,
Lets me be all alone.

White clouds spread across the sky,
There is dew on sedge and reed.
Heaven is verging toward calamity;
My lord makes no plan.

The Hu-tuo[1] northward flowing
Wets those paddy fields.
Full of woe is this song I chant,
Thinking of that tall man.

They have gathered that brushwood of the mulberry-tree;
High it blazes in the furnace.
To think of that tall man
Truly scorches my heart.

Drums and bells in the house!
One can hear them from outside.
Thinking of you I am in misery—
How you looked at me without love.

There is a pelican on the dam,
A crane in the wood.
Thinking of that big man
Truly frets my heart.

There is a mandarin-duck on the dam;
It folds its left wing.
My lord is not good;
Twofold, threefold he gives his favors.

Lopsided is that stone;
If you tread on it, it goes down.
My lord is estranged from me,
And leaves me to my misery.

In the last verse there are some puns, which I have explained in my textual notes.

1. In East-central Shanxi.

## 230 ✦ *Tender and Pretty*

Tender and pretty[1] are the yellow orioles
Perching on the side of the hill.
The way is long;
I am so tired. What will become of me?
"Let him have a drink, let him have some food,
Give him a lesson, scold him,
But bid that hind coach
Call to him and pick him up."

Tender and pretty are the yellow orioles
Perching on the corner of the hill.
How dare I shirk marching?
But I fear I cannot keep up.
"Let him have a drink, let him have some food,
Give him a lesson, scold him,
But bid that hind coach
Call to him and pick him up."

Tender and pretty are the yellow orioles
Perching on the side of the hill.
How dare I shirk marching?
But I fear I shall not hold out.
"Let him have a drink, let him have some food,
Give him a lesson, scold him,
But bid that hind coach
Call to him and pick him up."

## 231 ✦ *Gourd Leaves*

Flutter, flutter go the gourd leaves;
We pluck them and boil them.
Our lord has wine;
He fills his cup and tastes it.

1. *Mian-man* also suggests "on and on." The orioles find their perch; but the soldier is allowed no rest.

Here is a rabbit with a white head;[1]
Come, bake it, roast it.
Our lord has wine;
He fills a cup and proffers it.

Here is a rabbit with a white head;
Come, roast it, broil it.
Our lord has wine;
We fill a cup and hand it to him.

Here is a rabbit with a white head;
Come, roast it or bake it.
Our lord has wine;
We fill a cup and pledge with it.

## 232 ✦ *Jagged Are the Rocks*

Jagged are the rocks.
Oh, how high!
These hills and rivers go on and on.
Oh, how toilsome!
But soldiers fighting in the east
Have no time to pause.

Jagged are the rocks.
Oh, how steep!
These hills and rivers go on and on.
It seems as though they would never end.
But soldiers fighting in the east
Have no time to halt.

---

1. I should think a rabbit with a white head was lucky, because it meant that one
would live till one's hair went white.

We met swine with white trotters
Plunging in a herd through the waves.
The moon is caught in the Net.[1]
There will be deluges of rain.
Soldiers fighting in the east
Have no time to rest.

## 233 ✦ *Flowers of the Bignonia*

Oh, the flowers of the bignonia,
Gorgeous is their yellow!
The sorrows of my heart,
How they stab!

Oh, the flowers of the bignonia
And its leaves so thick!
Had I known it would be like this,
Better that I should never have been born!

As often as a ewe has a ram's head,
As often as Orion is in the Pleiades,
Do people today, if they find food at all,
Get a chance to eat their fill.

## 234 ✦ *What Plant Is Not Faded?*

What plant is not faded?
What day do we not march?
What man is not taken
To defend the four bounds?

---

1. The Net, i.e., the Hyades, connected by the Chinese, as by us, with rain. Swine with white trotters are also an omen of rain. Rain falling looks like a net cast over the landscape. The characters for "net" and "rain" are in their oldest forms very similar.

What plant is not wilting?
What man is not taken from his wife?
Alas for us soldiers,
Treated as though we were not fellow-men!

Are we buffaloes, are we tigers
That our home should be these desolate wilds?
Alas for us soldiers,
Neither by day nor night can we rest!

The fox bumps and drags
Through the tall, thick grass.
Inch by inch move our barrows
As we push them along the track.

# THE MAJOR ODES,
## POEMS 235–65

◆

The poems in "The Major Odes" (*Da ya*) are "major" in the sense that they interweave historical and legendary materials of the Zhou state into the concerns of the aristocratic society, giving the thirty-one poems a general sense of grandeur and retrospection. Again there is still a mix of poems contemplating daily events in the here and now, especially those of the clan and king. What is special about "The Major Odes" however, is the clustering of important narratives that tell the story of the origins and early struggles of the Zhou people. In these poems we have the creative imagining of the Zhou people as a cultural force. These works come closest in spirit to the epic narratives of other traditions, leading one modern critic to reconstruct from them a lyrical epic of the Zhou people.

Nothing is more important to that community and its celebration than "Birth to the People" (245), which plots the origins of the Zhou and describes their agricultural legacy to Chinese civilization. It is also one of the few poems in the strongly humanistic tradition of the Zhou that hints at a more magical beginning: "She trod on the big toe of God's footprint,/Was accepted and got what she desired [i.e., pregnant]." The long denouement after the birth of that child, Hou Ji, or Lord Millet, is filled with royal ancestors, timely migrations, and heroic conquests; yet overshadowing all of that is the presence of King Wen, the Civilized, whom Heaven selected to take up the rule of the whole world: "King Wen is on high;/Oh, he shines in Heaven!/Zhou is an old people,/But its charge is new" (235). From King Wen follows in quick succession the noble lineage of early Zhou dynastic rulers: King Wu, the Martial, who accepted the unpleasant but necessary task of smiting the Shang royal house; his brother, the beloved Duke of Zhou, who acted as sagely regent to the young king and graciously yielded power at the appropriate time; and young King Cheng, the Perfecter, who drew these various strands of leadership together into an enlightened reign. For these and other names see Important Legendary and Historical Figures, in the front of the book.

225

## 235 ✦ *King Wen*

King Wen is on high;
Oh, he shines in Heaven!
Zhou is an old people,
But its charge is new.
The land of Zhou became illustrious,
Blessed by God's charge.
King Wen ascends and descends
On God's left hand, on His right.

Very diligent was King Wen,
His high fame does not cease;
He spread his bounties in Zhou,
And now in his grandsons and sons,
In his grandsons and sons
The stem has branched
Into manifold generations,
And all the knights of Zhou
Are glorious in their generation.

Glorious in their generation,
And their counsels well pondered.
Mighty were the many knights
That brought this kingdom to its birth.
This kingdom well they bore;
They were the prop of Zhou.
Splendid were those many knights
Who gave comfort to Wen the king.

August is Wen the king;
Oh, to be reverenced in his glittering light!
Mighty the charge that Heaven gave him.
The grandsons and sons of the Shang,[1]
Shang's grandsons and sons,
Their hosts were innumerable.
But God on high gave His command,
And by Zhou they were subdued.

By Zhou they were subdued;
Heaven's charge is not for ever.
The knights of Yin,[2] big and little,
Made libations and offerings at the capital;
What they did was to make libations
Dressed in skirted robe and close cap.
O chosen servants of the king,
May you never thus shame your ancestors!

May you never shame your ancestors,
But rather tend their inward power,
That for ever you may be linked to Heaven's charge
And bring to yourselves many blessings.
Before Yin lost its army
It was well linked to God above.
In Yin you should see as in a mirror
That Heaven's high charge is hard to keep.

The charge is not easy to keep.
Do not bring ruin on yourselves.
Send forth everywhere the light of your good fame;
Consider what Heaven did to the Yin.
High Heaven does its business
Without sound, without smell.
Make King Wen your example,
In whom all the peoples put their trust.

1. The people overthrown by the Zhou.

2. Another name for the Shang.

## 236 ✦ *Major Bright*

Bright they shone on earth below,
Majestic they blaze on high.
Heaven cannot be trusted;
Kingship is easily lost.
Heaven set up a foe to match the Yin;
Did not let them keep their frontier lands.

Zhong-shi Ren of Zhi[1]
From those Yin and Shang
Came to marry in Zhou,
To be a bride in the capital,
And with Ji the king[2]
She joined in works of power.

Tai-ren became big with child;
She bore this King Wen.
Now this King Wen
Was very circumspect and reverent,
Toiled to serve God on high.
He received many blessings,
His inward power never failed
To protect his frontiers, his realms.

Heaven gazed below;
Saw that its charge had been fulfilled,
King Wen had begun his task.
Heaven made for him a match,
To the north of the River He,
On the banks of the Wei.

1. Tai-ren. She was presumably the daughter of a Shang grandee.
2. Wang Ji.

King Wen was blessed.
A great country had a child,
A great country had a child
Fair as a sister of Heaven.
King Wen fixed on a lucky day
And went himself to meet her at the Wei;
He joined boats and made of them a bridge;
Very dazzling their splendor.

There came a command from Heaven
Ordering this King Wen
In Zhou, in his capital,
To give the succession to a Lady Xin,[1]
The eldest of her family;
Who bravely bore King Wu.
"Heaven's protection and help are allotted to you
To assail the great Shang."

The armies of Yin and Shang—
Their catapults were like the trees of a forest.
They marshaled their forces at Mu-ye:[2]
A target set up for us.
"God on high is watching you;
Let no treachery be in your hearts."

The field of Mu-ye spread far,
The war chariots gleamed,
The team of white-bellies was tough,
The captain was Shang-fu;[3]
Like an eagle he uprose.[4]
Ah, that King Wu
Swiftly fell upon Great Shang,
Who before daybreak begged for a truce.

1. Or Shen; near He-yang, eastern Shaanxi. To give her succession as queen.

2. In northern Henan, near the Shang capital.

3. Known also as Tai Gong Wang; one of the companions of King Wu.

4. Very likely corrupt.

A large part of the human race at one time believed that mankind is descended from melon seeds. Dr. Alfred Kühn, in his excellent book on the origin-myths of Indochina,[1] mentions some twenty peoples who in one form or another hold this belief. A quite superficial search supplied me with two African examples.[2] I am told that the same belief existed in North America. The general form of the story in Indochina is summarized by N. Matsumoto in his *Mythologie Japonaise* as follows: "The human race is destroyed by a flood. The only survivors are a brother and sister, miraculously saved in a pumpkin. Very reluctantly the brother and sister marry, and have as their offspring sometimes a pumpkin, whose seeds sown in mountain and plain give birth to the different races of man, sometimes a mass of flesh, which the man divides into 360 parts."

In ancient China, as in modern Indochina, gourds were commonly used as lifebelts, and it is clear that in all these stories the gourd is merely a primitive equivalent to Noah's Ark.

The first line of the song which follows has always been taken as a simile, and no doubt it functions as one today. But in view of the facts mentioned above, it is most likely that embedded in this line is an allusion to a forgotten belief that "the people after they were first brought into being" were gourd seeds or young gourds. One has the impression, when reading the opening of this poem, that Dan-fu is an independent culture-hero, a rival, in fact, to Hou Ji. But tradition makes him a descendant of Hou Ji. He leads the people away from Bin, where their security is menaced by savage tribes, to Mount Qi, farther west.

The "as yet they had no houses" of verse 1 does not mean that they were incapable of making houses, but that till their houses were ready they lived in loess-pits, as many inhabitants of Shaanxi still do permanently. Compare no. 194, last verse, where a migration is also referred to.

1. *Berichte über den Weltanfang bei den Indochinesen*, Leipzig, 1935.

2. Among the Shilluk of the Sudan and the Songo tribe of the Congo. See H. Baumann, *Schöpfung und Urzeit des Menschen im Mythus der Afrikanischen Völker*.

## 237 ✦ *Spreading*

The young gourds spread and spread.
The people after they were first brought into being
From the River Du[1] went to the Qi.[2]
Of old Dan-fu the duke
Scraped shelters, scraped holes;
As yet they had no houses.

Of old Dan-fu the duke
At coming of day galloped his horses,
Going west along the river[3] bank
Till he came to the foot of Mount Qi.[4]
Where with the lady Jiang
He came to look for a home.

The plain of Zhou was very fertile,
Its celery and sowthistle sweet as rice-cakes.
"Here we will make a start; here take counsel,
Here notch our tortoise."[5]
It says, "Stop," it says, "Halt.
Build houses here."

So he halted, so he stopped.
And left and right
He drew the boundaries of big plots and little,
He opened up the ground, he counted the acres
From west to east;
Everywhere he took his task in hand.

1. I.e., the Wei.

2. Not the Qi of no. 281, but another Lacquer River in western Shaanxi.

3. The Wei.

4. Mount Qi, west of the capital city of Hao, was earlier the home of Zhou people, who had been led there from Bin by Dan-fu. See no. 270. *Ed.*

5. Tortoise shells were used as divination tools, particularly during the Shang period (as is referred to here); for example, see Kwang-chih Chang's *Shang Civilization* (New Haven: Yale University Press, 1980), pp. 31–42. *Ed.*

Then he summoned his Master of Works,
Then he summoned his Master of Lands
And made them build houses.
Dead straight was the plumb-line,
The planks were lashed to hold the earth;
They made the Hall of Ancestors, very venerable.

They tilted in the earth with a rattling,
They pounded it with a dull thud,
They beat the walls with a loud clang,
They pared and chiseled them with a faint *ping, ping*;
The hundred cubits all rose;
The drummers could not hold out.[1]

They raised the outer gate;
The outer gate soared high.
They raised the inner gate;
The inner gate was very strong.
They raised the great earth-mound,
Whence excursions of war might start.[2]

And in the time that followed they did not abate their sacrifices,
Did not let fall their high renown;
The oak forests were laid low,
Roads were opened up.
The Kun[3] tribes scampered away;
Oh, how they panted!

The peoples of Yu and Rui[4] broke faith,
And King Wen harried their lives.
This I will say, the rebels were brought to allegiance,
Those that were first were made last.
This I will say, there were men zealous in their tasks,
There were those that kept the insolent at bay.

1. The drummers were there to set a rhythm for the workmen. But they tired
more quickly than the indefatigable builders.

2. The shrine where the soldiers were "sworn in" for the combat.

3. The same as the Dog Barbarians?

4. In western Shaanxi.

### 238 ✦ *Oak Clumps*

Thick grow the oak clumps;
We make firewood of them, we stack them.
Great is the magnificence of the lord king;
On either hand are those that speed for him.

Great is the magnificence of the lord king;
On either hand are those that hold up scepters before him,
Hold up scepters in solemn state,
As befits doughty knights.

Spurt goes that boat on the Jing;
A host of oarsmen rows it.
When the King of Zhou goes forth,
His six armies are with him.

How it stands out, the Milky Way,
Making a blazon in the sky!
Long life to the King of Zhou,
And a portion for his people![1]

Chiseled and carved are his emblems,
Of bronze and jade are they made.
Ceaseless are the labors of our king
Fashioning the network of all the lands.

### 239 ✦ *Foothills of Mount Han*

Look at the foothills of Mount Han
With hazel and redthorn so thick.
Here's happiness to my lord,
A happy quest for blessings.[2]

---

1. Cf. no. 239.

2. Pun on *Han lu*, "foothills of Han," and *han lu*, "quest for blessings." Mount Han is in southwestern Shaanxi.

Fair is that jade-handled spoon[1]
And the yellow flood within.
Happiness to my lord,
On whom all blessings shall descend.

The kite flies up to Heaven;
The fish leaps in its pool.
Happiness to my lord,
And a portion[2] for his people.

The clear wine is brought,
The Ruddy Male is ready
For offering, for sacrifice,
That great blessings may be vouchsafed.

So thick grow those oaks
That the people never lack for firewood.
Happiness to our lord!
May the Spirits always have rewards for him.

Dense grows the cloth-creeper,
Spreading over branches and boughs.
Happiness to our lord!
In quest of blessings may he never fail.

## 240 ✦ Great Dignity

Great dignity had Tai-ren,
The mother of King Wen;
Well loved was Lady Jiang of Zhou,
Bride of the high house.
And Tai-si carried on her fair name,
Bearing a multitude of sons.

1. A libation-ladle with a straight handle of jade.
2. Reading very doubtful.

He[1] was obedient to the ancestors of the clan,
So that the Spirits were never angry;
So that the Spirits were never grieved.
He was a model to his chief bride;
A model to his brothers old and young,
And in his dealings with home and land.

Affable was he in the palace,
Reverent in the ancestral hall,
Glorious and regarded by Heaven,
Causing no discontent, protected by Heaven.
Therefore war and sickness did not destroy,
Nor plague nor witchcraft work havoc.

Without asking, he knew what was the rule;
Without being admonished, he admitted.[2]
Therefore grown men could use their Inward Power,
And young people could find work to do.
The ancient were well content;
And the doughty well employed.

### 241 ✦ *Sovereign Might*

God on high in sovereign might
Looked down majestically,
Gazed down upon the four quarters,
Examining the ills of the people.
Already in two kingdoms[3]
The governance had been all awry;
Then every land
He tested and surveyed.
God on high examined them
And hated the laxity of their rule.
So he turned his gaze to the west
And here made his dwelling-place.

1. King Wu, traditional dates, 1122–16 B.C.

2. The wise to his counsel? But the whole verse is probably corrupt.

3. Xia and Yin. (The ruling houses before the Zhou. *Ed.*)

Cleared them, moved them,[1]
The dead trees, the fallen trunks;
Trimmed them, leveled them,
The clumps and stumps;
Opened them, cleft them,
The tamarisk woods, the stave-tree woods;
Pulled them up, cut them back,
The wild mulberries, the cudranias.
God shifted his bright power;
To fixed customs and rules he gave a path.
Heaven set up for itself a counterpart on earth;
Its charge was firmly awarded.

God examined his hills.
The oak-trees were uprooted,
The pines and cypresses were cleared.
God made a land, made a counterpart,[2]
Beginning with Tai-bo and Wang Ji.
Now this Wang Ji
Was of heart accommodating and friendly,
Friendly to his elder brother,
So that his luck was strong.
Great were the gifts that were bestowed upon him,
Blessings he received and no disasters,
Utterly he swayed the whole land.

Then came King Wen;
God set right measure to his thoughts,
Spread abroad his fair fame;
His power was very bright,
Very bright and very good.
Well he led, well lorded,
Was king over this great land.
Well he followed, well obeyed,
Obeyed—did King Wen.
His power was without flaw.
Having received God's blessing
He handed it down to grandsons and sons.

1.  The subject of these verbs is "the people of Zhou." Possibly there is a lacuna in the text.

2.  I.e., a king below, as God is King above.

God said to King Wen:
"This is no time to be idle,
No time to indulge in your desires.
You must be first to seize the high places.
The people of Mi[1] are in revolt.
They have dared to oppose the great kingdom.
They have invaded Yuan and Gong."
The king blazed forth his anger;
He marshaled his armies,
To check the foe he marched to Lu,[2]
He secured the safety of Zhou,
He united all under Heaven.

They drew near to the capital,
Attacking from the borders of Yuan.
They began to climb our high ridges;
But never did they marshal their forces on our hills,
Our hills or slopes,
Never did they drink out of our wells,
Our wells, our pools.
The king made his dwelling in the foothills and plains,
Dwelt in the southern slopes of Mount Qi,
On the shores of the River Wei,
Pattern to all the myriad lands,
King of his subject peoples.

God said to King Wen,
"I am moved by your bright power.
Your high renown has not made you put on proud airs,
Your greatness has not made you change former ways,
You do not try to be clever or knowing,
But follow God's precepts."
God said to King Wen,
"Take counsel with your partner states,
Unite with your brothers young and old,
And with your scaling ladders and siege-platforms
Attack the castles of Chong."[3]

1. In eastern Gansu.

2. In eastern Gansu?

3. In Shaanxi? But this is now disputed.

The siege-platforms trembled,
The walls of Chong towered high.
The culprits were bound quietly,
Ears were cut off[1] peacefully.
He made the sacrifice to Heaven and the sacrifice of propitiation.[2]
He annexed the spirits of the land, he secured continuance of the
    ancestral sacrifices,
And none anywhere dared affront him.
The siege-platforms shook,
So high were the walls of Chong.
He attacked, he harried,
He cut off, he destroyed.
None anywhere dared oppose him.


The Magic Tower was built by King Wen near his capital at Hao,
close to the modern Xi'an. The Moated Mound was a holy place
surrounded by water, where the sons of the Zhou royal house were
trained in the accomplishments of manhood. We have no reason to
suppose that the young men were ever segregated there or that the
Moated Mound in any way corresponds to the Men's Houses and
Initiation Houses of contemporary primitives. Manhood initiation
in ancient China was, so far as we have any knowledge of it, a very
mild affair, not unlike Christian confirmation. An inscription[3]
describes an early Zhou king as boating on the waters of the Moated
Mound, where he shoots a large wild-goose. The Lord of Xing, who
follows him in a "boat with red banners," gives the bird a coup de
grâce, which suggests that the king had only managed to wing it.

## 242 ✦ *The Magic Tower*

When he built the Magic Tower,
When he planned it and founded it,
All the people worked at it;
In less than a day they finished it.

1. To offer to the ancestors. We are told that the character means "ears cut off";
but I suspect that, as its form would suggest, it originally meant "heads cut off."

2. To the spirits of the soil over which he rode. Compare no. 180.

3. Karlgren, B. 14.

When he built it, there was no goading;
Yet the people came in their throngs.
The king was in the Magic Park,
Where doe and stag lay hid.

Doe and stag at his coming leapt and bounded;
The white herons gleamed so sleek.
The king was by the Magic Pool,
Where the fish sprang so lithe.

On the upright posts and cross-beams with their spikes
Hang the big drums and gongs.
Oh, well-ranged are the drums and gongs,
And merry is the Moated Mound.

Oh, well-ranged are the drums and gongs!
And merry is the Moated Mound.
Bang, bang go the fish-skin drums;
The sightless and the eyeless[1] ply their skill.

## 243 ✦ *Footsteps Here Below*

Zhou it is that continues the footsteps here below.
From generation to generation it has had wise kings.
Three rulers are in Heaven,
And the king[2] is their counterpart in his capital.

He is their counterpart in his capital,
The power of generations he has matched;
Long has he been mated to Heaven's command
And fulfilled what is entrusted to a king.

Has fulfilled what is entrusted to a king,
A model to all on earth below;
Forever pious toward the dead,
A very pattern of piety.

1. I.e., blind musicians.

2. If we count Wen, Wu, and Cheng as the three kings, then this is Kang (1078–53). But I doubt if the song is as early as that.

Loved is this One Man,
Meeting only with docile powers;[1]
Forever pious toward the dead,
Gloriously continuing their tasks.

Yes, gloriously he steps forward
Continuing in the footsteps of his ancestors.
"For myriads of years
May you receive Heaven's blessing!

Receive Heaven's blessing!"
So from all sides they come to wish him well.
"For myriads of years
May your luck never fail!"


## 244 ✦ Renowned Was King Wen

Renowned was King Wen,
Yes, high was his renown.
He united, he gave peace;
Manifold were his victories.
Oh, glorious was King Wen!

King Wen received Heaven's bidding
To do these deeds of war.
He attacked Chong;
He made his capitol in Feng.[2]
Oh, glorious was King Wen!

He built his castle within due boundaries,
He made Feng according to the ancient plan.
He did not fulfill his own desires,
But worked in pious obedience to the dead.
Oh, glorious our sovereign and king!


1. With obedient *de;* i.e., with obedience.

2. West of Xi'an, Shaanxi.

Splendid were the works of the king.
Within the walls of Feng
All the peoples came together.
A sure buckler was our sovereign and king.
Oh, glorious our sovereign and king!

The Feng River flowed to the East
In the course made for it by Yu,[1]
Meeting-place for all the peoples.
A pattern was our great king.
Oh, glorious our great king!

To the capital at Hao, to the Moated Mound,
From west, from east,
From south, from north—
There were none that did not surrender.
Oh, glorious the great king!

Omens he took, our king,
Before the building of the capital at Hao;
The tortoise[2] directed it;
King Wu perfected it.
Oh, glorious was King Wu!

By the Feng River grew white millet.[3]
How should King Wu not be continued?
He bequeathed his teachings and counsels
That they might give peace and protection to his sons.
Oh, glorious was King Wu!

1. Great Yu, Controller of the Flood. *Ed.*

2. I.e., by divination with a tortoise shell. *Ed.*

3. I should imagine that it grew unplanted and was a portent. There are many similar portents in Chinese legend.

The legend which follows becomes more interesting if we connect its main features with parallels that, though they are familiar, may not immediately spring to the mind of the reader.

The hero is born of a mother whose barrenness is removed by a miracle. We are reminded of another "mother of nations," Sarah of the Bible, and of numerous folk-stories which begin with a king and queen who are glorious in every other way, but have no child. They always end by having a child, who becomes the hero of the story.

Hou Ji's mother obtains a child by treading on the mark of God's big toe. We could, instead of God, translate *di* by ancestor, meaning the spirit of a former king. Other versions of the story say "a giant's tracks." We are at once reminded that till recently childless women tried to remedy their condition by sitting upon the prehistoric figures of big men traced on chalky hills in various parts of England. The footprints of gods figure in many religions. Colossal footprints of Buddha were shown in several parts of northwestern India. Treading on a big toe can actually form part of the ritual of marriage, as, for example, among the Arapesh in New Guinea.[1]

The singularity of the hero is established by the fact that he was born of a barren or even of a virgin mother. It is confirmed by the fact that successive attempts to destroy him in infancy completely fail. Among famous infants upon whose lives fruitless attempts were made, either by exposure or other means, were Gilgamesh, Krishna, Moses, Cyrus, Oedipus, Ajātasatru, Semiramis, queen of Assyria, and Bao Si, queen of Zhou.

In our legend there are three successive attempts to get rid of the hero. This part of the stock heroic birth-legend was completely standardized and appears in almost identical sequence and rhythm in very widely separated parts of the world. Thus, to take a stray example, Prince Lai, a hero of a primitive Indian tribe, the Gonds, is put in the buffalo-shed. "They hoped the buffaloes would trample upon him. But a buffalo suckled him, so they took him to the goat-

1. See Margaret Mead, *Sex and Temperament,* p. 95.

shed,"and so on.[1] A first-century writer[2] tells how Dong-ming, hero of the Kokurye people in northern Korea, was "thrown into the pigsty, but the pigs breathed upon him and he remained alive. Then they moved him to the stable, hoping that the horses would trample upon him; but the horses breathed upon him, and he did not die."

In all such stories birds and animals (in our legend, sheep, oxen, and birds) help the child. They may even, as in the case of Romulus and Remus, act as foster-parents. But often there are also helpful humans, such as the woodcutters in our legend or Spaco and her husband in the Herodotean version of the Cyrus legend. Sometimes the human and animal foster-parents become confused. "Spaco" is explained to mean bitch; yet in Herodotus' narrative she figures as a woman. Hou Ji, however, was more miraculous than Cyrus. He did not need foster-parents, but provided in the most enterprising way for his own needs.

### 245 ✦ *Birth to the People*

She who in the beginning gave birth to the people,
This was Jiang Yuan.
How did she give birth to the people?
Well she sacrificed and prayed
That she might no longer be childless.
She trod on the big toe of God's footprint,
Was accepted and got what she desired.
Then in reverence, then in awe
She gave birth, she nurtured;
And this was Hou Ji.[3]

---

1. *Songs of the Forest,* Shamrad Hivale and Verrier Elwin, 1936.

2. Wang Chong in *Lun Hêng,* chapter 100.

3. "Lord Millet."

Indeed, she had fulfilled her months,
And her first-born came like a lamb
With no bursting or rending,
With no hurt or harm.
To make manifest His magic power
God on high gave her ease.
So blessed were her sacrifice and prayer
That easily she bore her child.

Indeed, they put it in a narrow lane;
But oxen and sheep tenderly cherished it.
Indeed, they[1] put it in a far-off wood;
But it chanced that woodcutters came to this wood.
Indeed, they put it on the cold ice;
But the birds covered it with their wings.
The birds at last went away,
And Hou Ji began to wail.

Truly far and wide
His voice was very loud.
Then sure enough he began to crawl;
Well he straddled, well he reared,
To reach food for his mouth.
He planted large beans;
His beans grew fat and tall.
His paddy-lines were close set,
His hemp and wheat grew thick,
His young gourds teemed.

1. The ballad does not tell us who exposed the child. According to one version it
was the mother herself; according to another, her husband.

Truly Hou Ji's husbandry
Followed the way that had been shown.[1]
He cleared away the thick grass,
He planted the yellow crop.
It failed nowhere, it grew thick,
It was heavy, it was tall,
It sprouted, it eared,
It was firm and good,
It nodded, it hung—
He made house and home in Tai.[2]

Indeed, the lucky grains were sent down to us,
The black millet, the double-kerneled,
Millet pink-sprouted and white.
Far and wide the black and the double-kerneled
He reaped and acred;[3]
Far and wide the millet pink and white
He carried in his arms, he bore on his back,
Brought them home, and created the sacrifice.

Indeed, what are they, our sacrifices?
We pound the grain, we bale it out,
We sift, we tread,
We wash it—soak, soak;
We boil it all steamy.
Then with due care, due thought
We gather southernwood, make offering of fat,
Take lambs for the rite of expiation,
We roast, we broil,
To give a start to the coming year.

1. By God. Compare no. 275, line 6.

2. Southwest of Wu-gong xian, west of Xi'an. Said to be where his mother came
from.

3. The yield was reckoned per acre (1 *mu* equals 100 ft. square).

High we load the stands,
The stands of wood and of earthenware.
As soon as the smell rises
God on high is very pleased:
"What smell is this, so strong and good?"
Hou Ji founded the sacrifices,
And without blemish or flaw
They have gone on till now.


246 ✦ *Wayside Reeds*

They are sprouting, those wayside reeds.
Let not the oxen or sheep trample them.
They are forming stem-shoots, they are branching;
Now the leaves are clustering.
Tender to one another should brothers be,
None absenting himself, all cleaving together.

Spread out the mats for them,
Offer them stools.
Spread the mats and the over-mats,
Offer the stools with shuffling step.[1]
Let the host present the cup, the guest return it;
Wash the beaker, set down the goblet.

Sauces and pickles are brought
For the roast meat, for the broiled,
And blessed viands, tripe and cheek;
There is singing and beating of drums.

The painted bows are strong,
The four arrows well balanced;
They shoot, all with like success;
The guests are arranged according to their merits.[2]

1. A sign of respect. Literally with "joined progress," i.e., never letting the heel of one foot get beyond the toes of the other.

2. They are asked, "Have you ever run away in battle?" and so on, and arranged accordingly. Compare *Li ji,* the section on shooting.

The painted bows are bent,
The four arrows, one after another, are aimed.
The four arrows are as though planted;
The guests must be arranged according to their deportment.

It is the descendant of the ancestors who presides;
His wine and spirits are potent.
He deals them out with a big ladle,
That he may live till age withers him,

Till age withers him and back is bent;
That his life may be prolonged and protected,
His latter days be blessed;
That he may secure eternal blessings.

## 247 ✦ *Drunk with Wine*

We are drunk with wine,
We are sated with power.
Here's long life to you, our lord;
May blessings be vouchsafed to you for ever.

We are drunk with wine,
All the dishes have gone the round.
Here's long life to you, our lord;
May their Shining Light[1] be vouchsafed to you.

May their Shining Light beam mildly upon you;
High fame and good end to all you do.
That good end is well assured;
The impersonator of the Ancient tells a lucky story.

And what is his story?
"Your bowls and dishes are clean and good;
The friends that helped you
Helped with perfect manners.

1. The blessings of the ancestors; spirits are often described as "bright." *Ed.*

Their manners were irreproachable;
My lord will have pious sons,
Pious sons in good store.
A good thing is given you for ever."

And what is this good thing?
"Your house shall be raised,
My lord shall have long life,
Blessed shall be his inheritance for ever."

And what is this inheritance?
"Heaven will cover you with rewards.
My lord shall live long,
Have long life, and a gift as well."

And what is this gift?
"He gives to you a girl.
He gives to you a girl,
That you may in due time have grandsons and sons."

## 248 ✦ *The Wild-Duck*

The wild-duck are on the Jing;[1]
The ducal Dead[2] reposes and is at peace.
Your wine is clear,
Your food smells good.
The Dead One quietly drinks;
Blessings are in the making.

1. A tributary of the Wei, in Shaanxi.

2. An impersonator of a former duke or ruler. I have omitted the adjective in the remaining verses. (The Dead One acted out the part of the ancestor in rituals of prayer and sacrifice. *Ed.*)

The wild-duck are on the sands;
The Dead One is calm and well disposed.
Your wine is plentiful,
Your food is good.
The Dead One quietly drinks;
Blessings are being made.

The wild-duck are on the island;
The Dead One is calm and at rest.
Your wine is well strained,
Your food well sliced.
The Dead One quietly drinks;
The blessings are coming down.

The wild-duck are where the streams meet;
The Dead One is calm, is at ease.
The feast is set in the clan-temple,
The place to which blessings descend.
The Dead One drinks quietly,
While blessings go on heaping up.

The wild-duck are in the ravine;
The Dead One is resting, overcome.
The good wine was delicious;
Roast meat and broiled, most savory.
The Dead One is quietly drinking;
We shall have no cares in time to come.

## 249 ✦ *All Happiness*

All happiness to our lord!
May he show forth his inward power,
Bring good to the common people and to the men of Zhou,
He shall get rewards from Heaven;
Safety, succor are ordained for him,
From Heaven held out to him.

Seeking rewards, a hundred blessings,
Getting sons and grandsons in their thousands,
Solemn and majestic,
Bringing good to lords and princes,
Never erring or forgetting
Following faithfully the old statutes.

Grave in deportment,
Of reputation consistent,
Without malice or hate,
Following the way of all his peers,
Receiving blessings limitless,
Chain-thread and master-strand of all the lands.

Their chain-thread, master-strand;
A comfort to his friends,
To all princes and ministers;
Loved by the Son of Heaven,
Never slackening at his task,
He in whom the common people put their trust.

Hou Ji's son Bu-ku retired to the "land of the barbarians," which presumably means that he settled farther north of the Wei. Bu-ku's grandson, Liu the Duke,[1] brought the descendants of Hou Ji back to Bin.[2] The place-names on which I make no comment are, in my opinion, unidentifiable. Many expressions like "wide plain," "southern ridge," and so on, may in reality be place-names. I should like to quote here what a very distinguished Chinese geographer of the sixth century A.D., Li Dao-yuan,[3] wrote concerning the place-names of this district: "Unfamiliar names of rivers and places are currently explained in a variety of different ways. Research in the classics and histories shows that these explanations could all be supported by one

---

1. I write it thus to show that the title and the name are in the reverse of the usual order.

2. This is usually placed to the north of the Jing; near San-shui. But I think the word has a much wider sense and means the territory between the Jing and the Wei.

3. A.D. 467–527.

ancient authority or another. My own knowledge is too shallow, my experience too superficial to justify me in deciding such questions."

### 250 ✦ *Liu the Duke*

Stalwart was Liu the Duke,
Not one to sit down or take his ease.
He made borders, made balks,
He stacked, he stored,
He tied up dried meat and grain
In knapsacks, in bags;
Far and wide he gathered his stores.
The bows and arrows he tested,
Shield and dagger, halberd and battle-axe;
And then began his march.

Stalwart was Liu the Duke;
He surveyed the people,
They were numerous and flourishing,
He made his royal progress, proclaimed his rule;
There were no complaints, no murmurings
Either high up in the hills
Or down in the plains.
What did they carve for him?
Jade and greenstone
As pairs[1] and ends for his sheath.

Stalwart was Liu the Duke.[2]
He reached the Hundred Springs
And gazed at the wide plain,
Climbed the southern ridge,
Looked upon the citadel,
And the lands for the citadel's army.
Here he made his home,
Here he lodged his hosts,
Here they were at peace with one another,
Here they lived happily with one another.

1. Stones that hung in pairs.

2. I have restored a stanza break here that was omitted—surely by error—in the original translation. *Ed.*

Stalwart was Liu the Duke
In his citadel so safe.
Walking deftly and in due order
The people supplied mats, supplied stools.
He went up to the dais and leant upon a stool.
Then to make the pig-sacrifice
They took a swine from the sty;
He poured out libation from a gourd,
Gave them food, gave them drink;
And they acknowledged him as their prince and founder.

Stalwart was Liu the Duke.
In his lands broad and long
He noted the shadows and the height of the hills,
Which parts were in the shade, which in the sun,
Viewed the streams and the springs.
To his army in three divisions
He allotted the low lands and the high,
Tithed the fields that there might be due provision,
Reckoning the evening sunlight,
And took possession of his home in Bin.

Stalwart was Liu the Duke.
He made his lodging in Bin,
But across the Wei River he made a ford,
Taking whetstones and pounding-stones.
He fixed his settlement and set its boundaries;
His people were many and prosperous
On both sides of the Huang Valley,
And upstream along the Guo Valley.
The multitudes that he had settled there grew dense;
They went on to the bend of the Rui.[1]

1. The modern Black Water River, which flows into the Jing from the west.

### 251 ✦ *At the Wayside Pool*

Far off at that wayside pool we draw;
Ladle there and pour out here,
And with it we can steam our rice.
All happiness to our lord,
Father and mother of his people.

Far off at that wayside pool we draw;
Ladle there and pour out here,
And with it we can rinse our earthen bowls.
All happiness to our lord,
Refuge of his people.

Far off at that wayside pool we draw;
Ladle there and pour out here,
And with it we can rinse our lacquer bowls.
All happiness to our lord,
Support of his people.

The meaning of the comparison is, I think, that though our lord is
far above us, we are all able to share in his *de*.

### 252 ✦ *A Bend in the Hillside*

Through a bend in the hillside
A gust of wind came from the south.
All happiness to our lord.
We come to sport, we come to sing,
To spread his fame.

Carefree shall be your sport,
Pleasant and diverting your time of rest.
All happiness to our lord.
May your life be prolonged
That you may continue in the ways of former dukes.

Great and glorious are your domains,
And mightily secure.
All happiness to our lord.
May your life be prolonged,
You whom all the spirits serve.

Long will last the charge you have received,
In blessings and rewards you shall be at peace.
All happiness to our lord.
May your life be prolonged,
Deep bliss be yours for ever.

Flourishing, majestic,
Of great piety and inner power,
You shall be continued, protected.
All happiness to our lord,
A model to all the lands.

Raised aloft, exalted.
Like a jade scepter, like a token of jade,
Of good repute, of good fame.
All happiness to our lord,
Chain-string of all the lands.

The phoenix[1] is in flight,
Clip, clip go its wings;
It is here that it alights.
In their multitude swarm the king's good men;
But it is our lord that is chosen to serve,
For by the Son of Heaven he is loved.

The phoenix is in flight,
Clip, clip go its wings;
It is to Heaven that it soars.
In their multitudes swarm the king's good men;
But it is only to our lord that a charge is given,
For he is loved by all the men of Zhou.

---

1. The *feng-huang*, afterward classified as a mythical bird; but it would not seem to be so in this song.

The phoenix sings
On that high ridge;
The dryandra grows
Where it meets the early sun.
Thick-leaved the tree,
Melodious the bird.

Our lord's chariots
Are many in number;
Our lord's horses,
Well trained and swift.
So I have put together many verses
To make this song.


The following two poems are translated by Joseph R. Allen.

### 253 ✦ *Our People Are Exhausted*

Oh, our people are exhausted,
Would they have but a little respite!
Treat the middle kingdom[1] with kindness,
Then peace will reign in all the lands.
Do not indulge the wily or servile,
And even the wayward will take care.
Repress those tyrants and those thieves,
For they have shown no proper fear.
Treat tenderly the near and distant,
And with that our king will be secure.

---

1. The "middle kingdom" (*zhong guo*), which later becomes a term for China in
general, here refers to the central royal state to which the feudal states owed alle-
giance; I follow Waley's translation of the term, but without capitalization.

Oh, our people are exhausted,
Would they have but a little rest!
Treat the middle kingdom with kindness,
And our people will be drawn together.
Do not indulge the wily or servile,
And even the disruptive ones will take care.
Repress those tyrants and those thieves;
Do not bring our people to grief,
Do not abandon your own toil,
And then the king will find his rest.

Oh, our people are exhausted,
Would they have but a little leisure!
Treat the capital with kindness,
Then peace will reign in all the states.
Do not indulge the wily or servile
And even the lawless will take care.
Repress those tyrants and those thieves;
Do not let them ply their evil trade.
Take heed of your demeanor,
Be close to those of virtuous ways.

Oh, our people are exhausted,
Would they have but a little repose!
Treat the middle kingdom with kindness
And our people's grief will go away.
Do not indulge the wily or servile
And even the vicious will take care.
Repress those tyrants and those thieves;
Do not allow the proper ones to fail.
Though you are but a youngster,
Your power is still great indeed.

Oh, our people are exhausted,
Would they have but a little quiet!
Treat the middle kingdom with kindness,
And the states will not be cruel.
Do not indulge the wily or servile,
And the even the hangers-on will take care.
Repress those tyrants and those thieves;
Do not allow the proper ones to be overturned.
The king treats you as a treasure,
Thus I offer this dire warning.


## 254 ✦ *Distant*[1]

Oh, how distant is God on high,
The folk down below all suffer.
Your words bear no truth in them,
The plans you make are not farsighted.
Helpless are we without a sage to lead us,
Insubstantial is your honesty.
Since your plans are not farsighted
Thus I offer this dire warning.

Heaven has brought on this hardship;
Do not be so complacent.
Heaven has brought on this turmoil;
Do not be so garrulous.
If your words were harmonious,
Our people would join together;
If your words were uplifting,
Our people would be tranquil.

---

1. This poem suffers from many disputed (and often contradictory) readings, as does its title. Chinese commentators have understood the term to mean something like "contrary" or "perverse," while Karlgren has argued that it means "grand," parallel to the title of no. 255. Here and elsewhere I have tried to make some compromise.

Though the positions we hold are different,
Still we are both in the same office.
When I come to you with advice,
You listen only with arrogance.
My words could be of service,
Do not treat them as a trifle.
In former times was the adage,
"Always ask the wood-cutter."

Heaven has now become vicious
Do not be so silly and foolish.
Old men speak with conviction;
Younger ones are filled with arrogance.
My words are not old or dimwitted,
But you treat them in foolish jest.
There will arise a great clamor
For which there will be no cure.

Heaven has now become enraged;
Do not be proud or cringing.
In demeanor you are misled,
Good men are lifeless as the dead.
Our people have now become mournful,
And no one dares to care for them
Death and disorder ruin their stores,
No one treats our multitudes with kindness.

Heaven draws the people on
Like a clay whistle, like a bamboo flute,
Like a stone scepter, like a jade tally,
As if holding them, as if in hand,
In hand and with nothing more,
It draws people on with great ease.
The people can be very wayward;
You should not be wayward too.

Great men are our fence,
The multitudes our wall.
The powerful states are our screen,
The royal clans our rafters.
Those of virtue are our peace,
The clan heirs our fortress.
Do not let this fortress fall;
Do let Him stand alone in fear.

You should hold in awe Heaven's wrath,
And dare not be so playful.
You should hold in awe Heaven's changes,
And dare not be so bold.
Mighty Heaven, they say, is bright,
And with you wherever you go.
Mighty Heaven, they say, is enlightened,
And always with you as you sport.

✦ ✦ ✦

## 255 ✦ *Mighty*

Mighty is God on high,
Ruler of His people below;
Swift and terrible is God on high,
His charge has many statutes.
Heaven gives birth to the multitudes of the people,
But its charge cannot be counted upon.
To begin well is common;
To end well is rare indeed.

King Wen said, "Come!
Come, you Yin and Shang!
Why these violent men,
Why those slaughterers—
Why are they in office, why are they in power?
Heaven has sent down to you an arrogant spirit;
What you exalt is violence."

King Wen said, "Come!
Come, you Yin and Shang,
And hold fast to what is seemly and fitting;
Your violence leads to much resentment.
Slanders you support and further,
To brigands and thieves you give entry,
Who curse, who use evil imprecations,
Without limit or end."

King Wen said, "Come!
Come, you Yin and Shang!
You rage and seethe in the Middle Kingdom,
You count the heaping up of resentment as inward power;
You do not make bright your power,
So that none backs you, none is at your side.
No, your merit does not shine bright,
So that none cleaves to you nor comes to you."

King Wen, said "Come!
Come, you Yin and Shang!
Heaven did not flush you with wine.[1]
Not good are the ways you follow;
Most disorderly are your manners.
Not heeding whether it is dawn or dusk
You shout and scream,
Turning day into night."

King Wen said, "Come!
Come, you Yin and Shang!
You are like grasshoppers, like cicadas,
Like frizzling water, like boiling soup;
Little and great you draw near to ruin.
Men long to walk right ways,
But you rage in the Middle Kingdom,
And as far as the land of Gui."[2]

King Wen said, "Come!
Come, you Yin and Shang!
It is not that God on high did not bless you;
It is that Yin does not follow the old ways.
Even if you have no old men ripe in judgment,
At least you have your statutes and laws.
Why is it that you do not listen,
But upset Heaven's great charge?"

King Wen said, "Come!
Come, you Yin and Shang!
There is a saying among men:
'When a towering tree crashes,
The branches and leaves are still unharmed;
It is the trunk that first decays.'
A mirror for Yin is not far off;
It is the times of the Lord of Xia."[3]

1. The charge of drunkenness is continually brought against the Shang. Possibly the Zhou only used wine for sacrificial purposes, whereas the Shang used it as an everyday beverage.

2. In eastern Gansu?

3. The Yin destroyed the Xia because of their wickedness, just as the Zhou are now destroying the Yin.

## 256 ✦ *Grave*

Grave and dignified manners
Are the helpmates of power.
Men indeed have a saying,
"There is none so wise but has his follies."
But ordinary people's follies
Are but sicknesses of their own.
It is the wise man's follies
That are a rampant pest.

Nothing is so strong as goodness;
On all sides men will take their lesson from it.
Valid are the works of inward power;
In all lands men will conform to them.
He who takes counsel widely, is final in his commands,
Far-sighted in his plans, timely in the announcing of them,
Scrupulously attentive to decorum,
Will become a pattern to his people.

But those that rule today
Have brought confusion and disorder into the government;
Have upset their power
By wild orgies of drinking.
So engrossed are you in your dissipations
That you do not think of your heritage,
Do not faithfully imitate the former kings,
Or strive to carry out their holy ordinances.

Therefore mighty Heaven is displeased;
Beware lest headlong as spring waters
You should be swept to ruin.
Rise early, go to bed at night;
Sprinkle and sweep your courtyard
So that it may be a pattern to the people.
Put in good order your chariots and horses,
Bows, arrows, and weapons of offence,
That you may be ready, should war arise,
To keep at due distance barbaric tribes.

Ascertain the views of gentlemen and commoners,
Give due warning of your princely measures,
Take precautions against the unforeseen,
Be cautious in your utterances.
Scrupulously observe all rules of decorum,
Be always mild and good-tempered.
A scratch on a scepter of white jade
Can be polished away;
A slip of the tongue
Cannot ever be repaired.

Do not be rash in your words,
Do not say: "Let it pass.
Don't catch hold of my tongue!
What I am saying will go no further."
There can be nothing said that has not its answer,
No deed of Power that has not its reward.
Be gracious to friends and companions
And to the common people, my child.
So shall your sons and grandsons continue for ever,
By the myriad peoples each accepted.

When receiving gentlemen of your acquaintance
Let your countenance be peaceable and mild;
Never for an instant be dissolute.
You are seen in your house;
You do not escape even in the curtained alcove.
Do not say: "Of the glorious ones
None is looking at me."
A visit from the Spirits
Can never be foreseen;
The better reason for not disgusting them.[1]

---

1. Doing anything that would put them off from coming.

Prince, let the exercise of your inner power
Be good and blessed.
Be very careful in your conduct,
Be correct in your manners,
Never usurp or go beyond your rights,
And few will not take you as their model:
"She threw me a peach
And I requited it with a plum."
That kid with horns[1]
Was truly a portent of disorder, my son!

Wood that is soft and pliant
We fit with strings.[2]
Reverence and goodness so mild
Are the foundations of inner power.
Mark how the wise man,
When I tell him of ancient sayings,
Follows the way of inner power.
Mark how the fool,
On the contrary, says that I am wrong,
And that everyone has a right to his ideas.

Alas, my son,
That you should still confuse right and wrong!
When I have not led you by the hand
I have pointed at the thing.
What I have not face to face declared to you
I have hoarsely whispered in your ear.
You may say to me, "You don't know";
But I am already a grandfather.
The people are short of supplies;
Who knew it early but deals with it late?

1. Presumably a portent that had recently occurred.

2. Make into zithers.

Oh, high Heaven so bright,
My life is most unhappy!
Seeing you so heedless
My heart is sorely grieved.
I instruct you in utmost detail;
But you listen to me very casually.
You do not treat my talks as lessons,
But on the contrary regard them as a joke.
You may say, "You don't know";
But I am in truth a very old man.

Alas, my son,
What I tell to you are the ways of the ancients.
If you take my advice
You will have small cause to repent.
Heaven is sending us calamities,
Is destroying the country.
You have not far to go for an example;
High Heaven does not chop and change.
By perverting your inner power,
You will reduce your people to great extremities.

The following two poems are translated by Joseph R. Allen.

### 257 ✦ *The Mulberry's Tender Leaves*

Profuse are the mulberry's tender leaves,
Under them spreads an even shade,
But when picked there are only tatters left.
Torment comes to the folk here below,
Their hearts are filled with endless grief,
Distress is forever upon them.
Glorious is mighty Heaven,
Why does it show us no concern?

The four steeds onward dash,
Serpent and falcon banners flapping.
From disorder rises disaster,
No state is without upheaval.
Diminished are all the people,
Everyone consumed in this turmoil.
Oh please, have pity on us;
The state is on a perilous course.

The course of the state ruins our stores,
Heaven does not come to succor us.
There is no place to stop and rest;
Where should we go to reside?
Our lord, he should be the one
Who has a heart without violence.
Whence arises the instruments of evil
That brings this agony unto us?

My grieved heart is deeply pained,
Thinking of my old residence.
I was born under a bad star,
Encountering Heaven's deep wrath.
From the west and off to the east
There is no place to make our homes.
I have seen much suffering;
They harass even our borders.

Plan well and with sincerity,
And disorder will be trimmed away.
I urge you to take their grief seriously,
I advise you to order well your ranks.
Who can hold a scalding iron
Without first cooling one's hand with water?
If you wonder what good is it,
Then down you will go with the others.

Like running headlong into the wind,
Their breathlessness grows more intense.
People have thoughts of moving on,
But only this holds them back:
They are devoted to their life of farming,
Their work feeding each generation.
Farming is their very treasure;
Feeding each generation is their gift.

Heaven brought down death and disorder upon us,
Destroying our king already enthroned.
Bringing down a plague of locusts
To turn our farms to ruin.
Pitiful is the middle kingdom,
All its affairs lay in waste.
With no more strength to spend,
I turn to those high-vaulted heavens.

Here we would have a kindly lord,
To whom all the people look.
His heart full of far-ranging plans,
He selects his ministers with care.
There we would have someone perverse,
Thinking only he can do good,
Alone having his own thoughts,
He drives the people to this lunacy.

Look, there in those woods,
Herd upon herd come the deer.
But insincere are my colleagues,
Doing nothing to benefit others.
The people have a saying, I hear:
"Both forward and back is an abyss."

Here we would have a sage
Who looks out over a hundred leagues.
There we would have an idiot
Who finds delight in this lunacy.
Words are certainly *not* inadequate;
Why would one hold back in fear?

Here we would have a fine one,
Neither seeking gain, nor striving.
There we would have someone evil,
Always wanting, always waiting.
The people are needy and distressed;
What is it that causes such bitterness?

A gale wind finds its course
Through the steep, deep valley.
Here we would have a fine one,
Good in all his actions.
There we would have someone perverse,
Proceeding in his depravity.

A gale wind finds its course.
The covetous will ruin our lot;
They answer only when they want,
And act drunk when admonished.
They do not use the good,
But cause us such trouble.

Oh, you, my colleagues,
How do I not know what you do!
Like those flying pests,
You will be caught too.
I go quietly to your aid,
But you turn on me in rage.

The people know no proper limits,
Because the good are scorned.
The people do not profit,
As if nothing could be done.
The people have been turned,
Because of violence and abuse.

The people know no peace;
There are robbers, there are thieves
If someone says, "This will not do!"
You are scornful and you curse.
You may say, "But it's not up to me."
Nonetheless, I have made this song for you.

## 258 ✦ *River of Stars*[1]

Vast is that River of Stars,
Shining and turning in the sky.
The king cries out, "But alas,
What blame do you find with us?"
Heaven rains down death and disorder,
Hunger and famine year after year.
There is no spirit not praised,
No victim who is begrudged them,
Token and tally are all expended;
How can none of them hear our plea?

The drought is long and deep,
Burning heat, thunder, and sultry skies.
We have been unceasing in our prayers,
From the suburbs to the temple,
To heaven, to earth, offerings and burials;
There is no spirit who is not worshiped.
Still, Hou Ji[2] cannot help,
God on High does not come near.
Ruin and destruction on earth below;
Why does all this fall to us now?

The drought is long and deep,
It cannot be erased.
It is frightening, full of danger,
Like thunder, like lightning.
Of those who remain in Zhou,
There is none who is whole.
Mighty Heaven, God on High,
You have left us nothing.
Why should we not live in fear;
Our ancestors are in decline.

1. The "Han River in the clouds" is a term for the Milky Way.

2. Hou Ji, Lord Millet, the mythical ancestor of the Zhou people; see no. 245.

The drought is long and deep,
It cannot be curtailed.
It is parching, a burning heat;
We have no place to escape,
The hand of fate closes near,
There is none to look to, none to care.
The former ministers and their lords,
Even they do not give us aid.
Father and mother, and our ancestors,
How can you abandon us?

The drought is long and deep,
Parched and barren is the landscape.
The drought demon is vicious
Like a burn, like a blaze.
Our hearts are tormented by the heat,
Our grieved hearts as if aflame.
The former ministers and their lords,
Even they do not hear our plea.
Mighty Heaven, God on High
Why do you force us to flee?

The drought is long and deep,
We struggle to be rid of it;
How come we are afflicted with this drought?
We never understood the reason why.
Our spring sacrifices were done early;
The prayers of thanks were on time.
Mighty heaven, God on High,
Even you do not consider our fate
We have honored the radiant spirits,
So there would be no anger, no spite.

The drought is long and deep,
Scattering out, it has no design.
Troubled are the ministries,
Tormented, the Prime Minister,
Master of the Stable, Commander of the Guard,
Steward of the Table, and advisers too.
There is no one not included,
No place where this does not reach.
In high regard we hold mighty Heaven
Why do we have this anguish now?

In high regard we hold mighty Heaven,
Its stars sparkling faintly above.
Oh, statesmen and noble sons,
Come to us without exception.
The hand of fate comes near;
Do not abandon your obligations.
What is it that I seek for us?
Success for the ministries, that's what.
In high regard we hold mighty Heaven,
When will its kindness bring us peace?

## 259 ✦ *Mightiest of All Heights*

Mightiest of all heights is the Peak[1]
Soaring up into the sky.
The Peak sent down a Spirit
Which bore Fu and Shen.[2]
Now Shen and Fu
Became the sure support of Zhou;
A fence to screen the homelands,
A wall to guard the four sides.

1. North of Deng-feng xian, near Henan fu. Also called Song-shan and "Middle Peak."

2. Fu was a sister-state, just to the east of Shen [in southern Henan; see note p. 58. *Ed.*]. This is a type of origin legend which is very unusual in the Far East.

Diligent was the Lord of Shen[1]
In the service of the royal successors,
Having his castle in Xie,
A model to the lands of the south.
The king bid the Lord of Shao:[2]
"Make secure the Lord of Shen's home,
Let him receive this southern land,
Let his heirs for ever have charge of it."

The king[3] charged the Lord of Shen:
"Go to this southern country,
Approach these people of Xie,
Make there your appanage."
The king charged the Lord of Shao:
"Tithe the Lord of Shen's lands and fields."
The king charged his stewards:
"Shift his lordship's own men."

The Lord of Shen's palace
By the Lord of Shao was planned.
Stout were its walls,
And when the Hall of Ancestors was complete,
Complete in all its majesty,
The king gave the Lord of Shen
Four steeds high-stepping
And breast-buffers very splendid.

The king sent to the Lord of Shen
A state coach and a team of horses;
"I have considered where you should live:
There is nowhere like the southern land.
I give you a great scepter
To be your treasure.
Go, O father of the royal bride,
And guard the southern clime."

1. King Xuan's maternal uncle. *Ed.*

2. A general under King Xuan. *Ed.*

3. King You (781–772)?

Then the Lord of Shen indeed went.
The king drank the parting cup in Mei,[1]
And the Lord of Shen went back to the south,
To Xie he duly returned.
The king charged the Lord of Shao:
"Tithe the Lord of Shen's lands.
That he may be furnished with a store of grain,
And speed him on his way."

The Lord of Shen, hale and venerable,
Has made his entry into Xie
With followers stout-hearted, both riding and afoot.
There is joy throughout the lands of Zhou;
If war comes, they have a safe protection.
Glorious is the Lord of Shen,
The king's eldest father-in-law,
A pattern of valor and might.

The Lord of Shen's nature
Is mild, kindly, and upright;
His gentleness to all the lands
Is famous on every side.
So Ji-fu made this ballad,
Its words very grand,
Its tune long and lovely,
As a present to the Lord of Shen.

Ji-fu is a very common type of name, and it does not follow that this
Ji-fu is the same as the Ji-fu who fought against the Xian-yun.

1. This may be corrupt, as Mei was to the west of the capital, and not on the direct
route to the south.

## 260 ✦ *The People of Our Race*

The people of our race were created by Heaven
Having from the beginning distinctions and rules.
Our people cling to customs,
And what they admire is seemly behavior.
Heaven, looking upon the land of Zhou,
Sent a radiance to earth beneath.
To guard this Son of Heaven
It created Zhong Shan Fu.[1]

In his nature Zhong Shan Fu
Is a pattern of mildness and blessedness.
Good is his every attitude and air,
So cautions, so composed!
Following none but ancient teachings,
Striving only for dignity and good deportment,
Obedient to the Son of Heaven,
Whose glorious commands he spreads abroad.

The king commanded Zhong Shan Fu:
"Be a pattern to all the officers of Court,
Continue the work of your ancestors,
Protect the royal person,
Go out and in with the royal commands,
Be the king's throat and tongue,
Spread his edicts abroad
That through all the land men may be stirred."

1. Who appears in the *Guo Yu* as an adviser of King Xuan. His career probably
began under Li (878–842).

With due awe of the king's command
Did Zhong Shan Fu effect it.
If in the land anything was darkened
Zhong Shan Fu shed light upon it.
Very clear-sighted was he and wise.
He assured his own safety;[1]
But day and night never slackened
In the service of the One Man.

There is a saying among men:
"If soft, chew it;
If hard, spit it out."
But Zhong Shan Fu
Neither chews the soft,
Nor spits out the hard;
He neither oppresses the solitary and the widow,
Nor fears the truculent and strong.

There is a saying among men:
"Inward power is light as a feather;
Yet too heavy for common people to raise."
Thinking it over
I find none but Zhong Shan Fu that could raise it;
For alas! none helped him.
When the robe of state was in holes
It was he alone who mended it.

When Zhong Shan Fu went forth
His four steeds quivered;
His warriors so nimble,
Each determined to keep his place.[2]
His four steeds so strong,
The eight harness-bells tinkling.
The king charged Zhong Shan Fu
To fortify that eastern land.[3]

1. To assure one's own safety ("guard oneself") was one of the main avowed objects of Zhou morality. The phrase occurs on numerous bronze inscriptions. One assures one's safety by pleasing one's ancestors.

2. In the line of chariots. Literally "not to be caught up."

3. Perhaps to help the people of Qi to fortify their new capital at Lin-Zi, 859 B.C.

His four steeds so fine,
The eight harness-bells chiming,
Zhong Shan Fu went to Qi,
And swift was his return.
Ji-fu made this ballad
Gentle as a clean breeze.
Zhong Shan Fu has long been burdened with care;
May this calm his breast.

If you look up "Han" in any topographical dictionary, you will find
that the Han of this song is in Hebei, near Beijing. There is, however,
no real evidence that such a place existed. It has been invented by schol-
ars who could not bear to think of the people of Yan coming right
across two provinces, when they helped to fortify Han. But the Lord
of Shao brought his people much farther to fortify Xie; and Zhong
Shan Fu went all the way from Shaanxi to Shandong to fortify Qi.

In the opening words,[1] the king giving his commands is com-
pared to the Great Yu, who gave the streams and hills their present
form. The Mount Liang of ancient legend was the range on each
side of the "Dragon Gate";[2] through these mountains Yu cut an outlet
for the Yellow River. Han was a feudal state which lay chiefly in
southwestern Shanxi, near where the Fen runs into the Yellow River,
but also partly across the Yellow River, in eastern Shaanxi.

### 261 ✦ Han Is Mighty

Mighty is Mount Liang,
It was Yu who fashioned it;
High aloft are its paths.
The Lord of Han received a charge;
The king in person delivered it:
"Continue the work of your ancestors,
Do not neglect this my charge,
Day and night never idle,
Steadfastly fulfill the duties of your rank;
My orders cannot be slighted.
Lead unsubmissive lands
To the assistance of your sovereign lord."

1. Compare the opening of no. 210.

2. The northern Long-men, not the one in Henan.

With four steeds so splendid,
Very tall and broad,
The Lord of Han came to audience;
Bearing his great scepter of office
He had audience with the king.
And the king gave to the Lord of Han
An embroidered banner, with blazonry of pennons,
An awning of lacquered bamboo, a carved cross-bar,
A dark-red robe, crimson slippers,
A breast-buffer, a chiseled frontlet,
Leather-work for his front-rail, a short-haired skin-rug,
Metal-headed reins and metal yokes.

The Lord of Han went forth,
Went forth and lodged in Tu.
Xian-fu gave the farewell party—
A hundred cups of clear wine.
And what were the meats?
Roast turtle and fresh fish.
And what were the vegetables?
Bamboo-shoots and reed-shoots.
And what did he get as presents?
A team of horses and a big chariot.
The trays and dishes were neatly laid;
My lord and his people feasted and were at ease.

The Lord of Han took a wife,
Niece of the king at Fen,[1]
Daughter of Jue-fu.
The Lord of Han went to meet her
In Jue's domain,
With a hundred teams of steeds very strong,
The eight bells tinkling,
Glorious the brightness,
The bridesmaids that were with her
Thronging like clouds.
The Lord of Han surveyed them;
Their splendor filled the gates.

---

1. This almost certainly means King Li, who c. 842 B.C. was driven out of his capital
and took refuge at Zhi, in south-central Shanxi, on the banks of the Fen River.

Jue-fu was a great warrior;
There was not a land he had not reached.
But thinking of a place for his daughter Han Ji[1]
He could think of nowhere pleasanter than Han.
Very pleasant the land of Han,
Its rivers and pools so large,
Its bream and tench so fat,
Its deer so plentiful,
And black bears and brown,
Wild cats and tigers.
Without mishap she reached this lovely dwelling-place;
Han-Ji rested and was at peace.

Wide was that castle wall of Han
Completed by the hosts of Yan.[2]
Because of the charge given to his ancestor
He sheltered all the tribes of Muan.
And the king gave to the Lord of Han
The Zhui tribes and the Mo;
He received all the northern lands
And ruled them as their lord.
He built walls, he dug ditches,
He divided the land and apportioned it.
He sent to Court skins of the white wolf,
Of red panther and brown bear.

1. This is an odd way to speak of her, for she did not become Han Ji ("girl of the Ji clan married to the Lord of Han") until after her marriage.

2. In Hebei, near Beijing. Muan (I write it thus to distinguish it from the English word Man) and Mo were both very general names for barbarian tribes, irrespective of their locality. I doubt if these Mo are in any way connected with the Wei-mo of Korea in Han times. The Zhui are unknown.

### 262 ✦ *The Jiang and the Han*

The Jiang and the Han sweep along;
The warriors march on and on.
No peace, no play;
The tribes of the Huai are mustering.
All our chariots are out,
All our standards set.
No peace, no rest;
The tribes of the Huai are attacking.

The Jiang and the Han spread far;
The warriors march far and wide.
They secure the frontiers on every side;
They tell the king of their victory.
On every frontier there is peace;
The king's lands are all secure.
No longer is there any strife;
The king's heart can be at rest.

"On the banks of Jiang and Han"
(Such was the king's command to the Lord of Shao)
"You are to make new fields on every side;
You are to tithe my lands."
Then without delay, without haste
The king's domains were marked out,
They were divided and duly ordered
All the way to the southern seas.

The king charged Hu of Shao
(And his charge was published far and wide)[1]
"When Wen and Wu received their mandate
The Duke of Shao was their support.
Do not say I am a lesser descendent;
You have equaled the Duke of Shao.[2]
You have been zealous in deeds of war
And therefore I grant you a boon.

---

1. A mandate to this lord of Shao, couched in similar terms, will be found on the bronze inscription; Karlgren, B. 104.

2. A great supporter and possibly a half-brother of the second Zhou king, Wu Wang.

"I bestow upon you a jade scepter and a jade goblet,
And a bowl of black mead.
Announce it to the Mighty Ones
That I give you hills, lands, and fields;
That the charge which you receive from the house of Zhou
Is as that which your ancestor received."
Then Hu did obeisance and bowed his head
Saying, "Long live the Son of Heaven."

Hu did obeisance and bowed his head,
Then in commemoration of the king's bounty
He made the Duke of Shao's urn.[1]
The Son of Heaven—may he live for ever!
Illustrious is he, the Son of Heaven,
Famous for ever,
Spreading the Power of his governance
Everywhere throughout the lands.

## 263 ✦ *Always Mighty in War*

The king, majestic and glorious,
Charged his minister
Nan-zhong Da-zu
And his Grand Leader Huang-fu:
"Set in order my six armies,
Repair my war-chariots,
With due caution, with due care
Extend my favor to these southern lands."

---

1. Not necessarily the same one as Karlgren, B. 104.

The king told his officer
To charge Xiu-fu, Lord of Cheng:[1]
"Marshal the ranks to right and left;
Prepare my hosts and battalions,
Go along the shores of the Huai,
Destroy this land of Xu."
And without loiter or delay
These three ministers went about their task.

Majestic, terrible,
Very splendid, a Son of Heaven,
Our king quietly set to work,
Not idling nor loitering,
The land of Xu was mightily shaken;
Startled as by an earthquake was the land of Xu.
As at a roll of thunder, as by a clap of thunder
The land of Xu was startled, and quaked.

The king spread his war–might,
He thundered and raged.
Forward went his tiger slaves,[2]
Fierce as ravening tigers.
Everywhere he garrisoned the banks of the Huai,
Again and again took chieftains and captives.
He cleared those banks of Huai;
The king's armies encamped there.

The king's hosts swept along
As though flying, as though winged,
Like the river, like the Han,
Steady as a mountain,
Flowing onward like a stream,
Rank on rank, in serried order,
Immeasurable, unassailable;
Mightily they marched through the land of Xu.

1.  Cheng was a fief in Shaanxi; another Cheng near Luoyang in Henan also claimed to be the site of Xiu-fu's fief. The historian Si-ma Qian believed himself to be descended from him.

2.  Military officers.

The king's plans have been faithfully effected,
All the regions of Xu have submitted,
All the regions of Xu are at one;
It was the Son of Heaven's deed.
In the four quarters all is peace;
The peoples of Xu come in homage.
The regions of Xu no longer disobey;
The king goes back to his home.

The Xu people, who lived along the Huai Valley both in Shandong and Anhui, had been a great power in the early days of the Zhou dynasty. A remarkable number of Xu bronzes have been found.

The following two poems are translated by Joseph R. Allen.

### 264 ✦ *High Regard*

In high regard we hold mighty Heaven,
But even it is unkind to us.
We are forever without peace;
It brings down this scourge upon us.
All the states are filled with unrest,
Low and noble both suffer this disease.
As with parasites and pests,
There is no controlling it.
The guilty are not apprehended,
There is no respite, no cure.

The people have farm and field,
But these you seize without warning.
The people have working folk,
But these you commandeer.
There are some people quite innocent,
But still you have them jailed.
Then there are those with offenses
Whom you let go free.

A clever man builds a city;
A clever woman tears it down.
Oh, that clever woman,
She is an owl, she is a shrike.
The wagging tongues of women
Are the instruments of our decline.
No, disorder does not come down from Heaven,
Rather it is the spawn of these women.
You can neither teach, nor instruct
Women and their eunuchs.

They attack others in anger and spite,
Slander arises, backs are turned.
You ask if they are not right,
You ask what harm can they do.
They are like merchants with a three-fold profit;
Noble lords understand this well.
Thus no woman serves the public,
They stay with their weaving and their loom.

Why does Heaven so reprove you?
Why do spirits not give their blessings?
Because you pay the enemy no attention,
And yet view us with resentment.
This is neither good nor auspicious;
Your demeanor is not fitting.
People flee for their lives,
The state is injured and exhausted.

Heaven casts down its net,
Indeed it is very wide.
People flee for their lives,
Their hearts filled with grief.
Heaven casts down its net,
It is very close-knit indeed.
People flee for their lives,
Their hearts filled with melancholy.

The geyser spews high in the sky;
It must be very deep indeed.
Our hearts are filled with grief
Why has this come to us now?
And not before?
Or not after?
Expansive is mighty Heaven;
There is nothing it cannot assure.
Insult not the august ancestors,
And your descendants will be secure.

## 265 ✦ *Shao Is Foreboding*

Foreboding Heaven is a cruel affliction,
Bringing death in heavy waves.
We are stricken with hunger and famine,
People flee and run away,
Our homes and our borders all lay in waste.

Heaven casts down its web of blame,
Parasites wreak havoc within,
Palace eunuchs have no respect,
All is chaotic and in neglect.
How are they to bring our country peace?

They are insolent and slanderous,
Never knowing their own flaws,
They are frightening, full of danger,
The state is forever unsettled,
Our position is ever weakened.

They are like a year of drought
The grasses withered and dry.
Like straw high in the trees,[1]
This is how I see our country,
Everywhere now in chaos.

---

1. The imagery of this line is enigmatic at best. I understand it as an image of the
wind-blown landscape filled with drought; thus the grasses "roost" in the trees.

The blessings of the past
Were nothing like this;
The afflictions of the present
Nothing like then.
That grain in hulls, this grain refined.
Why do they not step down,
Instead only going on like this?

The pond is parched,
Nothing will come from its banks;
The spring is spent,
Nothing will come from within.
Widespread is this harm indeed,
And the situation only gets worse;
Will it not ruin our very lives?

The ancient kings received their charge,
As did the Duke of Shao.
Daily he enlarged the state by a hundred leagues.
Now daily these men make it smaller by the same.
Oh, how pitiful they are,
The people these days;
How we yearn for the glory of former times.

# THE HYMNS,
## POEMS 266–305

✦

The somber and liturgical section "The Hymns" (*Song*) is divided into three parts: two are associated with the royal houses—the Zhou (nos. 266–96) and Shang as preserved in the feudal state of Song (nos. 301–05)—and the third with the state of Lu (nos. 297–300), the home of Confucius. "The Zhou Hymns" is universally accepted as the oldest layer of *The Book of Songs,* while the other two sections of hymns are considered somewhat younger, perhaps contemporaneous with "The Major Odes." Thus, the cultural and critical weight of this section is squarely with "The Zhou Hymns," although special attention should be paid to the "Dark Bird" poem (303), which contains the origin myth of the Shang people.

The oldest hymns are like bronze vessels: staid, solid, and not for daily fare. Their most common subject is again the Heavenly charge received by the Zhou royal family, but here the poems are brief and elliptical, suggesting their accompaniment to the rituals of the ancestral hall. This is particularly true of the first decade of poems, which is closely associated with King Wen: "Our ritual is patterned/ On the rules of King Wen./ Daily we bring peace to frontier lands./ See, King Wen blesses us;/ He has approved and accepted" (272). Even when the poems lapse into air- or ode-like language and imagery, in the end they return to the solemnity of ritual; poems 290 and 291 both begin with a description of agricultural activities but conclude by making those activities a preface to the offerings to the "blessed elders" and "men of old."

# The Zhou Hymns, 266–96

✦

### 266 ✦ *The Hallowed Temple*

Solemn the hallowed temple,
Awed and silent the helpers,[1]
Well purified the many knights
That handle their sacred task.
There has been an answer in Heaven;
Swiftly they[2] flit through the temple,
Very bright, very glorious,
Showing no distaste toward men.

### 267 ✦ *The Charge That Heaven Gave*

The charge that Heaven gave
Was solemn, was for ever.
And ah, most glorious
King Wen in plenitude of power!
With blessings he has whelmed us;
We need but gather them in.
High favors has King Wen vouchsafed to us;
May his descendants hold them fast.

Kings rule in virtue of a charge (*ming*), an appointment assigned to
them by Heaven, just as barons hold their fiefs in virtue of a *ming*
from their overlord.

1. Feudal lords in attendance at the sacrifice.
2. The Spirits.

## 268 ✦ *Clear*

Clear and littering bright
Are the ordinances of King Wen.
He founded the sacrifices
That in the end gave victory,
That are the happy omens of Zhou.

These are said to be the words of a mime-dance (*xiang-wu*) which
enacted the battles of King Wen. This type of tradition is, however,
very unreliable. The piece reads like a sacrificial hymn.

## 269 ✦ *Renowned and Gracious*

Renowned and gracious are those rulers, those sovereigns
That bestow upon us happy blessings.
Their favor toward us is boundless;
May sons and grandsons never forfeit it!
There are no fiefs save in your land;
It is you, O kings, who set them up.
Never forgetting what your valor won
May we continue it in our sway!
None are strong save the men of Zhou,
Every land obeys them.
Nothing so glorious as their power,
All princes imitate them.
Ah, no! The former kings do not forget us.

## 270 ✦ *Heaven Made*

Heaven made a high hill;
The Great King laid hand upon it.
He felled the trees;
King Wen strengthened it.
He cleared the bush;
Mount Qi has level ways.
May sons and grandsons keep it!

Mount Qi is about seventy miles west of Xi'an, the capital of Shaanxi, on the north side of the Wei River. The "Great King" is Dan-fu, grandfather of Wen (the first Zhou king).

## 271 ✦ *High Heaven Had a Firm Charge*

High heaven had a firm charge;
Two monarchs received it.
Nor did King Cheng stay idle,
Day and night he buttressed the charge
By great endeavors.
Ah! The Bright Splendors
Hardened his will;
Therefore he could establish it.

The "two monarchs" are Wen and his son Wu, who conquered the Shang. Cheng (1115–1079 B.C., standard chronology), as his name implies, completed their work. The bright splendors are what the early Persians would have called the *hvarenô,* the magic halo of the former kings. See no. 266.

## 272 ✦ *We Bring*

We bring our offerings,
Our bulls and sheep;
May Heaven bless them!
Our ritual is patterned
On the rules of King Wen.
Daily we bring peace to frontier lands.
See, King Wen blesses us;
He has approved and accepted.
Now let us day and night
Fear Heaven's wrath,
And thus be shielded.

Heaven's "charge," as we shall see constantly in the songs which follow, is "changeable." Just as the king can withdraw the *ming* which entitles a baron to hold his fief, so Heaven when displeased can in a moment withdraw its dynastic charge.

## 273 ✦ *He Goes*

He goes through his lands;
May high Heaven cherish him!
Truly the succession is with Zhou.
See how they tremble before him!
Not one that fails to tremble and quake.
Submissive, yielding are all the Spirits,
Likewise the rivers and high hills.
Truly he alone is monarch.
Bright and glorious is Zhou;
It has succeeded to the seat of power.
"Then put away your shields and axes,
Then case your arrows and bows;
I have store enough of good power
To spread over all the lands of Xia."[1]
And in truth, the king protected them.

## 274 ✦ *Terrible in His Power*

Terrible in his power was King Wu;
None so mighty in glory.
Illustrious were Cheng and Kang
Whom God on high made powerful.
From the days of that Cheng, that Kang,[2]
All the lands were ours.
Oh, dazzling their brightness!
Let bell and drum blend,
Stone-chime and pipes echo,
That rich blessings may come down,
Mighty blessings come down.
Every act and posture has gone rightly,
We are quite drunk, quite sated;
Blessings and bounties shall be our reward.

1. China in general.

2. 1078–53 B.C. (standard chronology).

## 275 ✦ *Mighty Are You*

Mighty are you, Hou Ji,[1]
Full partner in Heaven's power.
That we, the thronging peoples, were raised up
Is all your doing.
You gave us wheat and barley
In obedience to God's command.
Not to this limit only or to that frontier,
But near, far, and for ever throughout these lands of Xia.[2]

✦ ✦ ✦

1. The ancestor of the Zhou people; the inventor of agriculture. See no. 245.
2. I.e., China.

## 276 ✦ *Servants and Officers*

Ho, ho, my servants and officers!
Be zealous at your tasks.
The king will reward your achievements;
Come and take counsel, come and take thought.
Ho, ho, guardians and protectors,[1]
The spring is at its close.
What more do you look for?
How goes the new field?
Oh, royal the wheat and barley!
You shall gather in its bright grain;
Brightly has shone God on high
Till yours now is a rich harvest.
Call all my men saying, "Get ready your spades and hoes;
Have a look, all of you, to your sickles and scythes."

## 277 ✦ *Come Now*

Come now! the victorious kings[2]
Are shedding their light upon you.
Lead those farm laborers
To scatter the many grains.
Work your private lands to the full,
The whole thirty leagues;[3]
And labor with your ploughs
Ten thousand of you in pairs.

---

1. I.e., of the people. I think this is only a name for the king's officers. But much in this song is uncertain and obscure.

2. The spirits of former kings. I do not think one king in particular is meant.

3. Compare no. 177.

## 278 ✦ *Flock the Egrets*

Flock the egrets in their flight
To that western moat.
My guest has come,
He too with like movements.
They there find no harm;
Of him here we shall never weary.
Through the day, into the night,
May he long keep holiday!

## 279 ✦ *Abundant Is the Year*

Abundant is the year, with much millet, much rice;
But we have tall granaries,
To hold myriads, many myriads and millions of grain.
We make wine, make sweet liquor,
We offer it to ancestor, to ancestress,
We use it to fulfill all the rites,
To bring down blessings upon each and all.

## 280 ✦ *Blind Men*

Blind men, blind men[1]
In the courtyard of Zhou.
We have set up the cross-board, the stand,
With the upright hooks, the standing plumes.
The little and big drums are hung for beating;
The tambourines and stone-chimes, the mallet-box and scraper.
All is ready, and they play.
Pan-pipes and flute are ready and begin.
Sweetly blend the tones,
Solemn the melody of their bird-music.
The ancestors are listening;
As our guests they have come,
To gaze long upon their victories.[2]

---

1. Musicians were generally blind men.

2. As re-enacted in our pantomime.

## 281 ✦ *In Their Warrens*

Oh, the Qi and the Ju[1]
In their warrens have many fish,
Sturgeons and snout-fish,
Long-fish, yellow-jaws, mud-fish and carp,
For us to offer, to present,
And gain great blessings.

## 282 ✦ *Solemn State*

He comes in solemn state,
He arrives in all gravity
By rulers and lords attended,
The Son of Heaven, mysterious:
"Come, let us offer up the Broad Male![2]
Help me to set out the sacrifice.
Approach, O royal elders,
To succor me, your pious son.
None so wise in all things as the men of our tribe
Or so skilled in peace and war as their kings,
Who now repose at august Heaven's side
And can lend luster to their posterity.
May they grant us long life,
Vouchsafe to us manifold securities.
May they help us, the glorious elders;
May they help us, the mighty mothers."

1. Northern tributaries of the Wei. They join and flow into the Wei about half-way between Xi'an and Wei-nan.

2. Compare the kennings in no. 211.

## 283 ✦ *So They Appeared*

So they appeared before their lord the king
To get from him their emblems,
Dragon-banners blazing bright,
Tuneful bells tinkling,
Bronze-knobbed reins jangling—
The gifts shone with glorious light.
Then they showed them to their shining ancestors
Piously, making offering,
That they might be vouchsafed long life,
Everlastingly be guarded.
Oh, a mighty store of blessings!
Glorious and mighty, those former princes and lords
Who secure us with many blessings,
Through whose bright splendors
We greatly prosper.

## 284 ✦ *A Guest*

A guest, a guest,
And white his horse.
Rich in adornment, finely wrought
The carving and chiseling of his spear-shafts.

A guest so venerable,
A guest of great dignity.
Come, give him a tether
To tether his team.

Here we follow him,
To left and right secure him.
Prodigal is he in his courtesies;
He will bring down blessings very joyful.

### 285 ✦ *Wu*

Oh, great were you, King Wu!
None so doughty in glorious deeds.
A strong toiler was King Wen;
Well he opened the way for those that followed him.
As heir Wu received it,
Conquered the Yin, utterly destroyed them.[1]
Firmly founded were his works.

This and nos. 293–96 are said to be words of the mime dance which enacted the victories of King Wu. They may ultimately have been used for that purpose, but I doubt if they originally belonged to the war-dance. There is a pun on the word I have translated "toiler" and the name of King Wen. One must read the first *wen* with the "heart" radical underneath.

✦ ✦ ✦

1. Usually interpreted "put an end to the slaughters." The Confucians created a myth that King Wu conquered by goodness and not by force. But compare *Shu jing* (Legge, *The Chinese Classics*, vol. 3, p. 482), "He exterminated his enemies."

## 286 ✦ *Pity Me, Your Child*

Pity me, your child,
Inheritor of a House unfinished,
Lonely and in trouble.
O august elders,
All my days I will be pious,
Bearing in mind those august forefathers
That ascend and descend in the courtyard.
Yes, I your child,
Early and late will be reverent.
O august kings,
The succession shall not stop!

This poem, along with nos. 287 and 289,[1] are all songs from the leg-end of King Cheng. It is said that when he came to the throne he was a mere child and had to be helped in his rule by his uncle, the Duke of Zhou. He also had wicked uncles, who rebelled against him, making common cause with the son of the last Shang king. The story in its main features is probably historical. But the part played by the Duke of Zhou has perhaps been exaggerated by the Confucians, who made the duke into a sort of patron saint of their school.

1. Also compare no. 155.

## 287 ✦ *Here I Come*

Here, then, I come,
Betake myself to the bright ancestors:
"Oh, I am not happy.
I have not yet finished my task.
Help me to complete it.
In continuing your plans I have been idle.
But I, your child,
Am not equal to the many troubles that assail my house.
You that roam in the courtyard,[1] up and down,
You that ascend and descend in His house,
Grant me a boon, august elders!
Protect this my person, save it with your light."


## 288 ✦ *Reverence*

Reverence, reverence!
By Heaven all is seen;
Its charge is not easy to hold.
Do not say it is high, high above,
Going up and down about its own business.
Day in, day out it watches us here.
I, a little child,
Am not wise or reverent.
But as days pass, months go by,
I learn from those that have bright splendor.
O Radiance, O Light,
Help these my strivings;
Show me how to manifest the ways of power.

---

1. Of God.

289 ✦ *Take Guard*

I will take warning,
Will guard against ills to come.
Never again will I bump myself and bang myself
With bitter pain for my reward.
Frail was that reed-warbler;
It flew away a great bird.
I, not equal to the troubles of my house,
Must still perch upon the smartweed.

In ancient Chinese myth, when the reed-warbler grows up it turns into an eagle. Till then it perches in a nest precariously hung between the stems of reeds or other water-plants, liable to be hurled to disaster at the first coming of wind or rain. So the boy king, when he gets older, will pounce upon his enemies. But for the present he must be content to "perch upon the smartweed," i.e., put up with his troubles.

## 290 ✦ *Clear Away the Grass*

They clear away the grass, the trees;
Their ploughs open up the ground.
In a thousand pairs they tug at weeds and roots,
Along the low grounds, along the ridges.
There is the master and his eldest son,
There the headman and overseer.
They mark out, they plough.
Deep the food-baskets that are brought;
Dainty are the wives,
The men press close to them.
And now with shares so sharp
They set to work upon the southern acre.
They sow the many sorts of grain,
The seeds that hold moist life.
How the blade shoots up,
How sleek, the grown plant;
Very sleek, the young grain!
Band on band, the weeders ply their task.
Now they reap, all in due order;
Close-packed are their stooks—
Myriads, many myriads and millions,
To make wine, make sweet liquor,
As offering to ancestor and ancestress,
For fulfillment of all the rites.
"When sweet the fragrance of offering,
Glory shall come to the fatherland.
When pungent the scent,
The blessed elders are at rest."[1]
Not only here is it like this,
Not only now is it so.
From long ago it has been thus.

---

1. Or, "are reassured"; *ning* is technical of visits to "reassure" the anxious. The
two sayings have the form of proverbs.

## 291 ✦ *Very Sharp*

Very sharp, the good shares,
At work on the southern acre.
Now they sow the many sorts of grain,
The seeds that hold moist life.
Here come provisions for you,
Carried in baskets, in hampers.
Their dinner is fine millet,
Their rush-hats finely plaited,
Their hoes cut deep
To clear away thistle and smartweed:
"Where thistle and smartweed lie rotting,
Millet grows apace."
It rustles at the reaping,
Nods heavy at the stacking,
It is piled high as a wall,
Is as even as the teeth of a comb.
All the barns are opened:
"When all the barns are brim full,
Wife and child will be at peace."
We kill this black-muzzled bull.
Oh, crooked[1] is its horn!
We shall succeed, we shall continue,
Continue the men of old.

## 292 ✦ *Silk Robes*

In silk robes so spotless,
In brown caps closely sewn,
From the hall we go to the stair-foot,
From the sheep to the bulls,
With big cauldrons and little.
Long-curving the drinking-horn;
The good wine so soft.
No noise, no jostling;
And the blessed ancestors will send a boon.

---

1. The crumpled horn suggests "hooking on" one generation to another.

### 293 ✦ *Libation*

Oh, gloriously did the king lead;
Swift was he to pursue and take.
Unsullied shines his light;
Hence our great succor,
We all alike receive it.
Valiant were the king's deeds;
Therefore there is a long inheritance.
Yes, it was your doing;
Truly, you it was who led.

This is perhaps the most difficult poem in the whole book, and I am
not confident that I have understood it correctly.

### 294 ✦ *Bold*

He brought peace to myriad lands,
And continual years of abundance.
Heaven's bidding he never neglected.
Bold was King Wu,
Guarded and aided by his knights
He held his lands on every side.
Firmly he grounded his House.
Bright he shines in Heaven,
Helping those that succeed him.

### 295 ✦ *Bestowal*

It was King Wen that labored;
We, according to his work, receive.
He spread his bounties;
Ours now to make secure
The destiny of this Zhou.
Oh, his bounties!

## 296 ✦ Celebration

Mighty this people of Zhou!
It climbed those high hills,
The narrow ridges, towering peaks;
Followed gully and wide stream.
To all that is under Heaven
Is linked as compeer
The destiny of Zhou.

# The Lu Hymns, 297–300

✦

The next song is traditionally supposed to have been made by Ke, Grand Scribe of Lu, who flourished about 609 B.C., but lived on a considerable time later. The most natural explanation of it is to suppose that the Lu people had received a gift of horses (possibly from the Zhou State).

### 297 ✦ *Stout*

Stout and strong our stallions
In the paddock meadows;
Look what strong ones!
There is piefoot and brownie,
Blackie and bay,
Fine horses for the chariot.
O that for ever
We may have horses so good!

Stout and strong our stallions
In the paddock meadows;
Look what strong ones!
Brown and white, gray and white,
Chestnut, dapple-gray,
Sturdy horses for the chariot.
O that for all time
We may have horses of such fettle!

Stout and strong our stallions
In the paddock meadows;
Look what strong ones!
Scaly coat, white with black mane,
Roan with black mane, gray with white mane,
Fleet horses for the chariot.
O untiring
May these horses breed!

Stout and strong our stallions
In the paddock meadows;
Look what strong ones!
Gray and white, ruddy and white,
White shank, wall-eye,
Powerful horses for the chariot.
O without slip
May these horses sire!

## 298 ✦ Stalwart

Oh, stalwart, stalwart,
Stalwart that team of browns!
At dawn of night in the palace,
In the palace that is growing light,
There throng the egrets,[1]
Egrets that sink down.
The drum goes din, din.
They are drunk and dance.
Heigh, the joys we share!

1. As we have seen above (no. 136), dancers held egret plumes in their hands, and "the egrets" here means the dancers. They are compared to strong steeds; it is possible that they wore horse-masks or were in some way accoutred as hobby-horses. Not, however, quite in the way familiar to us; for the ancient Chinese drove horses, but did not ride them.

Oh, stalwart, stalwart,
Stalwart those four steeds!
At dawn of night in the palace,
In the palace, drinking wine,
There throng the egrets,
Egrets in flight.
The drum goes din, din.
They are drunk and must go home.
Heigh, the joys we share!

Oh, stalwart, stalwart,
Stalwart that team of grays!
At dawn of night in the palace,
In the palace a feast is set.
From this day as beginning
Every harvest shall have surplus,
Our lord shall have corn
To give to grandsons and sons.
Heigh, the joys we share!


## 299 ✦ *Waves of the Pan*

Oh, merry the waves of the Pan;
Come, pluck the water-cress.
The Lord of Lu has come;
See, there are his banners.
His banners flutter,
His bells tinkle.
Both little and great
Follow our duke on his way.

Oh, merry the waves of the Pan;
Come, pluck the water-grass.
The Lord of Lu has come
With his steeds so strong.
His steeds so strong,
His fame so bright.
He glances, he smiles,
Very patiently he teaches us.

Oh, merry the waves of the Pan;
Come, pluck the water-mallows.
The Lord of Lu has come,
By the Pan he is drinking wine.
He has drunk the sweet wine.
That will give him youth unending;
Following those fixed ways
He assembles the thronging herds.[1]

Reverent is the Lord of Lu,
Scrupulously he keeps his power bright,
Attentively he carries out every attitude and pose,
A model to his people.
In peace truly admirable and in war,
Casting radiance on his noble ancestors,
Pious toward them in all things,
Bringing upon himself nought but blessings.

Illustrious is the Lord of Lu,
Well he causes his power to shine.
He has made the palace on the Pan,
Where the tribes of Huai come to submit.
Valiant the tiger-slaves[2]
At Pan, offering the severed ears;
Our lord questions skillfully as Gao-yao,[3]
While at Pan they offer the captives.

1. Of his guests? Meaning very uncertain. Comparison with no. 180, verse one, suggests that they must be animals; or war-captives?

2. Military officers.

3. Legendary judge, whose portrait in after days was hung in law-courts. His name means "drum," or "drum-post."

Magnificent the many knights
Who well have spread the power of his desires,
Valiant on the march
They trimmed the tribes of the south-east.
Doughty and glorious,
Yet not bragging or boasting,
Not sharp in contention
By the Pan they announce their deeds.

"Our horn[1] bows were springy,
Our sheaves of arrows whizzed;
Our war-chariots were very steady,
Foot-soldiers and riders were untiring.
We have quite conquered the tribes of Huai;
They are very quiet, they have ceased to resist.
We have carried out your plans;
The tribes of Huai have all been dealt with."

Fluttering, that owl on the wing
Has roosted in the woods of Pan;
It is eating our mulberry fruits,
Drawn by the lure of our fame.
From afar those tribes of Huai
Come with tribute of their treasures,
Big tortoises, elephant-tusks,
And great store of southern gold.[2]

---

1. This expression evidently implies that horn entered into the composition of the bow; but whether as a strengthening to the tip or as part of the substance of the arc we do not know.

2. "Jin" may well not mean "gold." But archaeological evidence is not at present so complete that we can exclude all possibility of "gold" being mentioned circa 650 B.C., the probable date of this poem.

## 300 ✦ *The Closed Temple*[1]

Holy is the Closed Temple,
Vast and mysterious;
Glorious was Jiang Yuan,
Her power was without flaw.
God on high succored her;
Without hurt, without harm,
Fulfilling her months, but not late,
She bore Hou Ji,
Who brought down many blessings,
Millet for wine, millet for cooking, the early planted and the late
     planted,
The early ripening and the late ripening, beans and corn.
He took possession of all lands below,
Setting the people to husbandry.
They had their millet for wine, their millet for cooking,
Their rice, their black millet.
He took possession of all the earth below,
Continuing the work of Yu.[2]

1. For names herein, see Important Legendary and Historical Figures in the front
of the book. *Ed.*

2. See no. 261.

Descendant of Hou Ji
Was the Great King
Who lived on the southern slopes of Mount Qi
And began to trim the Shang.
Till at last came King Wen and King Wu,
And continued the Great King's task,
Fulfilled the wrath of Heaven
In the field of Mu:
"No treachery, no blundering!
God on high is watching you."
He overthrew the hosts of Shang,
He completed his task.
The king said, "Uncle,[1]
Set up your eldest son,
Make him lord in Lu;
Open up for yourself a great domain,
To support the house of Zhou."

So he caused the Duke of Lu
To be lord of the east,
Gave him the hills and streams,
Lands, fields, dependencies.
The descendant of the Duke of Zhou,
Son of Duke Zhuang[2]
With dragon-painted banners made smoke-offering and sacrifice,
His six reins so glossy,
At spring and autumn most diligent,
In offering and sacrifice never failing:
"Very mighty is the Lord God,
A mighty ancestor is Hou Ji."

1.  The Duke of Zhou.
2.  Duke Xi, 659–27 B.C.

Of a tawny bull we make offering;
It is accepted, it is approved,
Many blessings are sent down.
The Duke of Zhou is a mighty ancestor;
Surely he will bless you.
In autumn we offer the first-fruits;
In summer we bind the thwart[1]
Upon white bull and upon tawny.
In many a sacrificial vase
Is roast pork, mince, and soup.
The vessels of bamboo and of wood are on the great stand;
The Wan dance is very grand.
To the pious descendant comes luck;
The ancestors have made you blaze, made you glorious,
Long-lived and good;
Have guarded that eastern realm.
The land of Lu shall be for ever,
Shall not crack or crumble,
Shall not shake or heave.
In long life you shall be Orion's peer,[2]
Steady as the ridges and hills.
A thousand war-chariots has the duke,
Red tassels, green lashings,
The two lances, bow lashed to bow,
His footmen thirty thousand;
Their helmets hung with shells on crimson strings.
Many footmen pressing on
Have faced the tribes of Rong and Di.[3]
Have given pause to Jing and Xu,[4]
None dares resist us.

1. A bar placed on the horns, to mark the animals as sacrificial.

2. Similar formula are very common on bronze inscriptions. See Additional Notes.

3. The Rong tribes raided the Zhou capital in 649; the Di attacked central China at a number of different points toward the middle of the seventh century B.C.

4. Jing are the southern people known later as Chu. The Xu (in south-west Shandong and Anhui) were regarded as non-Chinese, but at this period often fought in alliance with the Chinese. We know from the *Zuo zhuan* that Duke Xi took part in an expedition against Chu in 656 B.C.

The ancestors shall make you glorious, shall make you blaze,
Shall make you long-lived and rich,
Till locks are sere and back is bent;
An old age easy and agreeable.
They shall make you glorious and great,
Make you settled and secure,
For thousands upon ten thousands of years;
Safe you shall live for evermore.

To Mount Tai that towers so high
The land of Lu reaches.
He took Gui and Meng,[1]
Then he laid hands on the Greater East,[2]
As far as the coast lands.
The tribes of the Huai River came to terms,
There were none that did not obey.
Such were the deeds of the Lord of Lu.

In his protection are Fu and Yi;[3]
In his hold the realms of Xu
As far as the coast lands.
The tribes of Huai, the Muan, and the Mo,
And those tribes of the south—
There were none that did not obey,
None that dare refuse assent.
All have submitted to the Lord of Lu.

1. Two hills near the Tai-shan. "He" is Duke Xi.

2. See on no. 203.

3. Hills in south-central Shandong.

Heaven gives the duke its deepest blessings.
In hoary age he has protected Lu,
He has made settlements in Chang and Xu,[1]
Restored the realm of the Duke of Zhou.
Let the Lord of Lu feast and rejoice,
With his noble wife, his aged mother,
Bringing good to ministers and commoners,
Prosperity to his land and realm.
Very many blessings he has received;
In his time of sere locks he has cut new teeth!

The pines of Mount Chu-lai,[2]
The cypresses of Xin-fu[3]
Were cut, were measured
Into cubits, into feet.
The roof-beams of pine-wood stick far out,
The great chamber is very vast,
The new shrine very large,
That Xi-si made;
Very long and huge;
Whither all the peoples come in homage.

Some critics make out that the last line but two must be interpreted "Xi-si made this song." Such a meaning can only be got by altering the text. Xi-si was a son of Huan, Duke of Lu (711–694 B.C.). This is a Court poem and very much exaggerates the military and political importance of Lu at this time.

1. Western Shandong.

2. Hills near the present Dai'an.

3. Also near Dia'an.

# The Shang Hymns,[1] 301–05

✦

301 ✦ *Fine*

Oh, fine, oh, lovely!
We set up our tambourines and drums.
We play on the drums loud and strong,
To please our glorious ancestors.
The descendant of Tang[2] has come;
He has secured our victories.
There is a din of tambourines and drums;
A shrill music of flutes,
All blent in harmony
With the sound of our stone chimes.
Magnificent the descendant of Tang;
Very beautiful his music.
Splendid are the gongs and drums;
The Wan dance, very grand.
We have here lucky guests;
They too are happy and pleased.
From of old, in days gone by,
Former people began it,
Meek and reverent both day and night,
In humble awe discharging their tasks.
May they heed our burnt-offerings, our harvest offerings,
That Tang's descendants bring.

---

1. These hymns are from the state of Song, whose people were descendants of Shang; while they probably contain older Shang material, they must date from Zhou times, perhaps the seventh century B.C. *Ed*.

2. Tang was the ancestor of the Shang people, said to have been enthroned in 1766 B.C. *Ed*.

## 302 ✦ *Glorious Ancestors*

Ah, the glorious ancestors—
Endless their blessings,
Boundless their gifts are extended;
To you, too, they needs must reach.
We have brought them clear wine;
They will give victory.
Here, too, is soup well seasoned,
Well prepared, well mixed.
Because we come in silence,
Setting all quarrels aside,
They make safe for us a ripe old age,
We shall reach the withered cheek, we shall go on and on.
With our leather-bound naves, our bronze-clad yokes,
With eight bells a-jangle
We come to make offering.
The charge put upon us is vast and mighty,
From Heaven dropped our prosperity,
Good harvests, great abundance.
They come,[1] they accept,
They send down blessings numberless.
They regard the paddy-offerings, the offerings of first-fruits
That Tang's descendant brings.

That the Shang were fundamentally different in origin from the Zhou
is suggested by the fact that they had a quite different type of origin
myth. The Shang were descended from a lady called Jian Di, into
whose mouth the "dark bird" (the swallow) dropped an egg. This is
the typical eastern Chinese origin myth. The ruling family of Qin,
which came from eastern China, gave an almost identical account of
their origin. In the origin story of the Manchus a magpie drops a red
fruit. In some Korean stories the egg is exposed just as the child is in
the story of Hou Ji, and in succession dogs, pigs, cattle, horses, birds,
so far from doing it injury, vie with one another in guarding and
fostering it.

1. The ancestors.

## 303 ✦ *The Dark Bird*

Heaven bade the dark bird
To come down and bear the Shang,
Who dwelt in the lands of Yin so wide.
Of old God bade the warlike Tang
To partition the frontier lands.
To those lands was he assigned as their lord;
Into his keeping came all realms.
The early lords of Shang
Received a charge that was never in peril.
In the time of Wu Ding's[1] grandsons and sons,
Wu Ding's grandsons and sons,
Warlike kings ever conquered,
With dragon-banners and escort of ten chariots.
Great store of viands they offered,
Even their inner domain was a thousand leagues;
In them the people found sure support.
They opened up new lands as far as the four seas.
Men from the four seas came in homage,
Came in homage, crowd on crowd;
Their[2] frontier was the river.
Yin received a charge that was all good;
Many blessings Yin bore.

## 304 ✦ *Always Furthering*

Deep and wise was Shang,
Always furthering its good omens.
The waters of the Flood spread wide.
Yu ranged lands and realms on earth below;
Beyond, great kingdoms were his frontier,
And when this far-flung power had been made lasting
The clan of Song[3] was favored;
God appointed its child to bear Shang.

1. Legendary date, c. 1300 B.C.

2. I.e., the Yin frontier.

3. From whom sprang Jian-di, the ancestor of the Shang.

The dark king[1] valiantly ruled;
The service of small states everywhere he received,
The service of great States everywhere he received.
He followed the precepts of ritual and did not overstep them;
He obeyed the showings of Heaven and carried them out.
Xiang-tu[2] was very glorious;
Beyond the seas he ruled.

God's appointment did not fail;
In the time of Tang it was fulfilled.
Tang came down in his due time,
Wise warnings daily multiplied,
Magnificent was the radiance that shone below.
God on high gazed down;
God appointed him to be a model to all the lands.
He received the big statutes, the little statutes,
He became a mark and signal to the lands below.
He bore the blessing of Heaven,
Neither violent nor slack,
Neither hard nor soft.
He spread his ordinances in gentle harmony,
A hundred blessings he gathered upon himself.

Great laws and little laws he received,
He became great protector of the lands below.
He bore the favor of Heaven.
Far and wide he showed his valor,
Was never shaken or moved,
Never feared nor trembled;
A hundred blessings he united in himself.

1. Qi, child of the lady who swallowed the egg.
2. Grandson of Qi.

The warlike king gave the signal;
Firmly he grasped his battle-axe,
His wrath blazed like a fire.
None dare do us injury.
The stem had three sprouts;[1]
None prospered nor grew.
All the regions were subdued;
Wei and Gu were smitten,
Kun-wu, and Jie of Xia.[2]

Of old, in the middle time,
There were tremblings and dangers.
But truly Heaven cherished us;
It gave us a minister,[3]
A true "holder of the balance,"
Who succored the King of Shang.

### 305 ✦ *Warriors of Yin*

Swiftly those warriors of Yin
Rushed to the onslaught upon Jing and Chu,
Entered deep into their fastnesses,
Captured the hosts of Jing,
Divided and ruled their places;
Such was the work of Tang's descendants.

O you people of Jing and Chu,
You must have your home in the southern parts.
Long ago there was Tang the Victorious;
Of these, Di and Qiang[4]
None dared not to make offering to him,
None dared not to acknowledge him their king,
Saying, "Shang for ever!"

---

1. The "three sprouts" must have been three kindred enemies, but who they were we do not know.

2. Xia was the dynasty that Tang the Victorious overthrew. We know very little about Wei, Gu, and the others.

3. The famous Yi Yin, who is connected with the Shang version of the deluge myth.

4. These are different Di from the ones mentioned above. They and the Qiang were related to the Tibetans.

Heaven bade the many princes
To make the capital where Yu wrought his work.[1]
The produce of the harvest they brought in homage:
"Do not scold or reprove us;
We have not been idle in our husbandry."

At Heaven's bidding they[2] looked down;
The peoples below were awed,
There were no disorders, no excesses;
They dared not be idle or pause.
Heaven's charge was upon the lands below,
Firmly were their blessings planted and established.

Splendid was the capital of Shang,
A pattern to the peoples on every side,
Glorious was its fame,
Great indeed its magic power,
Giving long life and peace,
And safety to us that have come after.

They climbed yon Mount Jing[3]
Where the pines and cypresses grew thick.
They cut them, they carried them,
Square-hewed them upon the block.
The beams of pine-wood stuck out far,
Mighty were the ranged pillars.
The hall was finished; all was hushed and still.

1. In the lands rescued by the Great Yu from the flood.

2. The ancestors.

3. In northern Henan. This ballad, ending with the building of a palace, is very similar to no. 300. It is not clear whether the palace here referred to is one built by the men of Shang in old days or one built by the men of Song, their successors, about the seventh century B.C.

# Waley's Notes on Books Used

✦

The following list with annotations is as it appeared in Waley's original edition; the order of texts is roughly chronological. Graphs for the Chinese titles and names can be found in Waley's Textual Notes, p. 32. I have updated the romanization only. *Ed.*

1. *Shang shu jin gu wen zhu shu*. Basic Sinological Series. By Sun Xing-yan (1753–1818). The most convenient text of the authentic (i.e., pre-Han) books of the *Shu jing*. Gives the more important variants. The editor's own interpretations are not, from our point of view, of much value.

2. *Jing yi shu wen*. Basic Sinological Series. Critical observations of Wang Nian-sun (1744–1832), recorded by his son Wang Yin-zhi (1766–1834). The section on the *Songs* contains some of the best linguistic work that has been done.

3. *Shuo wen tong xun ding sheng*. By Zhu Jun-sheng (1788–1858). A dictionary of the phonetic series, based on the *Shuo wen*. The best existing key to phonetic borrowing. Contains much original speculation.

4. *Shi Mao shi zhuan shu*. Basic Sinological Series. By Chen Huan (1786–1863). Absolutely tied down to Mao's glosses, but gives some of the more important variants. Mao's glosses are indeed almost always right, in the sense that when he says A=B, B really is one of the senses of A. But in cases where A has several meanings, Mao sometimes gives the wrong one, regardless of the fact that it makes nonsense.

5. *Mao shi yi wen jian*, in *Nan qing shu yuan cong shu*. By Chen Yu-shu (1853–1906). A study of different ways in which the same word is written in different parts of Mao's text. A little-known work which is very useful.

6. *Shi san jia yi ji shu*. By Wang Xian-qian (1842–1917); the author of well-known commentary on *Zhuang zi*. The most complete collection of variants.

7. *Zhong-hua da zi dian*. By Xu Yuan-kao and others. Four volumes, Shanghai, 1935. The fullest and best dictionary of early Chinese. Referred to as *Da zi dian*.

8. *Liang Zhou jin wen ci da xi kao shi*. By Guo Mo-ruo. 1935. A study of all the important Zhou inscriptions. Referred to as *Kao shi*.

9. References such as "Karlgren, B. 119" refer to *Yin and Chou Researches*, 1935. The word "Karlgren" alone refers to the *Analytic Dictionary*, 1923.

10. *Shuang jian chi Shi jing xin zheng*. By Yu Xing-wu (1936). Notes on the *Songs*, with special reference to parallels in Zhou inscriptions. Contains many emendations, all scrupulously supported by quotation. The same author's similar work on the *Shu jing* is also of importance; but both works are marred by disregard of Zhou phonology.

# Waley's Additional Notes

✦

The first figure is the number of the poem, the second that of the verse, unless marked as refering to the line.

3. "Horn-cup." Literally "drinking-horn," made of the horn of the *si*. This word may have originally meant rhinoceros. In Zhou times it meant wild cattle. To-day it again means rhinoceros. The link is that the hide of both animals was used for defensive armor.

27. 4. Literally "open-meshed fiber-cloth and wide-meshed fiber-cloth." The second word is etymologically the same as *qi*, "a fissure," "a crack" (Karlgren, 341).

34. She uses the unusual *ang* for "I" (first person singular) because she is addressing the boatman, a social inferior. Cf. the use of *ang* by the emperor when addressing subjects.

39. This poem has generally been supposed to deal with the visit of a wife to her parents' house; but this does not fit the wording. I take it that the lady had fallen in love with her future husband at the Wei capital, in northern Henan, and had afterward gone to live farther north. The only identifiable place-name is Mei, which was close to the capital. Cao must also have been near by. It cannot be the Cao on the far side of the Yellow River, which became the Wei capital after c. 600 B.C.

46. When Hui, still in his minority, succeeded Xuan as Duke of Wei in 699, the men of Qi, who at this period dominated the affairs of the central Chinese states, forced Hui's half-brother Wan to marry Hui's widowed mother, who was a Qi princess, in order to ensure a succession favorable to Qi interests. The princess was Hui's step-mother, and it is supposed that a dispute arose concerning the legitimacy of the union. Something

very shocking evidently transpired during the hearing of the case (if we accept that this explanation of the poem is correct). Presumably what transpired was that Wan had already had intercourse with his step-mother during his father's lifetime.

Zheng Xuan, in his commentary on the last words of *Zhou li*, chapter 26, says that the place where love-disputes were heard was "covered over on top and fenced in below." I take the *gou* of the present song as equivalent to the *zhan* (fencing) of Zheng's note. Both words mean trellis-work made of thin strips of wood. *Gou* is usually taken to mean the partition which divided the woman's rooms from the man's. But it was deeds, not words, which disgraced the harem. The "words" that were shocking were the stories told at the trial. My interpretation certainly makes better sense; but we know so little of these *yin song* (trials in camera) that I only put it forward as a hypothesis.

51. The character with which "rainbow" is here written means "spider" and is simply a phonetic borrowing for the "girdle" character. See textual notes. Characters for rainbow presumably have the "serpent" radical because at an earlier stage of their mythology the Chinese regarded the rainbow as a snake, a belief very common in Africa and elsewhere. For the rainbow as a woman's belt, see Phyllis Kemp, *Healing Ritual in the Balkans* (p. 199); Françoise Legey, *Folk-lore of Morocco*, p. 47 (rainbow as girdle of Mohammed's daughter). The fact that elsewhere than in China the rainbow is regarded as a girdle makes it unlikely that the "girdle" element in the Chinese character is simply phonetic.

76. The *tan* that means "sandal-wood" is derived from a Sanskrit word. The *tan* of the *Songs* may have been a kind of ash.

79. 3. "To signal with a circular movement of the flag" is the proper meaning of *xuan*. See *Shuo wen*.

80. "Give his life." See T. T. 2126. *She ming* also means "to disseminate royal edicts," as, for example, in the inscription on the tripod of Duke Mao (Karlgren, B. 143), but that has no relevance here. The tripod may well be two hundred years earlier than this poem and the context is quite different.

95. *Gan*. This is only another way of writing the word *lan* (Archaic, *klan*), which in later Chinese means the cultivated orchid. In early Chinese it is a general name for sweet-smelling herbs. The variants here and in no. 145 are due to the fact

that Han interpreters were not used to seeing *lan* written as it is written here.

Legge's "valerian" is based on a misunderstanding of a plate in an eighteenth-century Japanese book.[1] The plate is labeled *fujibakama*, which means "Chinese agrimony." The strongly serrated leaves are quite unlike valerian.

102. 3. "Side-locks looped" is the typical coiffure of a boy before he comes of age. The famous Japanese picture of Prince Shōtoku, the early patron of Buddhism, as a boy, shows him with his hair done like this. In China the "coming of age" rite for boys centered on the first wearing of a grown-up person's cap (*guan*).

106. 2. Dr. K. Kaku (in *Tōyō Gakuhō*, vol. 20, no. 3) holds that *sheng* originally meant "my sister's sons or daughters," the speaker being a woman. According to the *Er ya*, it means "my mother-in-law's children," "my father-in-law's children," "my wife's brother," "my sister's husband."

107. The *di* of the *Songs* is a belt-pendant and not a hair-pin, as in later times.

128. The results of recent excavation are likely, when fully published, to give us a much clearer notion of the Zhou war-chariot. I think the "flank-checks" in verse 1, line 4, were spiked balls, hung on the girth of the inner horse to prevent the outer horse getting too close to it. Something similar was used by the Assyrians. I do not doubt that the word usually translated "traces" means ropes or reins used to drag a chariot by hand, when the horses could not get it through muddy or difficult places. "Traces," in our sense of the word, seldom occur in antiquity.

Line 3. There is not the slightest evidence that *xu* can mean a ring. My translation of the poem is, however, merely provisional. It is very doubtful whether *wo* means silver-inlay (cf. J. G. Andersson in *Yin and Chou Researches: the Goldsmith in Ancient China*, p. 2); or indeed has anything to do with silver at all. It was about their own techniques that the Han commentators knew, and not about those of a previous period.

137. 2. I very much doubt whether *shi ye* can mean "in the market." I suspect that *shi* is corrupt.

---

1. *Mōshi Himbutsu Zukō*, by Oka Gempō, pictures by Tachibana Kunio, 1785.

137. 2. Yuan is a woman's family name, like Jiang and Zi in no. 138, Ji in no. 139, Jiang, Yi, and Yong in no. 48, Ji in no. 225, etc. Such names are often preceded by age-terms, such as Meng (eldest) and Shu (third daughter), or by local names, e.g. Bao Si, "The Si-woman from the land of Pao"; or by the father's title, e.g. (no. 225) Yin Ji, "The Ji whose father is a *yin* (i.e., an official or scribe)."

      Zi-zhong is a man's family name; compare the Zi-ju of no. 131. In the courtship and marriage poems men are usually referred to by typical names, which function like the Sepp or Hänsel of German traditional songs.[1] These names, however, are not personal names but relationship or age terms; for example, Shu (uncle), nos. 77 and 78, Bai or Bo (elder), no. 62.

144. The fact that the *Zuo-zhuan* chronicle (Zhao gong, twenty-third year) interprets the song in the same way as Mao (the earliest commentator) proves nothing. For the *Zuo zhuan*, in its existing state, is full of Confucian lore drawn from just the same sources as the traditional Confucian commentaries. What matters is not whether the chronicle supports an interpretation, but whether that interpretation is compatible with the wording of the text in question.

153. In the "Jin Sayings" of the *Guo yu*, Duke Wen of Jin is made to quote this poem while still in exile. That is to say, tradition associated him with the poem, though in a way different from that which I have assumed. The whole story of this ruler, both in the *Guo yu* and the *Zuo zhuan*, is interspersed with folklore elements: for example, his "ribs all in one piece," an obvious "invulnerability-motif." Certain facts about him (I think we may take them as such) facilitated the linking of his story with traditional folk-lore. His birth involved the breaking of a taboo, for his parents were of the same clan (*xing*), and this could be taken as putting him on a par with heroes whose parents were brother and sister, human and animal, or the like.

154. *Mei-shou*. This phrase means "great old age"; we cannot etymologize it any further. It is written in many different ways (on inscriptions never with "eyebrow" till Han times), suggesting pronunciations *men*, *wei*, *mei*, *mou*.

---

1. Or Iwantscho in Bulgarian, Jovan in Serbian traditional songs.

156. 4. The idea that *li* means "scent-bag" is due, I think, to a series of misconceptions.

167. *Xian-yun.* They are also mentioned in several bronze inscriptions (e.g. Karlgren, B. 107, B. 133, B. 205). The only place-name in those inscriptions which can be identified with certainty is "north side of the Luo" (B. 71), which can only mean north of the Northern Luo River in Eastern Shaanxi. Similarly, the only place-name in our songs with a certain identification is the "north side of the Jing" in no. 177. The Jing (cf. no. 188) is the next great Shaanxi river west of the Luo.

168. For an example of "trying" a defeated chieftain, see the inscription in Karlgren, B. 19. The defendant's plea is that he had been maltreated by a certain Zhou lord and had therefore thrown in his lot with the Shang. The farce of interrogation having been accomplished, the rebel chieftain was, of course, beheaded.

170. The interpretation of the last stanza is mere guess-work.

207. "The meshes of crime." The idea that sin is a net in which Heaven catches those whom it would destroy was very widely spread in antiquity. Scheftelowitz[1] has shown that it existed among the Sumerians, Babylonians, Indians (in the Vedas), and ancient Persians (in the Zend Avesta). It also occurs in the Bible.[2] It is therefore likely to be no accident that so many of the words connected with sin ["blame" *Ed.*] in Chinese are written with the "net" radical. Compare no. 264, "Heaven casts down its net," and no. 265, "Heaven casts down its web of blame." The ordinary character for sin (*zui*), which has the "net" radical, is said indeed to have been invented by the Emperor Shi-huang in the third century B.C. But it is much more likely that it was an old form, preserved in the State of Qin and made current in the rest of China when Qin established itself as supreme.

209. 4. "Hopes and rules." This is very likely corrupt; but to interpret it as "spring and sight" of a cross-bow, as does Xu Zhong-shu (*Academia Sinica*, 4.4, p. 422), is hazardous.

211. *He*, "crops," is very likely a corruption of *gua*, "melons." Cf. 190, 4.

214. I am not confident that I have understood this poem rightly.

---

1. *Das Schlingen und Netzmotiv . . .* , 1912.

2. Hosea 7.12; Ezekiel 12.13 and 17.19–20.

215. *Bu*, here as in no. 245 and elsewhere, represents a labial prefix, and is not a negative.

220. "Grandly, royally done." As we do not know what *ren* and *lin* mean, I have followed the traditional interpretation as preserved by Mao, simply in order to avoid leaving a blank. "Receive the pledge-cup." *Shou qiu* is corrupt, and impossible to emend with any certainty.

222. 2. Literally, "It is in teams . . . that (*suo*) the princes arrive."

236. 2. "There came a command from Heaven . . ." Here the song retraces its steps. This verse does not go on to a fresh narration, but echoes the last. The narrative songs developed out of lyric poems in which each verse deliberately echoes the last, and there are considerable survivals of this structure in the long ballads. There is not the slightest reason to suppose that two successive marriages are being spoken of. We may regard Xin (a domain of whose history we know nothing) as scarcely deserving the name of "great country." But compare no. 54, where another small state is conventionally spoken of as a "great country."

245. I take the particle *dan*, so frequent in this poem, to mean "truly," "verily," or something of that sort. I do not think Wu Shi-chang's recent study of the word[1] gets us much further.

246. "Shuffling steps." See Chen Huan's commentary, chapter 6, folio 10.

262. "All the way to the southern seas." This is probably merely a hyperbole.

262. Wen-ren. Cf. the *Wen-hou zhi ming* in the *Shu jing* and the well-known Shan tripod (Guo Mo-ruo, *Kao shi*, p. 65). We could translate "I have announced it to my Mighty ones."

263. I translate Tai-shi "Leader," i.e., war-leader and not "Master," because there is no evidence that the theory of three super-functionaries without definite duties (the Grand Master, Grand Helper, Grand Protector) existed before Han times.

270. This poem has recently been discussed by Yu Xing-wu, in *Yü Kung* for March 1936.

283. line 7. Ancestors were called *zhao* "bright" and *mu* "quiet," "solemn"in alternate generations. The *zhao* ancestral tablets were on the left, the *mu* ancestral tablets were on the right side of the ancestral temple. Thus father, grandson, great-great-

---

1. In the Yenching *Journal of Chinese Studies*, no. 8, 1930.

grandson[1] came together on one side. Son, great-grandson, great-great-great-grandson on the other. This no doubt merely reflects the original habits of the living; hence the double nomenclature of Chinese officials, scribe of the left, scribe of the right, etc. Compare the prohibition against a father carrying his son in his arms (separation of immediate male generations), or teaching him. All this implies an original system of exchange marriage between two matrilineal units. The odd generations would then all belong to one unit, the even generations to the other.

290. "Headman and overseer." *Ya* is literally "seconder." I take *lü* in the sense of government inspector, who sees that a due proportion of land is tilled for tithe purposes. See *Zhou li*, chapter 30, folio 1. But this is pure speculation. *Kao* means "deceased fathers," the term "father" including paternal uncles.

300. "You shall be [the star] Orion's peer." See Guo Mo-ruo, on the Zong Zhou bell inscription, *Kao shi*, 1, 53 verso. Some inscriptions have the character for "3" instead of the proper character for "Orion's belt," just as here. I only accept this explanation provisionally; the relevant inscriptions have not been satisfactorily deciphered.

1. I.e., son's son; son's son's son's son, etc.

# Appendix: Waley's Original Topical Categories and Order of Poems

✦

When he translated *The Book of Songs,* Arthur Waley arranged the poems according to seventeen topical categories, saying, "I would much rather have kept to the traditional order. . . . But after experimenting in this direction I came to the conclusion that the advantage of an arrangement according to subject far outweighed, for the purposes of the present book, the disadvantages of tampering with the accepted order." Recognizing the advantages to a topical order, I have here reproduced a listing of Waley's categories and the poems in the order presented. While the Chinese themselves are interested in topical categories (*lei*), the categories and listing used by Waley were his own devising. Needless to say, there is necessary arbitrariness in some of Waley's choices, but the reader will also notice high levels of correspondence between some categories and the original divisions of the text, particularly between Waley's Courtship category and the "Airs" section, and between his two Dynastic categories and "The Major Odes."

| 1. COURTSHIP | 111 | Secret | 78 |
|---|---|---|---|
| 94 | 138 | Courtship | 143 |
| 148 | 95 | 76 | 44 |
| 106 | 56 | 82 | 129 |
| 99 | 139 | 96 | 86 |
| 122 | 20 | 100 | 93 |
| 18 | 64 | 41 | 145 |
| 108 | 74 | 159 | 146 |
| 117 | 88 | | 87 |
| 137 | 98 | Separation/ | 3 |
| 147 | 42 | Hopeless Passion | 63 |
| 75 | 48 | 77 | 55 |

| | | | |
|---|---|---|---|
| 59 | 116 | 28 | 121 |
| 61 | 26 | 21 | 153 |
| 72 | 15 | 124 | |
| 91 | 43 | | **4. AGRICULTURE** |
| 102 | 32 | **3. WARRIORS** | 275 |
| 89 | 22 | **AND BATTLES** | 276 |
| 62 | 132 | 7 | 277 |
| 125 | 39 | 79 | 279 |
| 142 | 83 | 80 | 290 |
| 225 | 47 | 128 | 291 |
| | 24 | 31 | 154 |
| | 104 | 36 | 190 |
| **Broken Faith** | 57 | 37 | 211 |
| 45 | 1 | 110 | 212 |
| 34 | 9 | 156 | |
| 60 | 12 | 181 | **5. BLESSINGS** |
| 81 | 173 | 185 | **ON GENTLE** |
| 140 | 90 | 230 | **FOLK** |
| 73 | 228 | 232 | 4 |
| 226 | 14 | 234 | 5 |
| 27 | 118 | 167 | 152 |
| | 218 | 168 | 160 |
| **Desertion/** | 67 | 177 | 166 |
| **Love Suits** | 126 | 178 | 170 |
| 69 | 13 | 227 | 171 |
| 150 | 8 | 262 | 172 |
| 23 | 66 | 259 | 215 |
| 51 | 30 | 16 | 249 |
| 151 | 54 | 263 | 251 |
| 29 | 187 | 204 | 252 |
| 33 | 58 | 208 | 216 |
| 17 | 188 | 260 | 222 |
| 141 | 19 | 207 | |
| | 71 | 261 | **6. WELCOME** |
| | 35 | 169 | 278 |
| **2. MARRIAGE** | 201 | 162 | 284 |
| 105 | 229 | 10 | 53 |
| 101 | 176 | 133 | 123 |
| 158 | 2 | 149 | 130 |
| 107 | 6 | 68 | 182 |

161
175
186
213
214
134

7. FEASTING
231
114
115
174
221

8. THE CLAN
FEAST
164
165
217
246
144

9. SACRIFICE
209
210
239
247
248
302

10. MUSIC
AND DANCING
280
11
25
38
84
85
136

298
301

11. DYNASTIC
SONGS
266
267
268
269
270
271
272
273
274
281
282
283
285
286
287
258
289
155
157
292
293
294
295
296

12. DYNASTIC
LEGENDS
245
250
237
235
255
241
242
240

236
244
243
238
299
300
297
303
304
305

13. BUILDING
50
189

14. HUNTING
103
112
127
179
180

15. FRIENDSHIP
92
120
97

16. MORAL
PIECES
46
220
223
49
52
256

17. LAMENTA-
TIONS
40
65

70
109
113
119
131
135
183
184
200
202
203
205
206
219
224
233
163

UNTRANSLATED
191
192
193
194
195
196
197
198
199
253
254
257
258
264
265

# Postface: A Literary History
## of the Shi jing

### Joseph R. Allen

◆

This essay outlines the literary history of the *Shi jing* (The Book of Songs), including the text's origins and formulation, hermeneutic tradition, and poetics. It is intended both for the general reader who wants more historical information about the *Shi jing* and as a starting point for the student with research interests in the text. This essay should be read as a supplement to Stephen Owen's Foreword, which provides all readers with an engaging and penetrating analysis of the literary qualities of the poems. Following is an annotated, selected bibliography of materials in English that might act as an introduction to the rich secondary literature on the *Shi jing*.[1] My primary intent here is to summarize and integrate the writings and thoughts of others, with only an occasional interjection of my own.[2]

## Origins: From Song to Poem

In discussing the origins of the *Shi jing* we need to distinguish clearly between the origins of a text by that name and the origins of the poems that have come to form that text. Both of these questions are fraught with difficulties, but there is a lineage of shared assumptions that allows us to describe the origins coherently, if not necessarily with certainty.

Although there is little direct discussion of the issue in early commentaries, it is assumed that the songs emerge from different performance contexts, and pre-Han references to the songs should always be seen in the bounds of that type of environment. At the earliest stage this context would be entirely fluid and ephemeral; songs would not have existed beyond their momentary instantiations; they may have been repeated, but these repetitions would not be seen as versions of some fixed model. This type of performance context has been thoroughly investigated in the studies of oral formulaic composition, beginning with the work of Milman Parry and Albert Lord.[3] In that analysis, the performer constructs his song using compositional formulas that are melded with the formal demands of the genre, such as prosody and rhyme. The formulas, which have enough flexibility to allow for ad hoc accommodation, are shared by performers and help guide the composition along familiar plot and thematic lines. The audience shares passively in this oral tradition and finds the reiteration and combining of the formulas and patterns inherently pleasurable. While the Parry-Lord theory began with fieldwork in contemporary examples of oral composition, it was soon applied to written texts, most notably Homer's *Illiad,* where the remnants of the oral formulas were preserved. In turn, C. H. Wang applied the Parry-Lord methodology to the *Shi jing,* confirming the text's oral origins; Wang's statistical evidence allowed him to conclude that, at the least, the *Shi jing* is "conceivably oral, and demonstrably formulaic."[4] Wang clearly does *not* regard the texts of the *Shi jing* as "folk" or "primitive" poetry, but rather sees them as sophisticated products of a transitional period from an oral to a textual culture.[5]

While Wang's analysis demonstrates that formulaic composition is statistically significant in texts from all sections of the *Shi jing,* the "Airs" (*Feng*) shows this most strongly, followed closely by "The Minor Odes" (*Xiao ya*); this we might expect, and indeed it might not surprise even some traditional critics. Zhu Xi (1130–1200), whose contributions we will discuss below, said, "I have heard that of what are called the 'Airs' among the *Shi,* most come from the songs and ditties [*ge yao*] of village lanes. They are what men and women sang to each other, each expressing their feelings [*qing*] in words."[6] The logic of such statements by Zhu Xi and others in the end lead to modern studies that apply the analysis of comparative anthropology to describe more clearly the performance context for the songs, especially those in the "Airs." Foremost among these in the West is Marcel Granet's work of 1919 in which he describes the airs as examples of courtship and communal songs associated with seasonal festivals and fertility celebrations; he was particularly interested in the "matching song," where girls and boys sang in call and response.[7] While Granet's work is the best known, there were also Chinese scholars of the early twentieth century whose work forwarded similar arguments, particularly using comparisons with the culture of the

indigenous people of southwest China.[8] Perhaps the most impor-
tant result of these studies was the implication that village life of the
pre-Han period could have been radically different from that of the
imperial period.

Yet the performance environment of "village lanes" would not
seem to apply to the more elevated poems in the *Shi jing,* especially
the "Hymns." Zhu Xi himself is clear about this:

> The "Odes" and "Hymns" are all from the period when
> the Zhou dynasty was firmly established. The lyrics [*ci*]
> of this court and temple music have a language that is
> harmonious and heroic, and a meaning that is broad and
> dense; those who composed these songs were followers
> of the sages, thus they were able to offer models that did
> not change for ten thousand generations.[9]

Zhu is here clearly describing performances characterized by fixity
and repeatability, quite unlike the "Airs"; nonetheless, these perfor-
mances still could be structured by oral formulation, as C. H. Wang's
study suggests. Such an environment is best described by Walter Ong's
concept of "secondary orality." Unlike primary orality of a preliterate
society, secondary orality exists within the context of literacy; thus
consciousness is conditioned by the knowledge of written language.
This means that the consciousness of even illiterate people is affected;
they are aware of the possibility of written language even if they
cannot use it. For China of the Zhou dynasty that possibility is now
most easily seen in the inscriptions on bronzeware, but at the time it
was no doubt also seen on more perishable media. One of the cen-
tral changes in consciousness that knowledge of literacy brings is the
concept of the fixity of language (in written form) and thereby the
repeatability of materials verbatim.[10] From this we can posit the con-
cept of model and imitation that Zhu's remarks seem to address. While
performances of secondary orality exist throughout Chinese history,
the music of court and temple to which Zhu Xi refers may provide
some of the earliest examples.[11] Indeed, secondary orality might also
best characterize C. H. Wang's "transitional period," during which
he believes the *Shi jing* was formed.

Modern scholars have occasionally addressed the performance
environment from which these more ritualistic poems may have
emerged, and their thoughts inform the *Shi jing* more broadly as well.

Early in this century Wang Guo-wei, Wen Yi-duo, and Fu Si-nian all wrote separately on this issue. Recently Edward Shaughnessy has drawn on archaeological and phonological evidence to refine their arguments, concluding that the first decade of "The Zhou Hymns" (nos. 266–75) has vestiges of a very early, communal form of ritual, which by the end of the tenth century B.C. was replaced by another form in which principal figures *performed* the ritual for an audience.[12] It is in this latter form where one sees the role of the "impersonator" [*shi*]—Waley's "Dead One." C. H. Wang has summarized and integrated much of the earlier discussions of the impersonator into his reconstruction of a "ritual program," which he traces in texts primarily from the "Hymns." Following the lead of Liu Shi-pei's 1907 essay, Wang claims this program as a prototypical drama. He concludes:

> I have reconstructed a religious ceremony on the basis of some Confucian classics to demonstrate that Chinese drama, like its parallels in Europe, originates in ritual, and the lord impersonator is as much an important character among the *dramatis personae* on the first stage of Chinese drama as he is the "master" in the ancestral temple when the ceremony is called to order.[13]

Following others, Wang has also noted the importance of references to dance in these ritual poems and throughout the collection in general.[14] In Chow Tse-tsung's exhaustive essay on the meaning of *shi* (poetry) he says it is a term "with the meaning of a particular action in a sacrifice accompanied with a certain sign, music, songs, and dance."[15] Chen Shih-hsiang, on the other hand, wants to draw the linkage of dance, through the central concept of *xing* (see below), to the more communal and "primitive" side of the collection; he believes *xing* (and ultimately the songs) emerge from a communal performance of an "uplifting dance."[16]

While these studies hardly portray the entire catalog of performance environments from which the songs may have emerged, they do suggest the range of possibilities and the accompanying sediments of primary and secondary orality that would be found therein: from the festival round dance with its "heave-ho" refrains and the antithetical courting songs with their formulas of romance, to the solemn dramas of the ancestral temple with their concern for models and prescribed rituals.[17]

## *Whence the Text?*

When we wonder whether a *text* known as the *Shi jing* existed or not at a given point in time, we bring to that question substantial, often anachronistic, assumptions that condition our very asking. For example: Doesn't that question assume a physical text, something that we could put on a shelf or in a cupboard? Or could the "text" exist only as a memorized set of utterances available for repetition? If the text were physical, would there be multiple copies (or versions?) of it? Would we not assume that some person or group of persons was responsible for "making" the text(s)? Or could it have evolved in some more demiurgical fashion? And finally, who would possess the text, and why? Many of these questions are open to long debate, but they need to be kept in mind as we proceed.

First, some easy answers. If a text did exist in 500 B.C., let us say, then it would not have been called the *Shi jing,* since the Chinese canon, even this earliest layer, would not have yet been named—the term *jing* would not be used until the third century B.C.[18] Rather, the text would have been called the *Shi* (Songs) or *Shi san bai* (Three Hundred Songs). If the text did exist as a physical object, it would have been written on rolls of wood or bamboo slips, or perhaps silk; paper was not invented until the Han dynasty. So yes, you could put it in a cupboard, but it would have been bulky to carry around.[19] Texts of this type could have been in the possession of the important families of the realm, especially those of the royal and feudal courts, although it is likely that those texts would have been written in a variety of script forms.[20] We have as of yet no physical evidence for such archives from this early period, and it is unclear how such materials would have been used. Can we imagine, for example, someone literate and privileged "reading" these texts? And if so, to whom and why? In any event we should remember that in a culture of secondary orality it would have been the *performed* texts, with their inherent variety, that would have "circulated." This suggests the immensity of the leap that must be made when we move from discussing the possible origins of the songs to the existence of the text as a fixed and agreed-on collection of poems, but it is that leap that lies at the beginning of the history of the *Shi jing.*[21]

Traditionally, that leap was described in two separate stages that are logical in conception if not verifiable in specific manifestations. The comments are found in Han dynasty historical texts, and I would

like to consider them together here, even though they are not origi-
nally associated with each other.[22] The more recent comment con-
cerns how the "songs of village lanes" might have ended up in the
royal or state archives, where presumably texts of the more ritual-
ized sort would have been stored. The incident is related:

> In the first month of spring [that is, at the beginning of
> the year], when those who were living together were
> about to disperse, messengers would come along the road
> ringing wooden-clappered bells looking for songs to col-
> lect [*cai shi*], which they would present to the Grand
> Master. He would then set them to appropriate tones and
> pitches [i.e., tunes] and then have the Son of Heaven listen
> to them. Therefore it is said, "Without even peering
> beyond the window or door, the King knows [the con-
> ditions of] the empire."[23]

This passage has met with a great deal of skepticism, and we should
be especially concerned with the problem of anachronistic readings;[24]
nonetheless, I would suggest that the proposal is so unusual and
decontextualized (it occurs in a monograph on commerce) that it
suggests some core truth.[25] This is the point where C. H. Wang notes
a "process of transmission" as "many songs were edited and prob-
ably even rewritten to befit the specific musical and ceremonial
atmosphere of the court."[26] Presumably the "messenger" made the
first transcription, followed by later ones.

Let me here add two thoughts. First, we have no evidence for
any type of musical notation during the Zhou period (in fact, we do
not have such evidence until the sixth century A.D.);[27] thus "tran-
scription" could have been applied only to the lyrics of the songs.
We assume that music was performatory only.[28] Second, there is no
reason to assume that this practice of collecting poems would have
been limited to the Zhou royal house; given the practice, the feudal
states could also have used similar messengers to collect songs from
their environs. And with that we would have the beginning of
archives for the "Airs of the States."

Granted, these are speculative origins of the *Shi jing* as a written
text, but they are convincing in the sense that they suggest a begin-
ning that emerges naturally within the social-political framework of
the time, accounting for the leap from performance environments

of primary orality to those of secondary orality, and then on to a fixed text. Moreover, it suggests the very architecture of the collection as we know it, without venturing into the problematic discussion of authorship and intentionality of the corpus as a whole. Our next passage does just that, however.

### Enter Confucius

In the *Records of the Grand Historian* (*Shi ji*) (c. 90 B.C.) there is a passage that catapults us into the *Shi jing* as a text configured exactly as we now know it. In some ways the passage is too informative:

> In ancient times there were more than three thousand compositions [*pian*] associated with the *Shi*. From these Confucius eliminated the duplicates and selected texts that could be used with ritual propriety. The oldest materials deal with the dynastic founders Xie [of the Shang] and Hou Ji [Lord Millet of the Zhou]; the materials from the middle period describe the glory of the royal dynasties of the Yin [Shang] and Zhou; and the latest texts deal with the deficiencies of Kings You and Li. They began in celebration [?], therefore it is said, "The pattern in 'The Ospreys Cry' [1] forms the beginning of the 'Airs'; 'The Deer Cry' [161] is the beginning of the 'Lesser Odes'; 'King Wen' [235] is the beginning of the 'Greater Odes'; and 'The Hallowed Temple' [266] is the beginning of the 'Hymns.'"
>
> Confucius put all three hundred and five of the compositions to the music of strings and voice [*xuan ge*], and in doing so sought to fit them to the tunes [*yin*] of Shao, Wu, Ya and Song. From this the ritual music can be learned and performed; with this the kingly virtue is complete and the six principles [*liu yi*] are formed.[29]

This description has many signs of a reconstruction conditioned by contemporaneous literary culture; the early Han period was a time during which editorship and commentary on textual materials was an important activity. While we might imagine that some process such as described here occurred whereby we move from a fluid and undelineated tradition of songs to a corpus of *Songs,* that process was probably not as momentous as indicated here, but rather much more agglutinative and self-adjusting.

Si-ma Qian's description of the editorial process is true in this sense: by the time the *Shi ji* was written, Confucius, his disciples, and the texts associated with him were the principal voices behind the *Shi jing;* thus if Si-ma were to assume a single, intentional editor it would be from that lineage, and since the songs were by then considered canonical material it would behoove him to make that association as deep as possible. His reference to the musicality of the songs alludes to one of the oldest and most problematic aspects of the text as canon. His description of the *Shi,* on the other hand, including technical terms, the layering of textual materials, and the implication of moral import, certainly represented the parameters for an understanding of the text near to his own time. If we would ignore the reference to Confucius as a historical figure and substitute the concept of his school and legacy, as it evolved through the Warring States period into the Han, this description is probably quite accurate. It is *that* process, not the intentionality of a single editor, that best describes the formation of the text.

Steven Van Zoeren has traced in detail that process, which he calls a movement from a "weak text" to a "strong text," by which he means a movement from a "stable, reiterable discourse, usually although by no means always written" to a "stable text that has become central to a doctrinal culture and thus the object of exegetical exposition and study."[30] We could here posit C. H. Wang's period of "transition" and the emergence of secondary orality as the immediate preface to the earliest stages of Van Zoeren's weak text. In fact, early references to the *Shi* in the secondary materials, particularly the *Analects* and the *Zuo zhuan,* are ample evidence of that transition.[31]

Van Zoeren argues that when we position references to the songs found in the *Analects* against its supposed chronological layers, we can see a transformation of what constituted the *Shi* for the commentators. At the earliest level, presumably close in time to historical Confucius (551–479 B.C.), most references are to music and musical performance, especially the propriety thereof; little is said about the words themselves. This is true even when songs are mentioned by their titles, as in Confucius' famous remark, "The beginning by Music Master Zhi, the coda of 'The Ospreys Cry' [1]—how floodlike do they fill the ears."[32] At that point in time we would assume the song-texts were not yet fixed and would have been secondary to the music.

As a middle stage in the movement from weak to strong texts Van Zoeren identifies the citation and quotation of poems in politically charged situations of the early secondary literature; this is also mentioned by Owen in his Foreword. This practice, commonly called *fu shi* (recitation of poems), is especially prominent in the *Zuo zhuan* but occurs elsewhere, including in the *Analects*.[33] In the *Zuo zhuan*, for example, David Schaberg locates seventeen scenes of recitation, including references to nearly fifty poems; Qu Wan-li suggests that the text draws on 156 known examples from the *Shi jing*, in addition to ten references to lost poems.[34] What has most drawn the critics' attention in these accounts of *fu shi* is how the lines of the poem are quoted "out of context" to ornament an argument or to make a rhetorical point. There are also several passages in the *Analects* where we have a similar rhetorical usage of the poem. In those cases the concern is no longer with the music or musical performance but rather with the lyrics of the songs; yet the focus is not the "original" meaning of the words but rather the meaning they take on in the context in which they are quoted. This is what Van Zoeren calls the poem as "pretext"—there is a fixed language, but it is not language with a fixed meaning. The most famous example of that usage attributed to Confucius is when he cited the phrase *si wu xie* from poem no. 297 to characterize the *Shi*.[35] Traditional readers would have understood this to mean "In thoughts, there is nothing deviant"; yet within the context of the poem the word *si* (thoughts) is merely an introductory particle with no substantive meaning (as is very common in the *Shi*).[36] Clearly, Confucius knowingly quoted the line with its recontextualized meaning. Stephen Owen has called this the "application" of the poem to a context, which relies on an inherently open and indeterminant text; this was the norm, not the exception, in the early use of the *Shi*.[37]

In Van Zoeren's description of *fu shi* in the *Zuo zhuan*, he notes that the songs "serve as a rhetoric or source of usable phrases" and that their citation may have "served a function roughly analogous to the toasts or speeches made at diplomatic functions today," as well as opportunities for the application of more complex meanings and intentions.[38] One brief example cited by David Schaberg shows how *fu shi* worked on several levels. The scene is a banquet celebrating the signing of a treaty between the states of Chu and Wei in 541 B.C.:

> The Chief Minister of Chu feasted Zhao Meng of Jin and recited the first stanza of "Major Bright" (236). Zhao Meng recited the second stanza of "Diminutive" (196).
>
> When the affair was over, Zhao Meng said to Shu-xiang, a minister of Jin, "The Chief Minister presents himself as king. What will become of it?"
>
> He replied, "The King is weak and the Chief Minister strong. He can succeed at becoming king. But even if he does succeed, he will not come to a good end."
>
> Zhao Meng asked, "Why is that?"
>
> He replied, "When the strong man overcomes the weak and is contented with the situation, then the strong man is not righteous. One who is not righteous even though strong will meet with a speedy death. A song says, 'Majestic was the capital of Zhou, / But Lady Bao Si destroyed it.'[39] Zhou was strong but not righteous."[40]

The anecdote concludes with Shu-xiang explicating the meaning of these passages in reference to the inevitable downfall of the Chief Minister, including the direct application of the lessons learned from the story of Bao Si. Here we see a relatively conservative use of *fu shi*; poems and lines are quoted for their inherent political content, accompanied by an intratextual explanation of the use of the lyrics, as fully explained by Schaberg.[41] There are two relatively mundane points we should note here as they apply to the *Shi jing* as text and to many of the *fu shi* passages. First, songs are referred to by title and stanza (without lines cited), which clearly indicates a fixed, reiterable text—and most of those titles are ones now in the *Shi jing* corpus. Second, when lines are quoted (most often without an attached title), they are generally lines that we know from the extant text, verbatim or nearly so—again, another indication that by the time the *Zuo zhuan* was composed (if not actually by the time referred to in the passage), the individual songs had stabilized to such a degree that they were able to survive down into the Han, whereupon they were permanently recorded.

While *fu shi* was certainly a performance environment of secondary orality, it was not the same as singing or performing the music of the songs. In those performances the aesthetics and morality of the music provided the contextualizing frame. In the *Zuo zhuan* there is a famous passage that depicts this, at the same time providing more evidence of the progress toward a stable and strong text for the *Shi jing*.

In 543 B.C. Ji Zha, Ducal Son of the southern state of Wu visited Lu, the home state of Confucius and the alleged keeper of the flame of orthodox music. During his visit the Ducal Son asked his hosts if he might hear the Zhou music (*Zhou yue*), whereupon he was treated to a performance of the various sections of the *Shi* in their now common order: *Feng, Xiao ya, Da ya, Song,* followed by a series of dance performances, which were associated with the royal houses and rulers. After each section of the performance Zha commented on the character and quality of the music. Most remarkable about this scene is that the various "Airs" subsections are named in order and that the list is nearly identical with the one we now have.[42] For example, the second part of the performance reads:

> They sang from the Airs of Bei, Yong, and Wei for him. Zha said, "Beautiful! Very profound. They are somber, but not depressing. I have heard the virtue of Kang-shu of Wei and Duke Wu is like this; these are indeed the "Airs of Wei."[43]

There are no titles or verses named in any part of this exchange, and music is clearly the focus of Zha's comments. Nonetheless this passage refers to lyrics that are sung [*ge*] and offers us a larger framework into which songs and verses mentioned in other passages from the *Zuo zhuan* can be slotted. This provides us with the last element in the emergence of a stable, delineated text, which is the necessary prerequisite for the establishment of a strong text and its accompanying exegetical tradition.

## The Exegetical Tradition

During the Warring States period (c. 403–221 B.C.) the song-texts of the *Shi* came to be discussed quite disassociated from their performance contexts—that is, neither as music nor in rhetorical applications (*fu shi*) of the *Zuo zhuan* variety. Van Zoeren has plotted this new, text-based discussion through the pedagogical programs of Mencius (c. 372–289) and especially Xun zi (310–c. 211 B.C.), who declares the *Shi* a classic (*jing*) and moves the discussion ever closer to the status of doctrine. When we cross over from feudal to imperial China, the text is apparently fixed and becoming strong in the sense that it is moving toward being "central to a doctrinal culture and thus the object of exegetical exposition and study." The hermeneutical activities of the Han period established the importance of the *Shi jing,* and traces of those activities accompany the text up into the twentieth century.

The transition from feudal kingdoms to the central imperial rule of the Qin (221–07) and Han (206 B.C.–A.D. 220) was a bumpy one for many parts of the old society, not the least the textual traditions. The Qin openly banned and actively destroyed many texts associated with traditionalist thinking, and the early Han did not put much stock in those texts either. But gradually, with the stabilization of the empire, intellectual life grew in the official circles, manifesting itself in court-sponsored study and the controversy of the Old Text versus New Text schools of criticism. (Briefly, the Old Text school was more philological and text oriented, while the New Text school emphasized interpretational techniques, including cosmological speculation.[44]) This controversy involved a number of shared texts, including the *Shi jing,* which existed in at least four commentaries, three identified as New Text versions and one as Old Text.[45] In the *Han shu* bibliography the three New Text commentaries (of the Han, Lu, and Qi schools of *Shi*) were the officially accepted versions. As for the other version, the bibliographic notes says, "In addition, there is the school of Master Mao, which claims to have [the tradition] handed down from Zi-xia. Prince Xian of He-jian liked it, but it has not been established [in the official schools]."[46] Ironically, it is that Old Text version, the celebrated *Mao shi,* that survives today and to which we now turn our attention.[47]

We can view the exegetical tradition associated with the *Mao shi* as layers of self-referential materials, with each annotation often taking its topic of comment from the preceding layer(s) of material as much as from the poems themselves. This is even true during revolutionary moments in interpretation; Bernhard Karlgren's *Glosses on the Book of Odes* is nearly obsessive in this regard, for example. Here I would like to describe briefly the most important texts in those exegetical layers, giving some examples and commenting on the general lines of development. As an illustration I will refer to the

materials surrounding a short, simple poem, "Along the Highroad"
(81), which I offer in a revised translation that takes into account the
lexical glosses quoted below:

> If along the highroad
> I caught hold of your cuff,
> Do not hate me;
> Old ways take time to overcome.
>
> If along the highroad
> I caught hold of your hand,
> Do not be angry with me;
> Love takes time to overcome.

The earliest materials associated with the *Mao shi* form a com-
plex gestalt. Primarily there are two types: the philological glosses
and explications of the Mao commentary (usually called *Mao [shi]
zhuan*), and the various prefaces (*xu*) that carry the interpretation force
of the text. The Mao commentary, which is early attributed to Mas-
ter Mao (Mao Gong) and now dated to c. 150 B.C., contains both
short paraphrases and lexical glosses.[48] The need for detailed lexical
annotation is, of course, testimony to the linguistic difficulty of the
*Shi jing* even in the early Han period, a difficulty compounded by
shifts in orthography and the tumult of empire building. The Mao
commentary for "Along the Highroad" is only of this lexical type,
which we can see as a form of conservative, Old Text scholarship.[49]
These are the glosses for the first stanza, divided into couplets:

> (1) *zun* (along) means beside; *lu* (road) means way; *shan*
> (caught hold) means grab; *qu* (cuff) means fore-sleeve. (2)
> *zan* (no time to overcome) means hasty.[50]

This type of lexical glossing becomes an important aspect of subse-
quent *Shi jing* commentary, establishing one lineage of scholarship
for the text.

The prefaces, which begin another line of interpretation of the
poems, are of several parts. First, there is a division between the so-
called Great Preface (*Da xu*) and the Small Prefaces (*Xiao xu*). Since
the Great Preface offers a general rationale for the text, we will turn
our separate attention to it in the concluding section of the essay.
Here I want to sketch the nature of the Small Prefaces, which

accompany each of the 305 poems; they are one of the most distin-
guishing parts of the *Mao shi* gestalt and become fiercely debated in
the later history of the text.[51]

The Small Prefaces themselves are also of two parts, upper and
lower. The upper part is said to trace its lineage back to Confucius'
disciple Zi-xia, coming down to Master Mao, whereupon he, or more
likely Wei Hong (first century A.D.) supplemented it with the lower
part. The relationship between the two parts of the Small Prefaces is
much like that between commentary and subcommentary, where the
latter explicates or illustrates the former. This is the Small Preface
for our poem; the upper part consists of the opening general state-
ment, while the lower gives the illustrating historical example:

> "Along the Highroad" describes thinking of one's noble
> lord; Duke Zhuang of Zheng neglected the proper way
> and the noble lords abandoned him. The men of the state
> longed for them/him.[52]

While this "explanation" of the poem may seem forced, if not actu-
ally bizarre—in the Song dynasty Zheng Qiao would call these pref-
aces the work of a "rustic ignoramus"[53]—it is, nonetheless, a typical
example of a Small Preface. These prefaces have been much maligned
in modern times, but recent formulations have asked that we con-
sider them in their larger literary and intellectual contexts. For exam-
ple, Pauline Yu has argued that this type of interpretational strategy
is *not* a form of allegory or even allegoresis, as it is commonly called;
rather, it is a historical contextualization that fits well into the main-
stream of Chinese poetics, which treats its figural images as metonymic
truths of categorical correspondence (*lei*).[54] In this way they are similar
to the practice of *fu shi*—applications as much as interpretations of
the poems, establishing a context for the indeterminacy of the text.
Most importantly, these Small Prefaces became the orthodox doc-
trinal interpretation for the *Mao shi* and contributed substantially to
intellectual and political debate in China for many centuries. While
the Small Prefaces did not directly accrue any more exegetical layers,
their influence is seen throughout the later commentaries.

At the end of the Han dynasty the *Mao shi* acquired an annotation
(*jian*) written by the great literary and philological scholar Zheng Xuan
(127–200); this annotation contributed to the prestige of the Mao
text and may have been responsible for the fading importance of the
other, New Text versions of the *Shi jing:* by the Tang dynasty, only

the Han version would be extant, and that would subsequently disappear during the Song dynasty.[55] Zheng Xuan's work includes lexical annotation, often related to the Mao *zhuan,* but also takes its lead from the *fu shi* and Small Prefaces to offer paraphrase and comment.[56] His annotation of the first stanza of "Along the Highroad" illustrates the dual nature of his work, interweaving lexical glosses with interpretation. First we find a paraphrase of the first two lines: "Longing for one's lord, when seeing him on the road then one wants to grab hold his fore-sleeve to detain him." For the final two lines, to which Mao included only one lexical gloss, Zheng is more elaborate in his paraphrase. Borrowing from several glosses provided elsewhere by Mao, he paraphrases the poem, "You should not have hatred for me if I grab hold of your fore-sleeve; it is that Duke Zhuang did not hasten to the ways of the former lords that has caused me to do this."[57]

This Mao-Zheng commentary and annotation establishes the orthodox doctrinal line of early *Shi jing* scholarship and leads ultimately to the huge exegetical undertaking in the Tang dynasty: the *Mao shi zheng yi* (Correct Significance of the Mao Poems), imperially commissioned and edited by Kong Ying-da (574–648). Between those two moments of canonical formation and reaffirmation lie a period of *Shi* scholarship that mirrored the political fragmentation and intellectual heterogeneity of the time: the period of the Six Dynasties, when the Chinese central plain was divided into a series of northern and southern ruling houses who fought with each other and among themselves in quick, frantic succession. This was also when Buddhism took hold in China and when the esoteric Mysterious Learning (*xuan xue*) flourished, both of which involved philosophic and cosmological debates that indirectly encouraged similar speculations in the exegesis of the Confucian canon. Moreover, exposure to non-Chinese languages, especially Sanskrit, stimulated interest in philological matters, particularly in the area of phonology. This led to numerous insights and innovations, such as discussion of tones and the use of *fan-qie* spellings.[58] All of this affected *Shi* scholarship, although most of those effects have been melded into the syncretic work of Kong Ying-da.

Scholarship of the Six Dynasties period is conventionally divided into the Northern and Southern schools, which had obvious political analogs, contrasting an "austere, philologically and historically oriented style of exegesis with a scholarship that was visionary, specu-

lative, and inclined to discern hidden meanings in the text."[59] North-
ern scholarship, which traced its lineage back to Zheng Xuan, fo-
cused on problems of language and texts and yielded a new type of
commentary, the "explication" (*yi-shu*). In the explication, lexical
items were not merely glossed but also explored systematically and
thoroughly in their different aspects, such as etymology, usage, and
history; this produced wide-ranging comments and speculations that
also drew on the Southern style of scholarship. The form, in fact,
probably owes much to the influence of the Buddhist practice of
scripture explication (*jiang jing*).[60]

Kong Ying-da's *Mao shi zheng yi* was part of a huge project of
canonical scholarship begun under the sponsorship of Emperor Tai-
zong (r. 626–49). This included Yan Shi-gu's (581–645) definitive
editions (*ding ben*) of the Five Classics established and promulgated
in 633. Then in 638 a large committee, headed by Kong Ying-da,
was established to write subcommentaries for the Five Classics. This
resulted in the *Wu jing zheng yi,* of which the *Mao shi* was one. First
completed and approved in 642, it went through a series of rewrites
to reach the definitive form we now have, which was accepted by
Emperor Gao-zong (r. 649–83) in 653.[61] In his work, Kong Ying-
da sought to draw the diverging lines of scholarship found in the
voluminous and wide-ranging writings of the Six Dynasties into one
orthodox interpretation. In doing so, Kong needed a full account-
ing of all the often-conflicting materials, which led to a long, prolix
study noted for its rambling arguments. Again we can see how schol-
arship on the *Shi* mirrored the political landscape: a unified political
hegemony over China required a similar exegesis of the most impor-
tant Confucian classics; as the empire would unify a heterogeneous
and cosmopolitan population, so would the *Wu jing zheng yi*. Nomi-
nally the *Mao shi zheng yi* was written as a "subcommentary" (*shu*) to
the Mao-Zheng commentary and annotation, but it came to over-
shadow the earlier materials in its lengthy and syncretic expositions.
Steven Van Zoeren calls this the culmination of the trend that began
in the Han "to focus on texts in their 'textuality'—in their fixity and
in the details and form of their language."[62]

For the first stanza of our very simple poem, the *Mao shi zheng yi*
has a subcommentary approximately 275 graphs in length, which is
divided into two levels, separated by "nodes."[63] The first section is a
paraphrase and explication of the stanza itself; it draws the poem, the
Small Preface, and Zheng Xuan's comments into a convoluted whole:

To say [as in the Small Preface] "men of state long for the noble lord(s)" is to suppose that they are able to see him/ them. This is as if to say that beside the highroad, I my-self see the actual person of the noble lord, I would then grab hold of the cuff of the noble lord's jacket. If the noble lord were angry with me for detaining him, I would then explain to him: do not find some reason to have resent-ment and hatred for me; as for my detaining you, my reason is because Duke Zhuang did not hasten to the ways of the former lords. The logic behind referring to Duke Zhuang is to say that the Duke's not hastening to the way of the former lords is as if one does not hold the noble lords dear, which causes you to abandon them; this is why I detain you.[64]

From this small sample alone, one can see why Kong Ying-da's work might have been seemed too prolix, but this is nothing compared to the second level of annotation, which turns its atten-tion to the Mao lexical glosses, subjecting them to the rigors of the "explication" genre. These lexical annotations are explicitly keyed to the earlier Mao annotations. They draw on numerous texts—many no longer extant—to help contextualize the by-then very archaic language. As an example, this is the explication that deals just with the term "cuff" (*qu*):

The "Mourning Clothes" [chapter of the *Li ji*] says that the fore-sleeve [as the term is defined in the Mao com-mentary] is made of fabric; if a cuff is one foot (*chi*), two inches (*cun*) long, then it is a fore-sleeve. This is the base of a cuff; a cuff makes up the end of a fore-sleeve. For "Your Lamb's Wool" (120) of the "Airs of Tang," since the [Mao] *zhuan* says that the cuff is a fore-sleeve's end, then fore-sleeve and cuff are not the same. When it men-tions cuff and fore-sleeve, this is to say that the cuff and fore-sleeve both are part of the jacket sleeve; being the base and end is their only difference. Thus it uses their categorical correspondence to inform people. The "Airs of Tang" takes its significance from the [difference] between base and end, thus it says it is the fore-sleeve's end.[65]

This may be more explanation than we might think we need to understand the simple line "I caught hold of your cuff," but it illustrates the need of the *Zheng yi* to offer a full accounting of not only the poem but also the Mao glosses. Here the problem is why did Mao gloss *qu* (cuff) only as "fore-sleeve" (*mei*) for this poem when in no. 120 he clarified it as "fore-sleeve's end" (*mei mo*); the answer is that in no. 120 the difference between the two terms is part of the analogy that the commentary is drawing from the poem; thus it is significant there, but not significant here. In other words, this whole explanation is irrelevant to the poem at hand!

The *Mao shi zheng yi* also contains the phonological glosses of Lu De-ming (556–627), which have been taken from his *Jing dian shi wen* and inserted between Zheng Xuan's *jian* annotation and Kong Ying-da's *shu* subcommentary.[66] Lu's work is part of the legacy of increasing interest in phonology that emerged in the late Six Dynasties period. For our stanza the glosses include both six *fan-qie* spellings and one older *yin* homophone, applied to graphs from the poem and from the Mao *zhuan* commentary in equal proportions.[67] Such phonological glossing will remain a central part of the Tang and post-Tang exegetical tradition of the *Shi jing* and other texts.

## The Neo-Confucian Revision

The *Mao shi zheng yi* solidified—we might say ossified—the orthodoxy of the Mao-Zheng text, and in doing so created a large target for the iconoclastic scholarship of the Song dynasty (960–1260), which would establish a new, positivistic line of interpretation. In the end, this new style of interpretation would replace the Mao-Zheng orthodoxy with a new one. The object of that iconoclasm was not so much the long, tedious explication of terms, but rather the interpretations by historical contextualization that began with the Small Prefaces and continued to be filtered into all aspects of the exegesis. A famous remark by Zheng Qiao (1104–62), one of the most outspoken of these iconoclasts, sums up the frustration of the times, referring to the Small Preface's explanation that the poem "*Zhong zi*" (76) was, like our "Along the Highroad," about Duke Zhuang of Zheng, he said, "These are the words of a licentious eloper; they have nothing to do with the business of Duke Zhuang and Shu

Duan."[68] Somewhat more moderate in tone but more far-reaching in interpretational strategy was the remark by Ou-yang Xiu: "Those portions of the classics that can be understood without reference to a commentary are seven or eight parts in ten, while those that are confused and obscured by the commentaries are five or six in ten."[69] The details of the Song transformation of the *Shi jing* orthodoxy are complex, but in these two remarks by Zheng Qiao and Ou-yang Xiu are the outlines of the reforms, i.e., a suspicion of the historical contextualization of the Small Prefaces and an affirmation of the direct accessibility of the poems. This led in several critical directions, but principal to all of them was the foregrounding of the poems for direct comment and explication, with the subsequent devaluation of the intervening exegetical materials.

This new hermeneutic was interwoven with the evolution of Neo-Confucian thought that promoted the unobstructed mind's direct and deep engagement with a variety of materials, not the least being classical texts. For the *Shi jing* this was like a welcome breeze that brought the poems back to life. After centuries of ever-thickening interpretations of the *Shi,* dutifully followed by every degree candidate, the Mao-Zheng-Kong commentaries fell from favor; they seemed to have crumbled under their own weight. The range of responses in the Song dynasty to the earlier commentaries was broad, from cautious skepticism to outright dismissal, but for *Shi jing* hermeneutics (as for many other parts of the Neo-Confucian contract) the writing of Zhu Xi dominated the new interpretations; his explanations were refreshing and lucid, but not fanatically iconoclastic.

Even in its title Zhu Xi's edition of the *Shi jing* is noticeably neutral: *Shi ji zhuan* (Collected Commentary on the Songs). While Zhu Xi extracted the *Shi jing* from the hegemony of the Mao school, still he provided a "collected commentary" that also allowed room for materials from that school. This edition, which became the new textbook of the *Shi jing* and was memorized and examined as had been the *Mao shi zheng yi* before it, celebrated lucidity and promoted a study program that recommended the ease (*yi*) of the texts.[70]

Zhu Xi's entire commentary for "Along the Highroad," including *fan-qie* pronunciations and lexical glosses, is less than 115 characters; this pattern of simplicity is even more evident with other, conventionally more annotated poems. One can imagine the relief of the student who turned from the tortuous *Mao shi zheng yi* to this spare, clear text; the relief would not stop there, however. First, Zhu's

edition interpolates the *fan-qie* spellings directly into the verses them-
selves, immediately following each graph to be pronounced—these
spellings are largely repetitions of the ones used by Lu De-ming. Zhu
begins the commentary for each stanza with simple synonym glosses,
repeating a number directly from Mao but also adding his own, cre-
ating a relatively complete yet concise lexicon for the poem. For
example, he glosses even the "easy" words *gu* (old ways) and *hao*
(love). To this he adds a short paraphrase or explanation of the stanza;
here is where we find the more innovative moments of the text. Of
"Along the Highroad," he says:

> A licentious woman was abandoned by someone; upon
> the point of him leaving her, she grabbed his cuff in or-
> der to detain him and said, "Please do not hate me and
> leave; the familiar and old cannot be rejected." In a rhap-
> sody (*fu*) by Song Yu (fl. 275 B.C.), there is the line "Along
> the highroad,/ I grab hold of your cuff." These too are
> the lyrics of a love song between a man and woman.[71]

Thus the student has in a few short lines the technical apparatus to
read (and pronounce) the text, plus a succinct but clear recontextuali-
zation of the poem, which is now placed not in a frame of feudal
politics and exemplary behavior but rather in a little story of ordi-
nary people. That this poem, along with many others in the "Airs of
Zheng," has been accused of being licentious (*yin*) is closely associ-
ated with the Song critics' rereading of these poems. To the *Mao shi
zheng yi* commentators this explanation would have been a scandal-
ous interpretation of the canon. We must assume that everyone since
Zheng Xuan would have known Song Yu's use of the verses in his
rhapsody, but its context, in the "Deng Tu-zi Loves Sex Rhapsody"
(*Deng Tu-zi hao se fu*), would certainly have rendered it unaccept-
able as a gloss on the Confucian canon.[72] Zhu Xi's citation of the
Song Yu text not only implies that Song Yu's use is correct, thereby
enhancing his interpretation of "licentiousness" (*yin*), but also allows
him to draw the *Shi* into the realm of belles lettres; thus the quota-
tion of passages from the *Songs* by later writers could serve as legiti-
mate interpretations of the early, canonical materials.

While we may want to see Zhu Xi's affirmation of the licen-
tious nature of some of the poems in the *Shi jing* as a liberation from
Confucian morality, this would not be accurate. The Mao-Zheng

commentaries defused the scandalous nature of the poems by rewriting them into moral-political stories; the Neo-Confucianists, on the other hand, read these poems as negative didactic examples—the poems were licentious because they were composed during times when enlightened leadership had failed, and thus the poems were debauched. Zhu Xi therefore urged that the student not give too much attention to these negative examples: "What is the point of digging into the licentious songs of Zheng? If in one day you read five or six, that will be fine."[73] Moreover, we should remember that the majority of Zhu Xi's comments followed the standard Mao interpretations, though there was always an effort to clear away the debris of intervening commentaries and to encourage a direct engagement of the poems; he called more on the power of the subjective mind than on the interpretational layers to know the correct story. Zhu Xi also asked that the student be less concerned with reading in quantity and more concerned with reading well and thoroughly internalizing what he read. This philosophy is encapsulated in his aphorism *shao kan shou du* ("read less and recite until utterly familiar").[74] Of course, such idealism would ring hollow to the student when he came to take the imperial exam, for which he was expected to know the entire text.

Neo-Confucian thinking dominated the late imperial period, becoming more abstract and theoretical as it concentrated on self-cultivation, aesthetic appreciations, and moral rectitude. In terms of textual study, attention focused on the Four Books, which Zhu Xi had promoted as intermediate texts to the study of the classics, and less attention was paid the classics themselves.[75] A new orthodoxy came to dominate all aspects of elite culture, as seen especially in the emergence of the literati (*wen ren*) ideal during the Ming period. The subsequent fall of the Ming dynasty to the Manchus in 1644 brought much of this culture into question, whereupon aestheticism and amateur ideals of the time were criticized for fostering a weak state that was prey to the militaristic Manchus. This conventional understanding of the Ming state led to reactions in the Qing period; in literature and culture this was manifested in a *fu gu* (return to antiquity) movement that advocated the abandonment of Ming culture for earlier, particularly pre-Song standards.

Zhu Xi's promotion of the subjective engagement of the poem would be regarded with deep suspicion by the Qing textual scholars, who insisted that the inherent antiquity and difficulties of the text were addressed neither by the convoluted accounting in the *Mao shi zheng yi* nor by the naive optimism of the Neo-Confucians.

### Evidential Scholarship and the Shi jing

The Qing dynasty (1644–1911) was a golden age of textual scholarship in China. Important editions, collectanea, and studies were produced both under imperial sponsorship and in private literary circles, especially in the Jiang-nan (southeast Yangtze River) area. The emblem of the officially sanctioned scholarship was the compilation of the *Si ku quan shu* (Complete Library of the Four Treasures), in which a group of 700 state-supported scholars produced an annotated catalog of over 10,000 titles, and subsequently collated and recopied 3,593 texts (36,000 *juan*) to form an essential library of the empire.[76] In evaluating their collection, the compilers of that library relied heavily on the criteria of "evidential scholarship" (*kao-zheng*), which was the main thrust of the literary studies that arose in the private academies of the Jiang-nan area.[77] During the Qing period conditions in the southeast region of China produced phenomenal numbers of elite scholars whose talents led them toward textual studies, often in lieu of careers in the bureaucracy. Those scholars and their *kao-zheng* research wrote the final chapter in premodern history of the *Shi jing* and set the stage for modern Sinology.

The rise of evidential scholarship was in part a reaction to Ming Neo-Confucianism, which was seen as too removed from the essential aspects of thought and practice of the historical Confucius. Neo-Confucianism was accused of having been corrupted by the influence of Buddhist and Daoist thinking, especially in the form of cosmology and the "study of principles" (*li-xue*), all of which was viewed as empty speculation divorced from the Confucianism embodied in pre-Song texts. In the end, *kao-zheng* scholars would put their stock primarily in Han and pre-Han materials, earning the school the name "Han learning" (*Han xue*), as opposed to the Song learning (*Song xue*) of the Neo-Confucian scholars. These studies of Han learning took several forms, but for our purposes their work in philology is key.[78] "Evidence" for these scholars was primarily textual in nature; thus their overriding concern was language, both its referentiality and its inherent nature.

In their desire to return to an uncorrupted Confucianism, the Qing *kao-zheng* scholars studiously avoided the Four Books and returned to the Five Classics as established in the Han dynasty. Each of these classic texts posed different problems, but all these problems fell under the general concern of authenticity and the call for evidence. They sought this evidence in the oldest layers of the textual tradition, placing the highest value on Han and pre-Han materials. The further one moved from the time of the classic, the more suspect evidence became; speculations by Song scholars were generally dismissed completely. Not only should there be evidence, they believed, but evidence should also be cumulative and always cited in full to support a position. Song scholars were commonly faulted for their lack of sources or for basing their arguments on an isolated piece of evidence. In the Qing dynasty this search for evidence was supported by a rich culture of bibliography and printing, which allowed a wide range of scholars access to substantial collections of materials and provided opportunities of productive interaction.

The application of these methods brought numerous revelations in textual studies. Most important was Yan Ruo-ju's (1636–1704) investigation into the authenticity of the *Shu jing* (Book of Documents), which was considered the oldest text of historical writings. By comparing its passages with those from other, often noncanonical texts; by ferreting out chronological and logical inconsistencies; and by compiling statistical evidence, Yan proved that certain chapters in the standard *Shu jing* were later forgeries added to authentic pre-Han materials. Moreover, since among these forged chapters there were passages that the Neo-Confucianists had relied on to support their philosophic positions, Yan's arguments had wide-ranging implications in the debate over Confucian doctrine.[79]

Yan Ruo-ju's work inspired other analyses of the classics, including those of the *Shi jing.* Liang Qi-chao, for example, offers this evaluation of one such work:

> Wei Yuan (1794–1856) wrote *Shi gu wei* (The Ancient Hidden Meanings of the Songs), launching his major attack on the Mao Commentary and the Great and Small Prefaces, which he said were forgeries of a later origin. His arguments were erudite and convincing, like Yan Ruo-ju's elucidation of the *Book of Documents,* and he sometimes advanced new interpretations also. He argued

that poetry was not written to praise and blame [as advocated by the Mao Prefaces]: "It is certainly true that praise and blame are the order of the day with the Mao school . . . but the poet describes his emotions and stops when they are expressed. . . . How can there be genuine joy, sorrow, and happiness for subjects which require no emotion [as implied in praise and blame criticism]." This view has a deep affinity to the "art for art's sake" approach, and, in fact, breaks the fetters that had bound literature for the previous two thousand years.[80]

Considering Zhu Xi's original role in questioning the readings of the Mao prefaces, we can see Wei Yuan's position as a refinement of the Neo-Confucian view of the text, providing the next logical step in divorcing the poems from any exemplary contextualization (positive or negative) and placing the *Shi jing* in the mainstream of Chinese poetics, which emphasizes the expressive nature of art. As we shall see below, this emphasis ultimately derives from certain passages of the Great Preface itself, and Wei's description of the poet's emotion foreshadows our modern understanding of the *Shi jing*.

From Liang Qi-chao's description of Wei Yuan's work, one might get the impression that the basic arguments in Zhu Xi's *Shi ji zhuan* fared relatively well in Qing *kao-zheng* studies. That is not true. While certain critics, such as Yao Ji-heng,[81] directly attacked Zhu Xi, most new studies and editions of the *Shi jing* ignored Zhu Xi's text, reviving direct consideration of the Mao–Zheng annotations as better evidence for the meaning of the poems. This can be seen, for example, in two of the most important editions, Chen Huan's (1786–1863) *Shi Mao-shi zhuan shu* and Ma Rui-chen's (fl. 1850) *Mao shi zhuan jian tong shi,* both of which clearly affirm the Mao–Zheng commentary as their initial point of reference. They bring to the discussion of that commentary textual evidence cited from an array of early sources ranging from the canonical to the popular. Bernhard Karlgren has summarized the nature and importance of the *kao-zheng* scholars' work on the *Shi jing*:

Their great achievement concerned, above all, the interpretation of difficult words and phrases on the one hand, and variant readings (different versions) on the other. With indefatigable enthusiasm they traced and adduced all early

testimonies in the pre-Han and Han sources, rightly con-
vinced that the true meanings could never be guessed at,
in the fashion of Zhu Xi and his followers, at random,
but must be established through research into the earliest
texts, dictionaries, and commentaries, written at a time
not too far distant from that of the Shi poets, a time when
many a word which in Tang and Song time was entirely
obsolete was still a current colloquial word; or, at least, a
time when there was still a living and unbroken tradition
from Zhou time as to the meaning of unusual words and
phrases.[82]

We can see this, for example, in Chen Huan's treatment of "Along
the Highway," with his extended annotations on words and terms
deriving from both the poem and the Mao commentary. Chen cites
numerous sources, both those from the pre-Han period (Shang shu,
Er ya, and other poems in the Shi jing,) and those from early impe-
rial period (Shuo-wen, Wen xuan, and Lu De-ming's Jing dian shi wen).
As a sample, these are the opening lines of his subcommentary to the
Mao glosses:

The graphs "along" [zun] and "beside" [xun] had a simi-
lar pronunciation; therefore they were used as a gloss [in
the Mao commentary]. In the "Hong fan" [chapter of the
Shang shu] "Along the royal way" is also written "Along
the royal road." This shows that "road" [lu] and "way"
[dao] are the same.[83]

And this is just the beginning in Chen's systematic treatment of nearly
every gloss in the Mao commentary, supported by ample citation of
evidence, particularly from the Shuo-wen jie-zi dictionary of c. 100
A.D. Ma Rui-chen's comments are even more extensive (nearly nine
hundred graphs long), drawing on a even broader range of sources,
including the Yi jing; Meng zi; the Han, Lu, and Qi schools of Shi
commentary; and the later dictionaries Yu pian and Guang ya. Ma
pursues each gloss he raises with a vengeance, even when there is
little doubt about the meaning of the term; his discussion of the shan
graph ("caught hold") occupies a third of his commentary.

  Despite the objections of scholars such as Wei Yuan and Yao
Ji-heng, the kao-zheng scholars' renewed attention to the Han com-

mentaries often carried with it renewed credence for the Mao prefaces as well, thus eclipsing the radical rereading of some poems that arose in the Song period. Karlgren describes and laments this process:

> Unfortunately that same fusion of the Mao Commentary and the Wei Hong [Small] Preface . . . which had led Zhu Xi astray as to the value of the Mao commentary,[84] now entailed a similar fateful result in the works of the Qing scholars. Indignant at the arbitrary guesses and the lack of philological method and stringency of the Song school (Zhu Xi), they made it their aim to revert to the Han scholars—but while reinstating the Mao commentary and the Han, Lu, and Qi variants and glosses in their proper place, . . . they reestablished the moralizing scholastic construction of the *general purport of each ode,* such as it was expressed sometimes in the Mao, Han, Lu, and Qi commentaries, but above all in the Wei Hong preface.[85]

This can be seen clearly in Chen Huan's edition, which cites the Small Preface in full for each of the poems; for our poem Chen concludes his commentary with this paraphrase of the preface: "This is therefore a criticism of Duke Zhuang who lost the proper way and was unable to employ the noble lords, thus the noble lords left him and could not be retained."[86]

While there were spirited attacks during the Qing period on the Neo-Confucian understanding of the classics, Zhu Xi's *Shi ji zhuan* remained the "textbook" edition of the *Shi jing,* a position that it still holds to some extent today, despite the attacks of modern scholars such as Bernhard Karlgren. The reasons for that are not hard to understand. First of all, the hold of Neo-Confucian thought on the orthodox, bureaucratic world of Qing China was slow to loosen, and *kao-zheng* scholarship of the *Shi* had developed relatively late; thus imperial exams remained focused on the older editions. Moreover, for all their rigor and accuracy, the *kao-zheng* commentaries are extremely tedious affairs, often including long comments and citations on relatively simple issues—for example, that *shan* means "caught hold." A student preparing for an imperial exam seldom needed those details, but rather looked for a concise and reliable gloss; handy textbooks were not something that interested the *kao-zheng* scholars.[87] Thus Zhu Xi's text and its modern derivations remained the most common voices in the training of young scholars, including those who went on to the rigors of *kao-zheng* studies and modern philology.[88]

The central importance of the *Shi jing* poems to *kao-zheng* studies was not so much in the debate of their authenticity or meaning, but rather as their evidentiary role in the emergence of a subdiscipline of phonology. Pre-Qing commentators on the *Shi jing* were often perplexed by the "irregular" rhymes found in the poems, which led to some arbitrary graph substitutions to make the poems fit the established rhyme; Zhu Xi was accused of this practice.[89] Behind this problem lie two important phenomena. First, since the poems emerged from an environment of secondary orality (as songs), they were originally written down in graphs that were used for their sound value with little regard to semantic class—what are usually called loan graphs. In later times, with a more textual culture, these homophones would be distinguished by separate graphs; much of the early commentary was devoted to establishing those distinctions. Second, the diachronic shift in pronunciations was uneven; early homophones and words of a shared rhyme diverged with the passing centuries, so that graphs that would have rhymed at one time no longer did.

The *kao-zheng* phonologists attacked this problem. Building on Tang dynasty rhyme tables and earlier dictionaries (some with *fan-qie* spellings), they used the rhyme words in the *Shi jing* as their primary evidence of an even earlier pronunciation to establish patterns of rhyming, delineating the so-called early rhyme groups. This in turn allowed them to scrutinize graph substitutions in the commentaries to see whether they fit the earlier phonological patterns or belied belated pronunciations of the commentator. These studies laid the groundwork for modern phonological studies, particularly those of Bernhard Karlgren, who brought modern comparative philology to bear on the very difficult subject of Chinese language. The most important aspects of Karlgren's work were 1) to refine and supply phonetic value to the rhyme categories (i.e., finals) discussed in earlier works, and 2) to establish the phonetic value of initial consonants. Karlgren's research, along with the discovery of the oracle-bone texts at the beginning of the century, redefined our understanding of Chinese language and led to his rigorous and extensive glosses on the *Shi jing* itself. All subsequent studies of the *Shi jing,* in China and the West, take Karlgren as their point of departure.[90]

## The Poetics of the Great Preface

In addition to the Small Prefaces and the first layer of lexical anno-
tation and commentary, the original *Mao shi* was also accompanied
by the Great Preface (*Da xu*), perhaps the most influential essay on
traditional Chinese poetics. There is some disagreement of the actual
form of the Great Preface and its relationship to the first Small Pref-
ace (i.e., to "The Ospreys Cry"), but here I will treat the entire
document, including the comments on that first, important poem.[91]
Nor is there agreement on the degree of coherence of materials that
make up the Great Preface; some see it as a collection of only loosely
related comments, while others see a more integrated agenda. Haun
Saussy, who seeks integration, describes the variety of issues in the
Preface:

> In the space of a few lines, the Great Preface manages to
> put forth a psychological-expressive theory of art, a state-
> ment of the civilizing influence of art on the community,
> a plea for the special political status of the poet, a typol-
> ogy of genres and figural modes, an outline of literary
> history, a categorization of valid and decadent art, and a
> suggestion that doubtful poems must be interpreted ironi-
> cally (or allegorically, when content and not tone is at
> issue): lapidary answers to most of the questions posed by
> literary criticism and aesthetic theory.[92]

Lapidary these answers may be, but they are also maddeningly elu-
sive. There is, moreover, the question of the authorship of the Great
Preface; traditionally attributed (like the Small Preface) to Confucius'
disciple Zi-xia, it too was later attributed to Wei Hong, first century
A.D. Stephen Owen suggests, however, that the Great Preface is not
a composition in the sense of an individually authored piece, but rather
a "loose synthesis of shared 'truths' about the *Book of Songs,* truths which
were the common possession of traditionalists (whom we now call
'Confucians') in the Warring States and Western Han periods."[93]
Whether inherently cohesive or not, the Great Preface does articulate
a number of basic principles of Chinese poetics that become a con-
stant source of inspiration and debate in the following centuries; this is
especially true for its "psychological-expressive theory of art."

Since there are already three full treatments of the Great Preface in recent studies in English, I will not attempt a detailed accounting of all its passages here, but instead will remark only on the most salient lines.[94] The preface is conventionally divided into twenty-one sections:

1. "The Ospreys Cry" is the virtue of the queen.

This opening line reads exactly as if it were the upper part of the Small Preface for the first poem. In the subcommentaries the queen will be designated as the consort of King Wen of Zhou.

2. This is the beginning of *feng,* and it is the means by which the empire is swayed and the relationship between husband and wife is corrected. Thus it is used among village folk, and it is used among feudal states.
3. *Feng* means to sway, to teach. With suasion it moves them, with teaching it transforms them.

These two statements perhaps should be read as the lower part of the Small Preface. In any event, the key term here *is feng,* which is used in several ways. First, there is the self-evident truth that "The Ospreys Cry" is the beginning of the "Airs" (*feng*). Second, the term is also used as a pun with the sense of "influence" or "suasion," deriving from the common metaphor that the ruler influences his people just as the wind blows the grasses—hence my translation "sway." This in turn leads to the extended meaning of the first line: that is, "The Ospreys Cry" is also the beginning of the moral suasion of the *Shi,* which is essential to the Confucian understanding of the poems. This is all further clarified in section 3 with the identification of *feng* with *jiao* (to teach), and finally with *hua* (to transform). The assumption that poetry has the power to influence (both morally and politically) is pervasive in traditional Chinese poetics. We will meet *feng* again below in sections 10 and 15.

4. The poem (*shi*) is where intention (*zhi*) goes. While it is within one's heart it is intention; when it comes out in words it is a poem.

According to Zhu Xi, this section marks the beginning of the Great Preface. The opening statement is a reformulation of the earlier definition *shi yan zhi* (poetry [puts into] words intention), which is perhaps the most often-cited maxim of traditional Chinese poetics.[95] This near identity between poem (*shi*) and intention (*zhi*), between the inner heart (*xin*) and the outer words (*yan*) grounds much of later hermeneutics on Chinese poetry, especially when it develops into the assumed autobiographical nature of the lyric poem. For the *Shi jing* the identity of *zhi* and *shi* becomes interwoven with the power and result of the suasive nature of the poems. Poetry both reflects and manifests intention; it is both a window on the heart and a tool for its transformation. The term *zhi*, whose meaning oscillates between moral intent and worldly ambition, has been long discussed by critics as they wonder where exactly is intention to be found and how can it be accurately read. Presumably one purpose of the Small Preface was to establish the intent of the poems; Haun Saussy's work is particularly concerned with the nature of *zhi* in the *Shi jing* poetics; he wants to locate intention beyond the "composition" of the poem and posit it in its exemplary application.

> 5. When emotion stirs within, they take form in words. But if words are inadequate, then one expresses them in sighs. If sighs are inadequate, then one expresses them in singing. If singing is inadequate, then one quite unconsciously moves the hands in dance and stamps the feet in rhythm.

This formulation draws much on the musicology of the age; here it is singing (*ge*), not poems, that are the ultimate verbalization, and even it is finally overshadowed by mime and dance.[96] What the two different formulations of artistic production in sections 4 and 5 do share is a sense of the spontaneity of art; in the first case it is the inner drive (*zhi*) to which poems give voice, here the feelings (*qing*) burst through into different manifestations, ending in unconscious movement. The authentic spontaneity of poetry, as a criteria for genuineness of expression, will also become an underlying principal of Chinese poetics; artifice and fictionality are consistently dismissed in the promotion of the historical and/or biographical grounding of poems.

> 6. Emotion comes forth in sound, but when that sound is patterned, then we call this the musical tones (*yin*).
> 7. The tones of a well-managed age are peaceful and full of

joy; its governance is harmonious. The tones of an age of tur-
moil are resentful and full of anger; its governance is perverse.
The tones of a ruined state are grievous and full of longing; its
people are in distress.

This is a continuation of the analogies of emotion and music, but
the most significant point here is the clarification that music not only
manifests what is in a person's heart but actually can be a barometer
of social-political conditions. This leads to (or from) the interpreta-
tions of the Small Prefaces, where the success and failure of govern-
ment can be seen in poems whose topics are seemingly quite divorced
from politics, ranging from the supposed revelation of the general
high moral quality of King Wen to the poor choices in consorts and
entertainment of King You. Here too we find the logic in the refer-
ences to the collection of "songs from village lanes," whereby the
ruler is to be able to gauge the efficacy of his rule, not through songs
of explicit praise or blame but rather through poetry as a bellwether
of communal health.

> 8. Therefore, in rectifying gain and loss, moving heaven and
> earth, affecting ghosts and spirits, nothing approaches poetry.
> 9. The former kings used this to set a standard for husband and
> wife, to perfect filial piety and respect, to enhance human rela-
> tionships, to beautify the teachings and transformations, and to
> change the customs and habits.

These passages offer the reverse formula of the suasive power of
poetry. Not only does poetry inevitably reveal the times, it is also a
tool for correcting the times, first in matters of the spirit and then in
the matters of men. We should note that the term *feng* appears again
here in the sense of "customs," which becomes another gloss for the
genre: the airs are related to the customs of the folk.

> 10. Thus there are the six principles of poetry: the Airs (*feng*),
> expositions (*fu*), comparisons (*bi*), stimulus (*xing*), the Odes (*ya*),
> and the Hymns (*song*).

This apparently simple list of six principles, elsewhere called the
six types of poetry (*liu shi*), has nearly paralyzed discussions in Chi-
nese poetics, both ancient and modern. Three of the six seem self-

explanatory—they are the sections of the *Shi jing* that have been known at least since the story of Ducal Son Ji Zha's visit to Lu in 543 B.C. The other three terms are of modes of poetic composition. Why the list of three "genres" are divided by the three modes is a mystery and the cause of some consternation, but let us not dwell on that here. We have already encountered the term *feng* above, and there will be more to say below. *Ya* is generally understood as a term for "elegance" or as a reference to the civilization of the north China central plain, cognate with *xia* (often translated as "China"). In either case it designates a sense of heightened culture, perhaps associated with the music of the royal Zhou court. *Song* means to praise, as clearly it is used here, but Ruan Yuan has also glossed it as *rong* (countenance), associating it with ritual performance and dance; this leads to C. H. Wang's discussion of the countenance of the Zhou.[97]

The terms *fu bi xing* (in that order) have become nearly a single item referring to Chinese poetic composition. *Fu* has a rich history as a literary term, but here it refers to straight mimetic representation without figural speech, often translated "narration" or "exposition"; the poem "Along the Highroad" is an example of *fu*.[98] *Bi* means "comparison" and as a mode of presentation is often labeled "simile and metaphor": that is, figures of comparison where similarity is seen in difference, as in "Tossed is that cypress boat,/ Wave-tossed it floats./ My heart is in turmoil, I cannot sleep" (26). *Xing* is, however, the pièce de résistance of early Chinese poetics, leading to numerous essays and conclusions, many of them reviewed and evaluated in Pauline Yu's recent work on imagery in Chinese poetry.[99] *Xing* (stimulus, evocative image, allusion) is usually seen as an image of a natural object employed at the head of a poem or stanza when the relationship between the image and the topic of the poem or stanza is vague or open-ended; that is, when it is neither directly related to the scene (*fu*) nor part of an explicit comparison (*bi*). The basic meaning of the word *xing* (to rise up, to stir) has induced critics to focus as much on the affective power of the image (to cause an emotion to stir in the reader) as on this more formal aspect.

The prominence of *xing* results directly from the early use of the term by the Mao commentary to designate certain poems as *xing*-based (*xing ye*, heading the *zhuan* commentary); this in turn led Zhu Xi to give either a *fu, bi,* or *xing* designation to all the poems. A quick review of the comments of Mao and Zhu Xi will reveal that the mere designation of *xing* is very difficult to determine; its subsequent reading is no easier. The most often cited example of *xing* is the opening stanza of the first poem of the collection, which has been thoroughly explicated by Yu, Van Zoeren, and Saussy. As another example, I might suggest the opening stanza of "Magpie's Nest" (12):

> Now the magpie has a nest,
> But the cuckoo lived in it.
> Here comes a girl to be married;
> With a hundred coaches we'll meet her.

As with poem no. 1, we here have what appears to be a correspondence of bird and bride, but Stephen Owen has effectively exposed the difficulty of bringing that apparent analogy to a satisfying completion.[100] In fact, the inherent difficulty in bringing coherence to the relationship between image and referent is often the telling sign of a *xing* composition.

We should remember that Chen Shih-hsiang regarded *xing* as the essential character of the *Shi,* linking it finally to the "uplifting dances" of primitive communal life. C. H. Wang, on the other hand, suggested a formal relationship between *xing* and the incremental repetitions of orally composed verse. Finally, Stephen Owen has suggested that the *xing* image might be a device to set the rhyme for the poem or stanza; thus its function would be almost entirely formal and related to oral performance.[101]

> 11. Superiors use *feng* to transform those below; and those below use *feng* to criticize their superiors. Tempering their remonstrations with patterns of eloquence (*wen*), those who speak have no blame, but those who hear them are able to take warning. Therefore this is called *feng.*

Here the term *feng* is used in its homophonic sense "to critique" (now written with a "word radical"); this too will become one of the common glosses for the term. The extended discussion of *feng* suggests the concern early Confucians had with the inclusion of these poems in the collection, thus their incessant apologia.

> 12. When it came about that the royal Way declined, then ritual and righteousness were abandoned, governmental teaching was lost, the states changed their governance, and families altered

their customs. And with that arose the mutated (*bian*) Airs and mutated Odes.

The term *bian* (changed, mutated) was perhaps first a description of altered musical tones, implying the use of intervals (such as sharps and flats) between the notes of the orthodox (*ya*) pentatonic scale; such music was considered too elaborate (*xi*) and thus decadent.[102] Like other early musical associations of the songs that were transposed by inference to the texts, *bian* here is assumed to refer to the content of the song-texts. The outlines of this argument were adopted by critics who rationalized the editorship of Confucius, or at least the high moral ground of the text. Thus, when Zhu Xi declared that certain poems were licentious, he was able to justify their inclusion on the basis of negative example: the singer may have had licentiousness in his heart, but the editor included the poem only as a example of how bad government leads to such decadent art, from which the reader could then be instructed.

> 13. The state historians could clearly see the signs of gain and loss; thus they were pained by the abandonment of human relations and grieved by the cruelty of laws and governance. Thereupon they put feelings into song in order to sway their superiors. 14. They became aware how affairs had mutated and they longed for their old customs. Thus, the mutated Airs emerged from feelings, but still they stayed within the bounds of ritual and righteousness. That they emerged from feelings is because of the nature of people; that they stayed within the bounds of ritual and righteousness is by the grace of the former kings.

Revealing the pastiche nature of this preface, sections 13 and 14 introduce the role of the state historians (*guo shi*) in bringing the mutated airs to the court. In this discussion we sense a reference to the mechanism by which the songs became part of the states' archives and also an accounting for the layers of folk composition (from feelings) and elite editing (for ritual and righteousness) that lie behind speculations about the nature of the text. Yet the difficulty of this formulation is the implication that the historians were the actual authors of the airs, not the recorders and rectifiers (as their title would seem to imply) of the emotive songs of others.

15. Thus when the affairs of one state are embodied in the experience of a person, this is called a *feng* (air). But when they speak of the affairs of the entire empire or the customs (*feng*) of the four quarters, this is called a *ya* (ode).

16. The Odes are corrective; they speak of the means by which royal governments rise and fall. In governing there are both minor and major events; thus among these we have both the Minor and Major Odes.

17. The Hymns (*song*) praise the form and countenance of splendid virtue, and with these our achievements are told to the spirits.

18. These are the four beginnings; they are the perfection of the songs.

This series of statements form a coherent description of the four divisions of the *Shi jing*. Granted these are probably ex post facto descriptions by which the writer attempted to account for an inherited collection and order, rather than a contemporaneous rationale. Nonetheless, they articulate the earliest integrated statement of this sort and are the source (along with other passages above) of many later descriptions on the text. As described, the four divisions trace an expanding spiral of political power. Beginning with the concerns (*ben*) of a single person (*yi ren*) of a single feudal state (*yi guo*), each section widens its frame of reference to the empire (*tian-xia*)—that is, all the lands under Zhou feudal control; the four quarters (*si-fang*), including those regions with which the Zhou only had contact, such as the barbarian enemy, the Xian-yun; and finally the world beyond of deceased ancestors and spirits to whom the "Hymns" present the worldly glory of the Zhou. Note that the "Odes" are given special attention, including a lexical gloss (*song-zhe zheng ye*—the term "ode" means correct). The distinction between the minor and major odes is vaguely formed, but from the context we should probably understand this as a difference in the centrality of the political events described—thus my simple delineation above between the clan gathering and the royal legends.

The final remark on the ultimate "four beginnings," forming what is commonly assumed to be the conclusion of the Great Preface and echoing section 2, would be enigmatic without the clarification in the *Shi ji* (quoted above) where the term refers to the opening poems of the four sections, suggesting that they are the ultimate embodiments of the spirit of each section that they head.

19. The transformative power in the poems from "The Ospreys Cry" (1) to "Unicorn's Hoofs" (11) derives from the suasion of the king. Therefore these poems are associated with the Duke of Zhou. That they are called "Southerns" (*nan*) is because this transformative power proceeded from the north to the south. The virtue in the poems from "Magpie's Nest" (12) to "The Zuo-yu" (25) derives from the suasion of the feudal lords, which resulted from the teachings of the former kings; thus they are associated with the Duke of Shao.

20. The *Zhou nan* and *Shao nan* are the way of the correct beginning; they are the basis of the transformative power of the king.

By most accounts these passages regarding the special nature of the first two sets of poems in the collection (the pairs of poems named are the beginning and end of those sets) are not part of the Great Preface. They are important in reinforcing the alleged provenance of the poems, from the two ducal states of the Zhou royal family: the Duke of Zhou was the brother of King Wu and the sagely regent to young King Cheng; the Duke of Shao was Wu's half brother. The Duke of Zhou, through the promotion of the Confucian school, became a paragon of virtue in late classical and early imperial China, thereby adding additional weight to the first set of poems. Here we have another use of "beginning" to mark that special transformative quality.

21. Thus in "The Ospreys Cry" there is joy at finding a good girl to marry off to the lord and there is concern that the worthy ones be promoted; yet still there is no abandon in her beauty. There is grief in her seclusion, concern for her talent, but no harm to the goodness of her heart. This is the significance of "The Ospreys Cry."

Clearly this reads as the lower part of the Small Preface to "The Ospreys Cry." It provides an illustration of the transformative power of the *Zhou nan* poems and closes the frame on the Great Preface with a reiteration of the opening sections.

## Conclusion

As we have seen, the literary history of the *Shi jing* is long and complex, but from its multidimensionality we might draw certain constants that characterize the essential nature of the text and its history (see figure 1).

Foremost among those constants is the stability and integrity of the text itself. While the *Shi* in its earliest manifestations certainly was fluid and open, existing in a pretextual culture of formulaic composition and secondary oral performance environments, nonetheless, from the very earliest known sources we have references and quotations (to both the general shape and specific songs of the text) that we clearly recognize in the extant *Mao shi*. And once we enter the more text-based environments of the late Warring States period when its musicality was diminished, the *Shi jing* seems firm and enduring, as even attested by the recent archaeological discoveries (see note 19). Chinese literary history is known for its preservation of works and documents, but the integrity of the *Shi jing* is remarkable even within that tradition. Most critics have agreed it is a text whose formation begins around the sixth century B.C., preserving materials of early times in a form that betrays its complex political and social origins in the middle classical period.[103]

Yet even when the text became fixed and doctrinal (Van Zoeren's "strong text"), it retained something of its fluidity in the complexity of its form and the indeterminacy of the individual poems. This then led to a highly interpretative, ever-deepening exegetical tradition, a tradition of three major hermeneutic shifts, each addressing that indeterminacy in different ways. First, was the Mao-Zheng-Kong commentaries that read the poems as texts embedded in an exemplary moral-political order of elite culture—readings begun by the Small Prefaces and their elaboration. Next, the Neo-Confucian school, synthesized by Zhu Xi's *Shi ji zhuan,* rejected the elite orientation of the *feng* texts, suggesting they were "songs of village lanes"; his exegesis leads finally to the anthropological interpretations of the early twentieth century. Last, Qing evidential scholarship that criticized Zhu Xi's lack of philological rigor and returned to the Han lexical tradition was relatively neutral on larger interpretive schemes but passively re-established the readings of the Small Prefaces. Contemporary scholarship often combines these two methods, embracing the Han lexical annotations but rejecting the Small Prefaces in lieu of the more literary readings of the poems.[104]

The legacy of the *Shi jing* in Chinese culture is obviously pervasive, ranging from topics on the imperial exams to contemporary four-character aphorisms; but perhaps its greatest influence has been in determing how poetry, even all serious literature, was read in

| DATE | TEXT EVENT | COMMENT |
|---|---|---|
| 543 B.C. | Performance of Zhou music for Ducal Son Ji Zha of Wu | *Zuo zhuan* 29.13; includes comments on all sections of *Shi jing*, including "Airs of the States," but no poems |
| c. 200 B.C. | Xun zi declares *Shi* a classic (*jing*) | *Shi* is part of pedagogical program of early Confucians, including Meng-zi |
| 165 B.C. | Terminal date for Fu-yang text | Unearthed in 1977; 170 wood slips, with poems largely identifiable in *Mao shi* |
| c. 150 B.C. | Mao commentary (*zhuan*) | Attributed to Mao Chang; beginning of lexical annotation |
| 1st cent. A.D. | Mao Prefaces | Oldest layer attributed to Zi-xia, latter part to Mao; now considered to be by Wei Hong |
| c. 175 | Zheng Xuan (127–200) annotation (*jian*) | Helps establish *Mao shi* as dominant text |
| 6th cent. | Lu De-ming (556–627), *Jing dian shi wen* | Phonetic glosses incorporated into Mao text |
| 633 | Definitive editions of Five Classics established | Yan Shi-gu (581–645) |
| 641 | Kong Ying-da (574–648) *Mao shi zheng yi* completed | Revised, final version accepted in 652, orthodox version for Tang-Song period |
| 12th cent. | Zhu Xi (1130–1200), *Shi ji zhuan* | Challenges much of authority of Mao Prefaces, discusses the licentious poems (*yin shi*) |
| 1312 | *Shi ji zhuan* accepted as official text for examinations | Will hold this position for the duration |
| 1705 | Yao Ji-heng, *Shi jing tong lun* | Preface dated 1705, published 1836, highly skeptical commentary in textbook style |
| 1847 | Chen Huan (1786–1863), *Shi Mao shi zhuan shu* | Example of *kao-zheng* scholarship, includes the Mao Prefaces as part of text |
| c. 1889 | Ma Rui-chen, *Mao shi zhuan jian tong shi* | Most detailed *kao-zheng* treatment of *Mao shi*, published c. 1889 |

FIGURE 1: Chronology of Text Events in the Literary History of the *Shi jing*

China. Following the dictate of *shi yan zhi* (poetry puts intent into words) and its related formulations of the psychological-expressive theory of literature, poetry in China was seen not as the mirror of the deeds of men but rather as windows into their inner lives. The songs of the *Shi jing* were the first of those windows, looking in on the highly disguised inner life of King Wen's royal consort, or the inner life that informed the ad hoc application of the poem to a political argument, or that of the common folk who sang in "village lanes." In the main literary tradition, this produced a nearly chronic lyricism; even when the external world was the subject of literature— from poems on objects, to rhapsodies (*fu*) on the imperial hunt, to the biographies of great men—that external world was still seen as an omen of an inner one. When the Chinese readers turned to poetry they expected a perspicuity of language, an imagery of categorical correspondences, and a grounding in the mundane world; but in those they also found, or at least hoped to find, the intent (*zhi*) or feelings (*qing*) of the author. They read to feel those emotions, to know the man who wrote about them. It is this "way to read" (*du fa*) rather than a way to write that is the true literary legacy of the *Shi jing*.

JOSEPH R. ALLEN
*University of Minnesota, Twin Cities*
2000

## Notes to the Postface

1. Sources referred to in this essay are abbreviated if they appear in the bibliography; sources that do not appear in the bibliography—including all Chinese texts—are cited in full on their first occurrence.

2. There are a number of valuable encyclopedia entries on the *Shi jing*, such as those by C. H. Wang (*Indiana Companion*), Pauline Yu (*Masterworks of Asian Literature*), and Michael Loewe (*Early Chinese Texts*). Because of the context of their respective essays, Wang's is brief and relatively conservative, Yu's is comparative and pedagogical, and Loewe's has detailed technical and bibliographic information. I have drawn on these and other sources cited throughout this essay but have not been able to acknowledge that debt in every instance.

3. This work is best summarized in Albert B. Lord's *The Singer of Tales* (Cambridge, MA: Harvard University Press, 1960).

4. C. H. Wang, *The Bell*, p. x. Needless to say, the methodology and theory of oral formulation is complex and many faceted. Wang not only transposed this methodology to a disassociated literary tradition but also used it to ana-

lyze lyric rather than narrative composition, which stirred some controversy and challenges.

5. Wang insists on the characterization of "formulaic" and eschews all others. He has recently restated his case in "Oral, Folk, and an Unwanted Feud." For his thoughts on the transitional period, see *The Bell*, p. 29.

6. Zhu Xi, *Shi ji zhuan* (Taipei: Zhong-hua shu-ju, 1977), Preface, p. 2. Translation adapted from Steven Van Zoeren, pp. 228–29. As Van Zoeren points out, these thoughts ultimately derive from a passage in the *Han shu*, which I cite in my following discussion of the origins of the text. The actual language and conception of Zhu Xi's remark seems to echo, however, Shen Yue's description of Han dynasty *xiang-he* songs; see my *In the Voice of Others: Chinese Music Bureau Poetry* (Ann Arbor: Center for Chinese Studies, University of Michigan, 1992), p. 50.

7. Marcel Granet, *Fêtes et chanson anciennes de la Chine*. Granet has sometimes been accused of overzealously interpreting poems to meet his theory; for example see Bernhard Karlgren, *Glosses,* p. 75.

8. There is no general study of the "Airs," but the numerous essays collected in *Gu shi bian* (rpt. Taipei: 1970), vol. 3, use this conception and methodology, sometimes in a relatively casual manner. Most rigorous and extended is the work by Wen Yi-duo, who was well-versed in anthropological concepts; his speculations on totem figures are especially interesting; see his "*Feng shi lei chao*" in vol. 4 and various essays in vol. 1 of his collected works, *Wen Yi-duo quan ji* (Taipei: Kai-ming shu-dian, 1946). A review of Wen's myth study is available in my "The Myth Studies of Wen I-to: A Question of Methodology," *Tamkang Review* 8.2 (1982): 137–60.

9. Zhu Xi, Preface, p. 2. I understand the term *cheng Zhou* of the first line as a verbal phrase ("when Zhou reached completion") and not as the common term for the eastern capital; it seems unlikely Zhu Xi would have associated these materials with the disparaged Eastern Zhou.

10. Walter Ong, *Orality and Literacy: The Technologizing of the Word* (New York: Methuen, 1982). I am obviously oversimplifying Ong's arguments, which are subtle and far-ranging, including the discussion of secondary orality in contemporary modern society. He does occasionally speak of things Chinese, but not to the issues at hand.

11. This, of course, would also have been one of the most likely places where bronzeware texts would have been seen, if not read.

12. Edward Shaughnessy, "From Liturgy to Literature," *Before Confucius,* pp. 174–95; he works closely with the material of Fu Si-nian.

13. C. H. Wang, "Drama" in *From Ritual,* p. 51. One should also see his chapter "Ritual" in the same volume, or its original version, "The Countenance of Chou" (see note 97, below), which addresses a good deal of the same material. He cites the work of Wang Guo-wei and Wen Yi-duo.

14. Wang is following numerous earlier studies, whose references are found in the essays in *Gu shi bian*, vol. 3, and Wen Yi-duo, vol. 1. The three editions

of Arthur Waley's *The Book of Songs* include a short essay on the *wan* dance, pp. 338–40.

15. Chow Tse-tsung, p. 207.

16. Chen Shih-hsiang, p. 26, et passim. Chen writes much in the spirit of the early comparative anthropologists, although his work is primarily textual, especially in comparative folklore. The term "uplifting" (which is the primary meaning of *xing*) is borrowed from a study of European folklore by Sir Edmund K. Chambers.

17. Laurence Picken, p. 89, suggests that there was group singing of "The Airs of the States" and "The Minor Odes" at provincial banquets, which would certainly have been a middle ground in this range of performance environments. He derives his thoughts from a comment by Zhu Xi, so it is hardly solid proof; we do note the importance of the banquet (and presumably accompanying songs) in the *Shi jing* itself.

18. Steven Van Zoeren (p. 7) dates this terminology to use in the *Xun zi* of the third century B.C. Qu Wan-li, *Shi jing shi yi* (Taipei: Zhong-hua wen-hua, 1958), Introduction, pp. 1–3, has a detailed account of the names for the text; he dates the name *Shi jing* to the late Warring States period, i.e., third century B.C.

19. Descriptions of early writing materials can be found in Tsuen-hsiun Tsien's *Written on Bamboo and Silk: The Beginnings of Chinese Books and Inscriptions* (Chicago: University of Chicago Press, 1962). Recently approximately 170 wooden slips from a *Shi jing* text dating at least from 165 B.C. were unearthed in Anhui province; see Hu Ping-sheng and Han Zi-chang, *Fu-yang Han-jian* Shi jing *yan-jiu* (Shanghai: Shanghai gu-ji chu-ban she, 1988).

20. The various script forms (roughly analogous to different forms of the alphabet) of the Zhou period all seem to transcribe one "Chinese" language, although the problem of possible dialects is difficult to resolve.

21. Again we should be aware of the dangers of anachronistic evidence; for example, the mentality of the Han period, with its preoccupation with texts and writing, was light-years removed from the middle Zhou period.

22. See Van Zoeren's discussion of these two passages and a Tang dynasty text that links them, p. 149.

23. *Han shu* (Beijing: Zhong-hua, 1962), p. 1123. Compare C. H. Wang, *The Bell*, p. 28; he has a number of comments on this passage (as well as the following) that should be consulted. I should note again how our understanding of this passage is perhaps colored by descriptions of the Han dynasty Music Bureau and its alleged collection practices.

24. See C. H. Wang, *The Bell*, p. 28, n. 90.

25. Note that the reported incident of collecting songs should not necessarily be linked to the moral drawn from the passage (the secluded but perfectly informed ruler), which does strike one as reflective of the Han political agenda. The passage could very well have ended by noting how these songs were used for entertainment in the court.

26. C. H. Wang, *The Bell*, p. 28.

27. Kenneth Dewoskin, p. 127.

28. For a review of the importance of music in Chinese culture see Kenneth Dewoskin; he includes information on the *Shi jing*. For a specific discussion of the *Shi jing* texts, including speculations on accompanying music, see Laurence Picken.

29. *Shi ji* (Beijing: Zhong-hua, 1959), 47, pp. 1936–37. Embedded in this passage are many technical and borrowed terms from the exegetical writings on the *Songs*, some of which I discuss later in the Postface.

30. Van Zoeren, p. 25.

31. The *Analects* (*Lun yu*), nominally attributed to Confucius, is clearly an accumulation of comments by and lore about Confucius and his school that in itself betrays a long period of construction, perhaps coalescing in the third century B.C. (Van Zoeren, p. 26). The *Zuo zhuan* is a text of historical anecdotes of the feudal states covering the years 722–468 B.C., with strong linkages to the *Spring and Autumn Annals* (*Chun qiu*), which might have been written by Confucius himself; the *Zuo zhuan is* generally dated to c. 300 B.C. (Van Zoeren, p. 261, n. 44).

32. *Analects* 8.15; Van Zoeren, p. 31; here and elsewhere there are indications that the title was a tune title, rather than a song-text title, although it would be hard to keep that distinction clear for long. We might mention here that there are six titles cited in the literature that do not appear in the *Shi jing*, which has also suggested to some that these are references to tunes: see C. H. Wang, *The Bell*, p. 29. Van Zoeren notes that when lyrics are quoted in the *Analects* (six times), titles are not mentioned, and when there is a reference to the generic *shi* (the *Songs* or a song) it is usually clearly about language (pp. 31, 260, n. 27).

33. This practice is widely discussed in *Shi jing* scholarship; in addition to Van Zoeren, see, for example, Koo-yin Tam, "The Use of Poetry in *Tso chuan*: An Analysis of the 'Fu-shih' Practice" (PhD Diss., University of Washington, Seattle, 1975), and Haun Saussy; Tam has the most elaborate breakdown of the data.

34. David Schaberg, "Foundations of Chinese Historiography: Literary Representation in the *Zuo zhuan* and *Guoyu*" (PhD Diss., Harvard University, 1996). See chapter 4, p. 88, n. 192, for location and poems. Qu Wan-li, Preface, p.8; Qu's count is based on "situations that mention the *shi*" and does not list incidents; at that point he is making an argument for the stability of the text.

35. Van Zoeren, pp. 37–38; he also discusses a clearer, more developed example on pp. 35–36.

36. Van Zoeren, pp. 37–38, is not certain of how the quotation was intended; Owen, however, argues for the fully recontextualized meaning: "When the line was cited by Confucius, *si* meant 'thoughts'" (*Essays*, p. 75).

37. Owen argues that the basic indeterminacy of the text not only allows for this practice of *fu shi* but also encourages the many other different strategies for interpretation that accompany the text, from intratextual explanations

to the exegetical hermeneutics. I would note here that the indeterminacy of which Owen speaks is not the anxiety-filled indeterminacy of contemporary theory but rather one that provides a sense of richness of the text, of which the Chinese critic often speaks and celebrates.

38. Van Zoeren, pp. 43, 39. Along with discussing examples of *fu shi,* Van Zoeren (p. 42) also cites a *Zuo zhuan* passage that appears to establish the self-consciousness of the decontextualized quote; a speaker compares breaking a marriage taboo to this practice: "In reciting the *Shi,* I break off a stanza and take what I want from it." Cf. Owen, *Essays,* p. 74, n. 3.

39. *Shi jing,* no. 192, stanza 8.

40. *Zuo zhuan,* Zhao 1.3; Schaberg, chapter 4, p. 90, with my adaptation.

41. Schaberg does not note, however, that Shu-xiang's explanation of the passage plays on the critical question of the allegiance of the feudal lords and its abuse by the ruler in the Bao Si story. Excellent examples of *fu shi* passages, with accompanying explications, are also found in Van Zoeren, pp. 39–43, and Owen, "Application."

42. Qu Wan-li, p. 5, provides a convenient comparison of the differences; most noticeably, the "Cao feng" (which is a very small set) was not performed and the "Bin feng" appeared ninth in the sequence, instead of last.

43. *Zuo zhuan,* Xiang 29.8. A complete translation and explication can be found in Dewoskin, pp. 22–24; cf. Van Zoeren, p. 265–66, n. 39.

44. Van Zoeren, pp. 81–86, discusses the two schools; he notes in them a dichotomy that will be reconfigured throughout the following centuries between a stance of interpretative doubt, where there is a search for an "authentic" text and meaning, and a more optimistic approach, where understanding of the text is assumed and speculation thereupon encouraged.

45. Van Zoeren follows convention and describes these versions according to the New Text–Old Text dichotomy, but Robert Hightower, "The *Han-shih wai-chuan* and the San *chia shih,*" pp. 264–65, argues that this did not apply to the *Shi jing* because all texts were transmitted in memory and therefore would have necessarily been "new text." In any event, the point is somewhat moot, given the subsequent history of the text.

46. *Han shu* (Beijing: Zhong-hua, 1962), p. 1708; translation, Hightower, *Harvard Journal,* p. 256. The Mao text was first accepted as the official version during the reign of Emperor Ping (A.D. 1–5) but later withdrawn; see Hightower, p. 257, n. 53.

47. As explained by Hightower, the actual corpus of poems was for the most part shared by all these schools; it was the interpretational strategies that separated them. His study of the *Han shi wai-zhuan* provides clear evidence that not only are the poems shared but their sequence appears to be very close also.

48. Earliest references (in the *Han shu*) are to this Master Mao, later identified as Mao Chang, in the court of Prince Xian of He-jian; Zheng Xuan (A.D. 127–200) attributed joint authorship to Mao the Elder and Mao the Younger,

who were subsequently identified as Mao Heng and Mao Chang (Van Zoeren, p. 86; compare Loewe, "Shi jing"). It is interesting to note that this compilation date, 150 B.C., is very close to the date of the Fu-yang text (165 B.C.) that was recently unearthed.

49. For a fuller, more complex example of the Mao commentary, see Van Zoeren's translation of the entire *zhuan* commentary to "The Ospreys Cry" (1), pp. 87–88.

50. *Mao shi zheng yi* (Taipei: Yi-wen shu-ju, 1976), vol. 2 of *Shi-san jing zhu shu* (1815), p. 168. We must assume that these glosses, which sometimes now appear more difficult than the original terms, were useful and necessary. Many terms in the *Shi jing* have become well known because of the subsequent status of the text.

51. Originally the Great and Small Prefaces were said to be one piece, but Mao divided the material into separate prefaces and placed them before the individual poems, where they are generally still found. The prefaces are gathered together and translated in Legge, pp. 37–81.

52. *Mao shi zheng yi*, p. 168. References in the texts are somewhat ambiguous: what I translate as "noble lord(s)" (*jun-zi*) is sometimes rendered "gentleman," "superior person," etc. It is the common Confucian term for a man of impeccable virtue. Duke Zhuang ruled in Zheng 743–01 B.C.

53. Van Zoeren, p. 224, quoting Zheng Qiao's *Shi bian wang* (Beijing: Pu-she, 1933), p. 3.

54. Pauline Yu, *The Reading of Imagery*, Chapter 2.

55. A review of that history is found in James Hightower's "The *Han-shih wai-chuan* and the *San chia shih*." We should note that the *Han shi wai-zhuan* is neither poetic text nor commentary; rather it is a series of examples in the *fu shi* of *Zuo zhuan* manner. Zheng Xuan apparently drew materials from all *Shi* schools into his work; see Van Zoeren, pp. 272–73, n. 8.

56. Zheng Xuan also compiled a "Chronology of the Songs" (*Shi pu*), which dated and contextualized the poems, but it is no longer extant except in fragments; cf. Van Zoeren, p. 272–73, n. 8.

57. Zheng is here using the graph *su* ("haste") that Mao used to gloss the graph *zan* ("in no time") above, but it appears that the usage here is unrelated to Mao's gloss and is an example of Zheng's speculative reach.

58. Tones first came to the attention of Chinese poets in the sixth century A.D., as manifested in the prosodic rules promoted by Shen Yue (441–513). It is assumed that tones existed in Chinese long before then, but perhaps not in the earliest history of the language.

   "*Fan-qie* spellings" are the principal premodern form of phonetic glossing in China; two, presumably commonly known, graphs are used to "spell" a third, by combining the initial from the first and the final (including tone) from the second, such as Qi + jù = qù. These spellings are somewhat temporally bound, since a phonological shift in any component renders the entire formula invalid. Nonetheless, many dictionaries and annotations repeat *fan-qie* spellings from earlier materials, with little regard to those shifts.

59. Van Zoeren, p. 119; his chapter 5 has a detailed explication of this period and the nature of Kong Ying-da's text.

60. Van Zoeren, p. 124–25; he translates an illustrative example of the explication genre from a commentary on the *Analects*.

61. Details of this period of canonical scholarship, including information on the *Zheng yi* texts cited here, can be found in David McMullen's *State and Scholars in T'ang China* (Cambridge: Cambridge University Press, 1988), especially pp. 67–111.

62. Van Zoeren, p. 139.

63. Van Zoeren describes these *Zheng yi* commentaries typically in three parts; Sequence, Paraphrase, and Topic. Here we seem to have only the Paraphrase and Topic sections, perhaps because our poem is relatively simple.

64. *Mao shi zheng yi*, p. 168; the ambiguity of the term *jun-zi* ("noble lord(s)," etc.) is being used to draw the political story of Duke Zhuang and personal story of "me" (*wo*) together.

65. *Mao shi zheng yi*, p. 168. The gloss for poem no. 120 is on p. 224.

66. These glosses are sometimes marked by a *yin-yi* headnote; at other times they are merged with Zheng Xuan's commentary, usually separated by a "node" mark.

67. Lu De-ming includes a *fan-qie* pronunciation for the graph *xu* that does not appear in either the verse or the Mao glosses; this is apparently an error for the *xun* gloss by Mao. The glosses conclude with a note about variant graphs, in this case merely final particles.

68. *Shi bian wang*, p. 6, quoted by Van Zoeren, p. 226.

69. *Ou-yang Yong-shu ji* (*Guo-xue ji-ben cong-shu*), 3.36; quoted by Van Zoeren, p. 183, who notes that Ou-yang is much less iconoclastic than this often-quoted remark would suggest; in Ou-yang's actual exegesis of the *Shi* he frequently reaffirmed the primacy of the Small Preface, from which he felt Zheng Xuan and others had veered.

70. The *Shi ji zhuan* was promulgated as the official text for examination in 1312 (Wong and Lee, p. 223).

71. *Shi ji zhuan*, p. 51.

72. Whether the rhapsody is actually by Song Yu or not is difficult to say, but it is collected in the authoritative sixth-century A.D. anthology *Wen xuan,* chapter 19.

73. *Shi zhuan yi-shuo* (*Si-ku quan-shu zhen-ben*), 1.32; translated by Van Zoeren, p. 229, with my adaptions.

74. Van Zoeren, p. 231.

75. Kent Guy, *The Emperor's Four Treasures: Scholars and the State in the Late Ch'ien-lung Era* (Cambridge: Council on East Asian Studies, Harvard University, 1987), p. 41.

76. The project, begun in 1772, took twenty-two years to complete. As often alleged (and affirmed by Kent Guy's study), this was an opportunity for the Qing to revise or rid the empire of any anti-Manchu (especially Ming-loyalist) writings—perhaps as many as three thousand titles.

77. Benjamin Elman, *From Philosophy to Philology: Intellectual and Social Aspects of Change in Late Imperial China* (Cambridge: Council on East Asian Studies, Harvard University, 1990), p. 65.

78. Along with textual studies, there was a revival of practical learning, especially in the related areas of astronomy and math, but also in engineering, agriculture, etc. This interest in the physical world would later be reinforced by Western learning in the sciences. Benjamin Elman includes a discussion of this type of scholarship in his study.

79. Benjamin Elman, pp. 177–80, summarizes those arguments; throughout his study Elman discusses the exemplary role played by Yan's work on the *Shu jing*.

80. Liang Ch'i-ch'ao, *Intellectual Trends in the Ch'ing Period*, translated by Immanuel C. Y. Hsu (Cambridge: Harvard University Press, 1959), p. 90, with my alterations. Philip Kuhn discusses Wei Yuan's *Shi jing* scholarship as both political and progressive, in that Wei saw the lessons of the *Songs* as a "guide to action"; see Kuhn's "Ideas Behind China's Modern State" (*Harvard Journal of Asiatic Studies* 55.2), p. 305. In this sense Wei separates himself from the mainstream of *kao-zheng* scholars.

81. Yao Ji-heng (preface dated 1705) is particularly skeptical of earlier commentaries, including that by Zhu Xi. For example, his comments on "Along the Highroad" include dismissing the Small Preface as "without basis" (*wu ju*); pointing out the logical inconsistencies of Zhu Xi's paraphrase and his anachronistic use of Song Yu's *fu* as a gloss; and concluding that there is no way for us to know the actual circumstances behind this ancient love song; see his *Shi jing tong lun* (Hong Kong: Zhong-hua shu-ju, 1963), p. 104.

82. Bernhard Karlgren, *Glosses*; p. 74. Karlgren's Introduction provides an excellent, although somewhat loaded, review of scholarship on the *Shi jing*. Despite his description, the *kao-zheng* scholars do cite materials from the post-Han period, although not extensively.

83. Chen Huan, *Shi Mao shi zhuan shu* (Taipei: Xue-sheng, 1975), p. 214.

84. Karlgren suggests that Zhu Xi transferred his suspicion of the Small Prefaces to the Mao glosses; that may be true occasionally, but Zhu Xi often merely repeats the Mao-Zheng glosses, adding his own for other terms.

85. Karlgren, *Glosses*, p. 74.

86. Chen Huan, p. 214.

87. Again we should note the exception of Yao Ji-heng's text, which could have served very well as a student "textbook," but it was not actually published until 1837 (Michael Loewe, p. 421). It *has* been used extensively in modern editions of the *Shi jing*.

88. Modern Chinese *Shi jing* texts often draw on Zhu Xi's redactions, especially his paraphrases. This is true for example in Qu Wan-li's *Shi jing shi-yi;* yet Qu also extracts materials from the Qing scholars, especially Chen Huan and Ma Rui-chen; the recent edition by Cheng Jun-ying and Jiang Jian-yuan, *Shi jing zhu xi* (Hong Kong: Zhong-hua shu-ju, 1991), draws more on the Han, Tang, and Qing commentaries but does include citations of Zhu Xi; Cheng and Jiang are exemplary in their citation of sources.

89. Benjamin Elman, p. 215, describes this practice; he includes (pp. 212–21) a review of Qing phonology.

90. This is not to say that Karlgren is the last word on questions of early phonology; works by scholars such as Edwin Pulleyback, Li Fang-gui, Wang Li, and Ting Pang-hsin all have improved his work. The studies of W. A. C. H. Dobson are a rigorous application of modern linguistic descriptions and dating. Karlgren's glosses and translations are, however, the most acccessible application of modern phonology to questions of the *Shi jing.* The Selected Bibliography offers a review of more recent literary scholarship.

91. Zhu Xi designated the beginning and end of the preface (sections 1–3 and 19–21) as the Small Preface to poem no. 1, and the remainder (more general comments on poetry and poetics) as the Great Preface. Modern editions often follow this division.

92. Haun Saussy, pp. 84–85.

93. Owen, "The Great Preface," p. 38.

94. These treatments are by Stephen Owen, "The Great Preface," pp. 37–49, which discusses the text's relationship to other early examples of literary criticism and includes translations of supplementary passages (he also includes the Chinese text); Van Zoeren, pp. 95–97, who finds the text full of disjunctions but isolates three main themes that he constructs from different passages; and Haun Saussy, pp. 74–83, whose translation includes a full array of materials from the subcommentaries, including Ruan Yuan of the Qing dynasty. My translation is fully dependent on these three, although the phrasing is my own.

95. Owen, "The Great Preface," pp. 40–41, et passim, provides the context for those earlier formulations; he also discusses the subtle differences between those and the Preface's version.

96. For an extended discussion of early Chinese musicology, including an argument for the primacy of its role in epistemology, see Kenneth Dewoskin. The interwovenness of the music and poetry of the *Shi jing* is omnipresent in the critical literature; yet sections 4 and 5 seem to be quite separate articulations, perhaps deriving from quite different sources.

97. C. H. Wang, "The Countenance of the Chou: Shih Ching 266–296," *Journal of the Institute of Chinese Studies of the Chinese University of Hong Kong* 7.2 (1974): 425–49. This is reprinted in his *From Ritual,* pp. 1–35.

98. In early poetics *fu shi* is used as a verb meaning "to recite poetry," in the manner seen in the *Zuo zhuan,* discussed earlier; later (in the Han dynasty)

*fu* becomes the name of a genre, "rhapsody," often seen in the phrase *Han fu*. In all these cases the term is related to its basic lexical sense, "to display or unfold."

99. Pauline Yu, *The Reading of Imagery*, chapter 2, reviews a wealth of early materials to formulate a reconsideration of the *xing* in relation to early Chinese poetry in general.

100. Owen, *Essays*, pp. 101–03.

101. Owen, *Essays*, p. 95.

102. Kenneth Dewoskin, pp. 45, 92.

103. This dating is nearly uniform in the scholarship, with W. A. C. H. Dobson arguing most convincingly with linguistic evidence, but we must remember the difficult questions of dating texts that emerge from performatory and oral environments. If one is discussing a physically fixed text, then the evidence (as discussed by Van Zoeren) points more to the third century B.C. Bruce Brooks disagrees with that assessment, however, arguing that "the Shi is not only a Warring States *compilation* but a Warring States *text*. Its first (*Feng*) core is from 465 B.C.; its last (*Lu Song*) part was added, and the text fixed, by 321 B.C." (*Warring States Working Group, Note 30* [August 27, 1993]; I have transcribed Brooks' romanization and dating).

104. While both Chinese and Western critics alike now see the poems as "literary" products, we should note that this belief in the "original" meaning of the poems derives from an expressive, nearly romantic, theory of literature that may very well be anachronistic in its application to the poems.

# Selected Bibliography: Studies and Translations of the Shi jing in English

◆

Included here are the most important and readily available studies, excluding dissertations and theses. I have appended short comments to the entries that I thought deserved special attention. This list is intended as a starting point for a student interested in the text. Several of the studies have, as noted, excellent bibliographies of Chinese materials.

Allen, Clement Francis Romilly, trans. *The Book of Chinese Poetry: Being the Collection of Ballads, Sagas, Hymns, and Other Pieces Known as the* Shih Ching; *or,* Classic of Poetry. London: K. Paul, Trench, Truber, 1891.

Allen, Joseph Roe, III. "The End and Beginning of Narrative Poetry in China." *Asia Major* 2 (1989): 1–24. **A structural study of the narrative in nos. 58 and 245.**

Chang, Kang-I Sun. "The Concept of Time in the *Shih Ching*." *Tsing Hua Journal of Chinese Studies*. New series. 12:1–2 (December 1979): 73–85.

Chen, Shih-hsiang. "The *Shih Ching:* Its Generic Significance in Chinese Literary History and Poetics. *Bulletin of the Institute of History and Philology* 39 (1969): 371–413. Also in *Studies in Chinese Literary Genres*. Ed. Cyril Birch. Berkeley: University of California Press, 1974. 8–41. **A seminal study of the *xing* method of composition and its relationship to lyricism in China.**

Chou, Fa-kao. "Reduplicatives in the Book of Odes." *Bulletin of the Institute of History and Philology* 34.2 (1963): 66–98.

Chow, Tse-tsung. "The Early History of the Chinese Word *Shih* (Poetry)." *Wen-lin: Studies in the Chinese Humanities*. Ed. Chow Tse-tsung. Madison: University of Wisconsin Press, 1968. 151–209. **Exhaustive research on the archaic provenance and meaning of *shi*, including the oracle-bone script.**

Dembo, L. S. *The Confucian Odes of Ezra Pound: A Critical Appraisal*. Berkeley: University of California Press, 1963.

Dewoskin, Kenneth. *A Song for One or Two: Music and the Concept of Art in Early China*. Ann Arbor: Center for Chinese Studies, University of Michigan,

1982. **A general discussion of early music but contains much material related to the music of the** *Shi jing,* **including a translation of Ducal Son Ji Zha's comments from the** *Zuo zhuan.*

Dobson, W. A. C. H. *The Language of the* Book of Songs. Toronto: University of Toronto Press, 1968. **A technical, exhaustive study on word use and grammatical structures in the text.**

———. "Linguistic Evidence and the Dating of the *Book of Songs*." *T'oung Pao* 51 (1964): 322–43. **Argues for progressively older layers of materials, confirming standard dating of 1000–600 B.C.**

———. "The Origin and Development of Prosody in Early Chinese Poetry." *T'oung Pao* 14 (1968): 232–50. **A detailed description of prosody and arguments for the emergence of rhyme and regular form.**

Eoyang, Eugene. "Waley or Pound? The Dynamics of Genre in Translation." *Tamkang Review* 19.1–4 (Autumn 1988–Summer 1989): 441–65.

Francis, Mark E. "Canon Formation in Traditional Chinese Poetry: Chinese Canons, Sacred and Profane." *China in a Polycentric World: Essays in Chinese Comparative Literature.* Ed. Zhang Yingyin. Stanford: Stanford University Press, 1998: 50–70. **Considers the** *Shi jing* **as part of the early literary canon, in the context of later Chinese poetry anthologies.**

Granet, Marcel. *Festivals and Songs of Ancient China.* Trans. E. D. Edwards. London: Routledge & Sons, 1932. **A translation of Granet's seminal study** *Fêtes et chanson anciennes de la Chine,* **which treats the airs as communal poems associated with fertility festivals through comparative anthropological method.**

Hightower, James R. "The *Han-shih wai-chuan* and the *San chia shih*." *Harvard Journal of Asiatic Studies* 11 (1948): 241–310. **A detailed discussion of the schools of** *Shi* **scholarship during the Han; extremely valuable.**

———. Han shih wai chuan: *Han Ying's Illustration of the Didactic Application of the Classic of Songs.* Cambridge: Harvard University Press, 1952. **A translation with commentary and annotation of the** *Han shi wai zhuan* **text.**

Hung, William. *A Concordance to* Shih Ching: *Harvard-Yenching Institute Sinological Index Series, No. 9.* Rev. ed. Tokyo: Japan Council for East Asian Studies, 1962. **This is an extremely valuable research aid for study of the** *Shi jing;* **it is a complete concordance to a standard Chinese text, which is included in the volume.**

Karlgren, Bernhard. The Book of Odes: *Chinese Text, Transcription, and Translation.* Stockholm: Museum of Far Eastern Antiquities, 1950. **The most philologically accurate, though relatively awkward, translation in Western languages; includes the Chinese text.**

———. *Glosses on the* Book of Odes. Stockholm: Museum of Far Eastern Antiquities, 1942–1964. **A laborious, detailed discussion of many passages in the** *Shi,* **with comparison and evaluation of differing interpretations; absolutely essential for research.**

Kennedy, George. "Metrical 'Irregularity' in the *Shih ching*." *Harvard Journal of Asiatic Studies* 4.3–4 (1939): 284–96. **An important phonological analysis of prosody, arguing for strong regularity even in the face of apparent irregular lines.**

Legge, James, trans. *The* She King *or the* Book of Poetry. The Chinese Classics, vol. 4. 1871. Rpt. Hong Kong: Hong Kong University Press, 1960. **The translation is dated but it contains many useful passages and evaluations; includes the Chinese text and all the prefaces to the *Mao shi*, along with other background information.**

Liu, David Jason. "Parallel Structures in the Canon of Chinese Poetry: The *Shih Ching*." *Poetics Today* 4.4 (1983): 639–53.

Loewe, Michael. "*Shih ching*." *Early Chinese Texts: A Bibliographic Guide*. Berkeley: University of California Press, 1993: 415–23. **An excellent introduction, particularly on textual matters, including editions and translations.**

Mattos, Gilbert L. "Tonal 'Anomalies' in the *Kuo Feng* Odes." *Tsing-hua Journal of Chinese Studies* 9. 1–2 (1971): 306–25. **Builds on Karlgren in one of the few studies of "tones" in the *Shi jing;* extensive use of statistical data and charts.**

McNaughton, William. *The Book of Songs*. New York: Twayne, 1971. **A general study of themes in the text, plus a detailed study of rhetorical devices.**

———. "The Composite Image: *Shy Jing* Poetics." *Journal of the American Oriental Society*, 83 (1963): 92–103.

Owen, Stephen. *Essays on Ancient Literature*. Manuscript. Contents: "Reproduction," "Authority," "Application and Interpretation: A Hypothesis," "The Historical Imagination in the Interpretation of the Poems." **This set of essays is not yet available, but I include it here in anticipation of its publication. Owen has constructed compelling analyses of the nature of the *Shi jing* and its implications for Chinese culture and aesthetics, especially how the text manifests and affirms political power and cultural values.**

———. "The Great Preface." *Readings in Chinese Literary Thought*. Cambridge, MA: Council of East Asian Studies, Harvard University, 1992: 37–56. **A translation (with Chinese text) and a detailed annotation of the Mao Great Preface, including supplements of related texts in *Xun zi* and *Li ji*. Can be compared to translations by Saussy and Van Zoeren.**

Picken, Laurence E. R. "The Shapes of the *Shi Jing* Song-Texts and Their Musical Implications." *Musica Asiatica* 1 (1977): 85–109. **One of the few attempts to discuss the lost music of the *Shi*, by working backward from prosody and secondary remarks; necessarily tentative, but important.**

Pound, Ezra, trans. *The Confucian Odes: The Classic Anthology Defined by Confucius*. New York: J. Laughlin, 1954, 1959. **A complete translation in the Mao order; very creative and often compelling, especially with the courtship poems in "Airs"; not suitable for research, however.**

Riegel, Jeffrey. "Eros, Introversion, and the Beginnings of *Shijing* Commentary." *Harvard Journal of Asiatic Studies*, 57.1 (1997): 143–77. **An analysis of** a pre-195 B.C. commentary to poems 1 and 28 as found in a recently discovered manuscript, especially in comparison to later commentaries.

Saussy, Haun. *The Problem of a Chinese Aesthetic.* Stanford: Stanford University Press, 1993. **A very theoretical discussion of the *Shi* in early aesthetic theory; much detail on the prefaces. Extensive bibliography of Western sources.**

————. "Repetition, Rhyme, and Exchange in the *Book of Odes.*" *Harvard Journal of Asiatic Studies,* 57.2 (1997): 519–42. **Analysis of rhyme and other poetic structures as embodiments of thematic concerns central to Confucian ideology, especially the relationship between *he* (harmony) and *tong* (identity).**

Shaughnessy, Edward L. "From Liturgy to Literature: The Ritual Contexts of the Earliest Poems in the *Book of Poetry,*" "How the Poetess Came to Burn the Royal Chamber." *Before Confucius: Studies in the Creation of the Chinese Classics.* Albany: State University of New York Press, 1997: 165–95, 221–38. **An analysis of nos. 266–75 in terms of their function in ritual performance; and an innovative re-reading of the imagery in no. 10 as a metaphor for female sexual arousal.**

Sun, Cerile Chu-chin. "Two Modes of Stanzaic Interaction in *Shih-Ching* and Their Implication for Comparative Poetics." *Tamkang Review* 19.1–4 (Autumn 1988–Summer 1989): 803–33.

Svensson, Martin. "A Second Look at the *Great Preface* on the Way to a New Understanding of Han Dynasty Poetics." *Chinese Literature: Essays, Articles, Reviews.* 21 (1999): 1–33. **A critique of the interpretation of the Mao prefaces in the twentieth-century sinology, attempting to restore a reading according to the Han hermeneutics.**

Van Zoeren, Steven. *Poetry and Personality: Reading, Exegesis, and Hermeneutics in Traditional China.* Stanford: Stanford University Press, 1991. **The most extensive source on the literary and hermeneutic tradition of the *Shi jing;* extremely valuable and rich resource, illuminating many important areas of Chinese intellectual history. An excellent bibliography of Chinese and Japanese materials.**

Waley, Arthur, trans. The Book of Songs: *The Ancient Chinese Classic of Poetry.* London: Allen & Unwin, 1937. Rev. ed. New York: Grove Press, 1987. Foreword by Stephen Owen. **This is the work from which our edition derives (see next entry).**

————. *The Book of Songs: Supplement Containing Textual Notes.* London: George Allen & Unwin, 1937. **A 32-page booklet that gives many details on graph and textual problems and the author's solutions.**

————. "The Eclipse Poem and Its Group." *T'ien Hsia Monthly* October 1936, 245–48. **A brief discussion of fifteen poems that he omitted from his translation. Suggests a new date of 735 B.C. for no. 193.**

Wang, C. H. *The Bell and the Drum:* Shih Ching *as Formulaic Poetry in an Oral Tra-*

*dition.* Berkeley: University of California Press, 1974. **A ground-breaking study where oral formulaic theory is applied to the *Shi jing;* offers insights into the performatory origins of the text. An excellent bibliography of studies of the text, especially in Chinese.**

————. *From Ritual to Allegory: Seven Essays in Chinese Poetry.* Hong Kong: The Chinese University Press, 1988. **A collection of important essays on the poems and aspects of cultural identity: heroism, ritual, and origins. Most are reprinted from previous journal articles, which I have not listed here.**

————. "Oral, Folk, and an Unwanted Feud." *Tamkang Review* 16.2 (Winter 1985): 227–29.

————. "*Shih ching.*" *Indiana Companion to Traditional Chinese Literature.* Ed. William H. Nienhauser. Bloomington: Indiana University Press, 1986: 692–94.

Wong, Siu-kit, and Kar-shui Lee. "Poems of Depravity: A Twelfth-Century Dispute on the Moral Character of the *Book of Songs.*" *T'oung Pao* 75.4–5 (1989): 209–25. **A review of new interpretations concerning the purported depravity of "Zheng feng," particularly Zhu Xi's revision and rereading of the earlier commentaries; extensive citation of sources.**

Yang, Hsien-i, Gladys Yang, and Shih-kuang Hu, trans. *Selections from the* Book of Songs. Beijing: Chinese Literature, 1983.

Yip, Wai-lim. "Vestiges of the Oral Dimension: Examples from the *Shih-ching.*" *Tamkang Review* 16.1 (Fall 1985): 17–49.

Yu, Pauline; "Allegory, Allegoresis, and the *Classic of Poetry.* *Harvard Journal of Asiatic Studies* 43.2 (December 1983): 377–412. **An important study in which traditional methods of interpretation, especially in the Mao prefaces, are analyzed, with new insights into the early function of literature.**

————. "*The Book of Songs.*" *Masterworks of Asian Literature in Comparative Perspective.* Ed. Barbara Stoler Miller. Armonk, NY: M. E. Sharpe, 1994: 211–21.

————. *The Reading of Imagery in the Chinese Poetic Tradition.* Princeton: Princeton University Press, 1987. **Chapter 2 on the *Shi jing* integrates its use of imagery into the tradition of early Chinese poetry, especially its historical-biographical nature.**

Yung, Sai-shing. "Lyricism and Subjectivity in *Shih Ching:* Some Preliminary Observations." *Tamkang Review* 19.1–4 (Autumn 1988–Summer 1989): 875–87.

Zhang, Longxi. "The Letter or the Spirit: The *Song of Songs,* Allegoresis, and the *Book of Poetry.*" *Comparative Literature* 39.3 (Summer 1987): 193–217. **A comparison of exegetical literatures on these two texts, especially their anxiety with the poems' erotic surfaces.**